CUNNING

INFIDELITY - BOOK 2

ALEATHA ROMIG

NEW YORK TIMES AND USA TODAY BESTSELLING AUTHOR
OF THE CONSEQUENCES SERIES

CUNNING

Book 2 of the INFIDELITY series

Published by Romig Works, LLC

2016 Edition

ISBN 13: 978-0-9863080-7-9

ISBN 10: 0986308072

Cover art: Kellie Dennis at Book Cover by Design (www.bookcoverbydesign.co.uk)

Editing: Lisa Aurello

Formatting: Angela McLaurin at Fictional Formats

This is a work of fiction. Names, characters, places, and incidents either are the product of the author's imagin[illegible] resemblance to any actual persons, living or de[illegible]ntal.

This book is available in electro[illegible]

DISCLAIMER

The Infidelity series contains adult content and is intended for mature audiences. While the use of overly descriptive language is infrequent, the subject matter is targeted at readers over the age of eighteen.

Infidelity is a five-book series. The series is a dark romance. Each individual book will end in a way that will hopefully make you want more.

The Infidelity series does not advocate or glorify cheating. This series is about the inner struggle of compromising your beliefs for your heart. It is about cheating on yourself, not someone else.

I hope you enjoy the epic tale of INFIDELITY!

CUNNING

"He owns you. Whatever he tells you to do, you do".

One year. No future. A past that won't go away.

Lennox "Nox" Demetri broke his own rule by making a deal. It may not have been directly with the devil, but that doesn't mean Satan himself isn't watching. Was it fate that brought Charli into his life and his bed? What will happen when rules are broken and secrets are revealed?

"New rules… my rules."

Alex "Charli" Collins found pleasure with Nox like she'd never known. That was before she knew his last name. Now that Infidelity is involved and the rules have changed, what will result when real life and fantasy collide?

Is it really cheating if you're doing it to yourself?

From New York Times and USA Today bestselling author Aleatha Romig comes a sexy, new dominant hero who knows what he wants and a strong-willed heroine who has plans of her own. With classic Aleatha Romig twists, turns, deceptions, and devotions, the depth of this new, epic dark romance reaches new levels and will have readers swooning one minute and screaming the next.

Have you been Aleatha'd?

CUNNING is a full-length novel, over 360 pages, and the second of five books in the INFIDELITY series.

Infidelity - it isn't what you think.

CUNNING

Is it really cheating if you're doing it to yourself?

CHAPTER 1

CHARLI

"MR. DEMETRI?" I couldn't process more than to repeat his words. I was a parrot, not the strong confident woman I wanted to project.

"Yes, *Miss Collins.* New rules… *my* rules. You should say thank you."

I squeezed the phone tighter. The whiskey running through my veins had lessened my trembling but done little to slow my rapid heartbeat. I closed my eyes, trying to remember the man from Del Mar. The tone didn't match.

"Miss Collins, I said to say *thank you.*"

I wasn't sure if it was hearing his deep voice again or the difference in his demeanor, but my tattered nerves were ping-ponging between an emotional breakdown and a hysterical fit of laughter. I looked up at Karen, unsure if she could hear. When she nodded, I knew she could.

He owns you. Whatever he tells you to do.

"Thank you," I whispered, though unsure what I was thanking him for.

"By calling my number you broke our rule. I've mentioned I don't like to repeat myself, as well as how I'd respond if you ever again broke one of my rules. Do you remember?"

I remembered, but he hadn't said specifically what he'd do. Now didn't seem like the time to mention that. My chin dropped to my chest as I exhaled.

"Nox, please."

He cleared his throat. "*Mr. Demetri.* Listen closely. This is exactly what you will do."

I swallowed. The rush of blood coursing through my ears, my injured pride, and the multiple rebuttals forming in my head all worked together to dim the volume of his words. Nevertheless, I listened.

"Go down to the street. My driver is waiting. His name is Isaac, and he'll recognize you."

"I-I—"

"Miss Collins, your opportunity to negotiate has passed. It's time for our reunion. I paid handsomely for it."

I may have thought it before, but now it was official: Nox owned me. I'd sold my soul, but by the way my insides clenched, I knew that my companionship wasn't the only commodity Nox purchased.

After he finished speaking, I sat statuesque, holding the phone, waiting for anything, a goodbye, something. Instead, silence prevailed. When I turned the screen toward me only his name remained. He'd hung up.

Oh shit! Now what do I do?

As if reading my mind, Karen handed me the glass with the remaining whiskey, nodded, and said, "*Whatever* he tells you to do."

I took the glass and drained the contents.

Fire.

As I closed my eyes, tears teetered on the lids, and my lips burned. The liquor scorched everything in its wake. From my tongue to my throat, the heat left a blistering trail all the way to my stomach. And then the fire dimmed. Warmth radiated to my fingers and toes, leaving me calmer than only moments before.

Karen took the glass from my hand and asked, "Would you like another?"

Would I? Would I like to be so drunk when I reached Nox's car that I wouldn't process the shame that overwhelmed me? The idea that he, the one man I'd wanted, knew what I'd done was almost unconscionable. I'd told him I didn't sleep around, and yet he'd just purchased a year with me. If I had another drink, maybe then when I awoke in the morning, I wouldn't remember our reunion, *the one he paid handsomely for.*

I looked up at Karen's face. This was her job, what she did day after day. Yet the confident demeanor I'd witnessed yesterday was gone. In her eyes was something between pity and fear.

"Ms. Flores," I asked, "has Mr. Demetri been a client before?"

Her shoulders straightened. "All of our clients are covered by our confidentiality clause. I'm not at liberty to discuss Mr. Demetri with you any further than what we've already exchanged."

"That for the next year he owns me," I repeated her earlier words. "But yesterday you said this could take weeks. How? How did we go from weeks to less than twenty-four hours?"

Karen dismissively walked back to her chair. "Thank you, Alex, for coming to Infidelity. You don't need to return until your one-year anniversary. We'll be in contact with you and Mr. Demetri as that date approaches."

I stood, my volume rising with me. "What about training… or hell, I don't know…?" The whiskey gave me strength. "…therapy? Surely, a company as *successful…*" I used air quotes. "…as Infidelity has some plan or program to help its employees, to ensure we don't mess up or go insane."

"You're a Stanford grad and a Columbia Law student. Figure it out."

My forehead lengthened as my jaw dropped. "Figure it out? Figure it out? I feel like I'm being thrown to the wolves."

"Just one wolf, Miss Collins, and you're not being thrown. You walked in here of your own volition. You will walk back out of here to your client's waiting driver the same way—with your head held high. And you will not mention Infidelity to anyone—today or ever. You and Mr. Demetri are now a couple. When you're in public, you are his." She stood and leaned forward with her hands on the desk. "When you are in private, you are his. Currently, you're making his driver wait. I don't know Mr. Demetri well, but I'd venture to guess that he doesn't like to wait. I'd also venture to guess from what I overhead that you *do* know Mr. Demetri, don't you?"

It was my turn to be defensive. "Why, Ms. Flores, I thought that it was your job to know all."

"Tick-tock. Your client is waiting. Your income will be deposited soon."

She lifted a brow. "You're the employee; don't forget that."

I reached for my purse and turned to leave.

"Miss Collins?"

When I spun back, Karen's expression had softened.

"I wish you luck."

Luck?

"Thank you," I said, straightening my neck. *I'm going to need it.* I didn't say the last part aloud. Instead, I left her office with my head held high and found my way back to the secret elevator. Thankfully a badge wasn't needed to go down as it was to go up.

As the doors closed, I collapsed against the wall with a *whoosh* and tried to decipher what just happened. Though my mind told me to be nervous, upset, maybe even scared, because that was definitely the vibe I got from Karen, I wasn't. Well, maybe nervous. Perhaps it was the whiskey, but if I were honest, I was mostly excited. I didn't know how Nox did it or if he was a longtime client. I didn't know anything other than that soon I would be looking into the pale blue eyes I'd dreamt about.

I didn't ask him for help, but just as in Del Mar, he rescued me.

Maybe he *was* Batman.

While walking from the secret elevator to the main elevators within the catacombs of Infinity my purse vibrated. I stopped and moved to the side of the hallway as it vibrated again. I removed my phone from my purse and held my breath as I swiped the screen.

Am I ready to hear his voice again? Will he be upset that I'm making Isaac wait? Am I making him wait?

A lump formed in my throat until I saw the name: PATRICK.

"Pat," I whispered into the phone.

"So… tell me. I've been worried sick. Is there a problem?"

"N-No, I can't talk right now."

"But you're all right? Tell me you're all right," Patrick implored.

"Yes." The way my cheeks rose into a hint of a smile told me that I was—all right. This could have gone wrong in so many ways and instead had gone right beyond my wildest imagination.

"Tonight, girl. Tonight you're filling me in. Cy's out of town. It'll just be us and some wine. I'll cook—"

"I don't think I'll be there."

"What? Why? You're not going back to the house of horrors, are you? You can't. You signed—"

"No, I'm not. I-I met someone."

Patrick's voice lowered to a stage whisper. "You couldn't. It doesn't work that way—not that fast. I don't think that's even possible."

I looked around the hallway as people walked by. "Pat, I love you. I promise I'll keep in touch. Thank you for all that you've done. Really. This is good." My anticipation at seeing Nox again replaced the whiskey with adrenaline. "I need to go."

With each step toward the main elevators and the entire way down the thirty-seven stories my mind filled with Nox. The memories I'd kept at bay came rushing back. My cheeks reddened as the number of people around me grew. I was almost certain they could read my mind. The voices in my head were so loud.

I remembered his gaze and the way his pale eyes glistened with the menacing spark. I recalled his cologne, the woodsy scent that dominated my senses, and his touch, controlling yet adoring. I bit my lip to stop the sounds that longed to escape my lips.

This was my fantasy, my dream, and it was about to be my life. I should have thought about Bryce or the announcement Alton wanted to make. I didn't. My thoughts were too overwhelmed with Nox. Nox Demetri.

I shook my head. I now knew his last name.

The warm August air went unnoticed as I pushed my way through the revolving glass doors and onto the sidewalk. Parked along the curb was a string of black cars. I stopped and rolled my upper lip between my teeth.

What if Nox is inside one of the cars?

"Miss Collins?"

I spun toward the tall man dressed like Brantley. His attire of dark slacks, a white shirt, and jacket, was the signature unassuming uniform of drivers everywhere. By his shaved head and wrinkle-free face, he was younger than my stepfather's driver. He was also larger, with the muscled build of a bodyguard.

"Miss Collins, I'm Isaac. I believe Mr. Demetri told you that I'd be picking you up?"

"Yes. Is No… Mr. Demetri with you?"

"No, ma'am."

My earlier memories washed away in a wave of disappointment. I took a deep breath as I followed Isaac to the waiting car. When he opened the door to the backseat, I asked, "Where are you taking me?"

"I was told to ask you."

"Me?"

"Your things. I'm to take you to recover your personal items."

Isaac shut the door. My emotions were all over the place. One moment I was excited; the next I was scared. While Isaac walked around the car to the driver's side, I fought a new urge to run. If I opened the door, I could flee into the sea of people. What would Nox's driver do, tackle me? He was big enough to do that, but would he risk the scene?

"Which hotel?"

Isaac's question returned me to reality, while the motion of the car confirmed that I'd missed my opportunity to run. We were now easing into the afternoon traffic.

"Hotel?" I asked.

"Ma'am, where have you been staying?"

Did I want Nox to know that? Did I want him to know about Cy and Pat? Then again, we were now a couple, in private as well as public. That was what Karen said. I couldn't spend the next year with him and not tell him about my cousin. My stomach twisted. My cousin. Would that mean I'd tell him about all of my family?

"Miss Collins?"

"I-I'm sorry, Isaac. I wasn't staying in a hotel. I was staying with some friends: 1214 Fifth Avenue."

He nodded and guided us through traffic toward the Upper East Side. I wasn't a fan of being driven, but for once I didn't mind. It gave me time to think and plan.

To think about Nox.

Retrieving my things, even if it were only the clothes I'd taken to Savannah, made this real. I'd told Patrick I wouldn't be at his place tonight, but I wasn't sure I was ready to move out altogether.

With the effects of the whiskey waning, my mind began to overtake my body. Fright eclipsed excitement. Nox's voice was different on the phone. His words were clipped and tone was harsh. Maybe I should be scared. Obviously, Karen was. At the very least, she seemed intimidated.

I'd never felt that way around him—until now.

Isaac pulled into the small circular drive and handed me a card. "My cell phone number."

As he opened my door, he nodded. "Miss Collins, I'll be waiting. Mr. Demetri would like you to gather as quickly as possible only the personal items you need. He said that he'll send for the rest later. Tonight you have plans."

I wanted to ask what kind of plans. I wanted to ask a lot of things, but instinctively I knew my questions wouldn't be answered, at least not by Isaac. That wasn't how this worked. I was only too well aware of the protocol.

"I'll stay close," Isaac said. "Please call me when you're ready, and I'll be here." His eyes widened. "Do you need help? I can park and help you carry…"

"No, I'll be fine."

It didn't hit me until I entered Patrick's apartment that I didn't even know where I was going. I had orientation in less than two weeks, and I was being driven by someone I didn't know to an undisclosed location to meet with a man who, up until a few hours ago, had no last name.

I was breaking every rule in Jane's safety handbook. The thought made me scoff as I packed my things. Hell, since I'd left Montague Manor—only three days ago—I'd not only thrown that handbook out the window, I'd shredded it.

Hurriedly, I left Patrick a note on the kitchen counter.

Patrick,

I can't thank you and Cy enough for giving me a place to stay. For that, I love you.

I'll keep in touch. Hopefully we can still run on Saturdays.

Love,

Your little cousin

My heart ached as I took one last glance at Patrick's apartment. My thoughts and emotions were too jumbled to put it in words. Too many things had happened and too fast. My heart wanted what Pat and Cy shared. I didn't want to think about how they met or how Nox and I found our way back together. I wanted to think about the fairytale, the way Patrick and Cy looked at one another, and the way my tummy fluttered at merely the thought of Nox's gaze.

I couldn't think about my employment at Infidelity or about being owned. The way I was able to put one foot in front of the other was to look at everything in a new way. In my newly contrived perspective, I wasn't bought by Nox: I freely gave myself to him.

That was what I decided as I dialed Isaac's number.

CHAPTER 2

CHARLI

ISAAC BARELY SPOKE as he drove, leaving me time to think. I couldn't wrap my mind around what had happened, where I was, or even where I was going. The tumultuous tsunami of emotions billowed within me, the threatening winds frayed the edges of my well-bred façade. Nervousness and anxiety churned within me, their only outlet the uncharacteristic bobbing of my knee.

My current situation was almost unfathomable. I couldn't imagine how I'd feel if I were on my way to meet a stranger. How did that even work? Did the client and employee meet over drinks like a blind date? Surely they didn't move in together immediately. Nox was different. He wasn't a complete stranger. Granted, I only learned his last name today, yet I knew much more than a name.

I knew that he possessed an intensity that fascinated me. I remembered the way deep navy swirled in his pale eyes when his emotions ran high. I'd seen only a snippet of his anger or annoyance with Max at the pool and then again as he spoke to someone on the phone. However, mostly the navy I witnessed was brought on by desire—something he wore like cologne, the need emanating so strongly that it lingered in the air, filling my lungs and laboring my breathing.

My insides twisted and tummy fluttered as memories surfaced. I tried to come to terms with the reality. Soon, I'd be with him again. Unconsciously, I shifted on the leather seat, ashamed of how aroused I was by the mere thought. The tightening deep inside of me wasn't new, but it'd been absent since Del Mar. When Chelsea and I'd boarded the plane, I feared I'd never again feel this yearning. A small grin broke through my mask.

Isaac pulled the car over, making me aware of my surroundings. I hadn't expected to arrive so soon. Even with slow traffic, we hadn't traveled far from Patrick's building. I looked up at the front of the Mandarin Hotel.

"This is where you're taking me?" I asked, wondering how much Isaac knew about the situation.

"Yes, ma'am. Would you like me to help you with your bags?" he asked as he opened my door.

Taking his hand as he helped me from the car, I said, "No. I can get them. I only have the two." But before I finished my reply, he placed a room key within my grasp.

Isaac pulled an envelope from the inside pocket of his jacket and handed it to me. "This is from Mr. Demetri. He said to tell you not to open or read it until you're in the suite."

I took a deep breath.

He said to tell *me.*

That shouldn't make the butterflies in my tummy flutter, but it did.

"The room number is on the back of the envelope," Isaac continued, seemingly oblivious to my mental and physical state of both fear and arousal. "You have my number. If you need a ride anywhere, I'm at your service."

"Thank you, Isaac." I cleared my throat. "Mr. Demetri isn't in the room?" I didn't know if my words sounded as disappointed as I felt.

"No, ma'am. He's at his office. I believe the letter…" He tipped his head toward the envelope in my hand. "…will explain everything."

"All right. Thank you."

As I turned toward the glass doors, a small bit of Central Park caught my eye and I turned. The warm city breeze moved small wisps of my auburn hair around my face as I stared. It was exactly what I needed. My cheeks rose at the glimpse of trees. The green leaves reminded me where I was—that I was still here, still in New York City, close to my cousin, and near Columbia. No matter how surreal the last twenty-four hours seemed, I was still where I wanted to be. Lifting my chin, I nodded at the doorman and took a step closer to my goal.

Ornate lighting shone from a golden oval above my head and reflected onto the stunning marble floor of the lobby. The opulence neither impressed nor awed me as my gaze moved to a large staircase that curved up and behind the concierge's desk. Briefly, the staircase reminded me of Montague Manor, but this one was different, more modern with a glass banister.

The micro-thought of my childhood prison steeled my resolve. I might be an Infidelity employee; however, I was also a Montague. My new temporary role was for one reason—law school. I hadn't been forced to sign at Infidelity. I chose to do it, finding it the solution I needed. Waiting tables would never pay my tuition, let alone allow me money to live. My mother and Alton pushed my hand and underestimated my desire. I was doing it so I could continue my dream, not theirs.

Alex Collins was a survivor.

With my newfound determination, I stepped quickly to the concierge desk, allowing the click-clack of my heels to announce my arrival. When the concierge looked up, I smiled. "Could you help me with directions to my room? I'm staying in…"

Each word I uttered exuded Montague confidence, not the shame of an Infidelity employee. Immediately, the concierge called for a bellman. Despite my protest, he insisted that it wouldn't be right to allow a guest to roll her own luggage to the executive suite.

As the elevator ascended, I recalled something Karen said yesterday, why employees of Infidelity were expected to be well-spoken and successful. If they weren't, in this different yet similar world of smoke and mirrors, they'd be discovered. The companions on the arms of successful clients needed to be believable. Thanks to my Montague upbringing, when it came to illusion, I was a master.

I did my best to appear nonchalant as the bellman used my key to open the door of the executive suite. As he flipped the switch in the dark entry, I scanned the luxurious suite. Beyond the light illuminating the foyer, the furnishings appeared modern and sleek while the walls were covered in heavy drapery that kept the late afternoon sunlight at bay.

"Ma'am, I apologize," the bellman said as he hurried across the living room, "your suite has a spectacular view. Let me open—"

His feet and words stopped. My heart leapt to my throat. Stepping from a darkened doorway was a man who immediately dominated the executive suite.

"Sir, I didn't know that anyone…"

I no longer heard the man in the Mandarin uniform. Nox was all I saw. His silence filled the air, muting anything else. His pale eyes narrowed, capturing mine. Without words his icy gaze bore through me, planting my feet and sealing my lips. Displeasure radiated from his every pore. Rage rippled from his chiseled jaw as the muscles in his face and neck flexed. My knees grew weak as I realized this wasn't the man I remembered, but rather the man whose voice I'd heard on the phone call.

Only minutes earlier there had been so many things I'd planned to say and questions that consumed me. Yet now with Nox before me, none of them surfaced or made their presence known; instead, the suite warmed as my heartbeat raced. I gripped tighter to my purse. With the winds of his displeasure swirling about the suite, I needed an anchor, something to ground me.

For only a second, I considered turning and leaving. Would he stop me with the bellman as a witness? And then just as quickly I knew it wouldn't matter. Nox Demetri had influence, more than I'd realized. I took a deep breath. I wouldn't be outrunning the powerful man before me, not for a year.

Let the dog-and-pony show begin.

Nox reached into his pocket, removed his money clip, and handed the bellman a few bills. Finally, he spoke, shattering the silence with the power and majesty of rumbling thunder. Deep echoing words, not even directed at me, set my nervous system on high alert. To the outside world, the window coverings were just draperies, but inside they were the boundary containing the brewing storm, one that had already eclipsed the sunshine. Like other forces of nature, its strength was beautiful and frightening. The question, I wondered, was what destruction would be left in its wake?

From my peripheral vision, I saw the bellman's lips move as he backed away. When Nox spoke, the meaning of his words was lost. The tenor and tone reverberated through me, leaving my mouth dry and insides clenching. Before I could process, the click of the closing door signaled that we were now alone—I was alone with the man I'd dreamt of, the man who fascinated me, the man who currently owned me.

While we stared in stunned silence, the temperature of the room continued to rise. This wasn't the reunion I'd imagined or dreamt about. Closing my eyes, I inhaled. The woodsy scent of his cologne brought back memories, clouding my thoughts and tingling my skin.

Blinking my eyes, I tried to swallow, to speak, but I couldn't. The last few hours left me bewildered while his unexpected presence rendered me mute. I thought I had time before I would face him. Isaac said Nox was at work. He'd said he wouldn't be here, but here he was.

"Miss Collins." Nox's frosty greeting stilled the heat bubbling within me, covering everything in a layer of ice. I stepped back, trying to focus on his eyes, wanting to see the pale blue.

Nox had other plans. Before I could process anything, he was in front of me. A gasp escaped my lips as his large hand encircled my waist and pulled me forward. The touch was electric, sending sparks in every direction. It was the lightning to his thunderous voice, and I was in the eye of the storm.

"Miss Collins, answer me. Do not make me repeat myself."

I lifted my gaze as he pulled me closer, and our bodies melded together.

What question did he ask?

Though his words were cold, his touch was hot, blistering my skin. The stark contrast incited prickling goose bumps upon my flesh. Our hearts beat erratically as our chests united.

"Nox," I finally managed.

Roughly capturing my chin between his thumb and forefinger, he corrected, "Mr. Demetri. We've had this conversation already."

I tried to nod willing the tears of the last few days to remain at bay. "Mr. Demetri."

Brushing my long hair over my shoulders and away from my face, Nox continued to stare. Imprisoned in his grasp, I stood still as my eyes adjusted, and the strain of his expression became clear: the pulsing of the vein in his forehead and neck, the clenching and unclenching of his jaw.

I wanted to touch him, to remember and for him to remember me. As I lifted my fingers toward the stubble of his cheeks, I recalled his directive on the phone, telling me to thank him. The words were once again on the tip of my tongue. However, before I could touch him, Nox released my chin and seized my hand. His grip tightened painfully around my fingers.

"No," he said, his face moving closer to mine, "Miss Collins, new rules. *My* rules."

With our lips close and his warm breath bathing my cheeks, his curt tone and clipped words created a new chasm between us. Though we were only inches apart, our separation seemed wider than it had been since the day we parted.

"Speak, Miss Collins."

I watched his full lips as his unfamiliar tenor filled my ears.

"I've yet to hear anything from those beautiful lips except my name."

Whatever he tells you to do. Karen's words repeated like a sickening cadence in the recesses of my mind.

"Thank you," I whispered, the words cracking with pent-up emotion.

Nox took a step back, his stare never wavering. Slowly, the tips of his lips curled upward. It wasn't the sexy, menacing grin I'd learned to adore. This was different or maybe it was his eyes. The pale blue was glacier ice, absent of the navy swirls, absent of emotion. Calculation and determination shone in his gaze, sizing me up, scanning for weaknesses, and searching for secrets. I'd seen that stare before. I'd lived with it.

My neck straightened and stance stiffened as I swallowed my last drop of saliva. "Thank you, Mr. Demetri."

"For—?" he encouraged.

"For helping me."

The heat of his grasp disappeared as he released my waist, throwing me off balance and causing me to stumble backward. My shoulders collided with a wall awakening me to my surroundings and the fact that we were still in the entry.

With all things Nox, I hadn't realized that we hadn't even entered the suite. The dark rooms beyond our bubble grew more ominous as Nox paced a small circle before stopping in front of me.

Looming nearer, he replied, "Wrong answer, Miss Collins. I am *not* helping you. I'm helping myself. That's what I do. What we had in Del Mar…" He gestured between us. "…what we did, that wasn't me, not the me who succeeds in this filthy world. That was the me who believed he'd met a princess who enjoyed being treated like a slut." His lips pressed together as he slowly shook his head. "You deceived me."

I opened my mouth to disagree, to explain that I never deceived him, not about who I was, not about who I was with him. Then he uttered the one word that silenced me.

"Charli."

The weight of my one-week nickname crushed me.

"N-Nox, let me explain."

"The truth seems to be the opposite." His chin rose defiantly as he turned toward the darkened living room. "Come, Miss Collins. You have rules to learn and penalties to experience."

CHAPTER 3

CHARLI

A COLD CHILL ran through me as I willed my feet forward. Déjà vu bogged my steps, as each one sunk deeper into invisible quicksand. I couldn't survive a year with this Nox—no, with this Mr. Demetri. Somehow I had to revive my Nox.

He stopped and turned on a lamp near the sofa, illuminating a small portion of the darkened room. Sitting within the circle of soft light, he leaned back and unbuttoned the grey jacket of his suit, revealing a white linen shirt and light blue tie. The tie moved as his wide chest expanded and contracted with each breath. All the while his stare drank me in.

"Come closer. I want to see you and appreciate my investment."

Slowly, I moved forward. His eyes unashamedly scanned up and down, lingering on some areas longer than others. The trail burned, not as it had before, but with a scalding sense of shame. Silence continued to tick away as I stood before him. Uncertainty filled my thoughts.

When Nox shifted, his physical reaction was visible.

"May we discuss—" I began.

"No. Do not speak."

I blinked my eyes and took a step toward the sofa.

"Stop."

I did, mid-step. Merely a foot away was the man to whom I'd given my body and heart, and yet it wasn't him. I didn't know who this man was.

"Rules, Miss Collins. New rules."

I lifted my chin. "So you've mentioned."

He tilted his head to the side. "Make me a drink."

I followed the direction he'd indicated. There was a bar, complete with many bottles of liquor.

"A-A drink?" I asked with audible confusion. It wasn't the first thing I'd thought he'd want me to do.

"I know you saw doctors at Infidelity. Did they check your hearing?"

I straightened my neck and found my most placating tone. "What kind of drink would you like, Mr. Demetri?"

"Scotch, on the rocks."

So this was this my new job—to be his waitress?

Swallowing my pride, I walked to the bar and read the different bottles. I wasn't a scotch drinker, but I found a bottle I recognized from Alton's personal favorites. Thankfully, the ice bucket was full. I filled the bottom of a cocktail glass with the square cubes and poured the strong liquid over the top. The smell reminded me of the drink Karen gave me earlier in the day. Once I was finished, I turned back around.

Nox merely nodded.

I handed him the glass. "Your scotch, sir."

He swirled the ice and amber liquid, momentarily mesmerized by their dance, and then his pale eyes were back to mine.

"Take off your clothes."

Shock undoubtedly showed in my expression and tone. "What?"

After taking a drink, he sat the cocktail glass upon the table and grinned. "Come here."

My eyes narrowed. "Why?"

"My days of making exceptions are over. It's time you learn my rules and what happens when you disobey."

I inched closer. "I-I haven't..."

He lifted his hand, palm up, beckoning me closer. Like a spider to a fly, his silent invitation enticed and excited me. For reasons I couldn't comprehend, in Nox's presence my will to argue waned as my desire to please grew. Slowly, I reached for his fingers and placed mine in his. As he encased my smaller hand, just like the first time, our connection formed a conduit, a portal for energy to flow from one to the other. Heat flooded my circulation, warming everything from my fingers to my toes. My gaze flew to his, and in that millisecond, I saw the navy I adored. No matter what he was trying to prove, our connection wasn't gone.

His Adam's apple bobbed, and with a blink the navy disappeared.

"Closer, Miss Collins. I'm going to show you what happens when my commands are met by questions. This should remind you to end your rebellious ways."

My steps stuttered.

"Over my knee."

Is he fucking kidding me?

"What?"

In one fell swoop, he tugged my hand, pulling me closer and capturing me over his lap.

"No! Nox, I'm not doing this. I won't."

He didn't speak as I protested in vain. His erection prodded my stomach, as I went over his knee. Visions of Alton came raining through my mind. My mother's headaches and the days she couldn't make it out of bed. I wouldn't live that way, not for a day and definitely not for a year. My limbs stiffened as I thrashed about.

"Asshole, let me up."

I was no match for his strength. With his left arm pushing against the small of my back and his right leg keeping my kicking feet back, I was effectively pinned, balanced in a way that provided me no leverage—no escape. The dimmed world around us was a blur seen beyond the veil of my hair brushing the floor. Panic overtook me as I felt him lift the hem of my dress. My reaction was primal. I was in survivor mode and did the only thing I could think to do. Reaching for his ankle and lifting his pant leg, I bit with all of my might.

"Shit!"

His curse echoed as he pulled my hair to force me to release my bite and pushed me from his lap. Almost immediately, I was on the floor.

"What the fuck do you think you're doing?" he barked, reaching for his ankle.

Scooting away as fast as I could, I replied, "What the hell do *you* think you're doing?"

He stood and took two steps until he loomed over me. "Give me your hand."

My lip disappeared between my teeth as I stared at his palm once again being offered. I shook my head. "I don't want to be hit. I won't agree to that. It's my hard limit."

"Come here." This time his request was less cold than just moments earlier.

Unable to resist, I reached out and Nox helped me to my feet.

His large hands framed my cheeks as he searched my eyes, less scrutinizing and more curious than before.

"My tastes—"

"Are unique," I said, finishing his sentence. "I remember."

"What you did—signing with Infidelity—was unacceptable."

I sucked my lip back between my teeth and tried to comprehend his words. My signing with Infidelity was what brought us back together. Was being with me unacceptable? Would he prefer to be with someone else? He didn't have to buy my agreement. Why did he?

"Are you listening?" he asked.

I wasn't.

"No. I'm trying to understand. No one forced you to buy my agreement. If you didn't want me—"

His grip on the sides of my face tightened as he walked me backward. Once my shoulders were against the wall, Nox released my cheeks and pinned my wrists above my head. The vein in his forehead pulsated with life, as he asked, "Did I say that? Did I ever say I didn't want you?"

I swallowed, my emotions tugging my heart in too many directions. "I-I don't understand." I tried to free my hands. "And you're hurting me."

Ignoring my plea, he pulled my hands higher, making me shift to my toes. His shoulders broadened and neck straightened. "Come now, Miss Collins. From what I've heard, you're a Stanford graduate on your way to Columbia. That sounds like you're an intelligent woman. Prostitution shouldn't be too difficult for you to comprehend."

Heat bubbled from the floor, not erotic but stifling. I blinked my eyes, each time slower than the last, regulating my breathing and wishing to escape. My hands were beginning to feel numb as the grip on my wrists increased.

If my childhood fantasies were true, I could click my heels together three times to escape. The only problem with my solution—and the difference between Dorothy from the Wizard of Oz and me—was that I didn't want to go home. I wanted to go back to Del Mar and away from the decision I'd made.

"Companionship," I whispered.

"Excuse me?"

"Companionship, not sex, not prostitution," I said louder, forcing my eyes to meet his.

"Are you insinuating there's a difference?"

I lifted my chin defiantly. "Yes."

He released my wrists and led me to the sofa. I followed, mindful of his hands and doing my best to avoid landing across his lap again. This time we both sat.

"Let me tell you what *I* understand," Nox said.

I nodded, rubbing the circulation back into my wrists as the woodsy scent I'd missed settled around us.

"For the next year, you're mine. Tell me why."

I swallowed the bile bubbling from my stomach. "Because you bought my agreement."

"*You*. Not an agreement. I bought *you*."

If he wanted me to feel cheap, he was succeeding.

"Say it," Nox commanded.

"You bought me." The words came out stronger than I felt.

I flinched as he reached toward my cheek.

"No." The velvety tenor washed over me. "Don't flinch. Charli, I don't *hit*. What I wanted to do—and still plan to do—isn't hitting. I plan to spank that beautiful round ass. Do you know why?"

My body was defying me. Spanking was hitting. I knew that. I also knew the soft yet breathy tone that Nox was now using. That tone, combined with the way his warm touch caressed my cheek and neck and teased the neckline of my dress, brought my insides back to life. I moaned as he tugged my hair, pulling my eyes to his.

"Answer."

"You said," I began, "it was because I signed with Infidelity. But," I added quickly, "if you don't like it, why are you a client?"

His gaze narrowed as he painfully wound his fingers in my hair. "New rules."

My lips came together, the pressure on my scalp keeping me mute.

"My rules," he went on. "When you signed your name on that agreement, you forfeited the right to question. You forfeited your hard limits. Your job for the next year is to say, '*Yes, Mr. Demetri.*' Can you do that?"

I swallowed as he tilted my head back farther, and his lips found the sensitive skin behind my ear.

"Miss Collins," he spoke between demanding kisses, "answer."

"I can," I replied, "but it depends on what you want."

"No, it doesn't."

My eyes opened wide. His tone had again changed. "Nox, I do have limits, hard limits."

His assault on my neck ended. "No, Miss Collins, you don't. I own you—one hundred percent—for the next year. What I say goes without question. You will show me the respect I deserve as your client. You are mine to do with as I please. Is that clear?"

"Yes," I replied, the word choked out as resentment boiled within me.

Nox cleared his throat. "You've just added more swats to your ass, not that I mind, but you will. Would you like to try that answer again?"

I couldn't believe what I was hearing. It wasn't just my ears; it was my all of my senses. This wasn't my prince. He was a dick. I worked to hide any sarcasm. "Yes, Mr. Demetri."

I lowered my eyes, unknowingly shaking my head.

Nox tugged on my hair, lifting my gaze. "Tell me what you're thinking."

I fought the tears that welled in my eyes and the cries that festered in my throat. Ignoring his fist in my hair, I looked into the icy blue. "You have no idea how difficult this was, how heart-wrenching. When I began to make the call and your number appeared…" I took a deep breath. "…I was relieved, but now…" I searched for any sign that my words were affecting him. "…now you're making me feel cheap." My volume rose. "If that's what you want for the next year, a cheap whore, then you're succeeding."

One side of his lips quirked upward. "New rules, as I was saying. I always succeed. I always win. Know that, remember that." He released my hair and fluffed it over my shoulders. "Also remember, you're not a cheap whore."

My chest clenched. "I-I'm not?"

Nox lifted my hand, encouraging me to stand. When I did, he tugged and I was once again across his lap. This time I didn't fight. That didn't mean I approved of what he was about to do. I didn't. It meant that his next words sapped the fight from me. They hurt me more than his hands ever could.

"No, Miss Collins. I paid a fortune for you. You're the most expensive whore I've ever met."

I closed my eyes as he lifted the skirt of my dress, bunching it at my waist and pulled my panties down to my knees.

A low whistle filled the air before he said, "You do have a fine ass."

As he rubbed my behind, his erection grew against my stomach. The first slap of his palm against my exposed skin echoed through the room as blood rushed to my ears and copper filled my mouth. My teeth clamped as I pierced the inside of my lower lip. Tears fell from my eyes, but I refused to allow myself to cry out.

He punished and then would tease, spank and then caress. The opposite sensations produced an array of emotions. I hated the abuse to my ass, but loved what his fingers were doing. My vow of silence didn't last long. Soon, both moans and whimpers filled the suite, punctuated by the sound of slapping skin.

I didn't only utter sounds. Nox made me repeat phrases. If I did, I was rewarded with his fingers within my folds. If I was too slow or not loud enough, the sting of his hand returned.

By the time he was done, I'd admitted that he owned me, that I was his for the next year, and that my limits no longer existed but were his to decide. I'd agreed to all things in private and public. He was my job, and I belonged to him.

I'd said what I was required to say. That didn't mean I agreed. In Del Mar I'd given him my heart. I knew that now, because today he'd broken it.

Once he was satisfied that I was demeaned enough, he pushed me from his lap and callously said, "I'll be back. Read my instructions and be ready. I want my money's worth."

His words hung in the air to taunt me as he left me alone to gather the aching shreds of my heart. After the door shut, I slipped to my knees. Reaching for the lamp—currently the only source of light—I flung it against the marble floor. Sparks flew seconds before the room went dark.

CHAPTER 4

CHARLI

I COULDN'T PROCESS the downward spiral of the last few days. With my panties secured in their rightful place, I eased my sore body against the wall in the dark suite and hugged my knees to my chest. Tears coated my cheeks as I worked to fit the pieces of the puzzle together.

Memories, like slivers of my broken heart, scattered through my thoughts. Time lost meaning as my recent and long-ago past intertwined until I wasn't sure what was real and what were memories. I remembered the card Karen gave me this afternoon.

Could I call the number? Could I be the first to ever claim abuse? Or was this an injustice like others I'd suffered, ones where resolution never came?

The room blurred as more unshed tears raced for release. The entire scenario—Infidelity, Nox, and what he'd done—was embarrassing and degrading. I detested corporal punishment as a child—hated it—and yet at some point with Nox, it became erotic. My temples throbbed, ass hurt, and insides twisted with unfulfilled need. My body's reaction was as upsetting to me as his actions.

It was wrong. He was wrong. I was wrong.

More and more memories swirled. The fragmented contrasts to childhood punishments churned the acid in my stomach. Those memories erased any desire Nox had elicited.

I closed my eyes and gave in to a recollection I hadn't thought of in years.

Not every punishment began as a family conference.

The distinctive click of the key turning in the lock echoed through my dark bedroom. Consciously, I held my breath, praying to stay silent. I should have gone into the closet.

Why didn't I go into the closet?

My current location was only hidden by darkness and the obstruction of my massive bed. With little light, I could barely make out the pattern of the floral bedspread or bed skirt. Nevertheless, the web-like pattern of the lace skirt allowed me a limited view of the door, something I wouldn't have had in the closet. Golden light from the hallway spilled over the carpet as the door slowly opened. I gulped my hiccupped cry, trying to stay hidden, waiting to see feet, and praying he wasn't returning.

My pulse raced as the shoes came into view. Black shoes, lady's shoes, and black slacks. I sighed with relief as my forehead dropped to my raised knees, and I braced my eyes for the flood of light. It didn't come. The door closed, and the familiar click of the lock let my heartbeat slow, closer to its normal rhythm. Sometimes I wondered if I wore a beacon. No matter where I was, Jane always found me.

"Child, what are you doing?"

I shook my head as she walked around the bed. Even with the thick carpet, the sound of her footsteps filled the room. I didn't want to look up. I wanted to disappear. If only invisibility were real, I'd do that. I'd stay invisible so no one could see me, and if I were lucky, I wouldn't see them.

"Alexandria, baby, I'm talking to you." Her tone was soft yet firm.

"N-No, you're not. I'm not here. You can't talk to someone who's not here." My words were muffled as I kept my head down.

"You're not here? Then where are you?"

"I'm invisible. You can't see me." At nine years old it made perfect sense. People did it in books. They used cloaks or took potions. Maybe if I believed, I could make it true.

"Invisible? If you're invisible, aren't you still here?"

I shrugged. She was right. Invisibility was the wrong wish. I wanted to be someone else in another life.

Jane eased herself to the floor beside me. As she did, she blew out a long whoosh of breath and moaned, settling into her new position. Warmth radiated from her skin and covered me with a different cloak, one that enveloped both of us and only us. My cheeks briefly rose in a small smile.

"I'm getting too old to be sitting on the floor." She rubbed the top of my head. "But I did it for you. Now look up at old Jane. I want to see those beautiful eyes."

I gave up on my invisibility, since it obviously wasn't working; however, I didn't look up as she asked. Instead, I fell across her chest, landing with my face against breasts as her arms encircled my shoulders.

"Shhh," she said as she stroked my hair. "What's this all about?"

It took minutes or longer before the words came. "Do you think I could move away?"

"Move away from Montague Manor and your momma? Do you want to do that?"

"I do. Will you come with me?" It was the first spark of hope I'd had since Alton entered my room, mad again at something I did or didn't do. I couldn't tell. As much as I loved when he was out of town, his return was rarely worth the days of reprieve. He came home angry, as if he wanted to still be gone. I wanted him gone too. Why wouldn't he stay gone?

There was always some unforgivable sin that I'd committed in his absence. Many times like this evening, I didn't even know what he was talking about. That didn't matter. I'd learned that pleading my case was the spark to his rage. Admitting my guilt and taking my medicine, *as he called it, was the quickest way to a speedy end. Tonight with his disgusting breath smelling like the drinks he always drank, he ranted on about how I was a disappointment—to Mother, him, and the Montague name. It was as if he blamed me that there wasn't another Montague heir to take my place.*

Jane's reassuring tone broke through my thoughts. "Now tell me how we're gonna live. And where do you think we can go where your momma won't find us?"

"We can change our names. I read a book about people who did that. You can work, and I bet momma doesn't look. He said she'd be happier without me."

Jane continued to rub my back. "Alexandria, your momma loves you." She tapped my chest. "In here, you know that. Don't you ever forget that. And one day you can move away." She lifted my chin. "And when you do, old Jane will be so proud of you." Her warm lips kissed my forehead. "Not just then—now too. Right now I's proud of you. So is your momma."

I lowered my eyes. "That's not what—"

"Shhh. What did I say about that? You're as beautiful on the inside as you are on the outside. Some peoples not. Some people look pretty but they're ugly on the inside. Don't let that ugly inside of you. You keep it out." She tapped on my chest again. "That heart inside of you. Child, that's yours. You protect it. One day you may decide to share it, but don't do that because no one told you to. You do it because you found someone who is as beautiful on the inside as you."

I nodded and laid my head back against her chest. After a few minutes, I confessed, "I really hate him. I do."

"No, there's no room in that beautiful heart for hate."

"He hates me."

She took a deep breath, making my head moved up and down. "I'm sure he'd say he doesn't. Just remember, you are Alexandria Charles Montague Collins. Those gates out there… what do they say?"

"Montague Manor," I mumbled. I'd heard this before.

"Whose name is that?"

"Momma's and mine."

Jane nodded. "Just remember that."

"I wish I could forget it."

I took a deep breath and stood, doing my best to ignore the lingering soreness. Stepping over the broken lamp, I opened the drapes and blinked. The memory from my childhood and of *Storm Nox* dissipated as bright sunshine flooded the executive suite. Gazing out over the park, I looked to the northeast, toward Patrick's apartment.

His proximity gave me strength. Despite what Nox might think, I wasn't alone. Soon I'd be starting classes. My world would grow. I'd done it before. I'd do it again. If my childhood hadn't broken me, Nox Demetri wouldn't. The memory I recalled was right. Jane was right. It was *my* heart. It wasn't up to Nox or anyone else who I gave the power to break it or heal it. It was up to me, and I'd protect it.

With each passing minute, I bargained with myself and made myself a deal. I'd recover my heart and put the pieces back together. The job of the heart was to pump blood. I'd glue the pieces of my heart using blood and tears, but they wouldn't be my own. They'd come from those who'd wronged me—from Alton, my mother, and now Nox.

When a year was up, I'd be the one to walk away but not until I had Nox Demetri completely under my spell. Not until he was the one who would need to pick up the pieces of his heart. In doing so, I'd also secure my schooling and determine just how much of myself I was willing to give to Montague. Alton might believe he won, but he didn't know the truth. He's the one who made me a fighter, and this fight wasn't over.

I opened the door to the balcony and inhaled the summer air. Each moment in the sunlight invigorated me. I'd lived behind smoke and mirrors my whole life. I could handle one more year.

As I stared out at the park, I remembered the envelope Isaac gave me. Walking to the bar, the one where I made Nox a drink, I poured myself a glass of moscato—after all, by Montague Manor standards, it was still white-wine time—and sat carefully on one of the sofas as the warm air from the open door blew gently through the suite.

Retrieving my purse, I found my phone and the envelope. I checked the time; it was nearly four-thirty. On the outside of the envelope was the room number. Tentatively, I ripped the seam and pulled the pages free. The first page was a handwritten letter. Though I'd only seen Nox's handwriting on the note he left for me the first morning I awoke in his bed, I knew this note was penned by him.

My steeled heart ached to flutter. Who handwrote notes anymore?

And then I saw the second page. It was a photo—of me. By the outfit, I knew it was one of the shots taken yesterday at Infidelity, one that Karen said was for my profile. It wasn't on photo paper. As a matter of fact, the page was creased throughout, as if it had been wadded and then straightened.

The hairs on the back of my neck prickled as I began to read his words.

Charli, or should I say Miss Alexandria Collins?

I imagined our reunion and waited for my phone to ring. Never in my wildest imagination did I envision this (see picture). For the record, prostitution doesn't become you… too much makeup can't cover the beautiful princess in my memory…

The paper blurred in my trembling hand.

…Del Mar was a dream. Reality is here.

If it's a whore you want to be, then I'm your man. I told you my tastes were unique. We've only scratched the surface. Miss Collins, you're mine—body and soul—for the next twelve months. In Del Mar you gave me two nights; now I've purchased 365 more. They're mine and only mine.

Your ability to question or dispute me in any way was relinquished the moment you signed that agreement.

Alexandria Collins, I'm a businessman. I don't make bad investments. I will get what I paid for.

The butterflies I'd imagined at his handwritten note evaporated, washed away by a deluge of bile and contempt. How dare he address me in this manner? He doesn't know with what I was faced. He doesn't know me. Besides he's obviously an Infidelity client. That negates his ability to act superior.

Fuck him!

I forced myself to continue reading.

I look forward to tonight—not to fucking a princess who enjoyed being treated like a slut but to fucking a slut who for a week pretended to be a princess.

You have more instructions in the bedroom.

Do not disobey me.

~Mr. Demetri

I took a ragged breath, swallowed the contents of my wine glass, and stood. The shakiness of my knees wasn't brought on by sadness, though I admitted it was there along with hurt. No, the trembling was rage. I balled the letter and the picture, smashing it into submission.

After pouring another glass of wine, I made my way to the bedroom with a tug of my suitcase. It was still in the living room where the bellman had left it. Focusing on the bed, I barely noticed the luxury of the room. Upon the bed was a black dress. Reading the label, I recognized that it was a very nice black dress. Next to the dress were a pearl choker necklace, a shoebox, and another note.

I ran my fingers over the pearls. The necklace was stunning, but in an odd way reminded me of a collar. Surely, that wasn't his intention, was it?

I lifted the page in disgust.

You have a five o'clock appointment in the hotel's spa. Don't be late. They have instructions on what to do. Don't change them.

Later tonight you will go to Mobar, the bar here in the Mandarin. Be there by eight. Wear what is on the bed and only what is on the bed. Order a lemon drop martini. Do not drink. Nurse it, play with it, run your fingers around the rim of the glass. Other than the bartender, don't speak to anyone. As your finger slides circles over the smooth rim, imagine my fingers circling your tits, teasing your clit, and plunging deep in your pussy. I want you wet and ready for me.

I've never picked up a prostitute at a bar. I will tonight. (You see? My investment is already paying off. I have many more fantasies, and I've paid well to have them all come true.)

In this outfit, no one else will know what you truly are. They'll see the princess.

Reality will be our secret.

In the handbag is cash. Use it to pay for your drink and keep the rest. That's what you wanted—to be paid. I'll pay, and you will obey.

It wasn't signed.

Dick!

I ground my teeth together as I stared at the sexy dress. He was right. No one would know. Well, the hell with him. I wasn't that easily intimidated. He had a fantasy about picking up a prostitute? Fine, I'd role-play. But Mr. Nox Demetri was going to learn that despite his earlier show of force, I did have hard limits. I'd play his games but on my terms.

I picked up the phone and hit the button for the front desk.

"Hello, Miss Charli."

That must have been the name Nox gave when he registered. "Hello, can you please connect me to the spa. I need to cancel my appointment."

CHAPTER 5

NOX

I COULDN'T CONCENTRATE. Shit, I could barely function. Thoughts of Charli consumed my mind—her gorgeous eyes, the way she looked at me when I came out of that room and our gaze met. I hadn't planned on going to the Mandarin yet or being there when she arrived. I had things to do, but I couldn't stay away. I couldn't *not* see her. The attraction was too strong.

That was what she did to me. She made me lose focus on the world and see only her.

In only the short time we'd been together, she'd gotten under my skin like no one else, even Jo. I'd never fallen so fast or so hard. I didn't do drugs, never had. Nevertheless, I imagined that Charli was like cocaine. One casual hit at a party—that was all I was after in Del Mar. One hit, one week. Since returning to New York, I'd tried to deny my addiction. Each day we were apart was another day *clean*, another day *sober*. I was able to detox because she was out of my life.

That was then.

This is now, and now she's mine.

Deloris said her name was Alexandria, or Alex, but that didn't change anything. We'd confessed that our names were nicknames, and to me she'd always be *my* Charli. I just wasn't ready to let her know that, not yet. For the time being, we'd stick with formality. From the moment Deloris showed me that envelope with her picture and told me that Charli had a profile, I'd been consumed, overpowered by the need to save and protect her from Infidelity as well as teach her a lesson.

What she'd done—going to Infidelity and signing an agreement of intent—was stupid. It was dangerous. It was unacceptable. What would have happened if Deloris hadn't discovered her profile?

I knew what would have happened.

She would have ended up in someone else's bed. I believed her in Del Mar when she said she didn't sleep around. What I needed to know was how the confident, intelligent, breathtaking woman I'd met in Del Mar was lured into the sordid world of Infidelity.

I wasn't sure why she wanted to reduce herself to a whore, but if that was what she wanted, I was her man. With me, she'd stay safe. The possibilities of what could have happened if she'd truly gone into Infidelity sickened and enraged me. I couldn't move forward until I'd punished her for her poor decision-making.

Now that was done, and the new rules could begin.

The reality was too obvious to deny. I was an addict in need of one person—Charli.

Now that I'd seen her, touched her, and heard her voice—and moans—I'd do anything within my power to have more. In the few short hours since Deloris's bombshell, Charli had me acting out of character. Never did I leave the office in the middle of the day. Never did I cancel meetings for personal reasons. And never did I travel without Isaac.

My driver-slash-bodyguard was with her, and that thought consumed me. I wanted—no, needed—to be the one with her. Making my way back toward my office because some things couldn't wait, I rode in the back of a taxi, another thing I rarely did. Shaking my head, I stared down at my hand.

My cheeks rose at the tingling in my palm. Closing my eyes, I sighed. Damn, I was still hard thinking about the way her tight round ass reddened and the way she grew wet. She said she didn't like it, but her body told me another story. I could listen to her sensuous body tell me bedtime tales for eternity.

From her reaction alone, it seems that Miss Alexandria Collins and I have not even begun to discover her limits. Ideas of possibilities added to my uncomfortable situation. I couldn't dwell on those thoughts, or I'd never be able to walk from the taxi to the office. The anticipation of what I could do to her may be the death of me—death by blue balls.

One year wouldn't be enough.

I was done with Infidelity. I didn't care how financially beneficial it had become: Demetri Enterprises was walking away before Infidelity imploded. Once I was out and no longer associated with it, that was what I planned to have happen. The bigger it grew, the more of a risk it presented. Already poor decisions had resulted in issues. I wanted out.

My thoughts went back to Charli. I wanted to believe that she was lured, tricked, or scammed into signing with the agency. I didn't want to believe that she stooped to sell her greatest commodity—herself. The cold, hard reality was that she had. She'd signed the agreement of intent. She'd signed a one-year commitment. What she didn't realize was that it no longer existed.

I didn't own her as she thought, not really. Hell, I didn't want that. I only planned to let her think that I did for a while, so that she could fully experience the consequences of her actions.

When I spoke to Ms. Flores this morning, I didn't rent Charli for a year: I freed her. It cost a damn fortune, but I did it. I also told her to let Alexandria believe it was business as usual for Infidelity. I wanted Charli to think the deal was complete. And then, as soon as our conversation was done, Deloris deleted all of Charli's files. There was no record of Alexandria Collins anywhere on the Infidelity network. I'd made myself very clear: Alexandria's employment was terminated. The transaction cost me the entire year of her agreement, a bonus for expediting the process, as well as the additional fee for keeping the whole deal confidential. Fuck, I'd almost paid more for Charli than Demetri Enterprises originally invested in Infidelity. She was expensive, but I refused to allow her to be a whore.

The taxi stopped outside the building housing multiple floors of Demetri

Enterprises. As I glanced up at the glass structure, I realized that I'd accomplished nothing during the drive, not even looking at my phone. Running my hand over my face to refocus, the lingering scent of Charli almost derailed my efforts. Damn, I needed to get my head on straight or the next few hours would be a disaster.

Oren was in town.

If it weren't for my dinner plans with dear old Dad, I would have stayed with Charli. My father's timing couldn't be worse. Or maybe it was Charli's timing. Either way, I needed to get my head back in the game. Oren Demetri required one hundred percent concentration. If he didn't have it, he'd sense it like a wild predator sensed weakness. I'd seen him mercilessly eat adversaries alive and spit out their bones, all the while keeping a smile on his face. I wouldn't let Charli or anyone else allow me to slip up around him.

For the next few hours I needed to push her to the back of my mind. That was all right. She had instructions, and as long as she followed them, her evening would be occupied until we met again. As I rode the elevator high into the sky and tried to concentrate on business, one final realization hit me: I didn't own Alexandria Collins. From the first time I saw her in Del Mar, she owned me.

My assistant, Dianne, looked up from her desk as soon as I entered her office, the area immediately outside of mine.

"Mr. Demetri, thank goodness. I've been trying to reach you."

I straightened my shoulders, forced myself back to reality, and reached for my phone from the pocket of my jacket. Swiping the screen I saw the number of missed calls and texts. "I told you that I'd be temporarily unavailable."

"Yes, sir," she said, following me into my office. "It's Mr. Demetri. He's called for you several times, and now he's here."

I stopped walking near the large windows. The tinted glass kept the sun's rays from penetrating, but the shimmering buildings reflected the August heat. With her words, the buildings no longer registered. I ran my hand through my hair and shook my head as I spun back toward Dianne. "Here? Where?"

"The receptionist just called from the ground floor. She said he's about three minutes behind you."

"Shit. I'm supposed to meet him for dinner in an hour. I wonder what's so damn important it couldn't wait."

"Also, Senator Carroll called. He'd like you to return his call today."

I nodded. "Don't mention that in front of my father."

"Of course not. Would you like me to tell Mr. Demetri that you're unavailable?"

I would, but it wouldn't stop him. He'd barge right in even if I were in a meeting. It wouldn't matter to him who I was talking to. After all, he was Oren Demetri. It's his damn name on the letterhead.

"No. I have a few minutes before my meeting with Ellis. Send him back."

"Yes, sir."

I took a seat behind my desk as Dianne closed the door giving me a moment of peace. Demetri Enterprises comprised three floors of the seventy-nine-story building, the fifty-sixth through the fifty-eighth floors. The elevator ride alone could take a while.

The commotion beyond my closed door alerted me that it hadn't taken as long as I'd hoped.

"…Mr. Demetri, Mr. Demetri is here—" Dianne said as she opened my door, her voice disappearing into the booming tenor of my father.

"Yeah, yeah, he knows who his father is. Lennox, can't you train your girls better than that? I'm the CEO. I don't need an introduction to you or to anyone in this damn company."

I'd moved from my desk and nodded toward Dianne. Her expression was classic Oren encounter. By the way her eyes glazed over, she looked as if she'd just narrowly missed being hit by a bus.

"Welcome, Oren. My office is your office." I then added with all the sarcasm I could muster, "Feel free to barge in anytime." I turned toward Dianne. "Thank you, Ms. O'Neal, my *assistant.* Tell Ellis our meeting may be a few minutes delayed. I'll be in the conference room shortly."

After the door was closed, I turned to my father. "*Girls.* Jesus, Dad, are you wanting a sexual harassment suit? Have you checked the calendar lately?"

He waved toward the door dismissively. "You never did have what it takes to run a tight ship. Besides, when I was your age, my girls knew what was expected of them and what would happen if they disappointed me."

The muscles in my neck tensed as I took a step forward, unwilling to let him run his little tyrant show in my office. "I'm sure Mother appreciated that."

"You're not married, not anymore. A little discussion of company rules with that pretty little thing might loosen you up a little."

My teeth clenched. I'd been in my father's presence for barely a minute and I wanted him gone. Thankfully, he was usually in London. We worked much better with an ocean between us. "Why are you here?"

"Direct. Maybe there is hope for you."

I fought the urge to move closer. If I did, he'd pat my shoulder or some other pretense of affection. It wasn't affection. It was his posturing technique, one he'd undoubtedly perfected in the eighties.

"I wanted to hear about your time in Del Mar."

What the fuck?

"Del Mar? I told you about the meetings."

"No," Oren said as he settled into a chair in the corner of my office. The seat he chose was near a sofa and faced the door. Oren Demetri never sat with his back to the door. Rule number sixty-two: know your surroundings and have the exits and entrances in view at all times.

Sitting at one of the chairs opposite my desk would have violated that rule. Rules can't be violated. "No, son. You gave me the CliffsNotes. The shit with the Senate is too important to receive the condensed version. I get it. I do. You don't trust the security of Demetri." He cocked his head. "I know it's safe on my end, but maybe that girl you have running your side of things isn't as capable as you think."

I sat on the sofa, unbuttoned my suit jacket, and leaned back with a huff. "I met with Senator Carroll on two occasions."

"Two?"

"Two," I went on. "The House bill is currently being run through the Senate Finance Committee. Senator Carroll agrees with our proposal. The

House bill would result in an exorbitant tax levy for us and corporations like ours. In this financial climate, the taxpayers are tired of big businesses getting breaks. The election is coming. However, with the global economy, even insinuating that businesses should up their tax burden is like showing us the door of the country. Hell, we can do business anywhere."

"So if he agrees, what's the problem?"

"The problem is that others got to the House Ways and Means committee before the bill was drafted. Tobacco and alcohol have been taxed to death with the sin tax. They're rebelling. Senator Higgins from Georgia is one of the biggest proponents for the current wording. It cuts the sin tax by almost three percent and uses the wording in this new bill to make up the proposed lost revenue. The president won't sign a bill that will add to the overall debt. It's the wording. On face value it doesn't look like our increase would be significant, but Carroll laid it out. It is. It could be crushing."

I was already getting too technical for Oren, and I knew it. There was part of me that wanted to go on, to talk particulars, but by the way his eyes wandered about, I knew it wouldn't serve any purpose other than to stroke my ego. Furthermore, it would delay my meeting with Ellis, my dinner with Oren, and most importantly, the meeting I was anticipating with Charli.

"Then stop it."

I nodded. "I've made calls. The hearings will start soon. We have experts lined up to speak and answer questions. Carroll isn't alone. The Finance Committee is pretty evenly divided."

Oren slapped the arm of the chair. "This shit didn't get out of hand when I was running the U.S. side of Demetri. I had a handle…"

I clenched my jaw. This was bullshit. He never had a handle on any of this. If he had he wouldn't have almost lost everything in 2009. He was just lucky to have started Demetri at a time when the government was doling out tax breaks like candy on Halloween. If I had to spend another minute with him now and then dinner, my blood pressure would be through the roof. That would undoubtedly not bode well for Charli.

When he paused, I stood. "Dinner? Let's make it early. I have plans."

"You? You haven't had plans…"

…since Jocelyn.

Well, even he had the decency not to complete his comment, not after what he'd said earlier. "I have plans. I can meet you at six o'clock."

"Four Seasons. I'll be waiting."

That meant he'd have an hour drinking lead on me. Great. I nodded, grabbed the folder on my desk, and made sure the screens on my computer were locked. "Show yourself out."

"Son, that wasn't the only meeting in Del Mar I wanted to hear about."

My feet stilled. "What are you talking about?"

"I know you met with Peterson." He lowered his voice and nodded. "Working both sides of that sin tax—you're starting to get this."

I shook my head. He had no idea of my intentions. "We can discuss it tonight."

Just before I reached the conference room, my phone buzzed. Normally I wouldn't check, but it could be Isaac. I slowed my steps and checked the screen. It was a text from Deloris.

Deloris: "THREE UNSUCCESSFUL ATTEMPTS TO LOG ON TO YOUR OFFICE DESKTOP."

My father's a fucking idiot. If he thought I would give him carte blanche in my office, he was dumber than his Neanderthal attitude.

Me: "OREN'S IN THE BUILDING."

Deloris: "WILL KEEP WATCHING AND STOP FROM MY END."

Me: "HE'LL NEVER CRACK YOUR SECURITY. BUT KEEP WATCHING."

Deloris: "I ALWAYS DO."

Pressing my lips together, I held back the smile. She was better than the lackluster security he had in London. As a matter of fact, unbeknownst to him, a few months back she upped their security and replaced a few questionable employees, saving his ass again.

Then I saw a message I'd missed.

Isaac: "MISS COLLINS CANCELED THE SPA APPOINTMENT. SHE JUST LEFT THE HOTEL ON FOOT. WILL FOLLOW."

I took a deep breath. Maybe our afternoon discussion of rules wasn't enough. Though my hand would miss the delightful sensation, my belt would be more effective.

CHAPTER 6

CHARLI

AT 7:45 I STEPPED from the suite with my head held high. Nox left me five one-hundred-dollar bills, and while my plan was to save every penny, that wasn't starting yet. Instead of going to the spa appointment, I used my time wisely, walking to a few different stores, purposely avoiding the higher-end clothing. Nox may have said I wasn't a cheap whore, but he purposely made me feel that way. I intended to deliver.

The off-the-shoulder skater dress was perfect—red and barely reaching the middle of my thighs. It was too short to follow Nox's directions. I wasn't obeying anyway. One more violation wouldn't matter. Near the back of the store, I found a cheap gold armband that added to the illusion. Determined to avoid everything lying upon the king-sized bed, I found some strappy patent leather, high-heeled sandals and a matching purse, complete with a gaudy gold chain strap that matched my new armband.

My makeup was a work of art. Golden shimmery eye shadow and heavy black eyeliner made the woman in the picture in Nox's letter look like she'd been without makeup. Of course I found a lipstick to match the bright red of my dress. I curled and teased my hair, keeping one of my favorite childhood movies in the back of my mind. By the time I was done, Julia Roberts and

Richard Gere would have been proud and offered me a role in *Pretty Woman.*

The closer I came to Mobar, the faster my pulse surged. Twice he'd written not to disobey him. I'd disobeyed him on every count, and I had two more directions to defy before I was done. I just hoped Nox wasn't there yet, because when he arrived, I planned not to be sitting alone. I also wasn't planning on spending my time running my finger over the rim of a glass… and it wouldn't be full either.

I stopped at the entrance of the bar and scanned the room. There were tables with couples and more with groupings of people. I smiled at the clientele: mostly men and women wearing suits, probably visiting New York on business. I took a deep breath. It was showtime and my main audience had yet to arrive. That was good. I needed another drink before that reunion.

CHAPTER 7

NOX

THE MUSCLES IN my neck twitched as I made my way toward Mobar. My note had been very specific as to attire and directions. Charli was mine for the next year. I planned to make her think she was completely at my disposal.

Isaac told me that she'd already defied my orders by canceling the spa appointment. I also knew she'd walked to some nearby stores. After her spanking this afternoon, the idea that she was purposely defying me had me both pissed and aroused.

I knew her dress size from Del Mar, but Deloris was the one who learned her shoe size. I didn't read it, but apparently, Infidelity's profile was extremely thorough.

The black dress I had sent over from Saks was beaded, short, and dipped in the front and back. She couldn't wear a bra, and I left explicit instructions for her not to wear anything else. The shoes were black with high heels and reminded me of the ones she'd displayed on the dashboard of the Boxster. I was fucking getting hard thinking about it. In the matching handbag was five hundred dollars in cash. It wasn't as if she'd need to pay for anything. It was simply a reminder that I paid for her—she was mine.

I would most definitely be fucking her tight pussy, but first I would fuck her mind.

The upscale bar with the red walls and golden booths created the perfect ambiance. It was like walking into a 1950's film, and Charli was the starlet. Every man's fantasy was my reality. I was ready to see if she followed directions as well in New York as she had in Del Mar. My jaw clenched as I approached the bar. Charli didn't see me. She couldn't with the men on either side of her.

What the hell?

She wasn't wearing the black dress. I could only see a portion of the red material that hung from her slender shoulder as I moved closer. My entire body trembled. The walls and her dress weren't the only red I saw… rushing blood tinted my vision as my teeth clenched. My day had gone from bad to worse, and soon hers would too.

I laid my hand on one man's shoulder and motioned with my head for him to get lost. For only a second he looked as though he might argue. Charli flinched, but didn't turn toward me. One down, I then placed my hand on the other man's shoulder, the one seated beside her. My words came out more as a growl. "You have my seat."

He looked from me to Charli. She smiled at him, and the heat boiling from my collar told me that my face joined the party of red. If this asshole didn't move in the next three seconds, I wasn't responsible.

"Goodbye, Chad," Charli said. "Thank you for the drink."

"Is this the guy you're waiting for…?"

"Your three seconds are up, *Chad*." My nostrils flared with exaggerated breaths. However, instead of decking him—as I wanted to do—I reached for Charli's forearm. "We're leaving. Now."

"Do you know this jerk?" Chad asked, standing and meeting me chest to chest.

If he only fucking knew how pissed I was, he'd be running with his tail between his legs. I stood taller, dwarfing him by at least six inches. When I turned toward Charli, I couldn't believe my eyes. She wasn't wearing anything that I'd bought. Under my grip was some cheap gold jewelry that looked like a snake twisted around her forearm. Her eyelids sparkled. She was made up like some kind of eighties' throwback punk-rocker.

"We're leaving," I again growled.

Chad's hand came to my chest. The man had balls—I'd give him that. "I asked the lady if she knew you."

Charli's bright red lips pursed in defiance, but under my grip her pulse thumped erratically. It would be easy to allow mine to do the same, to be what she remembered—what I remembered. Touching her ignited something inside of me that I was trying to pretend didn't exist. Now, as my fingers surrounded her forearm, the connection was undeniable. Her agreement was for one year. I couldn't let her go after a week. After a year would be impossible.

But first she had a lesson to learn.

"I thought I did," Charli replied.

Chad couldn't hear the hurt and disappointment in those words. They weren't meant for him. Well, too bad. I was disappointed too.

"You thought?" Chad asked. "So you don't?"

The fucker was persistent. "She knows me. And we're leaving. Now."

"Thank you again for the drink," Charli said, calling over her shoulder as I pulled her from the stool and walked her out of the bar. Her cheap heels skidded across the floor as she moved to keep up with my determined gait.

I needed to get her up to the room. If we weren't alone in seconds, I'd explode. Leaning down to her ear as we neared the elevator, the muscles in my neck strained as I snarled, "Do you think this is funny?"

Charli made several attempts to free her arm, but my grip was iron. She would undoubtedly have a mark, probably the imprint of the ugly jewelry and maybe a bruise from my hold. But at that moment I didn't give a fuck. She'd be lucky if it was the only mark I left on her skin by the time this night was done.

"Let me go," she whispered, still as determined as she'd been in the bar.

"Never."

When the doors to the elevator opened, I walked us to the rear wall as other passengers entered. Each one stood near the doors with their backs toward us. I didn't give a shit about the other people as I turned my back on them and stared down at Charli. With my body as a shield, she was caged.

My mind was fighting an epic battle, and I didn't know which side would win. On one hand, I wanted to rip off the ugly red dress and fuck her into submission. My hand was done with its morning workouts, and seeing her, touching her, being this damn close to her, my cock was ready to get the party started.

On the other hand, I wanted to punish her for her blatant disobedience. I wanted to redden her perfect round ass again. This time I'd use my belt, and she'd remember exactly what happened when she didn't listen to me.

We stared in silence as the elevator made its painfully slow climb. Finally the last couple got off, and we were alone with over fifteen floors to go. I squeezed tighter on the jewelry, feeling the metal bend. "I asked you a question. Do you fucking think this was funny?"

CHAPTER 8

CHARLI

FUNNY? NO I didn't think any of this was funny.

Defiantly, I stared up into Nox's eyes. The cold glacier blue of this afternoon was gone. Navy swirled in their depths. I was playing with fire, and I knew it. However, the longer we stood, our lips a whisper apart, his warm breath skirting my cheeks, and our hearts beating erratically against one another's, I didn't care if I got burned. No, I *wanted* to be burned.

"Your caveman routine is getting old. Unhand me. Now."

His nostrils flared as the tendons in his neck flexed. Nox was a bull ready to charge and in the dress I purchased, I was the red cape. From the cyclone in his eyes to the force of his grip upon my arm, I watched the millions of thoughts swirling through his mind, thoughts that should scare me, but they didn't. I was mad and hurt by his words. I wasn't letting him off the hook that easily.

"What the fuck were you doing down there? You're mine." The last part came as a low, menacing whisper that reverberated through the elevator.

His declaration was both fire and ice, sending a chill down my spine while striking a match to the fire deep inside. Taking a step closer, his hard body pressed against mine to pin me to the wall, his chest flattening my breasts and his erection pushing against my tummy. Without warning his lips captured mine, their warmth setting my insides ablaze as our tongues battled. Tenderness was forgotten as he unapologetically took what he claimed to be his.

The emotion he'd tried to contain earlier in the day exploded in the fury, washing over us as we melted together. It was as if he'd needed to taste me, to know I was real.

When the elevator stopped, Nox stepped back, and I sucked my bruised lips between my teeth. His stare held me in place. In his eyes wasn't the menacing gaze that melted my insides. This was different, new, unyielding. Without words, he dared me to speak, and I wanted to, but my mind and body weren't sure what to say. At the moment they couldn't reach a consensus. The doors opened. He seized my hand and wordlessly pulled me toward the suite.

As my feet hurried to keep up, I reached for the arm cuff and tried to twist. The cheap metal wasn't merely around my forearm: it was painfully digging into my skin. His grasp had bent the fake gold, turning my arm the same color as my dress.

Once we were behind the closed door, Nox said, "Go wash that shit off of your face."

Is he serious?

"What—?"

The word was barely out before he again had my hand and pulled me toward the bathroom.

"Nox, what the hell are you doing?" I asked as he turned on the shower.

Water rained from multiple directions as he turned his attention back to me. Pinching my chin, he lifted my eyes to his. His tone was a low rumble, and his words came clipped. "*Mr. Demetri.* Say it."

I stiffened my neck as the grasp on my chin tightened. "Mr. Demetri," I repeated.

"Apparently, this afternoon wasn't enough for you to learn your lesson. Do we need to repeat it?"

"No," I answered defiantly, though the thought of him spanking me again did something to me that I didn't want to admit.

"Miss Collins, this is *my* year. I paid for it. When I tell you to do something, you do it. Do not question, and do not make me repeat myself. Is that clear?"

My lips were glued shut. I couldn't answer if I'd wanted. His eyes never left mine as he removed his suit jacket and threw it on the floor. By the steam gathering upon the inside of the glass doors and mirrors, the water had warmed.

Nox reached under the spray, adjusted the temperature and reached for my hand. "You are so fucking stubborn. I don't do stubborn."

"Well, then you bought the wrong girl." I didn't know where the words came from, but they were out, and I couldn't take them back.

Tension crackled through the steam-filled air as his defined jaw clenched and unclenched. Before I realized what happened, Nox stepped into the shower and pulled me in with him. Fully clothed, complete with shoes we stood under the multiple sprays.

Looking at our feet, I shook my head. I might be wearing cheap clothes, but he wasn't. His leather loafers alone probably cost a thousand dollars. His sexy gray suit pants were getting wetter by the second as they clung to his body and revealed his growing desire beneath.

"You're crazy!"

"You're right," he confirmed. "I've been fucking crazy ever since I met you." He thrust a washcloth at me. "Don't make me repeat myself, Charli. Wash that shit off your face. I'm barely holding on here."

Charli?

My once teased hair was now soaked and lying flat against my head. I twisted the excess water from the cloth and did as he said. The more I scrubbed, the more the white cloth filled with black and sparkles. No doubt, with the excessive eyeliner I'd used, the shower had turned me into a raccoon.

When I was done, I handed the cloth back to Nox. Without saying a word, he wrung it out, covered it in bodywash, and gently cleaned around my eyes. As he did, the atmospheric pressure shifted. The storm of raging tension that had surrounded us since our eyes met in the bar changed. The intensity was still off the charts, but this was something different. Whatever it was affected us both. Our breathing suddenly took effort as both of our chests rose and fell.

"Take off that dress."

Nox's command echoed throughout the glass stall. I considered arguing, but common sense stopped my rebuttal. I'd already pushed him far enough. Starting at the neckline, I slowly exposed myself, inch by inch. His gaze followed the soaked material. As I revealed my breasts, my nipples hardened, and he let out a low growl. Down the dress went, exposing my tummy and red lace panties.

Shaking his head, Nox ran his finger along the edge of my panties. With his large hands now at my hips, he asked, "Did you do *anything* I told you to do in my note?"

"No." My honesty left a trail of vulnerability and shame.

In one quick motion, Nox ripped the lace, and the shredded panties joined my dress on the shower floor. I blinked away the water as he tipped my face upward.

"No more disobeying. Do you understand?"

I nodded—not in acknowledgment of his words, but in response to the rush from once again being in his presence. Nox electrified me in a way I'd never known, and even in the absurdity of our current situation, he was doing it again. The way he scanned my nakedness as his Adam's apple bobbed tingled my skin.

He hadn't released my chin. "Say '*Yes, Mr. Demetri.*'"

My chest hurt. "N-Nox."

His grip tightened.

"Yes, Mr. Demetri."

He released my chin with a shove. "Undress me. I'm going to fuck you."

I shouldn't like his demands, but part of me did. As I started with his shirt, memories of Del Mar played in my mind. He'd told me that he didn't usually ask for sex. He had in California. Nox had. But this wasn't him—this was *Mr. Demetri*, and he wasn't asking. By the way my insides twisted and thighs slid over one another, I wasn't protesting.

The shower's spray made his shirt transparent and the buttons slick. I released them one by one, as more and more of his muscular chest became visible. It was as if he'd spent the last six weeks upping his workout. Once the buttons were undone, I shamelessly ran my hands over his defined torso. My bright red nail polish contrasted with his tanned skin.

Seizing my hands, Nox stopped my exploration. "No. My rules. You'll do what I say, when I say. I didn't tell you that you could touch me. Now, get down on your knees and undo my slacks."

Biting my lip, I knelt before him and found myself eye level with a prominent bulge. I reached for his belt.

"You're lucky," he said.

Turning my attention away from the task at hand, I looked up at his serious expression, unsure at that moment why he considered me lucky.

Nox's hand covered mine, the one on his belt. "I was very close to using this on your ass."

Even under the spray, my eyes widened as my heart rate skyrocketed.

He isn't serious, is he?

He released my hand and caressed my cheek. "Oh, princess, I'm fucking serious."

How does he do that?

"Keep working on that belt. I've decided there are other ways to punish you."

My hands trembled as I continued working and asked, "Wasn't that what this afternoon was about?"

When I lowered the zipper, his heavy erection sprung free between his muscular thighs. Saliva pooled over my tongue. Silently, I swallowed. With everything in me, I wanted to take him in my mouth. I would have, but he'd just told me not to touch him. My chest ached with indecision, unsure what he wanted or what I should do.

Nox opened the glass door, kicked off his shoes and threw his soaked shirt and slacks onto the floor. When he turned back around, my breath stuttered. The menacing gleam was back in his eyes.

"This afternoon?" he asked. "Princess, that's a question. Something you're not supposed to ask. Just to clarify, for the next year, I can punish you anytime I want for any reason."

He reached for my hand and helped me stand. My high-heeled shoes slid on the wet tile.

Nox continued, "I can punish you simply because I want to watch that firm ass turn red." He palmed my ass and pulled me closer. Even with the shoes on I had to look up. "But…" he continued, "…that's not the current reason. Tonight I'm accumulating a long list of offenses, all equally deserving of punishment. Let's start with that stupid stunt you pulled downstairs in the bar."

I lifted my chin and straightened my spine. Granted, with the way my nipples stood at attention, I didn't appear as convincing as I would have liked. "You called me a *cheap prostitute*. So that's what I gave you."

His head moved slowly from side to side as he backed me against the tile wall. "No." His velvet tone rolled like thunder as he tweaked an erect nipple. "I. Said. You. Weren't. *Cheap*."

I gasped as he leaned down and nipped the sensitive skin behind my ear. His long fingers painfully dug into my behind as his erection prodded my stomach.

Looking down at me, he said, "I paid a fortune for you. Princess, you're the most expensive whore I've ever known."

He spun my shoulders toward the wall as his words demeaned me. His actions were fast and rough, mixing pleasure with pain. But that wasn't what I concentrated on. It was his voice, the way it reverberated through the humid air to my core. I listened to the sound and timbre—not the words—as he found the silver packet and my new punishment began.

THE LAST FEW days had been too much: my parents, Infidelity, and Nox—Mr. Demetri. By the time we made it to bed, I'd lost count of the number of times he'd taken me to detonation. Physically unable to do more, I surrendered to sleep, too tired and emotionally spent to endure more of Nox's unique and not at all unpleasant punishment. He'd said it was all about him, how now it was my job to pleasure him, not the other way around.

That was what he said.

It wasn't what he'd done.

My body responded to Nox Demetri in a way I couldn't explain. With mere words or glances from him, I was putty, and he was the sculptor. Yes, he had his share of orgasms, but I'm most certain that if it were a contest, I would've won.

During the night, I woke and instinctively cuddled closer to his warmth. The woodsy scent of his cologne lingered on the pillowcases while the musk of our passion saturated the air. I hated that he considered things different, and at the same time, I was in heaven being back in his arms. He'd told me more than once that my little stunt—as he referred to it—was juvenile and stupid, and he was probably right.

And then I began to remember how angry—livid—I was at his note and his afternoon show of force. If I were completely honest with myself, I was hurt more than anything else. Disobeying every directive in that damn note was my way to rebel. I'd been told for most of my life that I was defiant and had authority issues. I wasn't and I didn't. When I was at the academy or at Stanford, I had no problem with teachers or professors. I did, however, have issues with assholes. Assholes like Alton.

No longer wanting to be near Nox, I scooted away and rolled the other direction. In that note and yesterday afternoon, he'd been an asshole—a dick. In Del Mar I'd willingly given him control. I could do that again—give control to the sexy, seductive man who was also protective and sweet—but what he'd done and said yesterday was wrong.

Calling me a whore—expensive or cheap—was neither protective nor sweet. Mr. Demetri had no idea what had taken me to Infidelity. He didn't know my dreams or goals. My signing at Infidelity wasn't about money—not really. It was about the same thing as my dressing like a cheap prostitute. It was my refusal to play by unfair rules.

I'd willingly sold—or rented—myself for a year to spite my stepfather. Nox could demean me all he wanted—I'd lived through it before—as long as I had the ability to accomplish my goals. The more my mind pondered everything that happened, the more elusive sleep became. My body chilled with the realization that my consciousness had made a comparison that up until yesterday seemed impossible.

Nox was behaving like Alton.

He was. The difference was that I liked Nox.

Is that past tense?

Fine. If Nox Demetri wanted to punish me for taking the opportunity to achieve my dream, so be it. I'd take his damn punishment, one orgasm at a time, and in one year I'd walk away with my tuition money in hand.

If that made me a whore, then so be it.

Letting out an exaggerated huff, I threw back the covers. As soon as I did, my gaze shot to the other side of the bed, praying I hadn't awoken Nox. I didn't want to talk to him. For the first time since his shadow covered my legs in Del Mar, I wasn't sure I wanted to be with him.

As I quietly made my way to the bathroom, I winced at the tenderness in my muscles. It was the same as I'd experienced in Del Mar. Damn, I should start running with Patrick. Maybe then my legs could handle Nox's punishment.

Finding a plush robe hanging on a hook, I wrapped it around me. Despite being upset with myself and angry with *Mr. Demetri*, when I saw the woman in the mirror, I smiled. Her wavy hair was wild from the shower and then the bed, and she had a lazy, satiated glaze to her golden eyes. My mind told me that I shouldn't want Nox as much as I did or like the things he did and said. Alex knew it was wrong, but the woman in the reflection wasn't complaining.

As the memories came back, my body overtook my mind. I began wondering if he'd want to punish me again. Now that I'd had a nap and even though my body ached from the last round, I was pretty sure I was ready. Nox did that to me. Even if my mind didn't agree, my body would always want more.

When I stepped back onto the plush carpet of the bedroom, Nox's demanding tone cut through the darkened silence. "Don't even think about leaving while I'm asleep."

My feet stilled at his suggestion. "I-I'm not."

By the illumination of a distant electronic glow, I could see Nox sitting against the headboard, blankets bunched around his waist and his arms crossed over his bare chest. The myriad of emotions that man evoked in me was perplexing. My lungs forgot to inhale as I studied his handsome face. His chiseled jaw, covered in the perfect amount of stubble, mesmerized me as it clenched and unclenched.

What is he thinking? And why does that question both scare and excite me?

CHAPTER 9

CHARLI

WHEN I DIDN'T speak or move, Nox demanded, "Come here. We didn't do much talking last night. We have rules to discuss."

Rules. I rolled my eyes.

He was right. We hadn't talked last night, not really. Walking to my side of the bed, I climbed in. With my robe still on, I mirrored Nox's stance, pulling the covers over my waist and sitting against the headboard.

He reached for my hand and tugged. "*Here,* princess, means next to me, not three feet away on the other side of the bed."

I scooted a little closer. "Nox—Mr. Demetri," I corrected. "I don't know what you want from me, but I think you should know, I don't follow directions well." *Especially when they're delivered by assholes.* I didn't say that last part.

He moved closer, removed the pillow from behind my head and laid me back. With his handsome face hovering above mine, he smoothed my unruly curls over the pillow. In the darkness, I saw the hint of a grin pulling at the corners of his lips, and my heart leapt with the hope of Nox, the man I'd known in Del Mar.

"I'm rather perceptive. I've noticed your flaws." As if opening a present,

Nox untied the sash from around my waist and exposed my nude body. The intensity of his gaze electrified my skin, peppering it with goose bumps and turning my nipples to pebbles. He sucked on his finger and then traced a circle over my areola. The glint came back to his pale eyes. "I've also noticed your assets."

My back arched as his voice rumbled through me, awakening my tender core. No longer concerned about the punishment he'd delivered the night before, I felt my insides clench with the promise of more.

A moan echoed from my throat as he lowered his lips to one of my nipples. Sucking, he skillfully circled it with his tongue. His warm mouth pulled away leaving it slick, and then he blew, the contrast was almost painful.

"We're going to discuss my rules. First, forget the *Mr. Demetri.* My name is Lennox or Nox in private."

His torment of my neck, breasts, and tummy punctuated each statement. The stubble of his cheeks scratched while his teeth tantalized my taut skin.

"I want to hear that you're listening," he said. "Say '*Yes, Nox.*'"

My voice came in breaths. "After last night, I was expecting *Yes, sir* or maybe *Yes, master*?"

He bit my nipple, sending shockwaves directly to my core.

"Keep baiting me, princess."

That was another direct order I planned to ignore.

"Yes, Nox. My name is Alexandria, but I prefer Alex."

His lips moved lower. If he was trying to distract me, he was doing a good job.

"Where did Charli come from?"

"My middle name is Charles, after my grandfather."

He nodded, delivering more abuse with his coarse stubble. "That's good. I was concerned it was an outright lie. As I mentioned when we first met, truthfulness isn't debatable. We both know what will happen if you lie to me."

Shit! His fingers joined the battle for my attentions. My legs willingly parted as I tried to concentrate on my answers.

"Oh! Y-Yes, Nox. I didn't lie. It's a nickname."

"Tell me about Columbia."

I didn't want to talk about anything. My hips moved as his hands and lips moved in tandem, their rhythm monopolizing my thoughts.

"Columbia, Charli." His reminder refocused my mind, though my body was lost to his ministrations.

"I-I start in less than two weeks."

"What if I told you no?"

The euphoria he'd created evaporated. My body stiffened as I pulled away from his touch. "Y-You can't." My volume rose. "No. It was in my profile, my hard limits." Panic washed over me. He *was* like Alton. "Karen said—"

"Stop," Nox said, touching a finger to my lips. "Suck."

Without thinking, my lips parted, allowing his finger access, covering my tongue with the taste of my own essence. His erection throbbed against my hip.

"I told you, your limits are now mine to define; however, I'm not saying no," he whispered, his tone softening as he retrieved his finger.

"You're not?"

"No. I think it's fantastic that you've been accepted to Columbia Law. I just want to know how someone as intelligent as you obviously are, is stupid enough to work for Infidelity."

I clenched my teeth to halt my reply. Our gazes locked. Nox was only inches away—our noses nearly touched as he awaited my response.

The muscles in his neck strained. "Answer me."

I was probably poking the proverbial beehive, but I couldn't stop myself. "You're a hypocrite. You're awfully high and mighty for a *client*."

"What?" he asked, pulling up as if to see me more clearly.

"You act like Infidelity is bad."

"It is."

"Then why are you one of its clients?"

Nox shook his head and ran a hand over his stubble. "What I do is none of your business. What you do is mine."

"That's not fair."

"Sorry, princess. Life's not fair."

Reaching under my shoulders, Nox lay back and rolled us both until I was lying on top of him, skin to skin, nothing separating us. Unexpectedly, he swatted my behind.

"Ouch!" I squealed, though the sting was more of shock than pain.

Nox raised his brow. "I told you, I don't repeat myself. I'll spank you harder if you don't answer my damn questions the first time."

Not wanting to look into his pale eyes as I told him my story, I lowered my cheek to his chest and began, "I graduated from Stanford last spring. I'd always wanted to be an attorney. I wanted to do something good. When I was young, I believed in fairytales—until I didn't.

"Even when I knew they weren't real and couldn't happen to me, I still liked them. In them, the good people always won. Even though I learned that wasn't true in real life, I wanted to make it true.

"That's why I want to practice law. I want to help defenseless people—people who can't help themselves…" *Something I couldn't accomplish when I was the one who was defenseless.* "…and I want to stop the bad people. I imagined that one day my career would be my own fairytale."

When Nox didn't respond, I took a deep breath and continued, "I worked hard at Stanford." Remembering our last conversation, I added, "I was honest when I told you I didn't sleep around. I mostly studied. Chelsea gave me a hard time, but I think my dedication helped her, too."

"Your sister?" His chest vibrated with his words.

I looked back to his eyes and braced myself for another swat to my ass. "No."

The spank didn't come, although a question did. "No?"

I shook my head. "No. Chelsea is my best friend. We call each other sister, but it's not biological. We met our freshman year at Stanford."

"Interesting," Nox said. "We'll talk more about that another time. Now back to Columbia and Infidelity."

I settled against his chest again and sighed. "I graduated with honors and was accepted to two of the top law schools in the country, Columbia and Yale. When I was young, my grandparents created a trust fund for me. It was supposed to pay for my education. I thought it would last through law school, beyond even."

"But it didn't? What happened?"

I wasn't ready to get that personal, not yet. I shrugged. "Bad investments, I don't know the details. I was just informed that my first semester was paid, but that was all. No living expenses, nothing."

"All right, that would be shocking, but surely you had other options. Student loans?"

I fought the onslaught of emotion that this subject evoked. Everything was still too raw; my mother's actions still hurt. I couldn't deal with that and Nox's accusing tone. He had no way of knowing that I'd only learned of the loss less than a week ago or that the money wasn't really gone, only being held hostage by my family. "I-I…" I took a ragged breath as I desperately tried to suppress the tears I'd allowed to flow after his punishment yesterday. "…please. I was without options. Everything I'd worked for…" A renegade tear slipped onto his chest. "I don't want to talk about it."

Nox's strong arms embraced me, wrapping around me and cradling me against his chest. I became lost in him, overwhelmed by the beating of his heart, warmth of his skin, and masculine scent. We lingered unmoving for what seemed like ages. Beyond the heavy curtains of the hotel suite, darkness gave way to dawn.

And then as if a switch had been flipped, Nox's body stiffened and he rolled me back to the bed. With his head propped on his elbow, he stared at me.

"Listen and listen carefully."

Welcome back, Mr. Demetri.

"Here are my new rules…"

It was surreal how he morphed from one man to the other. In his arms, I was Charli, and he was Nox. Listening to him now, he was Mr. Demetri, and I was his whore. The dichotomy both frightened and reassured me.

Is that what he wants, to elicit two such different emotions?

"…three more days, then you'll move into my apartment."

My pulse quickened again. "Where do you live?"

"Westchester County."

"I-I have classes. I have an apartment near campus. Maybe we could work…"

Nox shook his head. "No. My rules. Break your lease."

"B-But that's too far away…"

"Arguing isn't permitted."

My heart thumped against my chest. *Westchester County… how?*

"Yes, Mr. Demetri." I hoped he heard the dripping sarcasm.

His eyes narrowed, twisting my insides. "I should punish you for that."

Okay, he heard it.

"Perhaps there's another…" I didn't know what to ask or what to say.

"I also have an apartment on West 77th."

Oh thank God.

"It's where you'll stay—where we'll stay." He wasn't giving me a choice. "I rarely go to the house in Westchester. The apartment is closer to my office, and it's not far from Columbia. I'll get you a driver and a car."

I shook my head. "I don't like drivers."

"You don't?" he asked with a smirk. "Was Isaac so offensive? He's usually pretty quiet."

I wasn't thinking of Isaac, but his response made me smile. "No, Isaac was fine."

"Well, princess, how many drivers have you known?"

Nox didn't know me at all. If he wanted to believe this money thing was new to me, I wasn't going to burst his bubble. "It just seems like that would be intrusive. I mean, as if I was being watched."

"Oh, you will be."

"What?"

"You *will* be watched."

His words prickled my skin. Everything he said had a definitive edge, almost daring me to question. This time I took the bait. "W-Why?"

"Because you're mine."

"I'm yours for the next year. I know that. What does that have to do with my being watched?"

"Exactly what I said. I don't make an investment without protecting it.

You're mine. From what I've seen, you've demonstrated your inability to make reasonable judgments. For the next year, your decisions, your safety, and even your sensibility are all up to me."

"Nox, I'm not a child."

"No, Charli, you're not. If you were, I'd ground your round ass to this suite and make you write a thousand times that signing that agreement with Infidelity was stupid. Maybe by the time you were done, you'd understand it to be true."

I pressed my lips together to stop my rebuttal. He was a goddamned client. His hypocritical view didn't make sense. Placing my hand against his chest, I tried another approach. "I can take the subway or the bus." I willed my sarcasm to stay hidden. "Despite your lack of respect for my decision-making skills, I can manage mass transportation. I earned an A in my urban planning class at Stanford." *Okay, the last part was a bit much.*

"This isn't debatable. I'm involved in some dangerous things. If you're in the public eye as my..." He paused. "...*companion*, then you need to be protected. We're not discussing it. Besides, it's already begun. It started yesterday."

"I-I don't like that."

"Too bad. I didn't ask you. I bought—"

"I know," I quipped. "You bought me."

"My security detail is excellent. Most of the time you won't even know they're around." Nox scoffed. "Well, last night, they did almost blow their cover in the bar. Chad was about to get more than he bargained for."

"Yesterday? So you knew? You knew I didn't go to the spa?"

Nox nodded as his forehead wrinkled. "I knew. I wasn't aware of how far you'd strayed from my orders." He reached for my chin and pinched it between his thumb and finger. "Remember that. Think about it the next time you decide to go rogue. I'll have a fuck'n GPS tracker placed in you if I need to. Don't push this."

I swallowed. Security that sees without being seen—the Montague staff all over again. My stomach twisted. This would be a dream for most people. This was what Patrick enjoyed. Hell, Chelsea would be in heaven. I hated it. It was what I left in Savannah. "Nox, can we please talk about this?"

"No. Keep me informed of your schedule and I'll do the same. You have things you need to do for school—get them done. Just remember we're a couple. Don't do anything that would make people question that. Your freedoms are yours until you squander them."

"What does that mean?"

"It means, princess, I will ground your ass here or in my apartment, or anywhere I choose, if I need to. Don't make me need to. I know you're not a child." He sat up and raked my body with the tip of his finger, from my collarbone to my core, stopping short of where he'd been before. "You're a sexy-as-hell woman, and that alone makes the idea of having you tied up in my bed awaiting my return all the more appealing." His lips quirked upward, and the menacing gaze that swirled with navy shimmered in his eyes. "Go ahead… do something like you did last night, and we'll see how fast your freedoms disappear."

I didn't respond. I wasn't sure what to say. It was the new internal battle that his words and actions waged within me. Alex didn't like it, but Charli's tummy was doing flip-flops with the memory of the satin binding in Del Mar.

He brushed a finger between my folds and his grin blossomed to a full smile. "Maybe I'll need to think of a different punishment. It seems as though you like the sound of that one too much."

I started to sit up. "This is bullshit. This isn't what I signed up for."

Nox seized my shoulders and pushed me back to the mattress. "You're wrong. It's exactly what you signed up for. And you got me. That fairytale you spoke about—I want that for you. I want you to get your law degree. Just never forget, fairytales don't really exist, and the world's not black and white. One person's good is another person's bad. I can make the next year of your life as pleasant or as miserable as I want. As I've mentioned, my tastes are unique, and to me, tears of pain taste as sweet as tears of joy. You signed the agreement, and it wasn't to star as Cinderella. I'm about as far from Prince Charming as you're going to find."

My mouth dried as a cold chill settled over the room. This wasn't the man I'd met in Del Mar.

"I'm also a selfish bastard. I don't share well. Never have. You're going to learn to behave, and in public, you'll be my queen—my princess. In private, you're mine, which means whatever I want it to mean. I'm warning you: I'm not a good person, but I'm the only *bad* I want near you. Don't mention the security again. Is that clear?"

"Yes, Nox."

He sat up. "You have my number. Use it, but not frivolously during the day. I have work, but if you're unsure if I'll approve of something, call me. Keep in mind that my calls are all monitored. Don't do anything stupid like sexting. My security will only see you naked if I want them to see you."

What the hell?

He picked up his phone. "Work is where I need to be. We're going to try our plans for last night again tonight. Do you think you can manage to follow my directions or would you prefer my belt?"

"Are those my only two options?" I asked with a sultry twang.

Nox stood, in all his incredible naked sexiness. "Tonight, seven o'clock, Mobar—*take-two.*"

"Yes, sir, *Mr. Demetri.*"

"Watch it." He tilted his head toward my side of the bed. "Your phone's plugged in. I turned off the sound again. The vibrating woke me."

Nox wiggled his brows. "That reminds me of something, but we'll discuss it tonight. I'm taking a shower. Isaac will be here soon."

I wasn't exactly sure how this worked. "Do you want company?"

He walked toward me with his lips pursed together. Taking my hand, he helped me stand. His gaze burned as he slowly spun me around. "Do you still want me? After all of that?"

I did. I shouldn't, but I did.

"Yes, Nox," I said the words he'd told me to say.

He kissed my neck sending chills over my heated skin. The erection that had faded twitched against my hip.

"If I touched you, would I find you're still wet? Would your pussy be eager for me?"

I nodded.

"Words, Charli."

"Yes, Nox."

His large hands trailed down my arms, a whisper of a touch. His gruff tone, now gone, was replaced by velvet words. "What do you want?"

"You."

"Who owns you?"

I closed my eyes. "You do."

"Who is the only one who can bring you pleasure?"

My head became heavy on my spine and fell backward. "You."

"And what do you want? Be specific."

Nox was killing me. His warm breath on my skin, ghostly touch, and raspy tone had me piqued, twisted, and ready to combust.

"Your cock," I whispered. I sounded like the whore he said I was. The word repulsed me, but what he was doing was turning me on more than I cared to admit.

Nox's breath disappeared. His warmth was gone, and the coolness that comes from being alone settled around me.

"No." His voice came from the other side of the room.

My eyes popped open. "What?"

"Was that a question, Charli, or did you not hear me?"

"I-I…"

What the hell?

He stepped closer, pulling my eyes to his. "My year, my rules. I said *no*. I'll decide when you deserve my cock and when you don't. Tonight, if you're a good girl and do as you've been told, by the time we get back to this suite, you won't whisper your request. You'll scream it."

I swallowed, but my mouth was again dry.

"In the meantime," Nox continued, "do not take that responsibility into your own hands. You're mine—all of you. The only one pleasuring that pussy for the next year is me."

Dick!

His game made me dizzy. His words dripped with ice while the menacing gleam in his eyes sent heat through my body, causing synapses to spark and crackle along the way. It was like power lines I'd seen on the news that exploded in the dead of winter. The heat running through the wires combined with the frigid temperatures made a lethal combination.

"Oh," he added, "if you're looking for your vibrator, well, that's now in my possession. I'm sure I can come up with some inventive ideas for its use." With that he turned and walked toward the bathroom.

Asshole!

My body trembled with the combination of rage and unmet need. The physical chill made my fingers cold. I reached for the robe, the one I'd worn earlier. As I did, I saw my phone. Under it was a note and something under the note. I lifted the page to reveal ten hundred-dollar bills—fanned out for effect.

Charli~

Go shopping. Buy what I'd like, what I'd approve of. To the world you're my queen. Only we know what happens behind closed doors.

Wrapping myself in the robe, I fought the rising bile burning my throat. Grabbing my phone, I stormed out of the bedroom. I may have to live with him, but it didn't have to be in the same room.

In the living room of the suite, I found the Keurig and made a cup of coffee. The thought of making two was easily dismissed. I was Nox's whore, not his damn maid or cook.

With the robe around my body and the cup in my hands, I stood at the massive window and watched as sunlight and people brought the park back to life. When had I been on those paths with Patrick? It didn't seem possible that it had only been a few days ago. How had everything gone so terribly wrong?

I refused to cry. I couldn't let him see that. Instead, I settled on a sofa and picked up my phone. When I pushed the button, multiple text messages as well as Facebook notifications popped onto the screen.

Perhaps it was time to change my relationship status. However, I didn't think Facebook had *expensive prostitute* as an option.

Two of the text messages were from a number without a name. My stomach sank. Should I put Bryce's name in my phone? If I did, at least I'd know not to answer his calls. Maybe I should block the number. As I debated, I saw that the last text message I received was at nearly three in the morning. It was from Chelsea. Three o'clock in New York would've been midnight in California.

I sighed. I hadn't spoken or texted her since I signed the agreement. We rarely went a day, much less three, without talking. I was afraid to call. Afraid I'd blurt out the truth. Afraid of what she'd think, afraid to admit both how ashamed I felt and how disappointed I was in Nox.

Fighting the tears, I swiped my screen.

Chelsea: "ALEX, I HAVEN'T HEARD FROM YOU IN A FEW DAYS. THE MOVERS ARE COMING TOMORROW. I'M READY. I NEED TO TALK TO YOU. CALL ME."

CHAPTER 10

Unknown

Blocked number: "IT'S DONE."

Burner phone: "YOU TOOK CARE OF HER?"

Blocked number: "I FOLLOWED YOUR DIRECTIONS."

Burner phone: "GOOD. I'LL BE IN TOUCH."

Blocked number: "THANK YOU, SIR."

CHAPTER 11

Twenty years ago

ADELAIDE

I PULLED MY gaze away from my friend and looked toward my daughter running and laughing in the plush green grass with her nanny, Jane. Sipping my sangria, I contemplated calling down and reminding them that a refined Southern lady didn't chase little boys, even if she was only three, almost four years old. And then I remembered Russell's insistence upon allowing Alexandria to experience childhood.

Of course she'd experience childhood. Everyone did.

It didn't matter; I couldn't make him happy.

The constant tension, the lies, the masks—it all mocked me, reminding me of my duty, my birthright, and my slow death. Turning back to Suzy, I concentrated on my friend's words and tried not to think about how sweaty or dirty Alexandria would become. It was Jane's doing. She'd be the one to give her a bath.

I shook my head. It was too hot to run. It was simply too hot.

The humid Savannah air filled my lungs, weighing me down, suffocating me. I wasn't even thirty and I was old, not just physically, not just mentally, but socially and spiritually. Nothing within me held the light and colors of youth. I was the shell of their creation and yet it was all

I knew, all I'd ever known.

Who am I to assume it could be any better?

I blinked my eyes as sun filtered through the pagoda and listened to my best friend. Sometimes the suffering of others helped me reevaluate my own. I still had time to save my marriage; hers was beyond repair. I wanted to save mine, not only because of the fallout Suzanna was experiencing, but also because it was my duty, my job, and I couldn't face my father if I failed. It was plain and simple—and sad—but even as an adult, I wanted him to be proud. I wanted him to be content with his only heir. I couldn't help that I wasn't a male, but I could do my best in my non-existent brother's stead.

"Are you sure Jane won't let them get too close to the lake?" Suzanna asked. "I don't know what it is, but I've always been wary of it."

This time, we both looked out over the stone patio to the lawn below. It was easily another hundred yards to the lake from where the children ran circles around Alexandria's nanny.

I took another sip of my sangria, thankful I wasn't the one running after the children. Russell might insist on childish activities, but I didn't want to be the one participating. I would just as soon get my exercise running on the treadmill or swimming. "We used to swim in it when we were their age." The memory brought a smile to both of our faces.

"I don't know why. I mean the pool is so much nicer."

"Honey," I said, drawing out the endearment with just the right amount of Southern drawl, "how are you doing?" My second glass of sangria gave me the courage to attack head-on the subject we'd avoided thus far.

Suzanna shrugged. "At least I'm sitting here at Montague Manor with my best friend. The whole world hasn't ostracized me."

"No one is ostracizing you. It's not your fault. Besides, I never liked Marcel anyway."

"I know you're just saying that." She looked down and then up. "No one really knew him. But still, I'm the one who has to explain to Bryce that his father isn't coming home. Every night I have to…" Her words faded away as she straightened her neck and pressed her lips together.

It didn't matter how many times I held her hand and told her that she wasn't the talk of every social gathering or that the women she considered friends weren't saying terrible things about her behind her back, she knew I was lying. She knew the women we considered friends and have for most of our lives were like rabid beasts when it came to scandal.

"This isn't the turn of the century. I don't see why divorce is still considered such a failure."

I leaned back and inhaled. My chest rose and fell yet the air didn't come. It was this world—the world we were born into—where life was unforgiving, and if I didn't do something soon, I would become another one of its casualties.

"Suzy," I said with my painted-on smile, "you're here. Russell and I are here for you. My mother loves you like the daughter she never had."

"Stop that. You know that's not true."

I widened my eyes. "It is true. It's fine. This will blow over."

"I just worry about what it'll do to Bryce. He needs a father."

"Marcel is really giving up custody?"

Suzanna nodded. "He…" She looked all directions. "Where are your parents?"

"Mother's in the house and Father's at work."

"I swear, he's going to work at Montague until he dies. I thought maybe after Russell was involved for awhile, he'd slow down."

I pursed my lips. "And give up control? Have you met my father?"

Suzanna grinned. "What about Russell?"

"He's at Montague too." I leaned forward, studying her serious expression. "What is it?"

"Marcel wants a paternity test."

I gasped. "No! He couldn't think—"

"He does. He's thought it for years." Her hands flew to her chest. "Can you imagine?"

I shook my head. I couldn't imagine. Sex wasn't that great in the first place. Why would he ever suspect that Suzanna would want to do it with someone else?

"Is that why he left?"

Her head bobbed as she replied, "All those years of knowing about him and his flavor of the month and he had the audacity to accuse me. He threatened to make it public if I didn't agree to the divorce."

"Make what public? Let him have the test. I mean look at Bryce. He looks like Marcel—blond hair and gray eyes. He even acts like him."

Suzanna laughed. "Oh, I hope not. I hope he doesn't act like him."

"The good him," I corrected. "But Bryce does have a temper."

"So does Marcel. He just does a better job of hiding it than some."

I reached out and covered Suzanna's hand. "Honey, I'm sorry. I know you don't deserve that. Marcel just couldn't handle it. I mean the Carmichael name requires a lot of… pretense."

"Russell seems to be handling the Montague name all right."

I shrugged and looked out to the children now sitting in a circle, engrossed in some story that Jane was telling. "I swear, she fills those children's heads with the strangest ideas. Sometimes I wonder if she's good for Alexandria."

Suzanna smiled. "Oh, on days like today, when Bryce's nanny is off, I'm perfectly happy with whatever stories she wants to tell."

"Is Bryce doing all right?"

"He is. My father's been a big help—when he's not giving me the evil stare."

A chill ran through me. Both of our fathers had that look down to a science. In a room of people, they could telegraph it in some way that blinded everyone else in the room, but didn't stop it from reaching its desired recipient. Whether the target was my mother or I, when it came to Charles Montague II, the arrival was paralyzing.

RUSSELL'S GAZE NARROWED as he opened our bedroom door and our eyes met. Trying to ignore his stare, I concentrated on the lotion I meticulously rubbed into my hands. After my shower, I'd used the same lotion on my arms and legs. The rosewood scent lingered around me like a cloud. I waited for him to speak, to say something, but as the silence grew, I finally turned his direction.

"What? Why are you looking at me like that?"

"Like what? Like I'm surprised to find my wife in a nightgown in our bed?"

I sighed, placed the lotion bottle on my nightstand and pulled the blankets to my waist. Resting my head lightly against the headboard, I allowed my long brown hair to flow over my shoulders and said, "Russell, please."

"Did you say goodnight to Alexandria?"

"Earlier, yes."

"Earlier, when Jane took her for her bath, or earlier, once she was in bed?"

I reached for the light near the bed and turned the knob. "I can't seem to do anything right in your eyes."

"Why are you here? You haven't been in our bedroom in a week?"

When I didn't answer, his look of discontent morphed into a cocky grin. Standing straight, he bowed at the waist in a grand gesture. "Let me rephrase. Mrs. Collins, to what do I owe this pleasure? And don't insult either of us with Southern charm. Try for once in your adult life to be honest."

"My father."

Russell shook his head and walked to the dresser. He didn't say a word as he removed his watch and unbuttoned his shirt. Only two years my senior, Russell Collins was a handsome man, yet as he disrobed my blood turned to ice. The solid no longer flowed through my veins as I waited for his response.

"Your father? I guess I asked for the truth. So you're telling me that I have Charles Montague II to thank for a woman in my bed?" He scoffed. "If I'd known he had that kind of power, I would've been more specific with my request."

Though his insinuation hurt my pride, I continued with my honesty. "The staff told him I wasn't sleeping in our room while you were in town."

With his shirt now gone, Russell turned my way, walking closer and closer toward our bed. There was a time I found him attractive, maybe even sexually appealing. That time was over. "What did dear old Daddy tell you to do?"

I swallowed the bile that came with that answer. "He told me to make it right."

"Aren't you the perfect daughter? Daddy tells you to spread your legs and here you are."

"Do you have to be so crude? I want to be with my husband. What's wrong with that?"

"It's a little late for that, don't you think?"

"No. It's not," I protested. "I can't… I won't… Suzanna was here today. Do you realize what the others are doing to her? They're persecuting her, making up lies, shunning her. I'm a Montague. Our marriage can't end like theirs. I'll do whatever you want."

"You're pathetic. I don't give a damn about Montague anymore. It's not worth it." He lifted his hands and gestured around. "This house, your father, the money…" His hands dropped. "There, I said it. I fucking said it. I don't give a damn anymore about the money. I can't live like this. I won't. And furthermore, neither will Alexandria."

With each insult, each word, my chin fell toward my chest… until the last phrase. I snapped my face toward his. "What did you just say?"

"You heard me. I'm taking her, and we're leaving."

"Y-You can't. I-I can't…" My chest ached. "…you know what the doctors said. You know I can't have more children. She's the only heir. She has to stay here." My temples pounded. "And I don't want you to leave." I lowered one strap of my satin nightgown.

Russell's laughter filled the room. "Good try, sweetheart. I might have fallen for that a year ago, but I'm done. I'm not fucking an ice princess just because her daddy told her to lie there and take it. Sex isn't our only problem, and it sure as hell isn't our solution."

"We can't get a divorce, and under no circumstances can Alexandria leave Montague Manor. She's the only thing I've ever done right."

"Whose words are you using, yours or his?"

Both, I was using both. My father blamed me when we first learned Alexandria was a girl. She was supposed to be a boy, a grandson—a Montague grandson. Then, when we learned there couldn't be any more, that the complications with her birth were too extreme, she became my greatest accomplishment.

"She's my daughter, our daughter," I protested. "You can't take her away from her mother. My father will never allow it. The courts won't allow it."

"Really? You're going to let me drag this through court?" He shook his head. "I don't think so. I think I know too much about Montague Corporation and too much about this fucked-up family. Quiet and quick is the way this will be done. I don't want any money. I have money. I don't want a damn thing from this house or this family except my daughter."

Lifting back the covers, I lowered my feet to the floor and steeled my expression. From the time I was a child, I knew how to use my looks and my body. Whether it was a pout or flirtation, I had it mastered. I could do alluring. It worked before. "Russell," I whispered as I bravely walked toward him. "I'm sorry if you haven't been happy, if I haven't made you happy." I lowered the other strap over my shoulder and let my nightgown fall to the floor. Stepping from the satin puddle, I walked fully nude toward my husband, my flesh covered in goose bumps as the cold air hardened my nipples. Feeling them tighten I looked down and then up. "See what you do to me, what you still do to me?"

My heart seized as he took a step toward me, his body's reaction becoming more prominent. Reaching behind my neck, Russell fisted my hair and pulled my head back. With a deep guttural edge to his voice, he lowered his lips to my neck. "You're a fucking goddess. You know that. You know how beautiful you are." He shoved me backward as I fell against the bed. "It's all on the outside. I'm done."

He walked toward the bedroom door. "I have a business trip tomorrow, and when I get back, Alexandria and I are leaving."

"Where are you going now?"

"There are over ten bedrooms in this place. I think I can find one."

"But the staff—"

"I don't give a fuck what you tell dear old Daddy." He winked. "Don't worry about Alexandria. I'll take Jane too. Alexandria won't even notice you're missing."

The door slammed, leaving me cold and alone. After a few minutes, I pulled myself together, put my nightgown back on and covered it with a robe. Making my way through the outer room of our suite, I opened the door and peered down the hallway. Thankfully it was empty. Quietly, I walked toward the stairs on my way to the wine cellar. If anyone saw me, I'd retrieve two glasses. They didn't need to know one was for my right hand and the other for my left. Let them draw their own conclusions.

As I passed Alexandria's door, a thin ray of light leaked into the hallway and I heard Russell's voice.

"…I love you, and I'll be back soon."

"I love you too, Daddy."

She was nearly four, and her vocabulary had always been advanced.

"Remember what I said, you're as pretty on the inside as you are on the outside."

Alexandria's laughter filtered through the open door. "Daddy, stop tickling me."

"What's the rest? Tell me," he coaxed.

"My outside is pretty, too," her little girl voice squealed over his laughter.

"That's right, princess."

I walked silently toward the stairs.

CHAPTER 12

NOX

HAVING CHARLI IN my bed was supposed to eliminate the morning jerk-off session, not make it worse. Damn, it was all I could do to get in the shower and not lose it all over the bathroom floor, especially as our wet clothes from last night's shower greeted me, sprawled all over the floor.

Earlier this morning, I'd sent a text to Isaac to have him send me another pair of shoes. I'd planned for clothes, but who in the hell stepped into a shower with their shoes on? The answer would be me. Not that I'd ever done anything like that before. Then again, I'd never been so fucking drunk with the combination of passion and rage that I didn't know if I was coming or going. Last night I was on the edge of control. Desire and wrath made a lethal concoction, and in the heat of the moment, I wasn't sure who would survive. Thankfully the only casualties were my Italian loafers.

That was what Charli did to me. She made me into someone else.

Stepping under the cool spray, I fisted my length and closed my eyes as scenes from the same shower the night before played behind my closed eyelids: that ugly red dress falling from her shoulders, exposing her sexy body. Her gaudy makeup and those cheap high-heeled sandals that kept her balance in my control.

My cock hardened as my hand became an unacceptable substitute for her tight, wet pussy.

From the moment I saw her in the bar, I knew I was going to take her hard, but never in a million years did I anticipate how ready she'd be. Her slickness took away any resistance as I spun her around and took what was mine. Unapologetically, I filled her—no warm-up, no being sure she was ready. I pushed balls deep as each thrust drove into her, and my fingers dug into her hips. Primal need told me to pull out, rip off the condom, and release all over her soft skin. I wanted to mark her. I wanted the world to know she was mine. Instead, as soon as I was surrounded by her, I was lost.

Thrust after thrust—she was heaven and I couldn't or wouldn't leave.

My balls tightened and fist moved faster. Biting my lip, I recalled her moans echoing throughout the shower stall. Her pussy milking my cock as her body stiffened and her head fell forward. Giving her pleasure wasn't my goal. Taking it was. However, over and over she imploded. Apparently, even angry sex was beyond description with Charli.

"Fuck." My forehead hit the wall as string after string of come painted the tile. "Shit," I murmured as my shoulders shuddered and I blinked, bringing the world around me back into focus.

I might have told myself I was punishing her by withholding my cock, but standing under the cool spray, it was pretty fucking obvious that she wasn't the only one suffering.

Stepping back upon the soft carpet of the bedroom, dripping wet, I was happy to find the room empty. I'd tried to stay quiet, but with what only thoughts of her did to me, I'd probably failed. The last thing I wanted was for her to know the power she had or how badly I wanted her.

Once I was dressed for work, I took a deep breath and headed for the living room. With the door barely opened, I stopped to appreciate the view. She was a vision, sitting on the sofa with her knees near her chest and her phone in her hand. Charli was so engrossed in whatever she was reading, she didn't see or hear me. I stared, wondering if she had any idea how gorgeous she was. Had anyone ever told her? Maybe her unpretentiousness was part of her allure. Somehow, with that beautiful hair, now sexy and wild, her mesmerizing eyes, and perfect body, she didn't seem to realize what she did to me.

The idea that she needed all that makeup or a garish outfit to stand out was absurd. It was wrong on her. Alexandria Collins—my Charli—exuded elegance and culture with the perfect hint of sexy vixen. It was a unique blend of perfect qualities. I didn't know anything about her, not really. I knew that for a week I'd made her a princess, and with everything in me, I wanted that title for her for a lifetime.

When she looked up and her eyes met mine, I consciously returned my expression to one of disinterest, the exact opposite of what I felt. Though difficult to maintain, I resisted the urge to smile. Judging by the way she frowned and lowered her eyes back to her phone, I'd succeeded.

I could have walked out. I could have avoided twisting the proverbial knife, but I told her the truth when I said I was bad. I had one of the best teachers and too many years to perfect the craft. The words and cold tone came with ease.

"Coffee?" I asked, nodding toward the cup on the table beside her.

"Yes. You're incredibly perceptive. Was it the cup or the aroma that gave it away?"

"Very funny."

"I'm not laughing."

"Neither am I. Tomorrow you'll make my cup first. I take it black."

Her golden eyes swirled with sadness as they found mine, yet her words were crisp and precise. "I remember how you like your coffee. I didn't realize cook and maid were part of my job description."

Damn, her spunk turned me on. I moved closer and gestured for her to stand. When she did, the robe she wore gaped open ever so slightly, allowing me a glimpse of her tits. They weren't as visible as I would have liked, but with only the sides of her round globes showing, my cock thickened, twitching back to life. Lifting her chin, I brought her eyes to mine, and my tone turned purposely condescending. "Yes, Nox," I began, "I'll make you coffee and do whatever else you tell me to do."

Her stance stiffened before she repeated my words.

"Was that too difficult? If it was, I'd be glad to bend you over this sofa…" I looked out the large windows to the park and beyond. "…in front of half of New York City and give you a reason to remember."

"No, it wasn't difficult."

Releasing her chin, I brushed her lips with mine. My grin grew. "I think I'd like that. I'd like to bend you over the arm of the sofa, lift this robe…" I teased the lapels and dragged my finger from her tits up to her collarbone. "…and admire your round ass. Then, I'd decide if I would spank you or fuck you."

Her eyes closed as her head wobbled.

"Next, I'd decide if I'd leave you that way, your ass exposed and thighs slick, or if I'd allow you to cover yourself up before my security arrived."

Charli's eyes opened wide as she took a step back. "What? No."

I lifted my brow. "Excuse me?"

"You said I don't have a say in my limits, but I still have them. I'm with you. Only you."

"Says the woman who signed away her rights. Says the woman who had a man on each arm last night." I pulled her close. "I told you, I don't share. No one but me can or will touch." Her body relaxed in my embrace. "Looking, on the other hand," I shrugged and went on. "…well, we'll see how well you can follow my directions. Tonight?"

"Yes, Nox. Tonight, Mobar at seven o'clock. I'll be there."

"And tomorrow morning?"

"I'll make you a cup of coffee." Her eyes fluttered down.

I rubbed her cheek as a knock echoed from the door to the suite. "That's a good girl. Are you sure you don't want to give my security a show. We could just—"

Charli looked up, and on her lips was the first smile I'd seen all morning. My heart stuttered. The honest pleasure made her eyes light like golden reflections from the crowned jewels.

"Oh my God," she exclaimed. "You're in socks."

"How very perceptive of you." I couldn't help but send her words back at her.

She stifled a laugh. "That's why your security is coming here. You don't have shoes to wear."

"I'm glad you find this humorous."

She shook her head. "I-I do."

"Go answer the door."

Her expression turned suddenly sober as she looked down at the robe. "But, Nox, I'm not decent."

"You're also not bent over the sofa, but it can be arranged."

"They'll know…"

"That you spent the night with me," I said, finishing her sentence. "My security will know that I fucked you?"

Another knock came from the door.

"Yes," she answered, pink filling her cheeks.

"Door or sofa? They can know it or see it. Your choice."

Charli pulled the lapels together, attempted to smooth her long hair, and tightened the robe's sash as she walked toward the door. After a glance though the peephole, she turned back my direction, her expression confused. "It's Mrs. Witt. I thought you said it was security?"

"Open the door, Charli."

CHAPTER 13

CHARLI

ASSHOLE!

If I weren't afraid that Nox would follow through on the sofa threat, I would've told him to shove it up his ass. But since yesterday afternoon, I wasn't sure of anything. Taking a deep breath, I pretended I wasn't wearing a robe and reeking of sex, plastered a confident smile to my face, and opened the door.

"Mrs. Witt," I said, waving toward the suite. "It's nice to see you again. Come in."

In her closed-lip smile, I read the judgment she wasn't voicing. In her eyes I was taking the walk of shame, even though I hadn't left the suite.

"Miss Collins, nice to see you again."

I reached for the bag she was carrying. "Would you like me to take that? I assume it's for No—Mr. Demetri?"

Her lips turned upward as she presented the handles of the paper bag my direction and looked toward Nox. "Yes, I was told there was an unfortunate mishap with his shoes."

"Yes," his deep voice came from behind me as his warm breath tickled my neck. "I believe it was a puddle or something."

"Oh," Mrs. Witt replied. "I don't remember it raining."

I craned my neck backward. In Nox's pale eyes was the smirk of amusement I'd missed. I didn't know who Mrs. Witt was or why he referred to this woman as *security*, but whoever she was, it was clear they shared a comfortable relationship.

I took a step back as Mrs. Witt came farther into the suite, and Nox shut the door.

"If you two will excuse me, I need to—" I began as I handed Nox the bag, ready to make my way back to the bedroom. A shower was in order.

"No," Nox interrupted.

I tilted my head. "No?"

He sat on the sofa, opened the bag, and removed a shoebox.

Where and how did she buy him new shoes at six-thirty in the morning?

As I pondered that question, Mrs. Witt sat on the edge of one of the chairs, and Nox spoke, "I'm on my way out. Charli, you remember Mrs. Witt?"

His perceptiveness was astounding. I just decided not to point that out once again. Instead, I nodded and smiled her direction. "Yes."

"Deloris," she corrected. "Call me Deloris. Now, is it Alexandria, Alex, or Charli?"

I narrowed my eyes, wondering how she knew so much about me. "My legal name is Alexandria. However, I prefer Alex. Charli is… well, it's a nickname." Though I'd only been *Charli* for one week of my life, even now I liked hearing it from Nox. I preferred it to *Miss Collins.*

Nox stood, his shiny new loafers in place. "Deloris, I'll speak to you later. Charli, remember everything we discussed."

Still standing, my knees grew weak as I wondered why he appeared to be leaving while she was staying.

"Charli?" he asked again, narrowing his pale gaze.

"Yes, I remember."

"Thank you, Deloris. I'm sure you can explain everything better than I." With that he reached for the door handle and disappeared.

As I turned back, Deloris Witt was smiling my direction.

"Mrs. Witt, I mean Deloris, I'm apparently at a disadvantage. What are you supposed to explain to me?"

"Alex, please sit down. We need to talk."

Securing my robe, I asked, "Would you like some coffee?"

She shook her head. "No, I can't stay. I just thought that perhaps Mr. Demetri might not have told you everything."

I sat back on the sofa. "I'm sorry. I'm confused, and you're right, he hasn't told me much. What do you know and why are you the one talking to me? I apologize if my forwardness is rude. I've had quite a week and my filter is obviously not working."

"It's not rude at all. As you may remember, I work for Lennox. I have for a long time. He mentioned that you assumed I was his housekeeper." Her smile broadened. "I'm not. Alexandria… I mean, Alex, am I to assume that you'll be with Lennox for the foreseeable future?"

"We're… dating."

"I realize it's against the rules. However, I am fully aware of the origin of your new agreement."

My pulse kicked up a notch or two. "We met in Del Mar, as you know. We planned on one week, but there was more. We decided not to fight it any longer." It was the story I'd conspired to tell Chelsea. For the first time from my lips, I thought it sounded plausible.

"Yes. That does sound good. Is that the story the two of you have agreed upon?"

"We haven't really discussed it."

Mrs. Witt nodded. "That's why I'm here. No one, not even Demetri Enterprises' public relations can know the truth. Your stories must be the same. I like it so far; however, there may be questions. The best policy is not to answer them. *No comment* is your friend."

"Questions? Who will ask questions?"

"Everyone. Anyone."

When I didn't answer, she continued, "It only takes a tweet or a picture posted on Instagram or Facebook to start the world talking. Lennox hasn't dated anyone with any regularity since… well, for years. We were able to keep

Del Mar off of social media and away from the reporters. That was one week. This will be a year. We won't be able to keep it hidden. Not that we're trying. As soon as you two appear together on a regular basis, the world will start talking."

The world?

My stomach twisted. My family was part of the world. Bryce was part of the world. Before I could comment, she went on.

"I've read your profile."

I couldn't hide my shock. "What? Why?"

"Lennox has not. He didn't want to learn about you from a file. He wants to learn about you from you."

Blood rushed to my cheeks. If there was one thing Lennox Demetri was good at doing—and there was definitely more than one thing—it was getting to know me.

"You were rather evasive about your family on your profile."

I sat taller. "I'd rather not discuss my family."

"So you do have one?"

"I wasn't found in a cabbage patch, if that's what you mean. We're not close."

"Alex, I run Mr. Demetri's personal security as well as the security for Demetri Enterprises. I'm Lennox's eyes and ears. I'll be perfectly frank. I knew your last name in Del Mar. My top priority is Lennox and that won't change. He wants you to be safe; therefore, you will. Today you'll have Isaac at your disposal. He's more than a driver. Isaac is fully capable of protecting you under all circumstances.

"Since he is usually with Lennox, I'm currently working to fill the position of your driver and bodyguard."

"I don't want any of this," I said, my voice as determined as I could make it. I remembered Nox's lecture earlier this morning; however, the thought of having someone watching me all the time made me physically ill.

"Demetri Enterprises is an umbrella." Her eyes narrowed. "Do you know what that means?"

"It has a wide range of subsidiaries?"

"Very good. There's no reason for you to be any more familiar with Demetri Enterprises than Lennox chooses to make you. That said, some of the people in some of the rather diversified affiliations have been known to be less than savory. Don't fight this, Miss Collins. You agreed to this year. Know that there are certain things with Lennox Demetri that are non-negotiable. Your safety is one."

As I tried to comprehend, she continued, "I also have things that I consider non-negotiable. I will not mention your family to Lennox unless he asks. I also will not tolerate anyone getting close to Lennox in order to cause harm to him or Demetri Enterprises. If I have reason to suspect that, I won't hesitate to rectify the decision I made in Del Mar when I allowed you to enter the presidential suite."

My head moved from side to side. "Why would you think…? I don't even know what you're talking about."

"I believe you. I also think you should be honest with Lennox about who you are."

"I'm not being dishonest. I'm Alexandria Collins. I don't understand why anything else is relevant."

She stood and smoothed the material of her slacks. "A few other things. Your income will be deposited into your bank account from an overseas account. Your interview and signing bonus will arrive today. Monthly payments will arrive on the fifteenth of each month, beginning next month. There won't be any way to track these back to Infidelity."

"Thank you."

"Also, if you'd like, I'd be willing to investigate the sudden loss of your trust fund. At first glance, it seems at the least questionable and at the most fraudulent, perhaps illegal."

"How do you know so much?"

"It's my job. I'm very good at my job."

"You care about him, don't you?" I asked.

"I do." Her expression softened. "In Del Mar, Lennox was someone I hadn't seen in years. He smiled more and worried less about business. He took time to relax, time to be… a man. If you can do that for him, then you have my full and unwavering support. If you hurt him, I'll be your worst nightmare." Deloris scoffed. "I realize I don't look like much, but power isn't all about appearances."

She was right. From appearances alone, I'd never imagine her to be anyone's nightmare. Yet there was something in her voice.

"I know all about power," I said. "I believe it's mostly about conviction. I believe you too. But let's be honest. There's no way to know what will happen between Nox and me. I know that Del Mar was the best week of my life, and the last week has been one of the worst. I know the man I met at the resort was a prince who took my breath away, and the man I met yesterday was not. I can't promise you that neither one of us will get hurt. I can promise you that who I am and who my family is have nothing to do with my meeting Lennox Demetri. I'd never heard his full name until yesterday.

"I want to go to law school. I want to succeed in life on my own merit. If anything beyond this year is meant to be with Nox, then so be it. If it's not…" I shrugged. "I've been disappointed before."

Deloris opened her purse and laid a business card on the coffee table. "Don't contact Karen Flores again. If you have any questions or concerns, call me."

I wanted to believe this was good. Yet for some reason it felt like a safety net had been pulled out from under me.

"Thank you."

"Good luck to you, Alex. I hope this works out well for everyone. Your trust fund?" she asked.

"You'll look into it without telling Nox?"

"Yes."

I nodded as tears prickled my eyes. "I never wanted to sign… If you're the reason Nox found me, thank you."

"I'll be in touch." Deloris took two steps toward the door and turned back around. "Give him some time. He's more complicated than you can imagine. That man from Del Mar cares about you. Don't rush him, and be patient. You awakened something in him that he forgot existed. For that reason, I'm here for you."

I nodded. "Thank you."

FRESH AIR FILLED my lungs as I walked the sidewalk along Central Park West and made my way back to the hotel. I wasn't purposely setting out to disobey Nox as I'd done the night before. This was different. I'd walked through Central Park only a few days ago. Walking along its perimeter with thousands of people wasn't any different.

When I left the hotel, I called Isaac and had him take me to Columbia. I needed to talk to the bursar's office and confirm that Alton hadn't gone back on his word. It was a pleasant surprise to learn that everything was a go for orientation in less than two weeks.

Then I walked from the campus to my new apartment, met with the broker, and acquired the keys. When I initially contacted the broker earlier in the day, I intended to follow Nox's suggestion and break the lease. When the broker told me it was empty and I could take immediate possession, I changed my mind. I'd made too many rash decisions in the last four days to make one more. Besides, my furniture was scheduled to be delivered, and seeing the deposit that Deloris mentioned earlier appear in my checking account convinced me I could afford the one-bedroom apartment. Besides, after a year I'd need someplace to live. From my perspective the apartment was my guarantee of next year's housing.

Although I hadn't seen Nox's apartment on West 77th, I was certain my little one-bedroom couldn't compare to it or to Patrick and to Cy's on the Upper East Side. Nevertheless, I liked it. With its wood floors, white walls, and a galley kitchen, it wasn't pretentious. It was cozy. From its large old windows, I couldn't see the park. Instead, they looked out onto a tree-lined street, and just down the block was Tom's Restaurant on the corner.

I planned to tell Nox—eventually.

Maybe once I had the keys and was ready to head back to the Mandarin, I should have called Isaac. But the sun was shining and I wanted to think. Deciding to enjoy the summer day, I chose to walk. Every now and then, I had the sensation of being watched. I probably was. Undoubtedly, Nox was receiving up-to-the-minute reports of my rogue behavior.

The entire scenario was suffocating.

Pausing, I sat on a park bench and checked my phone again. I was waiting for something from Chelsea. I'd sent her a couple of text messages, but I hadn't heard anything since the text I found this morning. Today was the day the movers were picking up my things. I even tried repeatedly to call her, but after three rings it went straight to voicemail.

I knew she didn't forget. Her text said she was ready. I just wanted to touch base. I wanted to hear her voice. Now that I had my story, I wanted to tell her about Nox.

Sighing, I got up and moved south along Central Park West. The energy of the city filled the warm air with excitement and anticipation. I'd been nervous about moving here, but Patrick was right. I smiled as his rendition of *New York New York* played in my head.

If I could make it there…

My thoughts went to Nox and his directions for tonight. I'd do it all, even the drink. We had a year. Baiting him at every move wasn't a wise decision. Up until now, Nox was my fantasy. Del Mar had been that. Now we had reality, and it was a new road for both of us. If I wanted to be sure he was the one who would want this to go past a year, then I needed to play his game.

I also contemplated calling Jane. Though I shouldn't, I worried about my mother. She hadn't tried to reach out to me since the confrontation in the sitting room. Unless Patrick told Aunt Gwen that I was here, my mother and Alton didn't even know I was in New York.

They could think I was back in California. That was the gist I caught from Bryce's last text. He said something about the time difference, wondering if that was why I hadn't responded. It wasn't the reason, and I still hadn't responded.

I didn't want to hear from Bryce or talk to him. When I did, I'd need to let him know about Nox and that I was in a relationship. Maybe I could just change that Facebook status after all.

Pulling me from my thoughts, my phone rang, the melody reaching my ears moments after the vibration alerted me of its approach. I stopped and looked at the screen. I didn't recognize the number, but I did know it was a California area code.

"Hello," I said. "This is Alex Collins." I stepped back against the fence separating the sidewalk from the park and allowed other pedestrians to pass.

"Ms. Collins," the unfamiliar voice said. "I'm Felix. Me and my partner are supposed to move your things today."

"Yes?"

"There ain't nobody here."

"I'm sorry. What do you mean?"

"I mean. We're here, at your apartment. We knock. Nobody answered. Ma'am, are you gonna be here soon? If not, we need to reschedule and there's a fee."

No, I'm not.

"Felix, I arranged everything with your company. You're not supposed to contact me. You're supposed to contact my roommate, Chelsea Moore."

"Yeah. We tried that. I called her. I hear her phone ringing. She ain't answering. If we don't get in your apartment, we're going to need to reschedule."

My pulse increased as his words echoed in my ear. "Wait. Please don't reschedule. Let me call the manager of the complex. She'll let you in. I'm sure there's just been some misunderstanding."

"We can wait a few more minutes. Then I need to call my supervisor."

I nodded, though he obviously couldn't see me. "I understand. Please don't leave before talking to me again. I'll call you back."

About ten blocks from the Mandarin Hotel, my heart raced. I could see the south end of the park. It was after one in the afternoon. That meant it was after ten o'clock in California. I knew Chelsea liked to sleep in, but she wouldn't still be asleep, not after her text. Speeding my steps, I called Chelsea again. Three rings and it went to voicemail. Instead of leaving a message, I scrolled my contacts and called our apartment complex's main office. When someone answered, I hurriedly explained my situation. My words were breathy as my pace increased.

"Please just wake her. I know she's there. The mover said he could hear her phone ringing."

The woman on the line began to lecture me on her responsibilities and how waking up tenants wasn't one of them.

Before she could go on, I interrupted, "I'll pay. I just need the movers to get in."

"Fine," she replied. "I'll call you as soon as we have your apartment opened."

This wasn't like Chelsea. She had her faults, but never in four years had she let me down when it was important. I tried her phone again. Voicemail.

Just as I was about to cross the street to the Mandarin, my phone rang.

"Miss Collins?" It was the same lady from the complex's office, except her tone was different.

"Yes. Did you open my apartment?"

"Your roommate…"

Oh my God.

My stomach dropped.

"What?"

"We've called an ambulance."

CHAPTER 14

NOX

I STOOD AT the tall windows overlooking the Financial District, completely oblivious to the scene before me. From fifty-eight stories up, I had a prestigious view of some of the most expensive real estate in the country, and none of it mattered. My mind was with Charli. If I weren't careful, my body would follow. Not exactly the best state of affairs for conducting business.

I'd managed to do that, but between each phone call or report, I'd slip back to the beautiful redhead and rehash her reasoning for Infidelity. I also wondered about her conversation this morning with Deloris. At least I'd know about that since I'd have my report soon. What I couldn't comprehend was Charli's reasoning.

The questions continued to haunt me.

How did she go from law student to prostitute? Why didn't she investigate other options?

There had to be more she wasn't telling me, probably more that Deloris knew. I wasn't sure how long my curiosity would allow me to stick to my previous plan. I wanted to know more. I just wanted to learn it from her. I needed that, to trust her.

Sitting back at my desk, I let out a long breath and rubbed my hand over my face. Trust. Could I do it? Was I ready to trust someone as I had with Jo? The painful pinch in my chest told me that I wasn't, or maybe it was saying it came with a price. I could use Charli, as stipulated in the agreement she signed, but I already knew that wouldn't be enough. She was under my skin from the first day I saw her.

Trust needed to go both ways. She agreed to trust me in Del Mar. Now, if this was going to work, I would need her trust every day. But I needed more than that. I needed to trust her, understand her, and take care of her.

It wasn't like I wanted to control her every move. I didn't. As a matter of fact, I loved her strong will and ambition and would support it. Not only financially. Hell, money wasn't an issue. I wanted to support her dream. Listening to her talk about all she'd worked to accomplish, I wanted her to succeed. But on a personal level, I needed control. I needed to know she was safe. It wasn't debatable. It was how I coped.

Arguing about security was absurd. That was why I called Deloris—for her to explain. The subject was too black and white for me. I couldn't have what happened to Jo…

This time I wouldn't back down. Charli would have her own security detail, whether she wanted it or not. Today it was Isaac, but soon she'd have her own people. Deloris would see to that, be sure Charli had the best. Though I wasn't currently acting as if I believed it, Alexandria Collins deserved the best.

Letting her know that would take trust. It would take time.

Considering what I learned in California, time wasn't a commodity that I had in excess, at least where some matters were concerned. Undoubtedly, there were things at Demetri Enterprises that warranted more attention than I'd given them—more than I'd given since Charli came into my life, even in California.

While I was there, I did the essentials. I went to the meetings with the senator, did my homework on the bill before the Senate Finance Committee, and met with Peterson. I just didn't go above and beyond. I usually knocked this shit out of the park. While in California, to continue the baseball metaphor, I'd simply covered my bases. I'd been too preoccupied with the first woman to catch my eye in years. Instead of plying Peterson for more information, I'd blown him off to relax in a beach cabana bed.

It was out of character, and Oren knew it.

My father questioned me. Not only did he ask me bluntly once, he'd also alluded to it multiple times during dinner. He pried, trying to get me to confess. One day he'd know about Charli, but I wasn't ready for that to happen. If I could keep the news of us from going viral for the next few days, then when it did, Oren Demetri would be back in London.

That was why we were staying at the hotel. He never stayed at my apartment, but that wouldn't stop him from coming by. Once he was gone, we'd go there. I'd meant what I said about keeping Charli away from *bad*.

Oren was near the top of that list.

"Mr. Demetri," Dianne's voice came through the speaker near my telephone.

"Yes?"

"Mrs. Witt is here for you."

I sighed. Good, maybe once this security issue was settled, I'd be able to relax enough to concentrate.

"Send her in."

I rose as she entered and moved to the front of my desk. "Deloris, we seem to be seeing a lot of one another lately."

She half-smiled. "It's your bubbly personality. I can't seem to stay away." She looked down at my feet. "I'd love to know the story behind your new shoes."

I lifted my brow. "And I'd like to hear how your morning meeting went."

"It went well. Isaac is with Alex today. Last I heard he took her to Columbia. He's been following her. I've searched through viable bodyguards and have come up with a short list of candidates. Do you want to see the list or meet them? Or would you like Miss Collins to interview them?"

"No. You take care of it. Do it today, and tomorrow her driver can come to the hotel and they can be introduced."

It was Deloris's turn to purse her lips and look at me knowingly. "May I suggest you give her some warning so that she could be dressed?"

Lifting my brow, the side of my grin rose. "I'll consider that."

She shook her head. "Before she knew what I did and what I know, she told me a nice story about how the two of you are now together."

"Let me guess. It's because of my bubbly personality?"

"She didn't mention that," Deloris said with a knowing gleam to her eyes. "Although I'm sure it played a significant role in her decision."

I shook my head, thinking about what an ass I'd been. "I doubt that. What did she say?"

"She said that you met in Del Mar. You agreed to one week. When she moved to New York, the two of you decided you wanted more." Deloris nodded. "I like it. It's simple and difficult to refute."

"Did you warn her about discussing it with others?"

"I did. I told her that *no comment* was her new best friend."

I took a deep breath. "Thank you."

"Lennox, she's young, and she's strong. Give her time. She's more complicated than Jocelyn. I don't believe everything is as it appears."

I narrowed my gaze. "What are you saying?"

"You don't want to know. You said that. I'm just saying that so far I like her—and I like the man you are when you're with her. Most people don't get a second chance at that kind of spark. Del Mar was something special. Now you have the chance for more. I would hate for your bubbly personality to ruin it."

There were few people I'd allow to speak to me in this manner—no, that was wrong. There weren't a few, there was one, and I was staring at her.

"Is that all?" I asked, making no attempt to feign that *bubbly* personality.

"No." She shifted slightly in her chair. "There's something else. You may want to sit."

I gripped the edge of the desk behind me as I leaned back. "I'm treading water here. I'm not sure if I can handle another bombshell."

"Not a bombshell," she replied. "It's more like mortar fire."

I sighed. "Charli? Infidelity? Oren?"

"As I said, my discussion with Miss Collins went fine. I've had my say. Besides, it appeared you're handling the situation in your own way. This is about Demetri Enterprises and Oren."

Despite her earlier chiding, her choice of words amused me. I was handling Charli *in my own way*, and by the state of her dress—or undress—this morning, it would have *appeared* so. "Tell me about Demetri Enterprises and Oren."

"Apparently, your father's not only in New York to visit his son." She woke her iPad. "After your dinner last night, he came back here to the main offices for a meeting."

What the fuck?

She continued, "The executive offices were empty, except for the janitorial staff. He told them to leave and then used your office."

The pounding in my temples reminded me to unclench my teeth. "In *my* office? A meeting? With whom?"

"Severus Davis."

"Refresh my memory. How do I know that name?"

"On the surface, he's a lobbyist. In reality, he's a political gun for hire."

"Thus the mortar fire?" I asked with a smirk.

"Yes. Unfortunately, if you're in Davis's sights, I recommend wearing a bulletproof vest. History has shown that advice to be literal. Of course, there's never any proof or connection; however, his opposition has disappeared more than once. The coincidences continue to surface."

This was why Charli needed security. Deals weren't made in boardrooms. They were made with handshakes and greased palms. Nothing was safe or easy. Quid pro quo had its consequences.

"I'm assuming Davis hasn't been on the Demetri payroll?" I asked.

"No, and I would know. That's what made your father's meeting rather odd. During the House Ways and Means Committee's drafting of House bill 770, Severus worked for the sin-tax opponents. He's made a name for himself on behalf of alcohol and tobacco. The ATF has him on a watch list."

"Why would Oren meet with Davis if he's working to push the bill through the Senate Committee with its current wording?"

"That's what I wanted to know. Everything I heard on the audio footage from your office was unrelated. It appeared the meeting was strictly an introduction of sorts."

I paced the length of my desk and back, pondering Deloris's information. My father, president and CEO of Demetri Enterprises, one of the biggest opponents to the current wording of House bill 770, met with an influential lobbyist for the proponents of the bill—essentially, his enemy.

"Why would he meet with him at Demetri? If it's illegal wouldn't he do it somewhere else?"

"Unless it was a show of strength. Oren's way of saying he's still in charge."

In name only. I was the one who did what needed to be done.

"I also believe," Deloris continued, "that Mr. Demetri thought it was safe. He doesn't approve of any surveillance equipment in his personal offices. I believe he expects the same from you, thus making your office safe."

"Arrogant ass. My office is safe—for me."

"I learned a few other things about Mr. Davis." She paused, gaining my full attention. "Infidelity. Mr. Davis is a recent client. What I learned in the last ten hours was that he and his wife have an understanding. She plays nice at social functions and does all that's expected of her in public. In private, they agree to be… well… non-exclusive. Unfortunately, Mr. Davis's most recent mistress retired, so to speak."

"Retired? What does that mean? Was she with Infidelity?" My gut twisted as I thought of Charli ending up with the likes of this man.

"No, she wasn't. It appeared it was an organic relationship. According to sources, his ex-mistress recently left for Europe to reevaluate her life. Not surprisingly, I can't locate her. However, I haven't had much time.

"The interesting phenomenon of Infidelity is," she went on, "in my opinion, the reason for its success. Severus Davis didn't contact Infidelity for himself. Marisa Davis did."

My eyes narrowed. "Is that his wife? Tell me, Deloris, don't you think that's a bit fucked up?"

"I think Infidelity fulfills a need. People are willing to pay handsomely to have needs met."

"How did you learn all of this? I thought you said Infidelity's information was secure?"

She gave me a sideways grin. "It is. I make sure of it."

I shook my head. "I'm glad you're on my side. I need out of that company. I never should have—"

"As of now," she interrupted, "Severus hasn't been assigned an employee."

"Well, good. Then he won't be disappointed when I shut the doors." I made my way back to my chair and sat.

Deloris shrugged. "His wife already paid the twenty-five-thousand-dollar deposit."

Yes. I was all too familiar with the amount of the deposit. "Why are you telling me this?"

"Because it seems that you have a valuable resource at your disposal. Who will be closer to him, other than his wife, than that employee?"

My eyes widened. "Are you suggesting that instead of getting away from Infidelity, we utilize it to our benefit?"

"It seems to me that not only has Demetri Enterprises invested in the company, but recently a large sum of money was transferred to its accounts. Though the source of that money is untraceable, I believe that wielding the right information, Demetri could use this to its benefit."

I shook my head. "The whole Melissa thing is still out there, then the thing with Charli. No this needs to be shut down before the shit hits the fan."

Deloris appeared unusually disappointed as she shook her head. "I don't know why Melissa was hired in the first place."

"Yes, you do."

"Yes, that *client*…" she said the word emphasizing the obvious bitter distaste she felt for him. "…was willing to pay extra for a younger employee."

"And you're defending this company?"

"No, Lennox, I'm not defending that particular set of circumstances. They should've told the client to go away. Unfortunately, he was willing to pay and she was willing to be paid. She was of legal age. I'm not blaming the victim here, but she's the one who strayed from her agreement."

"Has that been determined?"

"Everything appears as though she accepted a date with a graduate student, more than once. Her client, as you may recall, is married. Her services weren't required on a daily basis, only when he was in town. She is young, suddenly had money, and although a student, she had time on her hands. It appears as though the young man, not her Infidelity client, was the perpetrator.

"The issue is that Melissa's parents are encouraging legal action against the graduate student. The Infidelity client is nervous because he doesn't want to be associated with any of this, and the graduate student's family has the means to dig. That graduate student is denying everything. We worked to bury the story as did his family. Unfortunately, some small campus paper picked it up and it's swirling around again."

"Jesus, Deloris, let's close this down now."

"She isn't blaming her client. She knows that by dating she broke the agreement and lost the best source of income she'd ever known. Melissa is blaming the graduate student."

"It makes me ill. That could be the downfall of Infidelity right there. I want Demetri Enterprises out." I stood taller. "Wait. You got Charli's paperwork out of there. Can't you do the same to Melissa's?"

Deloris shook her head. "I could, but it's different. Alex just entered the system. Melissa was in it. She received pay. She'd been assigned. She was the one who chose to break her agreement."

"The graduate student is—"

I lifted my hand. "I don't want to know more about this. I want it gone, taken care of, but instead you want to utilize Infidelity?"

"Lennox, just hear me out. That situation will be resolved, but Severus Davis is a credible threat. Having someone on the inside with him could potentially be game changing."

"Do you have anyone in mind for the job? If Davis is as dangerous as he sounds, it would be a hazardous assignment. And please don't tell me that he has a thing for eighteen-year-olds."

Her lips flattened to a straight line. "No, thankfully, based on his retired mistress, I don't believe so. I wanted your approval before I started working on this. I need to study his profile and see what I can do. Then I'll get it in motion. I can't give you the particulars. If I did…"

A smile pulled at the corners of my lips. "I pay you to keep me protected. So don't say that if you told me *you'd have to kill me.*"

"Then, Mr. Demetri, I suggest you don't ask."

It wasn't the first illegal operation we'd entered into, and I was most certain it wouldn't be the last. But first I had to be sure of one thing.

"Charli's profile, you deleted it? It's totally gone from Infidelity's records, isn't it?"

"It is. If Infidelity would blow up tomorrow, she was never there."

I sighed. "All right, keep me posted."

"As much as I can," Deloris said with a tight-lipped smile.

"Thank you. Maybe we can go back to weekly or bi-weekly meetings."

She didn't respond as she stared down at the screen of her phone. I'd seen that look before. Something had happened.

I leaned forward with my arms folded on my desk. "Deloris?"

"Sir, it's Isaac. He's following Miss Collins."

"Following? Why isn't he driving her?"

Deloris's eyes opened wide. "Lennox, he thinks she's headed to LaGuardia."

CHAPTER 15

CHARLI

UNCONSCIOUS.

Chelsea was unconscious and admitted to Stanford University Medical Center. The woman from my apartment complex said the police were called. No one had answers. The door to our apartment was locked and there were no signs of forced entry. If the movers hadn't come, they might not have found her. The lady even said the apartment wasn't in disarray, except for the obvious packing. They couldn't tell if anything was missing, but said usual high-theft items like electronics and jewelry were still there. From all accounts it looked like a crime of passion, yet Chelsea wasn't seeing anyone.

I didn't care about any of the things in our apartment. I cared about Chelsea. Since we weren't really family, I couldn't learn anything from the hospital. They wouldn't release her information.

Paying the driver, I rushed from the taxi at the curb of LaGuardia through the glass doors with only a carry-on and my purse. After I returned to the hotel, I hurriedly threw some essentials into my bag and left. I didn't need to pack much; I had a whole apartment full of clothes and things in Palo Alto. My only thought, only concern, was getting to my best friend.

Although Chelsea wasn't close to her family, I called her mother. For one thing, she'd be able to get information. She and Chelsea's sister were on their way to Stanford Medical Center. It would take them a few hours to get there from their home, but they'd still make it before me.

Rushing around people who weren't in as big of a hurry as me, I bypassed the ticket counter and headed toward security. Thankfully, I found a direct flight from LaGuardia to San Francisco. Unfortunately, even without a layover, the flight took six and a half hours from coast to coast. As I searched the Internet, Nox's plans for tonight or even his reaction to my leaving New York weren't part of the equation. I found the flight and booked it. After the last week, thinking about anything else was more than I could handle.

Nox continued to enter my thoughts, and now that I had a minute, I let myself consider him. After the way he behaved yesterday and this morning, I couldn't dwell on him or how he'd react to my impromptu trip. I'd take that *medicine*, to use an Alton idiom, when I returned. Right now, getting to my best friend was my only concern.

It wasn't like I disappeared. I left him a note in the hotel suite with a brief explanation. I almost called Isaac to drive me to the airport, but I knew how this worked. Isaac was supposed to be at my disposal; nevertheless, if Nox told him not to drive me, I would have missed my flight. That was why I opted for a taxi. To that driver, I was nothing more than a fare.

Rushing toward security, I pulled up my ticket on my cell phone and freed my identification from my wallet. As the line inched closer to the TSA, my phone vibrated and rang with an incoming call.

Shit.

NOX- PRIVATE NUMBER covered the screen. With my pulse thumping loudly in my ears, I swiped the red *end call* icon. Of course he knew where I was. I didn't know if he'd seen the note, or he just knew I wasn't at the spa appointment. He'd said I was being watched. No matter how he learned, my not answering his call probably pissed him off more. I put my phone on silent and decided to worry about that later. I'd call him back once I made it to my gate. I couldn't have a call and my ticket up at the same time.

"Good afternoon, ID and ticket please."

I forced a smile and handed my phone and driver's license to the agent.

After he scanned both of them, he handed them back to me.

"Have a good flight, Miss Collins."

"Thank you."

My flight wouldn't depart for another fifty minutes, but with the way the rules were, I needed to be boarded by at least ten minutes before takeoff. My best friend was alone in a hospital, and I refused to miss my flight.

I continued to weave around people, dodging children and luggage as my carry-on's wheels spun, when my phone vibrated again. I didn't take the time to look at the name. I was pretty sure I knew who it was. Taking a deep breath, I juggled my purse and bag as I swiped the green icon. I might as well get this over with.

"I was going to call," I said breathlessly as I continued my race through the crowd.

"Alexandria? Is that you?"

My feet slowed as I moved to the side of the corridor and closed my eyes. I could hang up, but this conversation needed to happen sooner or later.

"Bryce?"

"I'm not sure I believe you," the unexpected voice said. "I guess I'm just glad you answered now."

"Believe me?"

"That you were going to call. Alex, talk to me."

"This isn't a good time."

"Apparently, there hasn't been a good time since I left you after your party. I thought… I thought it was a nice night, down by the lake…"

I shook my head. I couldn't do this, not right now. I should be telling him about Nox; instead, a question that had been nudging at me came to mind. I needed to hear his answer. "Did you know?" My question came with more emotion than I intended.

"What? All I know is you're gone again. And we want you back."

I swallowed the tears as a lump formed in my throat, and the betrayal of Montague Manor reemerged. "Did you know? Bryce, answer me. Did you know Alton's plans? Did you know about my trust fund?"

"Alex, there's so much for us to talk about. I thought we'd have the chance on Sunday night—"

"Answer my fucking question!" I looked up in time to see a woman give me a grimace as she hurried by with her child. I took a deep breath and lowered my voice. "When we were talking and reminiscing at the lake, when we were talking about Nessie and you were proclaiming your innocence, did you know what my parents had planned?"

"Is that why you're mad at me? You think I knew? I'm not even one hundred percent sure what you're talking about now. I know that when I showed up on Sunday, your mother was indisposed and Alton told me you left—again. He said you'd be back, but he wasn't sure when."

He's wrong.

Bryce went on, "I know that it's been almost a week and you're not back."

"I'm not going back. If you want to know why, ask Alton."

Bryce's tone softened. He was my childhood friend, the one I could rely on when no one else was there. "Ask Alton? Should I ask him about what happened while you were just recently home or when we were young?"

I clenched my teeth as my spine straightened. "Goodbye, Bryce. This isn't a good time. I really need to go."

"We need to talk in person. I'm tired of the no answers and unreturned text messages." His tone slowed. "Alexandria, you don't have to say anything. You know I'm the only one who really knows you, who was there for you. Let me be there for you now."

Shaking my head back and forth, I tried to remember the young man I wanted away from, the one who suffocated me at every turn and claimed me as his own. But in that moment, my mind focused on one truth: of all the things Bryce had ever done, spanking me had never been one of them.

A renegade tear slid down my cheek.

"Bryce." My voice cracked.

"Alexandria, don't throw us away. We're meant to be together. It's always been that way."

"I'm going to hang up," I warned. I couldn't do this.

"Wait. Let me tell you why I called."

I stood taller and replied, "Make it fast."

"I'm coming to see you. We need to talk in person. I need to tell you about your mom."

"What? What about my mom?"

"When are you leaving California?"

My eyes scanned the corridor. "How do you know about California?"

"What do you mean? You live there—at least until you move to New York. When are you moving?"

"Bryce, no. Just tell me about my mother."

"I already have a ticket. I've been trying to tell you, but you wouldn't answer or return my text messages. I'll be in Palo Alto tonight. I'm waiting for my flight out of Atlanta."

Shit!

"It's too late. I'm in New York."

"You've never been able to lie to me. I'll see you tonight."

"I am in—" He didn't hear me. Pulling the phone away from my ear, I stared at the screen. He'd hung up. As his number disappeared, the icon for missed calls came into view. Six missed calls: three from Nox, two from Deloris Witt, and one from Chelsea's mother, Tina.

I took a second to add Bryce's name back to my phone. That way I would at least know it was him. Then with my head pounding and a lump in my throat, I called Tina.

"Mrs. Moore, this is Alex. Have you learned anything?"

"We're not there yet. Kelsey had to get off work. She's working at the mall now—"

"Mrs. Moore, I'm about to board my flight. Why did you call?" I couldn't care less about Kelsey or her job or why Chelsea's mother would delay her drive to her injured daughter.

"The hospital called. Chelsea's responding."

"Oh thank God." I needed some good news.

"They said she doesn't have any broken bones, just a lot of bruising."

"Is she talking?"

"Not yet, but she's moving and responding."

"Thank you."

"Honey, you don't need to fly out here. She's going to be all right."

I thought about that. I could stay in New York and avoid Bryce. Then again, I wanted to be sure Chelsea was really all right. If I avoided Bryce in California, would he come to New York? That wouldn't be good, because… well, because of Nox.

I took a deep breath. "I'll see you in about seven hours. I need to go."

BOARDING HAD BEGUN. When I booked, I took the last seat on this flight, which had me seated in a zone that hadn't been called. As I waited, my stomach twisted with myriad thoughts turning cartwheels in my head. My mother? What did Bryce want to tell me about her? And then there was Nox. I needed to return his calls. I just couldn't be talking when they needed to scan my ticket. Therefore, I decided to wait until after I was in my seat.

With the announcement of my zone, I made my way forward. When I handed the woman my phone, instead of the little beep that I'd heard for the passengers ahead of me, the air filled with the shrill alarm.

"Just a minute, Miss Collins. It appears there's been a change to your ticket."

"What? There can't be. I just purchased it."

"Give me a moment, ma'am."

My jaw clenched as my hands began to tremble. *Damn, him!* This had to be Nox. It had to be. "Ma'am," I said, "It scanned fine in security. I need to be on that plane. I need to get to San Francisco." My sentences were clipped with desperation.

She pushed a few buttons. "Not to worry. It appears you'll make it. You're still on the plane." She smiled up at me. "It must be your lucky day. You've been upgraded to first class, seat 3D." She handed me back my phone. "Enjoy your flight."

My lucky day. Hardly.

I shook my head as I entered the long causeway toward the airplane. Maybe I was just being paranoid. After all, my nerves were stretched and my imagination was working overtime. Upgraded. It made sense. I usually flew first class, so it was probably a coincidence. That's what I told myself as I made it over the threshold, smiled at the flight attendant, and walked down the aisle to the third row. I lifted my carry-on up to the compartment above my seat and settled into 3D. As I sighed with relief at being on the plane and other passengers continued to board, I looked around the cabin. The rest of first class was already seated, except 3F. The seat beside me was empty.

I tried to ignore the odd sensation that something wasn't right. When I first booked the flight, the computer indicated that first class wasn't available. I pushed those thoughts away as I swiped my phone, took a deep breath, and returned Nox's multitude of calls.

CHAPTER 16

Twenty years earlier

ADELAIDE

"NO," I REPEATED, as my mother, Olivia, held tightly to my hand.

There had been so many conversation and decrees I'd heard while within the regal walls of my father's home office. For all of my life it had been his throne room, his center for control. From within this room he'd make decisions and pass judgment, but today was different. Charles Montague II wasn't telling. Like my mother and me, he was listening. Today's news affected us all.

"Mrs. Collins, the LAPD has significant evidence to believe the driver of the car was indeed your husband, Russell Collins."

"It can't be. He was just here. He's on a business trip. I spoke to him yesterday."

"What time did you speak to him?"

My mind was a blur. It had been later, after dinner. Our conversation was short, but words were exchanged. That made it a conversation, right? "I don't remember. After dinner."

"Dinner's always at seven," my mother interjected, as if our unyielding schedule would somehow help the detective piece together our sordid lives or Russell's death.

Detective Michelson nodded and wrote in his notepad. "We'll undoubtedly need to see your phone records."

"I spoke to him on his cellular telephone. I called from the line in our bedroom."

Michelson looked around as if taking in the grandeur of our home for the first time. "You have more than one telephone line?"

"Yes," my father replied. "Is that significant?"

"No, it's just common procedure in cases like this to clear the family."

Heaviness filled my chest as I thought about the man I married, the man with golden eyes and copper hair. The man I'd met at Emory with the background and breeding that pleased my father. I remembered who we'd been before we came back to Savannah, before we changed. I recalled his excitement when I told him I was pregnant. We'd never practiced birth control and yet it took us years and two miscarriages before I finally made it through the first trimester. Russell was elated to be a father. Even after the ultrasound that told us we were having a girl, he never wavered. To him, Alexandria wasn't an heir; she was his child, his little girl. Now I'd need to tell her that he was gone.

"Laide?" My father's voice pulled me from the past.

"What?" I scanned from my father seated on the other side of his desk, his eyes open wide in expectation, to Detective Michelson, a tall, balding man in a cheap suit who shifted from one foot to the other. "I'm sorry. Did you ask me something?"

"I apologize," the detective said. "I know this is a difficult time. I don't want to be the bearer of more bad news…"

Tears escaped my eyes as I stifled my cries. My hands trembled as the news registered. Russell was gone, forever. He'd never return. Each time my head bowed, my mother's grasp of my hand would squeeze, reminding me to keep my head held high. Improper etiquette was unacceptable for a Montague, even when learning that I was now a widow at the ripe old age of twenty-nine.

"The LAPD," the detective continued, "wanted you notified in person, before news broke."

Charles's head bobbed up and down. "We appreciate that, Detective Michelson."

"We know, Mr. Montague, how upsetting this is and what a shock it is. We wanted you to know the details before any different stories got out."

My gaze shot to the detective. "Different stories? What are you talking about? You just said my husband was in an automobile crash. What different stories could there be?" Something he'd said earlier finally registered. "And why would you need to *clear the family*? Of what?"

"Dear," my mother cooed. "Let the men do their jobs. I'm sure it was purely an accident."

"Of course it was." Turning my gaze toward Detective Michelson, I asked, "Are you insinuating that it wasn't? Do you think someone purposely…" I couldn't bring myself to say the words as my chin again dropped.

"No, ma'am. I'm only saying that before Mr. Collins's body can be brought back to Savannah, there needs to be a few tests. In cases like this, an autopsy is mandatory."

"N-No," I whispered. Gathering my strength and lifting my eyes, I looked across the large desk to my father, wordlessly pleading for his help. If anyone could stop this, Charles Montague II could.

"Laide," he said, his tone dripping with fatherly concern, "it's their job."

I shook my head. "I don't want them to cut him open. No. I'm his family, Alexandria and I. We're all he has… had. I say no. Can't I say no?"

"I'm sorry," the detective said again, though I doubted his sincerity. "It's protocol. As I explained, the car exploded upon impact. His body was burned beyond recognition. Though the car was badly damaged, it was a rental, and LAPD was able to trace it to Mr. Collins. Upon preliminary examination by the medical examiner, the man driving that car met your husband's description: height, weight, age, but his identity and cause of death can't be one hundred percent confirmed without the autopsy."

"Wait. What about dental records?" I asked.

"We've already subpoenaed those from his dentist. However, that won't confirm his cause of death."

I stood and paced a small track near the front of Charles's desk. My eyes filled with tears. "You said the car exploded. He couldn't get out. Wasn't that the cause of death?"

"On the surface. However, tests need to be done to confirm that there were no foreign substances in his system: drugs, excessive alcohol, anything. This isn't debatable. The medical examiner has already begun."

My stomach twisted. "Father? Isn't there something you can do? I don't want them to do this. He wouldn't want that."

Charles Montague II shook his head. "I think this is something that needs to be done. It will help with closure."

"Closure? Closure! My husband is gone. I'm a widow and not even thirty years old, and you're talking about closure. What about Alexandria? No matter what the results are, she'll never be able to say goodbye to her father. I'll never…" More tears flowed.

"Mrs. Collins, was it your husband's practice to drive at excessive speeds?"

I shrugged as I lowered myself back to the chair. "Russell liked fast cars. He never drove too fast with me or Alexandria." I remembered a gift I gave him when we were first married. "He did one of those race-car fantasy weekends once."

The detective continued to take notes as I spoke.

"But he wasn't a drinker. I doubt there's anything you'll find. He barely drank wine."

"I hate to ask, but your marriage? LAPD wants to know if there were problems."

My teary eyes opened wide. "No. That's absurd."

"I didn't mean anything by that. It's a standard question when life insurance is involved."

Charles sat straighter. "Detective, does it look like my daughter is in need of insurance money?"

The tall, balding man shook his head. "Not on the surface, but these are all questions that need to be answered."

"No," I said with more conviction than I'd previously mustered. "What *needs* to happen is that Russell is brought home. We *need* to arrange a funeral, and I *need* to explain to our three-year-old daughter that her father is never coming home."

"As soon as the autopsy—"

"Detective, I want my husband home."

My blue eyes met my father's. Slowly his lips formed a straight line and he nodded. I leaned back against the chair.

"Tell me when my daughter's wishes will be honored." It wasn't a question. Charles Montague II didn't ask. He proclaimed.

"As soon as possible. We'll contact LAPD and do all we can."

"Thank you, Detective Michelson. Please contact me with the results of any tests. I don't believe you'll find anything, but if you do, Montague Corporation needs to know what it's up against."

"Of course, sir."

As one of the biggest employers for the area and beyond, Montague Corporation's reputation was something the Savannah police would do all they could to maintain.

"If that is all," my mother said, "I believe my daughter needs some time. I'll be happy to show you to the door."

Detective Michelson nodded. "I'll be in touch."

"Olivia, please close the door."

My eyes looked nervously toward my father's as the door closed and silence prevailed. Listening to the police detective give gruesome details of my husband's death should turn my stomach, and it did. But not as much as being left alone with Charles's judgmental stare.

Willing my neck to straighten, I took a deep breath and tried to ignore that the trembling I'd experienced when I first entered his office had resumed.

Father stood and moved to the chair beside me, the one where my mother had been. "Don't worry."

It wasn't what I expected to hear.

"But if they…"

"They won't find anything out of the ordinary. Russell went for a joy ride. He lost control. Montague will make a public statement and ask for time—

time for grieving."

For the first time in years, my lungs filled as I inhaled. My chest rose and fell in rhythm as each breath delivered essential oxygen to my deprived bloodstream. Like water to the Georgia clay, it brought a seedling of hope where before hopelessness reigned.

Charles's words registered. His low monotone tenor infiltrated my new sense of freedom. "…a respectable time before you remarry."

My face spun toward his. "Why? I don't want to remarry."

"That's nonsense. Of course you'll remarry. I believe someone older than Russell. He couldn't control you the way you need."

I stood, my head shaking from side to side. "I can't bear children. There is no reason for me to remarry."

"Adelaide, sit down and lower your voice."

Slowly, I did as he said.

"I won't live forever. I need to know that Montague Corporation is in capable hands."

"What about me? What about Alexandria?"

"Don't be ridiculous. You had a mission—correction, two missions. You failed at both. The husband you chose was incapable. Maybe that was your real failure. Him. Russell Collins couldn't produce a son, failed as a husband, and was a disappointment as a businessman.

"The position of your husband is too important to allow for you to fail again. I'll find an acceptable man to oversee my empire."

"You're crazy." It was the first time I'd ever stood up to him.

"Excuse me?"

"*Your empire*? Heavens, who are you, the king of Savannah?"

"Adelaide." His tone threatened to still my unusual outburst.

Nevertheless, I continued, "You point fingers, yet you seem to forget. You only produced a daughter yourself."

"No." The one word came out as a growl. "I haven't forgotten. I'm reminded of that fact every day. That is why I'll be the one who oversees this next husband. Your job, your duty is to give me a son-in-law capable of the tasks before me. I won't risk your poor decision-making ability again.

"You said you married for love. Well, Daughter, how did that work for you? Montague Corporation, my empire, is too important to let emotion be a deciding factor."

No longer able to breathe, I sat mute as he went on and on about my future and that of Alexandria's.

"I could leave. I don't need to do this."

Father laughed. "Be my *guest.* Oh, that's right. You have been for twenty-nine years. The door isn't locked, but you're not taking Alexandria."

What the hell?

"You can't take my daughter away from me."

"They don't allow children in prison. That's what happens to women who kill their husbands."

I wasn't the one who commissioned his death. Charles knew that.

"I didn't! I didn't have anything to do with it. You just said that they won't find anything."

"They won't, unless I want them to."

Just like everything else, my opinion didn't matter. It was my duty. I'd been told that since the day I was born. Arguing would prove futile. After all, this was his empire. King Charles II, supreme ruler of Montague Manor and beyond.

"When do you plan for me to marry? What's an acceptable amount of time?"

His cold hand patted mine. "Don't worry about that. Daddy will take care of everything. You mourn. But when you do…" He waved his hand up and down. "…remember to keep yourself… appealing. Russell may have grown tired of you, but you won't let that happen again. You're a Montague. Don't ever forget that."

CHAPTER 17

CHARLI

"LADIES AND GENTLEMEN," the captain's announcement bellowed through the speakers. "We apologize for any inconvenience; however, the tower has informed us that there is a backup on the runway, and our departure from the gate will be delayed."

I looked at my watch. It was time to take off and yet the cabin door was still open. I might be paranoid, but the longer I was unable to reach Nox, the more my mind created ridiculous scenarios. It wasn't difficult for me to do. In first class I saw everything. I saw the string of unfamiliar faces that passed by after I boarded. I noticed when the passengers ceased boarding. I watched as the flight attendant began to close the cabin door and saw the attendant on the sky bridge, the one who does whatever happens outside the plane, whisper to the inside attendant. I noticed that they left the door open.

Now, with the recent announcement, I wasn't sure what to think.

Surely, a plane of two hundred passengers wasn't being delayed because of me. That idea was ridiculous. No one had that kind of power.

I looked again at the phone in my hands. It should be turned off, but then again, we should be in the air. Since I was seated, I'd tried twice to call Nox. Each attempt went to voicemail. I hadn't left a message. I didn't know what to say. After all, I'd left a note. It wasn't like leaving him in Del Mar. With our agreement, I knew I'd see him again, and I had the uncomfortable feeling that it would be similar to yesterday.

I shifted in my seat with phantom memories of the sting of that reunion.

The last thing I'd said to him was that I'd follow his directions and meet him in the bar at seven. I wasn't trying to disobey him at every turn; however, he'd probably see it that way.

Since the person in 3F never arrived, I unbuckled my seatbelt and scooted over to get closer to the tiny window. The view was my distraction, a way not to think about Chelsea and her injuries or Nox and his consequences. Instead, I concentrated on the people outside, the people on the ground scurrying about with carts of suitcases. The entire operation fascinated me. I didn't really care how my checked luggage got from one airport to the next, but the fact that it did was in and of itself a feat. There were times when I'd run full speed through large airports, barely making my connecting flight, and yet my luggage was almost always there upon arrival.

The vibration of my phone took me from the mundane thoughts of baggage and airports back to reality.

NOX - PRIVATE NUMBER

I swallowed and faced the music. "Hello."

"Hello? That's your answer?"

My heart sank at his cold tone. *What did I expect?*

"I've tried multiple times to reach you."

"As have I. Explain."

Okay. At least he is willing to listen.

"Do you remember Chelsea?"

"Your sister, who isn't?" Nox replied.

"Yes. I told you we lived together. We did, near Stanford in Palo Alto. Today was the day my belongings were supposed to be picked up by the movers and brought to New York."

"You don't need anything from California. I told you to shop today."

I closed my eyes and tried to keep my voice low. "Please listen." When he didn't answer, I went on, "I did—need things. I scheduled this move before…

before my life imploded. Anyway, today I received a call from the movers. They were there knocking and Chelsea wasn't opening the door."

"You're flying to California to open a fucking door?"

"Shut up!" I whispered through clenched jaws. I was tired of his attitude. "Just listen. I love her. She's more of a sister than I've ever had. I called our complex. They opened the door and found her. She was hurt. Nox, someone hurt her. They took her to the hospital and…" I tried unsuccessfully to keep the tears at bay. "…I need to see her. I need to be there. I'm sorry. This isn't about you or us or anything. I need to be there…" My words trailed away as a newly boarding passenger caught my eye. "Are you kidding me?" I asked as my eyes met Deloris Witt's.

"Is that question for me?" he asked. "The last time I spoke you told me to *shut up*."

I looked from Deloris to the seat beside me, stunned that she was there, and silently asking if she was supposed to sit in 3D. Shaking her head, she smiled and silently walked past.

Well, at least she smiled.

"Did you…?"

My words trailed away as the next passenger boarded. The handsome man holding a phone to his ear, the one who had to duck his head as he entered, took my breath away. I wasn't sure if it was due to the fact that he was there or how incredibly stunning he was in his suit. I wasn't the only one to notice, apparently, for the flight attendants quickly offered their assistance, taking his suit coat and hanging it in the small closet. Behind him was another man I also knew.

Smiling at the flight attendants, Nox's eyes found mine. Removing the phone from his ear, he nodded my direction, hit the disconnect button, and slid his phone into the pocket of his slacks.

I swallowed the lump in my throat, unsure what to do or say. Unable to comprehend, I sat paralyzed, my phone still to my ear. Nox whispered to Isaac, who nodded my direction before following Deloris farther back into the plane.

Nox's brow furrowed in question as he eased into the seat beside me.

Without speaking, he reached for my phone and hit the disconnect button. A second later he leaned closer, and his warm lips collided with mine as a cloud of woodsy cologne replaced the stagnant cabin air.

When he pulled away, navy swirled in the pale blue of his eyes. The menacing gaze that I adored bore into me, only inches away, speaking volumes that his lips had yet to utter.

The dam on my emotions broke. It'd been too much for too long. I fell forward as his arms surrounded me and tears dampened his white shirt.

"I'm sorry." My apology came out muffled by his embrace. "I shouldn't have left, but I'm so worried."

"How is she? Have you heard anything?"

I leaned back and stared at this beautiful man. From his expression, the tenderness in his touch, and the concern in his voice, he wasn't the man who'd left me this morning. He was the man from Del Mar.

Before I could answer, I turned toward the attendant closing the main cabin door. The captain's announcement came over the speakers. "Ladies and gentlemen, I apologize for the delay. It seems as though the tower is now allowing us to proceed. For those of you having a connecting flight, I believe with current weather conditions, we will make it to San Francisco on schedule."

I shook my head. "You delayed a plane?"

Nox reached for my chin and pulled my eyes to his. "You belong to me. I'm not letting you fly across the country by yourself."

"How?"

"Why?" he asked, without answering my question.

"I told you, Chelsea."

"Charli, she was attacked in *your* apartment."

I nodded.

"No, you're not listening. Someone attacked her, in your apartment."

"You knew? Before our call?" I asked, astonished.

"Deloris figured it out. Don't you see? Don't you see how dangerous this is? I'm not being a caveman or a dick or any other name you want to call me. I'm being cautious. Today you tried to lose Isaac. You must stay with your security detail."

"Is that why he's here?" I asked.

"For now. He's here for both of us. I'm going to go with you to visit Chelsea. If you decide to stay with her and I need to return to New York, Mrs. Witt will assure the safety of both of us."

I looked down as Nox reached for my hand and our fingers intertwined. The bright red nail polish from last night was gone, replaced with a new nude shade. The warmth of his touch flowed from our connection throughout my body, filling me with support I'd never known.

"What?" he asked.

"I was afraid you'd be upset."

He kissed my nose. "Upset that you're worried about your sister?"

I shook my head. "I told you…"

"Charli, a sister isn't just blood. I don't have any siblings, but there are people whom I'm closer to than my own blood. We'll go and make sure Chelsea is all right. Then, if you want, we can bring her back to New York and keep her safe. If she means that much to you, she means that much to me."

My head continued to move from side to side. "Who the fuck are you?"

Nox leaned close, his cologne clouding my thoughts. "I'm Batman, princess. Next time you want to fly across the country, tell me. I won't delay two hundred people's plans, and we can just fly in the bat plane."

He shook his head as the plane began to move and pointed his chin toward my lap.

"What?"

"Fasten your seatbelt."

Though I didn't want to let go of his hand, I grinned and did as he said. "Actually," I said, "I think I'm in your seat. Since this one was empty, I moved over to look out the window."

"You can keep the window seat." He reached again for my hand. This time, he lifted it to his lips and kissed my knuckles. "I prefer my current view."

After we were in the air, I leaned back and tried to make sense of everything. "Nox?"

"Hmm?"

"How did Deloris figure it out? Did she see the note I left you?"

"You left me a note?"

"Yes," I replied. "In the hotel suite."

"No. It was your phone."

"My phone?"

"Even though you tried to lose him, Isaac was watching you today. He said you were upset over a call and rushed back to the hotel."

"I wasn't trying to lose him. I wanted to walk, clear my head."

"Then inform him. Don't just go MIA."

Had he seen me at my apartment?

"Please keep going, but then I need to tell you something."

"Deloris checked your calls," he explained. "Since all of your recent calls, except those to me, her, or Isaac, were to and from California, she did a little more research. I don't know how she does what she does, but I know she's invaluable." He squeezed my hand. "What do you need to tell me?"

"You probably already know."

"Even if I do, I'd rather hear it from you."

My stomach twisted with what I was about to confess. I liked the man beside me, the one who was concerned about my safety, the one who listened and held my hand. If I told him I disobeyed his orders again, that I'd signed the lease and agreed to keep my apartment, would he morph into the man from yesterday and last night?

"I'm scared," I confessed.

The flight attendant smiled at Nox as she handed him our drinks. As Nox handed the glass of red wine to me, his cheeks rose. "Let's toast."

"To?"

"To us, together again in California." His smile broadened.

Our glasses touched, and we each took a sip.

"We could also toast to whatever it is you are about to tell me."

I sighed. "I don't think it's toast-worthy, but here goes. I didn't cancel my lease. I signed it today, in person, and have the keys to my apartment."

By the way he nodded, I'd been right. He already knew.

I gave him time to respond, but when he didn't, I asked, "What are you thinking?"

"I'm thinking about how fun it will be when I get you alone."

The tension I'd felt moments ago in my stomach moved lower.

"That's what scares me," I said, sounding more seductive than scared.

"Oh, princess," Nox whispered near my ear, "it should. It should. Your list of offenses never seems to end. If we were on the bat plane, I'd start your punishment now."

With each word, my breasts heaved and my breathing labored. His lips teased my neck as his warm breath skirted my cheek.

The low tone of his whisper rumbled through me. "You're fucking gorgeous when you're aroused."

"I'm not," I lied.

"You are. You're gorgeous," he paused for a moment and inhaled. "And you're so wet I smell it. Princess, you're not scared; you're turned on."

I took a deep breath and tried to pretend he was mistaken. Lifting my glass of wine, I bravely turned his direction, keenly aware of the friction caused with shifting. Staring into his eyes, I proposed, "Another toast. To knowing last names, *Mr. Demetri.*"

He grinned. "Using that name isn't going to save you."

CHAPTER 18

CHARLI

Nox ushered me from the plane, up the causeway. I hadn't had a chance to change clothes from the casual sundress and sandals I wore to Columbia this morning. It was fine for the flight, but now walking next to Nox in his silk suit and shiny new loafers, I felt woefully underdressed. We waited for Isaac and Deloris before we headed toward the exit.

While Deloris spoke on her phone, Isaac wheeled my carry-on.

I'd planned on taking a taxi to Stanford Medical, but as we stepped onto the sidewalk, Deloris nodded to a large black Suburban. As she did, the driver stepped out and opened the rear door. In minutes, Nox and I were settled in the backseat with Isaac in the front beside the driver.

"Where's Deloris?" I asked as we eased into traffic.

Though Nox was busy reading something on his phone, he answered, "She's taking care of our hotel rooms."

"I don't need a hotel room. I have an apartment." I looked up in time to see Isaac's eyes peer toward Nox's in the rearview mirror. Their unspoken communication pushed my wrong buttons. "I have an apartment," I repeated. "I didn't bring many things because I have them there."

Nox's large hand splayed over my thigh. "You're not staying in an apartment that was broken into or one that's a crime scene."

I exhaled. "I need things from there: clothes and other things."

"Deloris will take care of that."

"She'll go to my apartment? How will she get in?"

He sighed. "I'm certain that if she wanted into your apartment, she'd have no difficulty. After all, someone broke in there with Chelsea present. However, that's not her plan. As you can only imagine, the three of us had no time to pack." He shrugged. "We could have, but then those passengers would have all missed their connecting flights. Anyway, she'll have everything we need in the hotel rooms by the time we get there."

I fell asleep with my head on Nox's shoulder during the flight. After we landed, he hurried me from the plane. Now, with my immediate future apparently no longer in my control, I reached for my phone and took it out of airplane mode. In less than a minute, it came to life, popping like popcorn with incoming messages.

"Are any of those about Chelsea?" Nox asked.

Missed calls, text messages, and emails made their presence known. I'd been so overwhelmed by Nox's presence and his nicer attitude, that I'd forgotten about my conversation with Bryce—that was until his name appeared on my screen. Ignoring it, I replied, "I missed two calls from her mother. I'm going to call her now."

Nox nodded as I returned her call. Smirking, I turned toward Nox's grimace as Tina answered. Her shrill voice was loud enough for everyone in the SUV to hear. In the short time we spoke, I learned that Chelsea was now awake, drowsy and bruised, and she was answering questions.

When I hung up, I asked, "Would you like to know what she said?"

Nox laughed. "I think we all heard what she said."

"Yes, Chelsea had to get it from somewhere. Tina Moore is a little over the top."

"You're not actually sisters, so that woman isn't your mother."

"Oh, no. Not even close."

"What does that mean?"

I turned toward the window on my side and watched the familiar scenery.

I hadn't planned to return, not after what happened with my trust fund, but being back in Northern California felt right.

"Charli? What's the matter?"

I shook my head and feigned a smile. "Nothing. I just loved living out here. I'm going to miss it."

"Did you apply to Stanford Law?"

"No…" For the remainder of our drive we chatted about Columbia and Yale and why I'd applied to East Coast schools. We talked about my upcoming schedule as orientation began, and we even talked about my apartment.

"I hate to admit it…" Nox's eyes shimmered. "…because I would love to punish you for signing that lease, but I think it's a good thing you did."

"You do?"

"Yes. If you convince Chelsea to move to New York, she can stay there."

I hadn't thought of that. "I figured the location was great." I turned toward him animatedly. "It's right down the street from Tom's Restaurant."

He leaned down and kissed me. "You're so cute when you're excited. I'll remember, no fancy restaurants. Diners are more your style."

"No. I just think it's neat. I also figured law school will take three years to finish. I'll need a place to live in another year, so I might as well keep it."

The tendons in Nox's neck popped to attention as his Adam's apple bobbed. "Are you certain of that?"

"Yes." I looked his way and changed my mind. "No. Nox, I'm not certain of anything."

He took my hand. "I'm certain that I'm glad Chelsea is doing better. I'm certain that after your short conversation with that very loud woman, the worry that was in your golden eyes has gone away, making them stunning. I'm also certain that I can't wait until we're at the hotel."

His velvet tone rumbled through me like molten lava, melting everything in its path.

"So you can…?" I prompted.

He lifted his brow as his lips formed a lopsided smile. "Do whatever I want."

I wanted to ask him what he wanted. I wanted to tell him no or tell him yes. I wanted to say things that I'd never said to a man, but I didn't want to say them within earshot of Isaac and a driver I didn't know. As indecision flirted with desire, I lifted his hand to my cheek and inhaled the magical woodsy cologne.

"Is there a problem with that plan, Miss Collins?"

Is he asking me? Do I once again have that power?

"No, Mr. Demetri, no problem at all."

Nox smiled before our lips touched. The kiss was soft and chaste. Though my body ached for more, the spark in his eyes told me that the connection was only a taste of what was to come, an hors d'oeuvre before a five-course meal. As my mind filled with carnal possibilities of what Nox might *want*, my insides burned with hunger in anticipation of what was in store.

As the SUV headed north, Nox silently went back to his messages, and I went back to mine. Though I had two voicemails from Bryce, I chose not to listen. After the conversation with Tina, I didn't want the entire vehicle hearing everything he said. Both of his calls came within the last hour. I wasn't sure how long his flight took from Atlanta, but it must have been quicker than ours from New York. Then again, he probably didn't have anyone delaying his departure. If it weren't that he'd traveled from Georgia to see me, I would do my best to avoid him altogether. Since he had, I couldn't very well continue to evade him.

I opted for sending a text message.

Me: "I'M SORRY IF YOU'RE HERE. I CAN'T RETRIEVE MY VOICEMAILS. AN EMERGENCY HAS COME UP."

He responded immediately. Nox looked my way with the vibration. His expression morphed from one of concentration on his messages to one that questioned mine. I shook my head and turned off the volume.

Bryce: "WHAT KIND OF EMERGENCY? ARE YOU OK?"

Me: "I'M OK. IT'S NOT ME. IT'S MY FRIEND."

Bryce: "WHAT HAPPENED?"

Me: "I NEED TO GO. I'LL CALL YOU TOMORROW."

Bryce: "NO. I FLEW TO SEE YOU. I'M SEEING YOU."

Me: "NOT TONIGHT."

Bryce: "I'M WAITING AT YOUR APARTMENT."

Shit!

Me: "I'M NOT THERE."

Bryce: "I'LL WAIT UNTIL YOU ARE."

I gritted my teeth. This was ridiculous.

Me: "I DON'T KNOW WHEN THAT WILL BE. PLEASE. I'LL CALL YOU TOMORROW."

Though a message instantly appeared, I stopped replying.

AWAKE AND RESPONDING.

After a cursory knock, I pushed open the door to Chelsea's hospital room. The conversation ceased as all eyes turned our direction. Tina Moore's mouth opened, but instead of her customary shrill voice, nothing came out. Chelsea's sister, Kelsey, stilled her fingers hovering above her phone, and Chelsea blinked.

I rushed to my best friend's side, evaluating her injuries. One eye was blackened, and a bandage was wrapped around her head. Hugging her softly, I asked, "How are you?"

She looked past me toward Nox. "Delusional, I'm definitely delusional," she replied.

I grinned. "Chelsea, you remember Nox?"

She nodded. "Faintly," she replied with a smile. "Sorry, not that memorable."

Nox came closer to her bed, his menacing grin in place. "I'm glad you're all right. You had us worried."

She stared up at him and then turned her eyes back to me. "I'm having an amazing hallucination right now." She reached for my hand. "No, if I were imagining a tall, dark, and handsome man, I'm sorry, sweetie, I'd imagine him for me, not you."

Nox stepped beside me and wrapped his arm around my waist. "I'll take that as a compliment," he said with a smirk.

"Oh! It was meant as one."

We all turned toward Tina.

Nox offered his hand across Chelsea's bed. "Mrs. Moore. Lennox Demetri."

The same hazel eyes as Chelsea's stared, unblinking.

"Hello, Mrs. Moore," I said when she didn't speak. "Thank you for keeping me updated."

Kelsey popped up next to her mother and thrust her hand forward. "Hi. I'm Chelsea's sister, Kelsey."

Nox shook her hand as I nodded. It was the longest sentence I'd heard Chelsea's sister say in the four years I'd known her. Usually her face never left the screen of her telephone.

Though she was bruised, the spark I loved was back in Chelsea's eyes.

"So," she said, "I was going to get mad at you for not calling me for a few days, but…" She pursed her lips and furrowed her brow. "…since I'm going to assume you also have been comatose, I'll forgive you."

I laughed. "Not quite, but thanks. I'm sorry I haven't called. Can you tell us what happened?"

She leaned back on the pillow and closed her eyes. "As I told the police and everyone else, I really don't remember. I had everything packed and ready for the movers. I remember texting you and going to bed. I woke up, but I can't remember why. I don't know if I heard something…" She shook her head. "I walked into the living room and was hit by something or someone. That's where it all ends."

"You didn't see anyone?" Nox asked.

"I think so, but only briefly. I can't recall a face, just a presence." She closed her eyes. "I know that doesn't make sense."

"Was your door locked?" Nox asked.

"I thought it was, but the police say there weren't any signs of a break-in."

I shook my head. "We always locked the door. I can't imagine your not doing that."

Chelsea sighed. "Me either. I just don't get it. Everything is jumbled. The doctors say if I don't force it, I may remember more."

"What's your diagnosis? How long are they keeping you here?" I asked.

"She has a concussion and bruises." Tina said. "Luckily, nothing is broken."

"Alex, I'm sorry about your stuff," Chelsea said. "Mom said the movers didn't take anything."

"Are you kidding me? Don't worry about stuff. I'm worried about you!" I turned toward Tina. "You went to our apartment?"

"Yes, Chelsea wanted a few things. It's weird. There's no sign of scuffle. The only thing out of place is some furniture—I assume so they could wheel Chelsea out. All the boxes are still there."

"I'll get the movers rescheduled. The most important thing is that you're safe. Did it look like anything was missing?" I asked Tina.

She shook her head. "Not that I could tell, but you girls will need to look to be sure."

"Let me know what you think," Chelsea said. "Then again, all your things are packed. It would be hard to tell if anything is missing."

"Kelsey and I were planning on staying there tonight." Tina looked from me to Nox and back. "But if you don't want us to…"

"Is it safe?" Nox asked.

"The locks work."

"You're welcome to stay," I said. "We have a hotel room for the night. We didn't know if the police would allow anyone to be there." I turned to Chelsea. "How long do you need to stay here?"

"They're doing some tests tomorrow. It all depends on the concussion."

I bent down and kissed her cheek. "All right. I'll be back in the morning."

Nox took my hand as we said our goodbyes and left Chelsea with her mother and sister. Once in the hall, I giggled at everyone's reaction to Nox. "I think you made quite the impression on Chelsea's mother. She looked disappointed that we weren't going to have a big slumber party tonight."

Isaac followed two steps behind after leaving his post outside Chelsea's door. I wasn't sure I could get used to having him or anyone else omnipresent. It seemed more intrusive than the staff at Montague Manor. Maybe I'd grown used to them. Could I grow used to Isaac?

"As appealing as that sounded," Nox scoffed, "I think I'd prefer our own slumber party."

On the elevator with just the three of us, Nox pulled my hand behind my back as he held me close. His tongue teased my lower lip before he pulled away and stared down. The passion in his gaze was overwhelming as he drank me in.

"It's so nice to see the worry gone from your eyes."

"I was worried. Thank you for coming with me."

The tips of his lips quirked upward. "I wanted to be sure you didn't do something stupid."

"Such as?"

"Drink California wine," he replied with a smirk.

"Well, thank you, Mr. Demetri, for keeping me on the straight and narrow."

He leaned close and whispered, "Straight, not narrow, and I do intend to keep you on it."

Blood rushed to my cheeks as I giggled and looked at the back of Isaac's head. If he heard Nox's whisper, he showed no reaction. My laughter stopped short as a gasp escaped my lips when the doors opened, and my eyes met Bryce's.

Shit! What the hell is he doing here?

With my heartbeat quickening, Bryce took a step back and allowed us to exit. As he did, his chest widened, while simultaneously, Nox's grip of my hand tightened. Comprehension was out of reach. My feet forgot how to move; nevertheless, Nox's momentum pulled us forward.

"Alexandria," Bryce's speech was clipped. "I was told I might find you here." Red seeped from the collar of his shirt, moving up toward his clenched jaw as he nodded to Nox. "Mr. Demetri, I wasn't aware the two of you knew one another."

What the fuck? Bryce knows Nox?

"Edward. I wasn't aware of a connection to you."

Nox knows Bryce?

I stood mute, my eyes darting back and forth as my two worlds collided in some show of male standoff within the hallway of the hospital. When Bryce looked up after settling his gaze on where Nox and my hands were still connected, I replied, "Bryce, I told you I couldn't see you tonight."

"You told me there was an emergency. I was concerned. There was a woman at your apartment complex who told me about your roommate. I thought you might need some support."

"That job's already taken," Nox replied. "You're a day late and a dollar short, as usual."

Ignoring Nox's comment, Bryce said, "Alexandria, I flew all the way out here." He paused, softening his tone. "Give me a minute. You owe me that much."

Ice and fire radiated from Nox's grip. When I looked up into his steely expression, I saw his answer. Though he didn't say a word, I heard the response he wanted—no, expected—me to say. However, Bryce was right. He'd flown across the country to see me. I could speak to him for a minute. Plus, he'd said he had information about my mother. I nodded to Nox. "I'll be just a minute, if you and Isaac want to get the car."

"The car's waiting."

I released Nox's hand and touched his chest. The playfulness of seconds earlier was gone, replaced with the icy cold stare from yesterday. "Five minutes and I'll be out."

Capturing my waist, Nox pulled me close, our chests and hips colliding. In a deliberate display of affection—or was it possession—he covered my lips with his. As mine bruised from the force, I realized which it was. His kiss wasn't meant to be one of affection. It was a warning of things to come as well as a claim, purposely staked in front of Bryce. When I pulled away, our gazes locked. In that moment, I tried to tell him that I heard him loud and clear and I understood.

"Five minutes," I repeated, sucking my tender lip between my teeth.

He turned his clenched jaw toward Bryce. "Edward."

"Lennox."

CHAPTER 19

CHARLI

WALKING AWAY FROM Nox, I became acutely aware of everything around me: the slickness of the tile floor beneath my sandals, the contrasting scent of Bryce's cologne, and the burn of Nox's stare singeing my back. I fought the urge to turn around and explain why I owed Bryce minutes of my time, to make Nox see that this wasn't about him or about us. It was what I'd been raised to do and be, and I was about to end it all for good.

As we strode toward the small cluster of chairs, I reconsidered. Maybe this talk was about us, Nox and me; because of him, I could finally end this farce with my childhood friend, boyfriend, and sometimes tormentor. Though it may seem that the Infidelity agreement imprisoned me for a year, in reality I would finally be free.

With each step I consciously worked to keep distance between Bryce and me. That didn't stop the displeasure that emanated from his being. Confusion, hurt, and anger mixed together and swirled around us. When we reached the waiting area, Bryce grabbed my forearm and spun me toward him.

Through gritted teeth, he spat out his question. "What the hell are you doing with Lennox Demetri?"

My eyes went back toward the elevators. I didn't see Nox, but Isaac was watching, ready to intervene.

"Let go of me or that man over there will be here in two seconds, and you'll have more to worry about than who I'm dating."

His grip disappeared. As if I'd struck him, he took a staggering step backward. "Dating? You're *dating* Lennox Demetri? You can't." He ran his hand through his blond hair. "Alexandria, we're dating. How could you?"

"We are not dating. I'm not cheating on you. I'm seeing him."

"When? How?" He sunk down to a sofa, his elbows on his knees and back to Isaac. Bryce lowered his head to his hands and spoke. His voice was heavily laden with defeat. "I don't understand. I can't even comprehend how you'd meet him, much less that you're dating him."

I sat beside Bryce, perched on the edge of the sofa, close enough to keep our conversation private, but far enough to avoid contact. "We met on vacation, about two months ago."

"So when you were home, you were seeing him?"

"Bryce, I was going to tell you. Things between Lennox and I picked up again recently. It's really none of your business."

"None of my business? I get five minutes with you, the woman I planned to marry and he gets…" Bryce's eyes opened wide. "…don't tell me you're sleeping with him."

My eyes narrowed. "Why did you fly out here? You now have about three minutes."

Anger returned to his tone. "Alton told you to be in his office in five minutes, and it took you twenty. For Demetri you suddenly remember how to keep time."

I stood. "You're upset. I accept that I should've told you sooner. I, however, never agreed to date you or to be the woman you planned to marry. I agreed to stay in touch. We're in touch. Do you or don't you have information about my mother?"

Bryce stood. "He's dangerous. Why do you think he has that henchman with him, watching you? Demetri is dangerous. Even if you don't want to be with me, you need to get away from him."

"Goodbye, Bryce. I'll call my mother to learn whatever it is you won't tell me. Have a nice flight back to Savannah." I turned to walk away, when Bryce blocked my path.

His crimson cheeks and flaring nostrils moved directly in my line of vision, blocking out the world and making him the center. His words seethed with emotion. "You've been dating Lennox Demetri for two months, and your roommate is attacked. Don't you see the connection?"

"No, I don't."

"For God's sake, he killed his wife. He's involved in things of which you can't even comprehend—things a woman like you should never know. You need to come with me, now."

It was my turn to step back. "You're lying."

"Do you know? Has he told you?"

I shook my head. "No, I know he was married and now he's not."

"Jesus, Alexandria, have you even Googled him? The feds have been trying to catch him and his father at one of their many illegal operations for years. You said you want to be an attorney. You want to help the innocent. You balked at helping me with that slut's false accusations, and you're in bed with a murderer. What law firm is going to hire you when you have a past with a criminal?"

"Miss Collins?" Isaac called, reminding me of my time limit.

"I don't believe you," I said in barely a whisper.

"It's true. Come home. Go to Savannah Law, and get away from him now, before it's too late. Before God-knows-what happens to you. Montague can keep you safe. If you're afraid of him, tell Alton."

Nox wasn't the one who'd scared me, not really. The idea of going to Alton for help of any kind was ludicrous. "Goodbye, Bryce."

He reached again for my arm and almost simultaneously Isaac appeared at my side.

"Miss, are you all right?"

Bryce released his grip and lifted his hand, palm forward in the common sign of surrender. "Think about it," he said. "Think about what I said."

Isaac and I turned to leave as Bryce's accusations bounced through my mind.

He continued to speak. "I'm staying here for a few days. You have my number. I can help."

I didn't respond as my feet hurried toward the doors and my pulse quickened.

"Alexandria?"

I spun around but continued to walk backward. "Alex. My name is Alex."

"Alex, Adelaide is ill. She wants you home."

My feet once again stopped.

Do I believe him?

As I pondered, Isaac tapped my shoulder. I didn't say another word as I turned, and the open entrance filled my view. On the driveway beyond the panes of glass sat the large black SUV. With the sky dark and the windows tinted, I couldn't see into the backseat, but that didn't stop me from feeling the icy blue stare.

Could it be the stare of a murderer?

"Isaac?" I asked just before he opened the back door.

"Yes?"

"I don't know where we're staying, but please ask the driver to go to my apartment first."

"Ma'am, we'll discuss it with Mr. Demetri."

I'm back at Montague Manor.

My knees weakened when Isaac opened the door. The expression before me caused my breath to stutter.

"Get in," Nox commanded. "You need to explain."

A cold chill peppered my skin. My palms moistened as conversely my mouth dried. I tried to swallow. With my upper lip tucked between my teeth, I slid into the seat, settled against the soft leather, and fastened my seatbelt. I wanted to tell Nox so much, and then again, I didn't want to say a word.

His anger created static electricity that crackled around us. I knew when I agreed to speak to Bryce, I'd gone against Nox's wishes. He didn't need to say it. At the same time, Bryce's accusations bombarded my thoughts. Why would he accuse Nox of illegal dealings? More than that, why would he accuse him of murder? Why hadn't I researched Nox? What did I really know about the man beside me?

Silence settled around us as the Suburban moved forward. The atmosphere intensified, and sparks ignited as I waited for him to speak.

When it became too much, we both did.

I said, "I want to go to my apartment first."

He spat, "How in the hell do you know that scum?"

Both came simultaneously as we turned toward one another.

Nox's finger covered my lips, silencing my request as well as my answer.

"No," he replied matter-of-factly. "We're going to the hotel."

"But—"

My eyes flew to the rearview mirror, catching Isaac's gaze. With an almost imperceptible nod of his head, he told me that we wouldn't be going to my apartment, at least not tonight.

Nox's finger applied more pressure, encouraging my gaze to return to his. "The next sentence out of your mouth will be the answer to my question. I guarantee you don't want me to repeat it." He paused. "Nod if you understand."

With my nod, his finger released my lips.

"I've known Bryce all of my life. Our mothers are friends."

Mothers. Was mine really ill?

"You've known Edward Spencer your entire life? Correct me if I'm wrong, but I got the distinct impression that he thinks of you as more than a friend."

My head moved slowly from side to side. "You're not wrong."

"Is the feeling or was it ever mutual?"

"No," I replied honestly. Even in high school I didn't feel the way he did.

"There's more to it," he surmised. "More that you're not saying."

"I've answered your questions honestly. Will you answer mine?"

With the light of the passing cars, I watched as the muscles along his handsome face strained and his Adam's apple bobbed.

"This agreement that we have," he began, "puts me in control." His pale gaze turned to me. "Complete control."

With each phrase his words slowed; on the contrary, each one hastened my heartbeat.

"Yes, Nox." It was the response he told me to say.

"Even without the agreement, what was the one thing I demanded in Del Mar?"

"Honesty."

He reached for my hand. "I also told you I'd give it. I will. However, I'll decide what you need to know. If you ask me a question that I'm not ready or able to answer, I won't. I won't lie to you, and never lie to me. The difference between the two of us is that you don't have a choice in what questions you'll answer. The choice you have is what you just exercised tonight."

"What did I do?"

"You answered honestly, but withheld information."

He was right.

I looked down at our hands, mine in his. The swirling fury from seconds earlier had dissipated. Nox's touch was warm and gentle. Could the man who held my hand have hurt his wife? Killed her? My heart wanted to say no.

The entire scene at the hospital seemed unreal. I couldn't fathom that he and Bryce knew one another or why they disliked each other. Nevertheless, whatever the reason for Nox's concern, my answers had given him the reassurance he needed, and for that I was relieved.

"So," he said, pulling me from my thoughts. "If you understand that the questions you ask will only be answered at my discretion, go on."

My gaze moved from Nox to the men in the front seat. This wasn't the time to ask about his wife or even his business practices. No matter what Lennox Demetri did or had done, Isaac was loyal to him. Supposedly, I was under Isaac's protection, but if I were a risk, even if it meant I had knowledge, I had no doubt where Isaac's loyalty would lie.

"How do you and Bry—Edward know one another?"

"Business."

"Business?"

Nox lifted my knuckles to his lips. "Princess, that's my honest answer. For now it will have to do."

"And I got the feeling you don't care for one another."

"Was that a question?"

"No." I sighed. "I don't care anymore. I don't want to talk or think about him." The lights of San Francisco came into view. "Why did we come back to the city? Why not stay in Palo Alto?"

"Since I'm in California, I'm going to meet with a few people tomorrow. Isaac will stay with you and get you to and from the hospital. If you want to go to your apartment tomorrow, during the day, fine. He'll go with you." Nox laid his head back. His entire body relaxed against the seat. "It's been a long day. I'm ready to get to the hotel."

He was right again. It had been a long day, especially with the time difference. It was after midnight in New York.

"Thank you."

He leaned closer and kissed my cheek. "For what, princess?"

"For being here." My lips curled to a smile. "For delaying all those people's flight, for worrying about Chelsea, and for not being mad."

He smirked. "Oh, I was mad… more than once, but I think you know that."

"Well, you're not showing it."

"Not yet."

My tummy somersaulted with his threat. That was all it was, I told myself. Besides what could he possibly have planned?

He didn't bring anything with him. Deloris supposedly did all the shopping for us.

It wasn't like he'd ask her to buy satin bindings, would he?

Then I remembered the candles in Del Mar. Nox hadn't been the one to light them or the one to draw the bath. It was her.

Shit!

My nipples hardened beneath my sundress at the realization. He would. Nox would ask her to buy whatever he wanted.

CHAPTER 20

NOX

I COULDN'T HELP but stare as Charli dropped her purse, slipped out of her sandals, and walked to the table. Lifting the silver dome from the tray, she asked, "I thought we said we weren't hungry?"

"Deloris obviously decided otherwise."

Her tired grin enticed me, pulling me toward her like a magnet. Watching her walk away with Edward Spencer affected me more than I would admit. The way he looked at her and at me, rubbed me the wrong way. I couldn't stand there another minute. I had to get out of the hospital. If I didn't, I would have done or said something.

I didn't like Edward Spencer, even without his connection to Charli. He was involved with Senator Higgins with the House Ways and Means committee, but that wasn't all. We'd crossed paths before. His techniques were slimy and backhanded. The idea of him near Charli made my blood boil. That was why I left Isaac to watch over her. If he'd so much as brushed his shoulder against her, I would have had the motherfucker on the floor.

Her brevity in answering my questions calmed me. The way she met my eyes and willingly sat beside me in the SUV told me more about her than her words ever could. Alexandria Collins may acquiesce to my demands, but she was stronger than most, with a spine of steel and bigger balls than most of the people I crossed in business, more than Edward Spencer certainly. I demanded the truth, but I wouldn't have known what that was. However, as her golden eyes met mine, and her breathing calmed, I believed her. I would, until she gave me reason not to.

I moved close. The scent of her perfume lingered in the air as I wrapped my arms around her waist and pulled her close. "You're not hungry?" I asked as my gaze left her beautiful face to scan the array of crackers and different types of cheese—the perfect late-night snack.

Charli reached for a slice of what I assumed to be provolone and shrugged. "I didn't think I was, but with it here, I am. Dinner on the plane was a long time ago."

Before she could eat the cheese, I covered her lips with mine. Fever burned through me as she melted against my chest. One hand moved to her neck as the other held tight to her ass. She couldn't break away if she wanted, but by the way our tongues wrestled, getting away wasn't in her plans.

When we came up for air, I said what I usually don't. I confessed my feelings. "Watching you walk away with him pissed me off."

"I know." Her eyes fluttered downward as if she were suddenly interested in the cheese she was holding. "I knew you didn't want me to."

"But you did it anyway?"

Charli sighed. "Bryce is… part of the way I was raised." She looked up as shadows I didn't understand swirled within the gold. "He called earlier today… or yesterday. I don't know what time it is." She scoffed.

"What?"

Shaking her head, she said, "Nothing. It's just something he said about my ability to tell time. Anyway, he called and told me he was flying out here to see me."

My gaze narrowed. "Out here? You told him you were coming, and you didn't tell me?"

"No. I hadn't spoken to him since the last time I was in our hometown. I hadn't even told him yet that I'd moved to New York. He thought I was still here."

I released her waist and picked up the bottle of wine and read the label. Deloris was good. She'd selected a red blend from the Bordeaux region of France. "Go on."

Charli peered at the bottle. "Deloris knows you well, doesn't she?"

"Probably better than anyone. After you tell me more about Edward, tell me about your meeting with her this morning."

Charli huffed as she sat at the table and placed the cheese on a small cracker. "From now on, would you please warn me if I'm expected to meet with someone? I'd like to be dressed and maybe not reek of sex."

I poured our wine and laughed. "I wouldn't consider it reeking. You smelled fantastic. So good, as a matter of fact, that I want more of that lovely fragrance very soon."

She shook her head as her cheeks blushed. "The meeting was fine. I got the impression she's incredibly devoted to you and your company… Demetri Enterprises?"

"Yes, that's the name of it. I'm loyal to her too. She's one of the few people who's earned that."

"Is that how it works?"

We were sitting, eating, and talking, and damn, if it didn't feel natural. Other than Deloris, I rarely just sat and talked. It was always about business or with a goal in mind. This was different, relaxing and yet stimulating. "How what works?" I asked.

"Your loyalty and devotion. They have to be earned?"

I hadn't thought about it, but yes. "Either earned or lost. What about you? Do you just give them blindly?"

"No. I guess you're right. I've been burnt, and well, I think they do need to be earned. I'm sorry I took off today. I wasn't thinking about Deloris or you or Isaac. I was thinking about Chelsea."

"Don't do it again."

Her chin lowered. "I'll try not to. I can't say I never will." Only her eyes looked back up, veiled by her long lashes. "You said you want honesty. That's honest."

"You're avoiding the first part of this conversation."

"I'm not," she said with her most innocent expression. "I've told you. He didn't know I was in New York. That's how close we are."

"Why did he want to see you?"

She shrugged. "He and I dated in high school. He wants to date again. He thought we were."

What the fuck?

"You went to Infidelity even though you were in a relationship?"

"We're not. He wants to say we are. That's why as weird as tonight was, it was good that it happened. He now knows that I'm with you."

I leaned back and removed my tie. "I'm sure that made him happy."

Her cheeks rose as they blossomed with a hint of pink. "No, it didn't. I'm not sure which of you was more upset."

My lips quirked as I ran the length of my tie across my palm. "I think you know the answer to that question."

Charli's stare concentrated on the tie as she inhaled. Her chest moved, showcasing her hardened nipples as they tented the front of her dress. "I've apologized for leaving," she said mounting her own defense, "and I can't control what other people do or where they are. It's not fair for you to blame me because someone else showed up at the hospital."

I stood and walked behind her. Brushing her gorgeous hair away from her shoulder, I lowered my lips to her neck. As I began to speak and tickle her skin with my breath, she gasped, making my cock twitch. I wanted her more than I should, more than I could admit. My words became breathy. "I've mentioned before that life isn't fair." Goosebumps materialized as I gently nipped the sensitive skin. "And I'm not going to punish you because he showed up." More kisses and taunting. "I'm going to punish you because you knowingly went against my wishes by walking away from me to go to him."

"Nox…" She drew out my name, making it several syllables long as she tilted her head to the side.

"You also put yourself in danger."

She stiffened.

Did she agree? Did she know how important it was to keep her security detail with her? I caressed her breasts, knowing why I could see her nipples.

There was no bra under her dress. A new question monopolized my thoughts.

Is she wearing panties?

"Your security isn't debatable."

I helped her stand. In her bare feet, her face was even with my chest. She tilted her chin to look at me. "Tell me," I prompted.

"My security isn't debatable."

"The next time you purposely dodge Isaac or your new bodyguard, I won't spank your fine ass with my hand."

She swallowed as she contemplated my threat.

"Do you plan to eat any more?" I asked as I glanced toward the table.

Leaning into me, her heartbeat thudded with mine. I hardened at her proximity, my intention pushing against her stomach.

"I-I'm not hungry."

"I am." I tugged her hand toward the bedroom. "But not for food. There isn't much I've asked Deloris about your profile, just one thing."

Her eyes widened. "What?"

"It was your medical exam."

"What about it? Everything happened so fast, they didn't tell me."

"It's clear. I'm clear. And you're on birth control." My brows rose questioning. When she merely smiled, I continued, "From now on, I'm going to feel your tight pussy around my cock with nothing separating us." Her breathing deepened. "My rules." I reminded her. "My decisions. Complete control." With each word I backed her toward the bed. "What is the appropriate response, Charli?"

"Yes, Nox."

Her knees buckled, and she fell back. With the way her beautiful red hair fanned out over the bedspread, she was so damn gorgeous, so sensual, and fucking mine. If I had my way, she'd reek of sex every day and night. The next time she saw Spencer or any other man, she'd have my seed inside of her.

I reached for the hem of her dress and lifted it over her head. Her back arched allowing me to remove the material. Underneath she wore only pink lace panties.

"Scoot back, Charli. I want to see you."

As she moved I pulled down her panties and tossed them on the floor.

"Spread your legs for me."

Her breasts heaved as she obeyed, showing me her perfect pussy, glistening with her essence. I knew the answer, but I asked her anyway.

"If I touch you, will I find you wet and ready?"

"Yes, Nox." Her eyes closed as she leaned back on her elbows.

"Ready for what?"

Her hips bucked with only my voice, only words. She was ready and I knew it. I had no intention of teasing her like I'd done this morning. I planned on following through. Undoing my belt, I slowly pulled it from the loops. As I did, her eyes sprang open, large golden windows to her every thought. When her lip disappeared between her teeth, I knew she was thinking about my threat, and I let her, even though that wasn't my intention. Tonight's pain wouldn't be intentional. Tonight was about pleasure.

"Do I need to repeat my question?" I asked, running the black leather length over my palm.

"I'm ready for whatever you want."

"What do you want?"

"Your cock."

I fucking loved hearing her say that. My erection sprang free as I unbuttoned my trousers and pushed down my boxer briefs. My shoes and socks disappeared in a pile of clothes as I crawled across the mattress toward her, a lion sizing up my prey. Inch by inch, I made my way closer, until she was in front of me, her legs on either side. Dipping my head, I kissed the inside of her ankle, her calf, her knee.

She didn't fucking reek. She smelled amazing as I kissed and licked and teased. When I sucked her clit, the room echoed with her scream. The only pain I intended to deliver was that brought on by the intensity between us. I wanted every inch of her, inside and out.

Her legs stiffened and toes curled, but I wasn't ready to let her come.

"Not yet, princess. Get up on your knees, on all fours."

God she was stunning, doing exactly what I said as her body trembled in anticipation.

"Are you going to spank me?" She asked with her ass fully exposed.

I moved behind her, my finger dipping into her. Her face tilted upward as her mouth opened in pleasure. My fingers were slick as I circled her clit and her moans filled my ears.

"One more time, tell me what you want."

"Please, Nox, fuck me. I want you inside of me. I want to feel your cock, nothing separating us."

Fuck!

Stroking myself as she spoke, I eased inside of her. With each inch she squeezed and stretched. I held tight to her hips, driving deeper until my balls tightened and slapped against her ass.

"God! Princess, you feel so good."

She didn't answer as we fell into rhythm, her tits swaying as I thrust faster and faster. The friction built, a bubbling volcano ready to erupt. Higher and higher the pressure went as slapping skin and labored breathing dominated the bedroom.

Sweat covered our flesh as the temperature rose. My fingers bit into her hips as I bent forward and bit her shoulder, her resulting moans changing me from hard to stone.

Charli screamed my name as she came, her pussy hugging me through wave after wave of release. Her arms gave out as she fell onto the pillows.

I pulled out. My primal instinct was too strong to fight.

"Roll over."

When she did, our eyes met. Hers were hooded with wanton desire and satiation. She bit her lip as she watched. Faster and faster I pumped until my cock throbbed and exploded, covering her stomach with my seed.

Would she be upset?

I waited.

With a shy smile, Charli rubbed the wetness, like lotion, over her stomach and breasts. Without a word, she knew my intention. Licking her fingers, she said, "I'm yours. You just marked me."

Falling beside her, I kissed her lips. Our tastes intermingled. "Do you have a problem with that?"

Her smile grew as she rolled onto my shoulder, and I wrapped my arm around her.

"Not as long as it goes both ways."

"It does, princess. It absolutely does."

CHAPTER 21

Nineteen years ago

ADELAIDE

I STARED OUT the window at the bare skeletons of trees bending and swaying, pushed and pulled by the winter winds. They were like me and I was like them, a kinship of sorts, both submitting to external forces.

Do I have a choice?

Like the Tanya Tucker song said, be strong enough to bend.

Ignoring all else, I continued my voyeurism. The world beyond the windowpane sparked with electricity: a flash of lightning followed by a crash of thunder. The momentary strike brought light to the shadows, illuminating fallen leaves swirling in a primitive dance. Eventually the pounding rain brought their song to an end, capturing and damning them to the cold, wet ground. The Savannah temperature wasn't low enough to snow, yet the scent of winter hung heavily in the air. I couldn't fathom living farther north. Winters in Savannah were dreary and dismal enough. Snow would be more than I could handle—it would break me. Even standing in the sitting room with a raging fire in the fireplace, I was chilled to the bone. Unconsciously, I wrapped my long sweater around me, overlapping the lapels as torrents of rain beat against the window, blurring the gray world outside.

"Laide, don't look so upset. Your father allowed you to narrow it down."

I turned and stared incredulously at my mother. "This isn't a job interview. I'm not H.R. This is my life, my future. I should have more than a say in *narrowing the field.*"

Olivia Montague pursed her lips. Her tone dripped with Southern charm, but her words were harsh and condescending. "Before you get yourself all worked up, remember that you did, dear. You chose Russell. Must we keep reminding you of that?"

Tucking my fingers under the warm cuffs, I paced the length of the sitting room, stopping briefly before the roaring flames. Extending my hands, I searched for the warmth, but felt none. Though the opening in the stone fireplace was easily five feet tall and more than six feet wide, it was as if I were standing in front of a picture or videotape. I'd seen one of those on television, the videotapes of fires. I supposed they were for people who didn't have grand fireplaces in nearly every room. They essentially made a television into a fireplace, complete with the crackling and popping sounds.

As I stood numbly waiting for my father's decision, I imagined that I wasn't standing before a real fire, but one that only looked and sounded authentic. It was the only excuse I could fathom for the unmelting ice in my veins.

What is it like to live in a regular house with a fire only on a television?

My only experience to anything similar was in college, in my apartment. With one bedroom, a living room, and a kitchen, Russell and I were happy or at least content. Then we married. Our wedding was one of the grandest affairs Savannah society had seen in decades. Following it, we moved in here, to Montague Manor. Suddenly we had everything and nothing.

How would it be different with another man?

The answer twisted in my viscera. It wouldn't.

"Here," my mother said as she handed me a glass of cabernet. "This will take the chill off."

The thick red liquid sloshed within the confines of the crystal goblet. I placed a second hand around the long slender stem, trying to still my trembling.

"Laide, sit down over here by the fire. You never did like storms."

She was wrong. I did. I do. The raw energy and potential for destruction fascinated me. Nevertheless, as the obedient daughter I'd been raised to be, I mindlessly walked to the velvet sofa. Sitting by the fire with no warmth, I took a hearty drink of my wine and said, "Maybe I'm coming down with something."

Mother sat facing me, crossing her ankles and tucking them under the sofa. "You're not ill. You're distraught, and it pains me to see you this way. Look at you. You've lost weight and are too pale. Maybe we should fly someplace warm and get some sun on your skin."

I closed my eyes. I was about to learn whom I would marry and my mother wanted to go on holiday. I took another drink. "Did you want to marry Father?"

Olivia ran her finger over the rim of her wine goblet. "Of course I did."

"Then why can't you see that I don't want to do this?"

"I think you're looking at this the wrong way."

I turned away from her gaze toward the flames. The lack of warmth fascinated me, much like the storm outside. If the blaze didn't radiate heat, could I step into it? With each sip of my liquid courage, the urge grew stronger. I didn't want to burn, but in that moment I knew I wouldn't. How could a fire that didn't give off heat hurt me? How could anything hurt me any longer?

I'd lived through a loveless marriage and been a widow for over a year. In the last three months I'd begun dating, which mostly consisted of social events and family dinners. Was it dating when essentially my father was my pimp?

I'd not only thought that word, I'd said it to Suzanna. At first we'd laughed about it, but somewhere during the last three months I'd lost my sense of humor. I'd lost more than that.

I didn't try to meet new people. It wouldn't matter if I did. Charles had a plan. My wishes were inconsequential.

Mother reached for my hand, pulling me back to her and our conversation. I shook my head as the sitting room came back into focus. I was standing, mere inches from the hearth. When had I stood? I didn't remember standing. Yet here I was.

"Tell me about them," she bid.

I licked my suddenly parched lips. "Tell you? Who?"

"Laide, sit back down. Tell me about Marcus and Alton."

I closed my eyes and sighed. "You've met them, both of them. They've both been here for multiple dinners." I never knew for sure when Father would bring one of them around. Being constantly prepared was my duty.

"I supported you about Alexandria. I'm not sure if you knew that."

I shook my head. I didn't. I didn't know my mother ever said anything to support me to my father.

"Of course, he didn't say anything," she went on, "but you notice that he didn't push you."

"I didn't want her to become attached to either one, if it wouldn't materialize."

"What about you? Have you become attached?"

I shrugged. "I've known them both for years. I remember Mackenzie. We were friends. It's strange. Marcus and Mackenzie and Russell and I used to do things together. And now, Marcus and I are both widowed."

Mackenzie's death was slower and more painful. Their marriage appeared real. Then again, so did Russell's and mine. While an accident took my husband, cancer took his wife. I was younger than Marcus, by nearly ten years. Which was only two years less than the age difference between Alton Fitzgerald and me. Alton was never married. Neither man had children of his own. Though my father didn't say it, I believed it was part of his screening process—no stepchildren to expect inheritance.

At least Alexandria's interest appeared to be protected.

"So start with Marcus."

Olivia looked at me as if she were waiting for me to tell her a great fairytale or love story. Truth be told, of the two I liked Marcus more. There was a gentle air about him and when we were alone, he asked more about Alexandria and me. It was probably because we knew one another better and longer. He'd worked with my father for as long as I could remember. It may have even helped that I knew Russell had liked him.

I was afraid to voice that, because I felt as though in my parents' eyes, an endorsement from Russell would be the end of Marcus.

I tried reverse psychology. "I'd rather start with Alton."

"You would?" she asked, sitting taller.

"He seems very devoted to Montague."

"Dear, you're the one who said this isn't a job interview."

I stood and refilled my glass. As I did, I realized my trembling had stopped. The flames spit and sputtered as their warmth reached out to me. "The wood must not be dry enough." Sparks flew to the hearth leaving tiny embers that soon turned dark.

"Maybe some of the rain is getting through the flue?"

I turned my attention back toward the window. That made sense. It was raining cats and dogs. That combined with the wind made anything possible. Sitting back on the sofa, I slipped my feet from my shoes and curled my legs under me. "He's intense."

"What does that mean?"

I shrugged. "Like Father. I worry that it may be why Father won't choose him."

She perked up. "Laide, are you saying you want your father to choose Alton Fitzgerald? You're not concerned about the age difference?"

"Like you said, I married for love once. This is for Montague, besides he's only two years older than Marcus."

"Both men come from good bloodlines. The Fitzgeralds and the Stocktons are both upstanding families." She leaned forward. "Are you… Do… Have?"

"Are you asking me if I've slept with either one?"

"Yes," she answered sheepishly. "I've only… with your father."

I took a big drink of my newly filled wine glass. "Please, Mother. I can't have this conversation with you."

"Why not? I suppose you could with Suzy?"

"Yes, I could, but to answer your question, no, I haven't."

"Oh, Laide, that should have been part of your decision-making. After all, whether this is for you or Montague, you will be expected… you will be his wife."

My heart thumped against the inside of my breastbone so painfully I wondered if it might explode. I used to like sex. It was all right, before Alexandria was born. Something happened. The psychologist I'd recently been seeing said it was me. He said I psychologically shut down after learning I couldn't bear more children. I'd been told all my life that continuing the Montague name was my responsibility and since doing so was no longer an option, my body rejected sex.

I dried up—literally. For a year or two, Russell tried everything and anything to make it enjoyable. I even tried pretending. Finally, we both stopped. We stopped pretending. We stopped trying. I didn't miss the sex. I missed the intimacy.

Father was the one who insisted that I seek professional help. He said he wouldn't condemn any man to a loveless, sexless marriage. Apparently, he could condemn me, but he drew the line at his future son-in-law.

With the help of the therapist, I'd learned to embrace my sexuality, to think of myself as worthy of enjoying intimacy as well as sexual intercourse. He even encouraged me to masturbate. I was nearly certain that my mother would say my fingers would fall off or some other terrible consequence of such offensive behavior if she knew. I wasn't sure what my father would say, but it wasn't a conversation I intended to have.

Nevertheless, I was getting better at it. I'd even brought myself to orgasm, a feat Russell hadn't been able to accomplish since before Alexandria.

"I'm aware of a wife's duties, Mother. I think Dr. Sams has helped me."

Her lips pressed into a straight line. "Everyone thinks you're seeking help to deal with Russell's death." She fanned herself. "Oh, can you imagine the scandal if they only knew."

"No one will know. I've managed to avoid all scandals."

She nodded. "Yes, poor Suzy. If only she could've been as fortunate."

I couldn't believe my ears. My mother was wishing that my best friend had been widowed too, instead of dealing with a divorce.

"Is she seeing anyone?" Mother asked.

"Suzy? No one serious, but she does date."

"Seeing the gentleman in public more frequently will be the next step for you, once your father makes his choice."

My tongue darted out to moisten my dry lips. "That's what I was told."

"And for him to get acquainted with Alexandria," she added.

"What if the man he chooses doesn't connect with…?"

"Stop fretting. You worry too much. Your father will take care of everything." Standing, my mother walked closer and cupped one of my cheeks in her warm hand. "Look at you. I'm not sure if it's the fire, the wine, or thinking about Mr. Fitzgerald or even Mr. Stockton. Whatever it is, your cheeks are pink and your blue eyes have a glow. It's time, Laide. You need to start living again. You're too young to shrivel away. If Suzy were my daughter, I'd insist she do the same, but there's no talking to either of the Carmichaels."

"They're not opposed. They just aren't pushing her."

Olivia took a step back. "Dear, we're not *pushing* you. It's that you're not getting any younger. You're thirty, and well, neither are we—getting younger. Your father is over seventy. He… we would be happier knowing that you have someone to take care of you and that Montague Corporation is in competent hands."

I'd lost my fight.

That was what else I'd lost. My fight was gone. No matter the decision Charles Montague II reached, my future was set. I would be Mrs. Fitzgerald or Mrs. Stockton.

Closing my eyes, I said a prayer that it was Mrs. Marcus Stockton. As soon as the words were recited mentally, I recognized their futility. God hadn't listened before. What made me think he'd listen now?

"Mrs. Montague, Mrs. Collins," the young maid said. "Mr. Montague has asked for you both to join him in his office."

The crackling of the fire and the howl of the wind dimmed as the sound of blood coursing through my veins thumped in my ears. The increased speed of my circulation left me dizzy as I slipped my feet back into my shoes and stood.

One glance at the fireplace reminded me that I could leave. I could gather Alexandria and find a house somewhere with a television for a fireplace.

"Laide, it's time."

My thought was but a distraction. I was Adelaide Montague. It was a life sentence. Freedom wasn't an option. Charles Montague II would find me.

I gulped the remainder of my wine and handed the glass to the girl in the maid's uniform. I should know her name, but she was new. Mother ran the household staff, yet Father always had a way of finding the young and pretty candidates. Turning to her I said, "Bring me another glass in my father's office."

"Yes, ma'am."

Olivia reached for my arm, steadying my direction and propelling my steps. As we neared Father's office, we both stilled. He wasn't alone. Two deep, manly voices spoke, their words ending in a hearty laugh. They were congenially discussing a subject we couldn't decipher. One voice was my father's. The other was…

His blond hair did a good job of hiding the peppering of white. His gray eyes met mine as he stood and looked at me anew. From my toes to my head, he scanned, his chest rising and falling with shallow breaths.

Alton Fitzgerald had just won the lottery, and I was his winning ticket.

CHAPTER 22

CHARLI

"GOOD MORNING, MISS COLLINS," Isaac said as he opened the door to the black sedan.

"Please call me Alex. After all, I'm using your first name."

Am I? Or is Isaac his last name?

He winked and pointed with his chin toward the car. As I sat in the backseat, he confirmed, "Yes, Alex, you are." With his hand still on the door, he asked, "Shall we stop at your apartment before we go to the hospital?"

I glanced at my watch. "Mr. Demetri wants me to meet him for lunch, so let's go straight to the hospital."

"Yes, ma'am."

The door closed. As I settled against the soft leather, my mind went to my best friend. This morning, Nox again mentioned offering Chelsea my apartment. The idea made sense. The apartment was sitting there essentially empty. It would eventually have my furniture, and if Chelsea moved there, it could have more. Yet for some reason having her in New York felt wrong. It wasn't that I didn't love her and want her with me, but I'd been ready to make a clean break and move on to my new life.

As Isaac moved into traffic, my mind followed that same train of thought… moving on. It was too bad that not everyone was willing to do that. Most definitely, Bryce wasn't cooperating. This morning when I finally turned my attention to my phone, I was met with multiple text messages. As soon as they came on the screen, I sighed.

For someone who could be a self-centered dick, Nox noticed everything, almost as if he could read my mind. Not only did he see, but he also paid attention. It was especially true during intimacy. In only the short time we'd known one another, he knew exactly what to do to elicit my body's response. In many things, he knew better than I. However, that wasn't all. He listened—an unusual characteristic with most of the men in my life.

With only a sigh, he sensed my irritation. With a moan he heard my desire.

My reaction to the text messages wasn't meant as a conversation starter; nonetheless, that was what it became.

"What's the matter, princess? Is something bothering you?"

I looked up at Nox's expression, his furrowed brow and widened eyes. There were so many things that should be bothering me—the accusations Bryce made, Chelsea being attacked, and even my new employment. However, waking in Nox's arms, his warm body curled around mine, his arms around my waist, and his morning erection against my back, washed those concerns away.

Last night and this morning had been reminiscent of Del Mar. I was putty in his hands, fresh and pliable, waiting for the master sculptor to work his magic and create whatever he desired—or to show me what I desired.

Lying to Nox or dismissing Bryce's text messages never crossed my mind. Honesty—that was what we'd both pledged. As much as I wanted to believe Nox, I also wanted him to believe me. He said he wouldn't lie to me, nor would he tell me more than he felt was necessary. Nevertheless, when Bryce confronted me last night, he granted me something he never intended. Bryce opened the door for me to be honest with Nox about my childhood boyfriend.

It felt liberating.

I'd lived in smoke and mirrors for most of my life. I didn't want to do that any longer. Taking a deep breath of clear secret-free air, I answered Nox's question. "I have multiple text messages from Bryce."

I don't know what response I expected from Nox, but curiosity wasn't it.

"Is that a nickname?"

"What?" I asked, suddenly distracted by the broad shoulders and flexing biceps crawling across the large mattress toward me.

"His name is Edward Spencer," Nox explained. "Yet you call him Bryce.*"*

"I've always called him Bryce… since I was old enough to talk." I added the last part as a reminder that I'd known Bryce forever. "It's his middle name, one of them anyway."

"One of them? Who has multiple middle names?" Nox shrugged, falling beside me on my pillow. "My mother, I guess."

"Your mother?"

His pale blue eyes stared toward the ceiling while his warmth and intoxicating scent drew me closer. "She had her first, middle, and last name and her confirmation name. According to her that gave her four."

"Had?" I asked, detecting a hint of sadness in his tone and faraway gaze.

Nox's handsome features pinched as he pushed away whatever thoughts he was thinking and ran his hand over his cheeks. In less than a second, he scooted up the headboard, leaned over, and kissed my nose. "Let's hold off on some of that?"

Was he asking? After one of his recent speeches, I didn't think I had any choice in the matter; however, if I did, I'd take his offer of reprieve. I wasn't ready to go there either, not into our families, not with him or with me. We each carried enough baggage individually. It would be better to understand that before we added family.

Accepting his stay and before I opened any of Bryce's messages, I tossed my phone on the bed and rolled toward him. The solid muscles and defined torso beckoned me. I reached out, wanting to trail my hands over the ripples of his abs, but before my fingers connected, I stopped.

Nox reached for my hand, still lingering in the air. "Charli, it's all right. I'm fine. I'm just not ready…"

"No, I understand. I do." Wanting to explain my hesitation, I went on, "I was going to touch you, and then I remembered what you said about only touching you when you said I could."

He pulled my hand to his lips and kissed my palm before placing it on his chest. Tenderly he splayed my fingers until my hand settled over his beating heart.

"I was mad," he explained. "I still am about Infidelity, but I like your touching me." His eyes sparkled below his disheveled hair.

The sight of him with less than his normal GQ perfection made my cheeks rise. This sexier-than-hell man was with me, and I was seeing him as others didn't. Gaining strength from his words, I bravely lifted myself over him and with a smirk, pushed him back against the mattress. My long hair hung in auburn waves beside our faces as our noses touched and our bare chests melded together. After teasing his lips and neck with a peppering of kisses, I said, "I don't understand how you can say that about Infidelity, being a client and all, but… *" I added before he could speak. "…I'm still in a shock that I'm in your arms and your bed. After Del Mar, I thought we'd never see one another. I thought… I'd never again know the way you make me feel."*

His smile widened as his hand dipped down squeezing my behind and holding me close. "How is that? How do I make you feel?"

"Mostly like a princess."

"Mostly?"

I nodded. "You made a point when we first saw one another again." I swallowed and diverted my eyes from his gaze. "I get it, and I know I still owe you that night at Mobar."

Nox's chest rose and fell beneath me. "I could remind you that you owe me a lot more than that. You owe me a year… but I won't."

Asshole. You just did.

"Instead…" He lifted my chin. "…I'll remind myself how fucking glad I am that you're back in my arms and my bed."

I tried to smile. I wanted to believe he meant that in a good way. Before I could respond, he changed the subject. "Are you going to talk to Chelsea about moving to New York?"

I nodded.

He kissed me gently. "Good. I'd say from what little experience I have with your sister…"

I began to refute him as his finger touched my lips.

"…having her close will save time on cross-country trips."

I giggled. "She really isn't that high maintenance. Her mother…"

Nox shook his head. "Oh please. I don't want to know any more about that woman. She was… how do I put this?" His lips quirked from side to side. "Interesting."

"Yes, that's Tina Moore, interesting."

He kissed me again. "I'd love to show you exactly how a princess should be treated and spend the entire day in this bed or against the wall or over the sofa..." He added another kiss to my forehead. "...but you, Miss Collins, wreak serious havoc on my work ethic, and if this is our new reality—that I get to wake every morning to your gorgeous body against mine—we both have things that we need to do and places we need to be." He winked. "Knowing I'll have you back in my arms tonight makes it much easier to leave you now."

Nox rolled away, leaving me cooled by our sudden lack of connection. He stood, his boxer briefs tight and accentuating all the right parts, and then, as if the thought just occurred to him, he said, "Deloris bought you a few different outfits. Wear something nice and plan to meet me for lunch. I have an appointment. It's time to start being my companion."

Sitting back against the headboard, I pulled the sheets above my breasts. "What does that mean?"

"It means that I have a lunch meeting today with Senator Carroll. His wife, Shirley, often accompanies him. Today, I'll have my new girlfriend with me."

I liked the way that sounded. "Your what?" I asked, my smile broadening as my brow quirked upward.

He found his frosty tone, but the gleam in his eyes let me know he was teasing. "My... whatever I say."

"Yes, Mr. Demetri."

Nox shook his head. "I should spank you for that."

"I'm afraid that would make us both late for our appointed duties."

Smiling, he turned and walked toward the bathroom. His muscular ass, hidden behind the thin layer of material, thick thighs, and narrow waist held my full attention until he disappeared behind the door.

Just as I began to reach for my phone, Nox peeked his head out of the bathroom. His menacing smirk stuttered my breathing, causing my heart to skip a beat, and the temperature of the room to rise.

With his velvety tone, he said, "A shower with me or your phone with him? The decision is yours, Charli. Choose wisely. What will it be?"

Even now, riding north toward Palo Alto, fully dressed in the high-waisted blue skirted dress with a white linen bodice and matching blue pumps, my long hair secured in an Alexandria style and simple elegant pearl jewelry, the way my satiated body tingled, I knew I made the right decision. Even Bryce Spencer couldn't upset me after the way my day started.

No matter what Bryce said, I couldn't comprehend that the man who worshiped me, lavishing my mind with declarations and my body with magical detonations, could or would hurt his wife.

Thankfully in Bryce's text messages, he hadn't repeated his accusations. I had the feeling that my phone was now monitored. I never saw Nox look at it, but even if he didn't, I believed that Deloris had the ability to do so. After all, Nox said she'd figured out I was leaving to go to California through my phone.

"Miss Collins?"

Isaac's voice turned my mindless gaze from the passing landscape to him. "Alex," I corrected.

"Alex, the turn-off for your apartment is approaching. Are you sure you don't want to stop there before the hospital?"

"I'm sure. I want to get to Chelsea. We can stop by the apartment later."

"Yes, ma'am."

"Did Mr. Demetri tell you what time he wanted me to meet him for lunch?"

"Yes, we should leave Palo Alto no later than eleven. Traffic is unpredictable."

"Then, definitely, I don't want to waste time at the apartment now."

WALKING INTO THE hospital with Isaac, I saw Tina Moore seated in a large chair in the lobby. I went directly to her.

"Why aren't you with Chelsea? Are they doing tests?"

"No," she said, sipping a large white paper cup of coffee.

I stood taller, understanding why Nox didn't like to repeat himself.

"Then…" I prompted.

She stood. "I figured you'd know. She said she was a friend of yours."

"Who said?"

"The woman talking to Chelsea. She asked for privacy."

I shook my head. "Is she someone from our apartment complex or a friend from our classes?"

Tina shrugged. "I don't know. She's kind of old to be in class with you, but I guess anything is possible. I think she said her name, but honestly, I was thinking about another cup of coffee. It's still early."

"Is she still there?"

"I think she is. Chelsea said she'd text when she left." She pulled her phone from the back pocket of her jeans and swiped it with her thumb and shook her head. "I haven't received one."

I didn't have time to spare, not with my lunch date. "Well, I'll go on up. If it's someone we both know, there shouldn't be an issue."

Tina reached for my elbow and lured me a few feet away from Isaac. "Where's that hot guy?"

"Lennox?" I asked, as if I had so many *hot guys* buzzing around that I wasn't sure which one she meant.

"Damn, he is…"

This was my best friend's mother and while I agreed with her assessment, it made me more than a little uncomfortable to hear her go on about my boyfriend. I smiled at that title, or was it because he'd been the first to use the label. "He's working today," I said. "I need to meet him for lunch, so I'm in a hurry. I'm going to go on up to Chelsea's room."

Tina nodded with a grin. "Okay, honey. I'll stay here for a while longer."

A few minutes later, Isaac and I reached her door and I asked, "Would you like to come in?"

"No, I'll stay here."

I shook my head and opened the door, expecting to interrupt a conversation. Instead, Chelsea was alone, sitting on her bed and staring toward the window.

"Hi."

She turned toward me, her expression momentarily perplexed. "Hey. Where's Mr. Handsome? And why do you look like you just walked out of a magazine?"

I giggled. "Why do you look so confused? Who was your visitor?"

"Visitor?"

"Your mom said someone wanted to talk to you." I walked closer and inspected her blackened eye. "Does that hurt?"

She scrunched her nose. "Not really. Only when I move my face, you know, smile or frown."

"Honey, I'm so sorry. I still don't understand what happened or why anyone would come into our apartment and hurt you."

"I don't either," she admitted.

"How do you feel about going back to the apartment?"

She shrugged. "I don't know. Mom said it was fine last night."

I wanted to ignore the hint of trepidation in her normally bubbly voice, but I couldn't. I couldn't let my feelings of uncertainty about her moving to New York stop my invitation, not if she no longer felt comfortable in our apartment. "Would you feel better in New York?"

Her eyes opened wide and she grimaced.

"Sorry," I said. "Stop moving your face."

My directive made her laugh followed by another whimper.

"Stop it," Chelsea said, "I can't *not* move my face. What do you mean New York? Are you finally picking up on all the hints I've dropped?"

"Yes, but more than that, I miss you."

"You have Mr. Handsome. Surely you don't want me cramping your style."

I put my hands on my hips. "When have you ever cramped my style? I'd say I wouldn't have a style if it weren't for you."

She eyed me up and down. "You did, and looking at you, I'd say you've got it back."

I shrugged. "This is different. Nox asked me to meet him and a colleague for lunch."

"You carry the classy Alex as well as you do the sexy Charli."

I pulled up a chair and sat with a ridiculous grin on my face. "You know, I thought Charli was gone forever."

Chelsea shook her head. "I'm glad she's not. I like her smile."

Palming my own raised cheeks, I admitted, "I do too!"

After a few minutes of catching up, Chelsea asked, "So, tell me why, now that Mr. Handsome is here, your old beau showed up?"

My smile disappeared. I'd read Bryce's text messages this morning, and he didn't mention going to Chelsea's room. I hadn't replied to any of them. I didn't know what else to say except to tell him to *go back to Savannah*. "What do you mean?"

"He came here last night, not long after you left. As soon as he started talking, I knew he was the guy you were trying to dodge our freshman year. He said he was looking for you."

"That's ridiculous. We saw him downstairs. He knew where I was."

"He didn't act like it. He gave us a big story about how worried he was about your staying in the apartment. I remembered how hard it was for you to get rid of him. So I played along, trying to figure out his end game."

"Did you," I asked, "figure it out?"

That was one of her specialties, seeing people for whom they really were. Her freshness and realism were part of what drew me to her our freshman year. After living at Montague Manor, her ability to cut through all the pretenses was invigorating. It was also why she ended up with a major in psychology. She had an uncanny ability to figure people out.

"I got the feeling he wanted more information about when and where you were moving."

I ground my teeth. "I told him that I'd already moved. I know to him it doesn't look like it." I shook my head. "I'll talk to him. Besides, if you agree to New York, soon we'll both be there."

"I thought your apartment was too small for two people."

I tucked my chin down and looked at my best friend bashfully through my lashes. "I may not be using it."

Her eyes once again opened wide followed by the wince. "Stop making me do that!"

"I'm not making you do anything."

"Mr. Handsome? Really? Oh my God, Charli with an *i* is back and boy, is she moving fast."

I shrugged. "I mean, I could pretend to live in the apartment, but why?"

"Oh, girl! Why indeed? But… what about the bombshell your mom dropped on you? Did you tell Mr. Handsome? Obviously, he's able. Is he helping you?"

I shrugged. "Yes, he is." That answer was easier than explaining the truth about Infidelity.

"So you told him?"

"Not all of it. We're taking it slowly."

She pursed her lips. "Charli…" She drew out my nickname. "You just said you won't be using your apartment. Babe, that's not slow. And…" She became more serious. "I can't say yes to New York, not yet."

It was my turn to look surprised. "Why? Did you get a job?"

"Maybe. I had an offer. I need to think about it."

I sprang from my chair. "Chelsea, that's great. What? Where? Is it in counseling?"

"It's difficult to explain. I wasn't expecting it. The offer came out of left field."

"What offer? Tell me all about it."

"It's… I'm not sure."

"Why are you being so mysterious?"

"Well, it wasn't exactly an offer. It was an offer to interview. If I get it, I will live in Washington DC." She looked out the window for a minute. "I would be able to travel to a home base." Turning back to me, her hazel eyes sparkled, even though one was framed by the dark bruise. "New York would be a quicker commute than California."

"Oh, that sounds so exciting. I'm sure Nox would be willing to help with travel back and forth."

Chelsea shook her head. "I wouldn't need help. If I get it, the pay is more than I ever imagined."

"In DC?" I asked. "That sounds very exciting."

Her lower lip disappeared between her teeth as she inhaled and exhaled. “It could be.”

The door opened and a woman in scrubs, pushing a cart with a computer, came in. “Hello, Chelsea. I’m Madden, your day nurse. May I see your wristband?”

Chelsea held it up and answered all of Madden’s questions: name, date of birth, and last four digits of her Social Security number. After she passed the mini-exam, Madden said, “I’m sorry to interrupt, but it’s time for your tests. Your doctor ordered a full panel of tests and scans. It will take us a few hours.”

I squeezed Chelsea’s hand. “That’s all right. I need to go to lunch. I’ll stop by the apartment before I come back. Text me and let me know if you’re breaking out of here today.”

The nurse turned my direction “The results won’t be conclusive until tomorrow.” She looked at her computer screen again. “I’m pretty sure the doctor won’t authorize her release until at least then.”

“Maybe this time,” I said in a stage whisper, “I’ll need to be the one to break you out.”

Chelsea smiled. “No way, girl, I’m the one who kicks ass at jail breaks.”

CHAPTER 23

CHARLI

AS I LEFT Chelsea's room, I instinctively slowed, waiting for my shadow. Somewhere over the last few days, Isaac's presence had become my normal. Deloris promised I'd soon have my own bodyguard and driver. Part of me wanted to keep Isaac. There was something about him that I didn't mind. Maybe it was the way he made his presence known with Bryce. Maybe it was the realization that what happened to Chelsea could have happened to me. I didn't want to buy into Nox's paranoid mentality, but ignoring it didn't seem wise either.

My phone vibrated. Removing it from my purse, I hoped the call was from Nox.

BRYCE flashed on my screen and I sighed.

With Isaac by my side, I debated my options. I could let the call go to voicemail or excuse myself to the bathroom and away from listening ears. While those thoughts raced through my mind, my better sense told me to just rip off the Band-Aid. Now that my world included Deloris and Isaac, my ability to hide calls or anything else seemed remote. No matter where I took the call, Nox would know.

Taking a deep breath, I swiped the screen.

"Hello?"

"Alexandria," Bryce said, obviously unable to comply with my request for a shortened name. "Thank God you answered. I've been worried sick about you."

I clenched my teeth, suddenly seething with the need to defend Nox. "Stop worrying. Go home. I'm fine. As soon as Chelsea's out of the hospital, I'm going home."

"That's great," he said with a sigh. "Your parents will be relieved. It's too dangerous. You need to be home."

I looked up at Isaac, almost certain he could hear every word, and shook my head. Since we were still walking through the hallways of the hospital, I kept my voice low. "No, you misunderstood. I'll be going *home* to New York."

Momentary silence.

When I didn't say more, he asked, "Have you at least Googled Demetri? Have you called Adelaide to learn what's going on? Have you done any of the things I told you to do?"

I straightened my neck. "That you've *told* me to do? Welcome to the new world. I don't do what you tell me to do. You mentioned those things last night and since then I've been a little busy."

"Busy doing what, Alexandria? Screwing a murderer?"

"Goodbye, Bryce."

"No. Please, I'm sorry. I am." His words gushed through the phone, one running over the other. "I know your orientation at Columbia starts soon. Just spend a few days at home, learn the particulars of what happened, and you'll see that you belong in Savannah."

Isaac opened the car door. I nodded as I eased into the seat.

"You're talking in circles, Bryce. Please go home, leave my friend alone, and report back to Alton that I'm not returning. Tell him he lost. His power play didn't work. If you don't know what I'm talking about, ask Adelaide and Alton."

"I know what happened. I do. I also know it wasn't them—it was you." *What the hell?* "You can get it back. I overheard a conversation that I wasn't supposed to hear. I wanted to tell you in person, but damn, I'm getting desperate."

My chest ached with the reality of Montague Manor. I didn't know if I believed Bryce or if Alton purposely set him up to overhear something. Either way, I doubted it was an accident. Everything there was calculated.

"Desperate? Why do you care?"

His sigh filled my ears. "Why do I care? Alexandria, I care because I love you. I've loved you since we were children."

I didn't respond.

"I don't want to have this conversation on the phone, but you're not leaving me a choice."

I swallowed. The emotion in his voice was getting to me, finding the small place inside of me, the place I'd tucked away, the place that had belonged to him since we were children running around the yards of Montague Manor and Carmichael Hall.

"Are you listening to me?"

I nodded, a tear coming to my eye. "Yes, but I need to go."

"Let me say this… please."

"Hurry, Bryce."

"I've dated other people over the last four years."

I bristled. "Go back further."

"Yes, I've dated others. I'm not going to lie. None of those other women meant anything to me. They were for a purpose, my distraction. Demetri is your distraction. I get that. I won't hold that against you—against us. He caught your attention. But don't you wonder why? Don't you wonder why a criminal and big player in so many different scenarios would find *you,* Alexandria Montague Collins?"

What is he saying?

"He's using you. He doesn't care about anyone. He's a user and a killer. You're there for a reason. When that purpose is met, we can only hope he discards you, because, Alexandria, the other option scares the shit out of me. The other option is that you end up like his wife."

His volume rose. "That can't happen. We've been each other's destiny. I can't imagine my life without you in it. You're my everything… my past… my future… the mother of—"

I shook my head, unwilling to listen to his words anymore.

"Stop. Stop calling."

"Why? Because Demetri will be upset? Does he look at your phone? Does he tell you whom you can talk to? You shouldn't live like that."

"No," I corrected. "Don't call because it upsets me. Goodbye."

I disconnected the call and turned my eyes to the window. I didn't need to look into the front seat to know Isaac heard every word I said.

I turned off the volume on my phone and sent a text.

To: NOX- PRIVATE NUMBER:

Me: "WE'RE ON OUR WAY. I JUST SPOKE TO BRYCE. HOPEFULLY THIS SHIT WITH HIM IS DONE. I CAN'T WAIT TO SEE YOU."

New questions gathered with my usual swirl of uncertainty.

Was this smart? Could I find any shred of evidence that what Bryce was saying was true? Yes, he'd lied in the past, but did that mean I should disregard everything else?

Keeping my eyes away from Isaac's in the rearview mirror, I took a deep breath, opened the browser on my phone, and did what Bryce suggested, perhaps what I should have done as soon as I learned Lennox's full name.

I Googled Lennox Demetri.

Multiple articles appeared, only the first few words were visible on each one. Some had pictures. His handsome face and light blue eyes made my insides clench. I clicked to enlarge the first picture. The article began. I didn't mean to gasp, but I did. It wasn't just his image that took my breath away. Not his sexiness or magnetism, but who was with him.

Lennox Demetri recently seen…

Shit!

Deloris was serious when she said the *world*—the whole damn world.

The picture on my screen was a candid photograph, shot yesterday of the two of us standing in the San Francisco airport. I turned my phone to enlarge the image. My mouth dried. There was Nox, all attractive and GQ in his silk suit, and me, in a sundress, flat sandals, with my hair in a low ponytail looking like I just woke from a three-hour nap. The picture must have been taken while we were waiting for Deloris and Isaac to deplane, since we were alone.

I scrolled and read. The short article was mostly about me. Not my identity. It said my name, Alexandria Collins. Realistically, they could have gotten that from anywhere, including my airline ticket information. Whoever wrote the article was more interested in publishing Lennox's picture with a woman than researching the particulars. There was nothing about the delayed flight or my family. The emphasis was that Lennox Demetri, self-proclaimed bachelor since the death of his wife of four years, Jocelyn Demetri, was traveling with a woman.

Jocelyn… the name made my heart hurt, not in a jealous way. I recalled how he'd looked up at the ceiling blankly when he mentioned his mother. That millisecond of emotion saddened me. What would it be like to discuss this other woman, his wife? Who was she? Obviously, she was married to him for four years. Undoubtedly, someone he loved.

Not all marriages were about love—my mother was a prime example. No matter how long ago Jocelyn died, I knew Nox had only recently removed his wedding ring. How could a man who continued to wear his wedding ring, a man as hot and eligible as Nox, be accused of killing his wife?

Question after question bombarded my thoughts. The Northern California landscape that I adored was but a blip on my radar, unnoticed as we drove toward the city, the elevations, the bay, the beauty. None of it registered.

My pulse kicked up a notch when I noticed Jocelyn's name was blue, as opposed to the black type. It was a link—a modern day portal giving me access to the all the answers to my questions. All I needed to do was touch it. Apprehensively, my finger hovered over her name. Before I could activate the link, I recalled something Deloris said.

She said she'd read my profile, and even before that in Del Mar, she said she knew my last name. She left the distinct impression that she knew more, perhaps even that I was a Montague. Yet she made a point that Nox didn't want to know her insights. He wanted to learn about me from me.

Didn't I owe Nox the same consideration? Shouldn't I learn about Jocelyn from him, when and if he was ready to share? And then there was the fear of what I'd learn. What if what Bryce said was true?

Before I could be tempted further, I closed the browser.

When I turned to the window, we were already in the city. Beautiful building after building along the hilled streets brought back fond memories of San Francisco as I watched people and vendors filling the sidewalks.

"Miss Collins, we're about at the restaurant."

"Thank you. I texted Mr. Demetri to let him know we were on our way."

"Yes, ma'am, so did I. He said to tell you that they were already seated."

I looked at my watch, suddenly concerned with making a poor impression. "Are we late?"

"No. They recently arrived."

"HELLO, MISS COLLINS," Senator Carroll said, as I approached the corner table, led by a pretty young hostess.

Smiling, I nodded, but no matter how hard I tried, my attention was drawn to the pale blue eyes shining my direction. My heart fluttered like a schoolgirl's when Nox came closer, kissed my cheek, and pulled back my chair.

"You look stunning," he whispered.

His words filled my cheeks with pink as I turned back to the older gentleman across the table and the woman beside him. "Hello, Senator Carroll, Mrs. Carroll. Thank you for allowing me to intrude upon your meeting."

"Nonsense, dear," Mrs. Carroll said. "After all the years of listening to these two attempt to right the wrongs of politics and business, I'm thrilled to have someone else to share my misery."

Mrs. Carroll was easily the age of my mother, and while she seemed nice, she reminded me of the country-club crowd surrounding the Montagues.

"Don't listen to her. She is enthralled by our conversations as well as our solutions," Senator Carroll said.

"Solutions?" I asked, leaning closer to Mrs. Carroll. "Have they succeeded in righting the wrongs?"

She laughed softly. "Why, you know, I don't know. I have an awful habit of tuning it out."

I smiled. "That does sound enthralling."

"Actually," Senator Carroll said after the waitress took my drink order, "Lennox mentioned that you're a proud graduate of our state. Tell me why, after graduating from Stanford with honors, you'd leave this fine state to pursue education elsewhere. Keeping our finest graduates here is one of our top priorities."

When I glanced at Nox, I saw a strange bit of pride in his gaze.

"I adored living here. I hoped that after making my mark on the West Coast, I could tackle the East Coast."

"Besides, I'm on the East Coast," Nox added.

"It is hard to compete with that," Mrs. Carroll replied.

"So moving back to California after law school isn't out of the question?" the senator asked.

I shook my head. "I've recently learned that nothing is out of the question."

"Right you are. Perhaps you may even convince Lennox to move with you?"

I merely smiled at the senator. When I turned toward Nox, the way he was looking at me did things to my insides that were inappropriate for our lunch meeting.

"Which brings us to our next topic," Senator Carroll, continued. "I was just trying to convince this man to consider relocating a few of his distribution centers. Perhaps you'd be better at that persuasion than I. We have some prime real estate…"

I listened as the senator and Nox talked about location, taxes, and logistics. As I ate my salad and sipped my water, I began to wonder what exactly my purpose was at this luncheon. It wasn't that I didn't want to be with Nox, but I could easily be at the hospital or my apartment. Bryce's words about Nox using me came to mind. But that was ridiculous. How could my presence mean anything to a senator from California?

Mrs. Carroll reached for my hand and whispered, "See what I mean?"

I shrugged. "It's interesting."

"Oh, dear, you must be infatuated."

"Excuse me?"

"I don't blame you. I've known Lennox for a few years, and he's never brought a woman to a luncheon. He's obviously smitten with you…"

As she made small talk, Senator Carroll spoke to Nox. "…testimony will be starting soon. You know you have my vote. However, if I could go to a few other senators with rumors of relocation of those centers, I believe it would get the buzz going…"

"…our daughter will be attending Stanford…" Mrs. Carroll's words drowned out the ones I wanted to hear of her husband's.

"…House bill 770… Higgins is a strong opponent…"

"…any advice you would share…"

My attention was pulled back and forth. I wanted to listen to Senator Carroll and Nox's conversation, but with Shirley Carroll speaking near my ear, I was constantly pulled back to her. Had I heard the men mention Senator Higgins? Was that the same Higgins who was at my party in Savannah? What did that mean?

My stomach churned with Bryce's words, making the lunch before me less appetizing.

By the time we said our goodbyes, Nox led me away from the table, and we sat in the back of the waiting car, my thoughts were jumbled. It wasn't difficult to deduce that they were discussing more than moving distribution centers.

"Why was I there?"

CHAPTER 24

CHARLI

NOX LOOKED MY direction as Isaac moved the car into traffic. "Because I wanted you there."

I leaned back against the seat with my lips together and tried to calm my nerves. Surely I wasn't there because of some political struggle for votes. I never doubted Alton used my party as a means to influence Senator Higgins, but would Nox do the same thing?

"What's the matter, Charli? Is that so hard to believe?"

"Well, Nox." My volume was louder than I intended. "I don't know. I know next to nothing about you. I don't know anything about the House bill you two were discussing. Every time it was mentioned, Shirley Carroll had another story to share."

He reached for my hand. "I wanted to spend time with you. There was nothing more than that."

"So explain some of it. Tell me about the House bill."

"You don't need to worry about that. It would bore you. It's something that could affect Demetri Enterprises."

I took a deep breath. "Okay, tell me about Demetri Enterprises?"

Nox's brow lengthened. "Why?"

I exhaled. "Because you invited me to this lunch. I want to understand what was said or at least what my role was."

"Your role?" he asked incredulously. "Your role is to be whatever I say. Today you were my companion. You kept Shirley Carroll occupied so Senator Carroll and I could speak."

I folded my arms over my chest. "Arm candy. Is that it, Mr. Demetri?"

"Arm candy? Are you fucking kidding me? You don't think I could have all the damn arm candy I want? Well, I could and I don't. Not now, not ever. You aren't arm candy. You're intelligent and capable of carrying on a conversation with Mrs. Carroll…"

As he attested to my attributes, Karen Flores's comments came back to me. Everything Nox was saying was why she said I made a good Infidelity employee. With each word, the pressure behind my temples as well as that in my chest built.

"…Do you know the last time I took a date with me to an important meeting?"

It was Bryce's accusations combined with my luncheon role: I'd reached my boiling point. "No. As I said, I don't know anything, and you obviously don't want to tell me. I have no idea why you really wanted me there. I have no idea the last time you took a date to a meeting or whom. Have you taken anyone, or hasn't there been anyone since Jocelyn?"

The air throughout the car crackled with the electrical tension of before. As soon as the question tumbled from my lips, I regretted it. The metaphoric clear blue skies surrounding us filled with rumbling gray. For only a moment, he stared at me, his gaze holding me mute. Then his body stiffened, and he turned toward the window.

The loss of his stare allowed me to speak. "Nox, I'm sorry. I don't know any more than her name. I want to know more. I started to research and then I stopped. I don't want to learn something that important about you from the Internet. I want to learn about her from you." I reached for his leg, wanting to feel our connection.

Nox brushed my hand away. Turning, his voice again dripped with ice. "My rules—my information at my discretion. Why is that difficult for you to understand?"

I looked up to Isaac and back. "Please may we discuss this in private?"

"This is private." He reached for my chin, painfully pinching it between his thumb and finger as his words slowed to a low growl. "We're not discussing *her* in private or public. Don't ever mention her name again."

Tears bubbled in my throat as I maintained my Montague posture. When he released my chin, I turned toward the window. After swallowing the emotion, I modulated my voice. "I apologize, Mr. Demetri. I won't mention her name again. I'm sorry I overstepped."

"You did. Don't let it happen again."

It wasn't what I wanted him to say. I wanted him to apologize, to tell me he was sorry for overreacting. When I turned toward him, his entire presence was different. The familiarity we shared was gone. With his eyes focused beyond the window, he spoke through clenched jaws. "Whatever research you've done, you can't possibly know what happened. Leave it alone. It's none of your business."

I nodded, my gaze also focused beyond the car window. The scenes outside blurred as tears teetered on my lids. Silence settled heavily in the car as we traveled back toward Palo Alto. It seemed that despite all our progress, in one stupid move I'd sent us back to the beginning. With each mile, my posture remained rigid, unchanged despite the chaos of thoughts and emotions within me. Oddly, I found a strange comfort in falling back on my upbringing.

When we were over halfway back toward my apartment, Nox's words shattered the stillness but did little to ease the tension. "Take Miss Collins back to the hotel."

"Yes, sir," Isaac replied, easing the car to the right to be able to take the next exit and turn around.

I spun toward Nox. "What? No. I told Chelsea I'd be back to the hospital. I wanted to go to my apartment."

Nox sat unmoving, his eyes now focused on his phone.

After a moment, I gathered my strength. "Did you hear me, or do I need to email you to get your attention?"

Quicker than I could comprehend, Nox turned toward me. His words seethed with contempt as he captured my thigh, his painful grip stopping any further rebuttal. "Watch it, Miss Collins. I suggest you consider your answer to my next question carefully."

I tried to move his hand. "Stop it," I hissed so only he'd hear. "Let go of me."

"Who told you about her?"

His refusal to use her name didn't go unnoticed.

I tried again to loosen his grip. "You're hurting me."

He didn't repeat his question, but he did lighten his hold of my thigh as his eyes opened in anticipation of my answer. Not wanting to make him repeat the question, I swallowed and answered, "You."

He let go altogether. My answer wasn't what he expected.

Before he could question, I went on. "In Del Mar, when I saw the line of your wedding ring, you came to my suite and—"

"I didn't tell you her name."

I shook my head, ashamed I'd researched him and not granted him the same amount of privacy he'd given to me. "I read her name. I Googled you."

"Why?"

I shrugged. "I-I had—have—so many questions."

"Was this before or after I told you that my sharing of knowledge was at my discretion?"

We were now heading again back toward San Francisco.

"It's silly to take me back to the hotel. I'll take a taxi if I need to. I'm going to my apartment and to see Chelsea."

"No, you're not."

My eyes opened wide at the finality of his reply. He might consider this private, but I couldn't help but be keenly aware of Isaac and his occasional glance in the rearview mirror. I leaned closer and whispered. "I'm not a child. You can't forbid me from going somewhere."

"You're not and I can. I told you that your freedoms were yours until you squandered them. Consider this your first…" He scoffed. "…your *second* lesson in following my directions."

A lump formed in my throat. "W-What does that mean?"

"It means, Miss Collins, that I'm grounding your pretty little round ass to our hotel room. I have some business to attend to. You'll behave and do as I say, which means no more searching for answers that are mine to give. When I return and assuming you've complied, I'll decide what we do next. I suggest you spend your time reflecting on our new rules and the consequences for obeying versus defying me."

This was ridiculous. He was making me feel like a rebellious child. For a moment I was even afraid he was going to spank me. How ludicrous was that? Not as absurd as the tightening in my insides that accompanied that thought. I was demented, and if he thought he could treat me like a fourteen-year-old, he was equally as crazy.

Before I could refute him, Nox said, "It was Spencer, wasn't it?"

I turned his direction and blinked, digesting his words. "What was?"

"He said something about her, something to make you question. Was it today or last night?"

The accusation in his tone spoke louder than his words. Nox was accusing me of listening to Bryce, rather than to him. The hurt in his voice and the truth behind his claim stung, physically constricting my chest and limiting my ability to breathe.

I nodded. "Last night."

Isaac pulled the car in front of the hotel. As he did, Nox reached for my hand and leaned his lips to my ear. "I won't be long. Behave, or the thought you had a few minutes ago…" He cocked a brow. "…well, I'll be doing more than grounding your ass."

Hating that he could read me so easily, I pressed my lips together. Telling him he was nuts and that he couldn't speak to me like that were on the tip of my tongue. While at the same time, I was uncomfortably aware of my body's reaction to his threat.

He lowered his tone. "I'm not letting go of your hand until you say what I want to hear."

"Yes, Nox."

With each step across the sidewalk, through the doors, to the elevator, and down the hallway, my indignation grew. I came to California for Chelsea. I came to be sure she was safe and to stay at my apartment. And now I was being sent to my room like a teenager because I brought up a topic I wasn't supposed to discuss. Nox didn't have the right to tell me what to do or where to go. Nor did he have the right to limit or censor information.

What happened to Jocelyn? Why was he so sensitive about it?

Entering our suite, I threw my purse on the nearby sofa and kicked off my heels.

I opened the balcony doors and stepped out into the Northern California sunshine. The breeze off the bay was chilled for an August afternoon. The difference in climates between here and New York came to the forefront of my mind. Early this morning, the fog characteristic of San Francisco lingered near the water and hung ominously around the mountains. With the passing of time, the afternoon sun shone, burning through the moisture and giving way to the beauty of the scenery, yet the air wasn't hot or humid. I wrapped my arms around my own shoulders and sighed.

Deloris had provided both Nox and me with a mini wardrobe that suited every need. Just as I was about to change out of the dress and into jeans and a light sweater, one I'd seen hanging in the closet, I heard the vibration of my phone.

Walking toward the sofa, I imagined Nox or Deloris checking to be assured of my compliance. Well, guess what, I'm here. I'm just not sure I will be in another few minutes. I didn't know what I wanted to do.

When had simple decisions become so complicated?

JANE

I swiped the screen before her call could go to voicemail.

"Jane?"

"No, Alexandria."

The energy of the suite changed. My blood pumped with new force as the hairs on my arms and neck stood to attention.

"I was afraid you wouldn't answer my call," my mother said.

"Are you all right?"

She let out a hushed laugh. "Darling, I was calling to ask you the same question."

Maybe it was because she didn't say she was ill. Maybe it was because the last time I spoke to her she sent my world spiraling out of control. For whatever reason, my volume rose. "You called to learn if I was all right? Why, Mother? You didn't care if I was all right the afternoon I left Montague Manor?"

"That's not true. I've been worried sick about you. That's why Bryce offered to see you, to talk to you, but then he learned about the break-in. Alexandria… were you there? Were you hurt?"

"No. I wasn't there or hurt."

"Oh thank God. Obviously, it isn't safe for you to be with that dreadful girl. She must attract some unsavory people, people who'd do terrible things."

I clenched my teeth. "Chelsea, Mother, is that who you mean? Well, Chelsea is safe. She was hurt, but she's safe. Thank you for asking about my best friend."

"Darling, Bryce mentioned something else to me. We've decided not to say anything to Alton, not yet. I wish you'd told me."

This had to be about Nox, but I knew the game Mother was playing. I'd been raised to speak in circles and keep each word covered with sugar when in reality it was a ploy to discover more, to learn what was hidden. I had no intention of giving her more than she already knew.

"What? What are you talking about?"

"When we spoke to you about Bryce, about his situation and the two of you, why didn't you mention the young man you're seeing?"

She made it sound like a high school dance.

"You never asked me. None of you did. You all told me."

"According to Bryce, this man is dangerous. I understand your desire for independence, but seeking that in the company of an unsavory individual isn't the way to do it. I've talked to Alton about your trust fund. There's so much more that we need to discuss, things you need to know and understand. You rushed out of here too quickly. I know I didn't give you the support you wanted. For that, Alexandria, I'm sorry.

"Seeing what a strong young lady you've become has helped me too. That's why I'm calling you. I need to do what my parents never did. I need to explain everything to you."

"Mom?" There was something genuine about her voice. A different tone than I was used to hearing.

"Yes?"

"Why did you really use Jane's phone?"

"Darling, how long will you be in California?"

I shook my head, though I knew she couldn't see it. "I'm not sure. It depends on Chelsea." *And Nox.* But I didn't say the last part.

"Your father will be out of town for the next week. Will you please come here before you go to New York?"

I closed my eyes and bit my tongue, stopping myself from correcting her title of Alton.

"Where is he?"

"Oh, I'm not sure, New York, Seattle, somewhere."

Marriage made in heaven.

"You're not sure where he is, but you know he'll stay away?"

"Alexandria, Alton isn't the enemy. He isn't. He's raised you since you were young. I wish the two of you would try to get along."

Copper coated my taste buds as I bit harder on the inside of my lip, piercing it with the uncontrollable force.

"Are you ill?" I asked. "Bryce said you were."

"Not in the conventional sense of the word. I'm distraught. I need to speak to you, to explain. If that would be better without your father here, then I'm asking you to please come back and let me do that."

"Meet me in New York."

Silence.

"Mother, meet me in New York. Let me show you around Columbia. We can have dinner with Patrick and…" I debated about mentioning Nox. "…and we can discuss what you want to discuss."

"I-I don't travel much without your father."

"He travels all of the time without you. Do this, and we can talk."

I waited as silence prevailed. I even looked at my phone to be sure the call hadn't disconnected.

"He doesn't even know I called. That's why I used Jane's phone."

This time it was my turn to stay quiet.

"Alexandria, Bryce loves you. He always has. He wouldn't… it wouldn't be like…"

"Mother—"

"I'll do it. I'll be in New York on Sunday. I'll make reservations in Manhattan. I can't stay long. But, dear, Bryce needs you as much as you need him. Please listen to me and let me try to explain."

I didn't need Bryce. What made her think I did?

"Sunday. Let me know and I'll arrange to pick you up at the airport."

"Nonsense. I'll have a driver scheduled." Of course she would. Hell, I probably would have picked her up with a driver. "I'll let you know when I'll arrive."

"Thanks, Momma. If you come to me, I'll listen." I couldn't guarantee I'd do what she wanted, but I would listen.

"Phoenix."

"Excuse me?"

"He's not in New York. I just looked at his itinerary. Your father is in Phoenix."

I wished. At least Alton wasn't in New York.

The knock on the door startled me. "I need to go. Someone's knocking on the door."

"Be careful, dear. I'll see you in a few days."

"Please tell Jane I said hello."

"I will…"

Her words faded as I peered through the peephole. The blonde hair and ruddy complexion came into view. If he were forty years older he'd look like the man my mother continually referred to as my father. I couldn't remember Bryce's father or even what Marcel Spencer looked like, but from the red covering Bryce's cheeks and neck, I knew that the man outside the door was angry about something.

Shit! I can't let Bryce Spencer into Nox's suite.

CHAPTER 25

Nineteen years ago

ADELAIDE

MOTHER SQUEEZED MY hand, her usual Montague mask gone as her smile shone my direction. So much for reverse psychology. It was too late. She wouldn't be able to influence Father. His decision was set.

"Adelaide," Alton said with a grand gesture as he stepped forward and placed a warm kiss to my cheek.

I tried to remember Dr. Sams' therapy. I tried to take in this moment, not only with my eyes, but with all of my senses. Inhaling, I decided my future husband carried the aroma of expensive tobacco and whiskey. I recognized the whiskey. It was from my father's private collection. No doubt while my mother calmed my nerves with Montague Manor private reserve wine, Charles and Alton were crossing the *t's* and dotting the *i's* of their agreement while the whiskey flowed.

I smiled, feigning delight in what everyone in the room knew to be a business deal.

My senses.

Dr. Sams' voice played on a track only I could hear. "Don't forget about sight. It's second most important to smell. Our olfactory senses trigger the deepest memories, yet sight creates a picture. Look at your lover, inch by inch.

Appreciate the beauty of the human body."

Though I doubted he'd undergone the same therapy, it was what Alton had done when I entered the room, scanning me from head to toe. I returned the favor, beginning with his blonde hair. It was short, but not too short, parted on the side and combed back to perfection. His gray eyes reminded me of steel, glittering with small sparkles of blue and green. He was an attractive man with a confident smile. The paleness of his complexion lent itself to the rouge of blush as blood gathered in his cheeks. He was taller than Russell with a wider build.

At forty-three, he still looked quite good. I suddenly wondered why he'd never married. After all, he was successful in his own right. Not only a trusted vice president at Montague Corporation but also the only son of William Fitzgerald, real estate tycoon from Atlanta, who made his fortune in the 1960's. His only sister, Gwendolyn, was married to Preston Richardson. They had one son, Patrick.

I listened halfheartedly as everyone spoke. My mind was a symphony of thoughts: outside words, Alton's résumé, and Dr. Sams' homework all swirled together in an unfamiliar melody.

"While the engagement is slightly unorthodox, rest assured that I'm honored you want to be my wife." Alton's voice was deep and booming, much like my father's. Only the tenor was different, giving the song a new pitch.

"Laide?" Charles asked, bringing my eyes to his. It was the conditioned response I never questioned.

"Yes, Father?"

"Your fiancé is speaking to you." His lips smiled, but his blue eyes, the same color as mine, sent a warning. I was zoning out, lost in my senses. My attention was needed in the present.

Lifting my chin to the man by my side, I inhaled again. The Montagues made their name and fortune from the tobacco fields that still dotted our estate. It seemed only fitting that my husband carried the aroma. His, however, was spicy, aged, and refined. I thought of how happy that must make Charles and smiled. "Alton, I'm overwhelmed. This is… will be…" I swallowed. "…I'm happy to be your wife."

He reached for my hand.

Warm. Clammy.

No, Dr. Sams said to only think positive thoughts. Warm and *tender.* Yes, tender. Alton Fitzgerald was tender. That's what I told myself.

"I believe we should be upfront with my daughter, Alton."

"Yes, sir."

Father continued, "As Alton mentioned, this is unorthodox, but I believe it's in the best interest of everyone. The decision has already been made. You know that, don't you, Adelaide?"

With Alton still holding my hand, I decided it was comforting to have someone beside me as Charles began his speech. Looking to where our hands touched, I smiled. Turning back to my father, I replied, "Yes, I know. What's next?"

Yes, my fight was gone. I would be the perfect daughter and wife.

"You two will be seen more and more together. In the spring, you'll elope."

"Elope?" I asked.

"My dear," Mother chimed in. "We did the big wedding. Now it's more important to make it legal."

"I have not," Alton interjected.

I turned his direction, wide-eyed. "You've not what?"

"I've not had a wedding. I told your father I thought eloping was better than a courthouse wedding. It would give us a real wedding, something special, without the large fuss."

Slowly my head moved up and down. I liked that. Did that mean that Alton actually negotiated this with my father? He didn't accept everything on Charles's terms and yet my father agreed to Alton? I was curious. "What else was negotiated?" I asked.

"Adelaide," Alton said. "I'm afraid that term sounds too much like business legalities. I'd prefer you think of this as more personal, without deals and agreements."

There was a timbre to his speech, a rhythm that steadied me.

"Thank you, Alton. I appreciate that. However, no matter what my father's told you, I'm capable of understanding the part I play in the negotiations that occurred. I'll do everything in my power to make you a good wife. I'll also agree to everything, but I want to know… I need to know what has been negotiated."

He looked to my father. I followed back and forth as they wordlessly debated between themselves.

Finally, my father cleared his throat. "As I said, you will elope. There will be a prenuptial agreement."

I nodded, happy that my father thought to look out for my best interests.

He went on, "I won't bore you with the specifics, only the highlights. In the event of the death of either of you or divorce, all Montague holdings will revert to Alexandria."

"Wait! What? Either of us?"

"Yes," Charles said. "There's more."

I retrieved my hand and looked at Alton. "You agreed to this?"

"I did. We're both healthy, and I've waited until now to marry. I have no intention of divorce. That clause is a non-issue."

"But eventually… we won't live forever."

"Alexandria will be admonished to care for the remaining one of you," Charles added.

"By agreeing to this marriage, Alton accepts the fact that he'll never produce an heir of his own. He's aware of your inability to conceive."

I hated how clinical he made it sound. No wonder I had issues with sex. Besides, the man's forty-three years old. If he were to have children, he should have done it by now.

"Laide, what you are about to hear may not be repeated," my father warned. "Alton and I discussed this at some length, and I've decided that for it to work, you must be aware of the stakes."

"What?"

"Do you agree?"

Though my pulse increased, I nodded.

"As you mentioned, you and Alton won't live forever, as obviously, neither will your mother and I. Contingent upon Alton Fitzgerald agreeing to this marriage is the guarantee that his progeny will inherit the Montague name and status and all that comes with it."

I looked from person to person, unsure what I was missing. "Didn't you just say that you agreed to no more children?"

"We aren't discussing *more* children," Alton corrected.

I searched for answers. "Patrick? Your nephew?"

"No!" Alton said with a laugh. "As I'm marrying you to obtain Montague rights, I want to guarantee that my son has the same opportunity."

"Y-Your son?"

"Not opportunity," Charles corrected. "As this agreement with you is set, so is Alexandria's."

I stood and paced back and forth. "She's four years old. I've agreed to everything you've said. I understand it's my duty. But she's a… baby."

"She's a Montague. She's the continuation of the name. It's her duty as well as it is yours," Charles said.

"Son?" I turned to Alton. "Whom is Alexandria supposed to marry?"

Charles nodded at Alton, who returned the favor. Olivia stood and walked to the door. Everyone and everything happened in slow motion. I watched, detached, as if they all knew the stage cues and I was the only one without a script. So many emotions, so many lies. I wanted to remember Dr. Sams' instructions, *coping mechanisms* he called it. But in the time it took for my mother to open the door, my world shattered.

My best friend entered.

"Suzy?" I asked. "Why are you here?"

"Olivia and I will be outside." My father wasn't asking, and within seconds I was alone with my best friend and my fiancé.

Suzy's eyes were uncharacteristically red and puffy. "God, I hate you right now," she said as she hugged me. "But I'll always love you."

I couldn't comprehend. "Why are you crying?"

"We make sacrifices for our children. Right?"

"I guess," I replied. My eyes widened as I searched Alton and Suzy for answers. Slowly some surfaced, but they didn't make sense.

She reached for my hands and held them tightly in hers. "Bryce is my angel, my pride and joy. I suffered through the embarrassment of divorce and held my head high so he'd never be ashamed. Marcel was the loser, the one who abandoned us. He wanted a paternity test. I couldn't allow that. If I would have, Bryce would have known the truth. The whole world would have known. They never can. He never can."

Where the hell is that girl with my wine? I need the whole damn bottle!

My arms flung up and down as I walked in circles and wedged the pieces of this new puzzle into place. Bryce… paternity test… blood thundered through my veins, the echo reverberating in my ears. The wine I'd drank sloshed about my stomach as my understanding grew.

"Say it. Say it!" My volume increased. I was like a caged lion, a wild beast consigned to a box on display. It was wrong. The lion was a king and deserved to be on the plains of Africa; instead, he was trapped as entertainment and amusement. Some may even argue his captivity served the purpose of education, giving children the opportunity to learn about animals not indigenous to their world. Someone needed to explain that to the king of the jungle. To him it was injustice. I felt the same way. At that moment, I was the lioness, also confined to a cage, on display, asked—no told—what to say and what to do.

Suzy sniffled softly as Alton's neck straightened and chest grew.

"Edward Bryce Spencer is my son." His tone bubbled over with pride, completely devoid of remorse.

I looked into Suzy's eyes. "You never, ever said a thing to me. I'm your best friend and you never told me that you and…" I turned toward the man who'd slept with my best friend, who'd ruined her marriage. "…how didn't I know?"

"Laide, you knew Marcel and I weren't happy."

"Then why? After you and Marcel divorced, why didn't the two of you…?"

They exchanged a look, one only shared by intimate familiarity. It made my stomach retch.

"Oh my God." I took a step backward. "You two did. You have. Oh

God… you *are*…" My voice trailed away.

Suzy's head moved vigorously from side to side. "No, Laide, we *aren't*." She took a deep breath. "We were. We were about to make it public when Russell…"

My temples throbbed. *Where the fuck is my wine?*

"As soon as you told me what your father said, about remarrying, I thought of Bryce."

My knees gave out as I fell back to one of the chairs. "You thought of Bryce? My husband was dead. I was told I had to remarry…" I looked at her in disbelief. "…and you thought of your bastard son?"

Crimson seeped from Alton's collar, filling his neck and cheeks. In my altered state of understanding, I had images of cartoons I'd seen as a child. Ones with a funny little bald-headed man wearing hunting gear. When he was mad, the redness rose, much like a thermometer, until the top of his head blew. That was what I saw as I looked toward the man I was about to marry.

"Yes and no," Suzy said with authority. "I thought of Bryce. I always think of Bryce. However, he's *not* a bastard. Officially, he's the son of Marcel Spencer. And," she added with an air of confidence, "he *will* marry Alexandria Montague. He will hold claim to all of this." She motioned about with her arms as she turned a small circle. "Just as Alton will."

"You're what?" I asked in disbelief. "A damn martyr?"

Suzy held her chin high. "Yes. And I don't regret a thing. Marcel and I tried for years for a child. He blamed me, though he'd never go to the doctor to learn differently. I figured he was right; I was broken. Then after Alton and I… after we…" She at least had the decency to look down. "I became pregnant. It wasn't like Marcel and I weren't still… I was his wife. I told him Bryce was his. I believe Marcel wanted to believe. But with time, he couldn't."

"Are you two?" I moved my eyes back and forth. "…still?"

Alton knelt beside my chair. "No. You two are friends. I wouldn't do that. In a few months we'll be married. Suzy and I are done."

A tear descended my best friend's cheek.

"This is so sordid!" And then a new thought occurred to me. "My parents know?"

Suzy nodded.

"Why? Why did my father agree to this?"

"Because I'm not Russell. I have a vested interest in making this marriage work, as much as you do. I want this." He looked around the office and then peered at me with a raised brow. "Adelaide, I want you. I want Montague Corporation, but mostly I want to guarantee my son's future success. You'll never be able to give me a child. I can live with that, but I want to know that my son will have the best. This marriage will accomplish that."

"But Alexandria…?"

"Is a child," Suzy answered. "She and Bryce are best friends. Who better to marry than your best friend?"

I pinched the bridge of my nose. I wasn't about to marry my best friend. I was about to marry my best friend's lover, and my parents were okay with it. Shaking my head, I looked at Alton. "How did you and Father negotiate this? When are the children supposed to wed?" My indignation grew. "When they're eighteen? How about as soon as Alexandria has her period? Then she could reproduce."

"Laide," Suzy cooed, "don't be ridiculous."

I stood again and walked toward the windows. The storm had calmed, leaving the darkness of night looming over the Montague estate. In the reflection of the panes, I saw my likeness. But it wasn't me. My eyes were too narrow with dark circles below each one.

Alton's voice brought me back into the room. "After Bryce completes graduate school. We built in eighteen months. Hopefully, they'll be ready to marry sooner. If things go as they are now, it'll be organic."

I spun toward them. "What if it doesn't?"

"They don't have a choice," Alton said. "It's my hard limit for this marriage."

I felt it in my hands first, the trembling. His hard limit… to marry me.

"Is it that unappealing?" I asked louder than I intended.

My back straightened as Alton came closer. "No." His deep tone had softened as his gray eyes shone with flecks of blue and green. "Marrying you is very appealing. Marrying into your family is appealing, running Montague

Corporation is appealing. Guaranteeing that Bryce will have it all after we're gone is the icing on the cake." He leaned down and kissed my cheek.

From the corner of my eye, I saw Suzy quickly turn away.

"Laide," he said with a smile. "I like that name. We'll have many years together. This will be good. As parents we want what's best for our children. This agreement assures all of us of that outcome."

"But what if they don't? What if they fall in love with someone else?"

He shook his head. "Love has nothing to do with it. This is business. We can grow to love one another. They have the advantage of starting out as childhood friends. According to the agreement, if either marries someone else, refuses to marry by the defined time limit, or marry and divorce, Montague Corporation and all assets of Montague, including Montague Manor will be sold. The proceeds will be transferred to Fitzgerald Investments. Montague will cease to exist."

"No…" I shook my head. "My father would never agree to that."

Alton caressed my cheek. "He already has. He did because he has faith in us." He motioned to all three of us. "Faith that we'll keep Montague intact. Faith that Alexandria and Bryce will have a long, happy marriage and provide us with a home full of grandchildren."

My daughter was four years old and he's talking about grandchildren.

CHAPTER 26

CHARLI

I BRACED MYSELF, steeling my shoulders as I prepared to open the door. With my hand near the knob, I heard voices. The wooden barrier did little to muffle their words as the small peephole became my only view of the scene on the other side.

"May I help you?" Deloris's voice was sharp yet professional.

"No," Bryce dismissed her as he turned back, rapping his knuckles again against the solid door.

"Son." Her demeaning title made me smile. "You're knocking on my door. May I help you?"

Bryce took a step back, the crimson on his cheeks simmering in his new state of confusion. "Your door? I thought this was…" He stood straighter. "Is Alexandria Collins staying with you?"

"I'm not sure why *who's staying with me* is any of your concern. You are…?"

"I-I am Edward Spencer, and I'm looking for my fiancée."

His word made my stomach churn. It took every bit of self-control not to open the door and correct him.

"I assure you I don't know who you mean. If you'll excuse me, I need to enter my room."

"You do know who I mean. I saw you. You were at her roommate's hospital room this morning. You know Alexandria."

Deloris was at Chelsea's room? Why? When? Why was Bryce there?

"Son, I'll gladly call security if you don't step aside."

"This isn't…" He paused. "…this isn't Lennox Demetri's suite?"

Deloris's eyes narrowed. "Mr. Spencer, I'm not sure who you are or who you think you are, but this room is registered to me. I'm staying in this room, and you have three seconds to allow me to enter."

Not wanting to be standing and staring when she opened the door, I picked up my purse and hurried toward the bedroom. As I crossed the threshold, I suddenly worried that Deloris didn't have a key. Then I realized whom I was thinking about. Of course she had a key. A moment later the locking mechanisms turned, and the door opened. I waited unseen for the door to close. Once it did, silence prevailed.

With my shoes dangling from her fingertips, Deloris turned the corner and met me eye to eye. "Thankfully," she said, "he didn't pursue me. If he had, I'd need to convince him that four-inch navy pumps were now my shoe of choice."

I shrugged with a smile and reached for my shoes. "I remembered my purse."

Deloris sat on the edge of the bed and patted the mattress beside her. "Alex, we need to talk."

Taking a deep breath, I moved her direction and sat.

"He's mad at me."

"Mr. Spencer?" she asked with a furrowed brow.

I shrugged again. "Probably. But I don't care about that. Nox, I mean, Lennox, is mad at me. I said something I shouldn't have."

She nodded knowingly.

"You already know, don't you?"

"I do," she answered truthfully. "I was informed on my way here. Since Isaac is with him, Lennox didn't want you left alone." Her eyes widened as she tilted her head toward the living room. "I believe that was a good call. Please tell me that you weren't about to open that door."

I looked down at the shoes in my lap and sighed.

I was.

"You think you know him?"

"Bryce or Nox?"

"Mr. Spencer."

I swallowed. "Deloris, I do know him. I've known him my entire life."

"It's a common misconception. I've known Lennox for many years. I may know more about him than anyone, yet you know him in ways I don't."

My cheeks tingled with pink as I nodded.

"Knowing someone and *knowing* that person are two different things. How much contact have you had with Mr. Spencer over the last few years?"

"Very little."

"Alex, you have no reason to be honest with me, but I have no reason to be dishonest with you. Please tell me about Edward Spencer, the one you *know*."

I replayed the day's scenes in my head. "First, before I do." I reached for her hand. "I will. I'm not stalling. I just want to know what Bryce meant when he said he saw you at Chelsea's hospital room today?"

"I was there."

I waited. When she didn't offer more, I pried. "Why?"

"Because she was attacked in your apartment. Keeping you safe has become my job. I need to know all I can."

I nodded. That made sense. "Was it before or after… were you the person with her who asked her mother for privacy?"

A small grin came to Deloris's face. "Her mother is… it's easier to talk without her around."

I couldn't agree more. Tina Moore was annoying at best. "Did you say anything to her about moving to New York?"

"No. Why?"

"Nox… Lennox thinks I should offer her my apartment. He said it would save on cross-country trips. The thing is, she really isn't high maintenance. She didn't ask me to come out here. It was my idea. I wanted to be sure she was safe."

"I'm sure Miss Moore is debating all of her options. Now, please tell me about the man who claims to be your fiancé. You can see how that's a direct violation of the agreement you signed?"

I sighed. "Do you mind if I change into something more comfortable and we can talk?"

She patted my knee. "I don't mind. I'll be out in the living room."

"Before you go, please tell me… how mad is he?"

Her shoulders moved up and down. "I've seen him more upset."

"Why isn't that comforting?"

"Change clothes. Then we'll talk."

An hour later, with my legs curled beneath me, wearing jeans and a sweater and sipping a glass of moscato, I was all talked out on the subject of Bryce Spencer. I'd told Deloris everything about him that I could think of, from how we were friends since birth, our mothers inseparable, the best of friends. I even told her about us dating at too young of an age and how I expected my mother to protest, but she never did. The conversation was cathartic, allowing me to purge a part of my life, a part I was happy to leave in the past.

"Even while he was at Duke and I was still at the academy, he continued to pursue the relationship."

"You didn't fight it?"

"No. I can't explain it. There's something about being back in my hometown that is…" I looked out the window toward the bay. "…well, it takes away my ability to fight."

"Does Lennox do that to you?"

A grin pulled at the corners of my lips. "It's different."

"That makes me curious."

"While I was at Stanford, I worked to become someone other than the obedient daughter I was raised to be. I worked to be independent and have my own beliefs. I'm proud of who I became and what I did. I want to carry that on to Columbia."

I took a drink of my wine.

"With Lennox…" It was odd to use that name. "…I'm still the me from

Stanford. I want to please myself and have my own opinions, but I also want to please him." I tilted my head to the side. "I don't know if that makes sense."

"It does," Deloris said with a smile. "So you aren't engaged?"

"No."

"Never were?"

"No."

"Mr. Spencer is…"

"Obsessed," I volunteered. "I guess he feels entitled. If I never went away, if I'd attended Duke as he wanted, I probably would be engaged."

Deloris reached for my hand. "Is that what you want?"

"It doesn't matter, does it? You know about Infidelity. I couldn't walk away from Lennox if I wanted to."

"Do you want to?"

I stood and walked to the window. The early evening sun danced across the water. "No. I don't want to be with Bryce. I want to be with Lennox, but he also scares me."

"Lennox or Mr. Spencer?"

"Lennox."

"He frightens you?"

"That's the wrong word. I'm apprehensive. I shouldn't have said anything about his wife today. It was that Bryce said some things, and it had me thinking, wondering." I spun back around. "You know who my family is, don't you?"

She nodded.

"Does Nox?"

"I haven't told him. I recommend that you do."

"Is it that important?"

It was Deloris's turn to ask questions. "Do you know anything about Melissa Summers?"

I pursed my lips and tried to recall that name. "I don't. Should I?"

Our conversation ended as we both turned to the opening of the door.

The energy of the room immediately shifted. Power surged through the air, crackling the molecules and setting off electricity. With only his eyes on me, the hairs on my arm stood to attention. I tried to read him, to decipher his disposition.

Is he still upset?

"We're leaving tomorrow."

His proclamation did little to assure me of his mood, though it did bring my conversation with my mother to mind, reminding me she was supposed to be in New York on Sunday.

"Leaving? For…?" I asked, suddenly concerned I wouldn't.

"Back to New York."

I sighed.

In only a few elegant strides, Nox was across the room. My heart fluttered as I craned my neck up to look into his eyes. The anger from the car was gone but frost remained. I stiffened as he captured my waist and pulled me against him. "Have you behaved?" His question mocked me, reminding me of his directives and the grounding I'd just experienced.

Shivers tingled up my spine as I considered his other threat. "Yes."

"That's too bad," he replied, releasing his hold.

"I'm sorry…"

His finger stopped my apology. "It's done. Don't mention it again… ever."

I pressed my lips together, rolling them between my teeth. There was something in his demeanor that didn't invite a reply.

Nox turned his attention to Deloris.

"Commercial or private?" she asked after a moment of unspoken dialogue.

"Private. Take care of it. First, take Alex to her apartment and the hospital. Isaac is waiting."

I stared back and forth as Deloris simply nodded. "Wait. Now I can go? What about you?"

"Have her back before too late." He wasn't speaking to me.

"Nox, what the hell?"

He walked toward the bedroom, leaving us in silence.

I turned toward Deloris with questions hanging in the air.

"Come, Alex. We'll be leaving first thing in the morning."

I turned on my heels and followed Nox into the bedroom.

"Alex…" Deloris's warning trailed behind me as I opened the door he'd closed and stepped inside. He turned, our eyes locked on one another, my gold questioning and searching, while his blue cooled a few more degrees, accusing.

"Silent treatment?" I placed my hands on my hips. "Really? I never took you for the silent type."

"Don't," he spoke though his jaw barely moved.

"I said I'm sorry."

Two strides or was it three? I wasn't sure, but from where I was near the door and where he was near the bed, he was now before me, pushing me back until my shoulders crashed against the door. I gasped, trying to steady myself, confident Deloris could hear every sound.

"I. Said. Don't."

"Tell me what to do," I begged. "I don't like having you mad."

Securing my hands behind my back, he leaned closer, pinning me against the door. His warm breath bathed my cheeks as his nostrils flared. "Tell you what to do? I just told you to *fucking don't* and you didn't listen."

Though his grip of my wrists tightened, I kept my chin high, never releasing his eyes from my gaze. The ice melted as swirls of navy displayed his whirlwind of emotion.

"I should spank your ass for pushing this."

I straightened my shoulders, ignoring the pain in my wrists. "Do it."

I'd take the physical pain to get him to open up, to break this wall he was building around himself.

Nox released his grip and took a step back. "What the hell did you just say?"

I daringly stepped toward him. "I said *do it.*"

He ran his hand through his hair and turned away. "Fuck, Charli. Don't push me."

I quickly moved in front of him, poking the proverbial stick in the beehive. "Just look at me, please."

Is this stupid? Am I pushing someone who'd hurt his wife?

Once again our eyes met. "I'll go to my apartment and the hospital, but first, will you at least tell me that I didn't ruin everything? Tell me that what was happening between us, in Del Mar and beginning again on the plane… tell me it isn't broken beyond repair." With each phrase I stepped backward as he moved closer.

"I can't," he said, stopping his forward motion.

My chest ached. I would have rather had the spanking—physical pain wouldn't hurt as much as his words. "Y-You can't?" I repeated, hoping I'd heard him wrong.

"Trust. It's my hard limit. I told you that I'd be honest with you on my own terms. You broke that trust by searching on your own."

"And I'm sorry! How many ways can I say that? I'm sorry. All I know is her—"

My back collided with the wall. My gasp filled the air and the whoosh of blood coursing through my veins filled my ears. Nox's chest expanded and contracted, and the muscles in his neck tightened.

"I told you to not mention her." Spit escaped as his words hissed through closed teeth. "Simple instructions seem to be your downfall."

Tears stung my eyes, not from the new pain in my shoulders but from the pain in his eyes. I should have left with Deloris. What the hell was I thinking? I was only making it worse. I lowered my chin, unable to bear his gaze, as a tear escaped my now-closed eyes.

"You…" I searched for the right words. "Do you want to break the agreement?"

I was afraid to look up. I was afraid I'd see his pain replaced with relief.

CHAPTER 27

NOX

"DELORIS."

I didn't shout. I knew she was outside the bedroom door, ready to intervene, yet willing to allow me to make my own mistakes—again.

"N-Nox?" Charli's one-word question hung in the air.

I couldn't look at her. I couldn't stare into her golden eyes and see the hurt and disappointment. I was too busy feeling my own.

How much did she know about Jocelyn? Did she know what happened? She couldn't. It wasn't public knowledge. Even Jo's family didn't know. I didn't owe them that, not after the way they treated her and me. Even Oren didn't know the whole truth. Only Deloris.

"Alex," Deloris said as she opened the door.

Taking one step back from Charli, I stood still, not making eye contact with either one of them. Instead, I turned away, my chest heaving with the too many emotions Charli elicited in me, the ones I'd refused to acknowledge in years. Thank God for Deloris. Her calm settled me. I prided myself on self-control. I rarely lost my shit, but when I did…

Once they were out of the bedroom, I walked to the bathroom. The sound of my shoes upon the tile dominated my thoughts. I closed the door and sunk to the side of the garden tub, elbows on my knees and head in my hands.

Shit! Fuck!

I thought I had my shit together. I wouldn't have come back to the suite if I didn't. After I dropped Charli off at the hotel, I told Isaac to take me to her apartment. I wanted to see it for myself. The entire drive my fingers were sweeping the screen of my phone, searching the Internet, typing my own name, trying to find what she'd read.

Since the night I lost Jo, I refused to do what I did earlier today. I refused to read the stories and speculations. They were out there in news articles as well as social media. Though they'd lost their steam over the years, they resurfaced from time to time. The Internet was a damn cesspool of ignorant cowards, people who only had balls when sitting behind a keyboard. Just once I'd like someone to have the guts to say to my face what they feel entitled to say via the World Wide Web.

For years I'd ignored the accusations and moved on. I concentrated on Demetri Enterprises. It was easy to disregard strangers, but her family was different. The fuckers didn't come to her funeral; instead, they sent the police. The warrant they wanted was never issued. The Matthewses probably think I did something to stop it. The truth wasn't that convoluted. It was simple. There wasn't any evidence, only their pathetic lies.

If it weren't for the ambulance-chasing attorney the Matthewses hired, it would be over, but it wasn't. Their damn civil case was buried in so much red tape it would be at least a decade before it was ever seen by a judge.

By the time we made it to Charli and Chelsea's apartment, I was barely seeing straight. The memories were worse than the stories: Jo's long brown hair, the way her brown eyes sparkled when she was excited, and her continued promises that everything would be all right, that she would be safe.

Each article I read opened the damn floodgate until I was drowning.

As we stepped into the small two-bedroom apartment, my nerves were already a wreck. Seeing the little bit of furniture out of place switched my gears from Jo to Charli. Unconsciously, my hands balled into fists.

What if Charli was the one in the apartment instead of Chelsea? Was the attack because of me?

Senator Carroll wanted me to bring distribution centers to California. That wasn't all he wanted. Since the legalization of recreational marijuana in multiple states and the medical use in many others, including California, states were seeing the benefits—monetary benefits—in the way of tax revenue. Legalized marijuana was an even bigger cash cow than alcohol and tobacco. The market was ready for this untapped resource.

While fighting the wording on House bill 770, Senator Carroll was paving the way for increased revenue. The Napa Valley had the perfect growing climate. The distribution centers he wanted would begin with wine—California wine—and be ready for the impending marijuana industry.

The opponents of legalization and distribution weren't as transparent as the alcohol and tobacco giants who opposed the bill's wording, though they too were invested in the fight. No, the most dangerous opponents of legalization were the people the law would affect directly, the illegal drug cartels. The loss of income would start at the top and trickle down to the everyday dealer on the street. Most were well diversified into other forms of illegal drugs, but marijuana was still a viable income producer. The war was waging in multiple states, its armies not bound by maritime rules.

Unfortunately, due to previous dealings, ones that helped to get Oren up and running over thirty years ago, the Demetris were on the radar of the largest cartels. We'd paid our dues, but with them the ledger was never closed.

Getting involved in the legalization and distribution would upset people we didn't need to upset. My interaction with Carroll over the years made it look like I was in favor of his stance. I couldn't shake the feeling that the attack on Chelsea was a warning. Only I doubted Chelsea was the intended victim.

With each step around their apartment, my determination to keep Charli safe battled with my need to learn who broke in, who violated the place she called home. The only furniture out of place was where the paramedic's gurney came through to wheel Chelsea out. The tracks were still visible on the large rug in the center of the living room, as well as on the tile.

It didn't appear as though anything else was disturbed. The boxes that I assumed contained Charli's things lined the far wall, box after box with words labeling the contents: kitchen, bath, books. Hell, Charli had at least six boxes labeled *books*. How many books did she need?

I ran my hand over the cardboard trying to devise another reason for the break-in. In the bedroom, which I assumed to be Chelsea's since it still looked lived in, there was a laptop on a desk and jewelry on the dresser. In the living room was a flat-screen television with a sound system and video components. If robbery was the motive, the perpetrator failed miserably.

"Tell Deloris to have this all sent to my apartment," I told Isaac, motioning to the boxes.

"Yes, sir."

Once Charli decided what she needed with her, we'd have the rest sent to her apartment—correction, Chelsea's apartment.

If Chelsea agreed to the job proposal Deloris offered her this morning, she wouldn't be spending much time in the apartment near Columbia. Getting her to New York was the first step. The second would be passing the entrance interview. If the people from Infidelity met her mother, they'd reject her, but the woman with Charli in Del Mar would pass with flying colors. The trick was not letting anyone from Infidelity know that she was a plant. Once she was accepted, Deloris would work her magic and pair her with Severus Davis.

By the time we left the apartment, my nerves were shot. Thoughts of Jo combined with worry over Charli had me all over the place. I couldn't go back to Charli, not yet. Isaac knew what I needed—my release.

Before driving away, he removed a duffel bag from the trunk and placed it in the backseat. I didn't need to look. Just seeing the bag made my pulse slow a beat. Since Charli came back into my life, I'd skipped my morning workouts. More accurately, I'd exchanged one workout for another. I needed the old-fashioned kind.

That was exactly what Isaac found me. It wasn't a big gym with a million people in color-coordinated workout clothes. The place was out of Palo Alto, down side streets and out of the way, nothing more than a storefront on a deserted strip mall; however, as soon as he parked the car, I knew it was what I needed. I didn't want to be recognized or singled out. I needed to beat the shit out of a bag until my fists ached and my body stopped moving.

Moving from the sunlit street to the dingy sweat-permeated interior, I didn't say a word. Just inside the door was a small hallway with a tiny office to the side. I waited as Isaac spoke to the gray-haired man at the desk. The man's leathery skin was dented with wrinkles and creases and his hair was long, tied back at the nape of his neck. Though the years appeared to have been tough on him, he still had the build of a fighter. I'd place money on the fact the man knew his way around a ring or maybe it was the street. Either way, when his dark eyes scanned me from head to toe, I knew exactly what he was thinking.

I didn't need to say a word to refute the impression he had of me in my silk suit and Italian loafers. I was ready to let my fists do the talking. I don't know what Isaac said to him. I didn't give a shit. All I wanted to do was pass through the door and work off the multitude of emotions coursing through my veins.

The old man hit a button that filled the hallway with a shrill buzz as the door at the end opened. Stepping through the doorway I inhaled the scent of hard work and testosterone. This was the kind of gym that had been my home away from home when I was young. While Oren was busy building a name for himself and doing anything to get rich, I was left to my own devices. It didn't matter how much money I had or what deals my father was brokering if I couldn't stand up for myself.

Oren thought it was a disgrace, and my mother was oblivious to my pastime, but as my father was making the Demetri name known, so was I. As a teenager, Lennox "Nox" Demetri was one of the top MMA fighters in New Jersey.

It'd been a long time since I'd stepped into the octagon, bare-fisted, with nothing but my muscle shirt and track pants. It started as a pastime, a way to burn off steam, but the better I became, the more I was wanted. Studying business during the day and beating the shit out of thick-necked cocky bastards at night kept me busy, until it didn't.

Everything about it was dangerous. Each fight was riskier than the one before. The bigger my name, the more cocksuckers who wanted a piece of me. It worked until the day Oren's world and mine collided. Cartels don't limit their investments to illegal drugs. I came out alive, barely. The other guy didn't fare any better.

Staring at the boxing ring, I felt a pang of disappointment that it wasn't the chain-linked octagon. I hadn't fought like that since I was twenty years old when the name Nox disappeared from the circuit and from my life. And then one day I told Jo about it, and she liked the nickname. Instead of associating it with a shadowy past, it had new meaning. I hadn't used it again until the day I took off my wedding ring—the day I met Charli.

In a more refined sport of abuse, after I changed out of my suit into sweats and a t-shirt, I donned a pair of boxing gloves. Though I was confident I could take either or both of the posturing peacocks currently in the ring, I concentrated on the bag. My training came back. Pay attention. Keep my balance. Only move my feet when I'm not punching. Punch the damn bag—don't push it. Breathe. Snap punches three to six reps. Move my feet. Find my rhythm.

Before I even realized it, my punches were flowing. Sweat saturated my shirt as I moved effortlessly around the bag. My power built, the snap keeping my combinations flowing. It wasn't long before I had an audience.

When I took a breath, I noticed Isaac off to the side holding a bottle of water and talking to the man from the front.

He stepped forward, handing me a towel and placing the straw near my lips. "He said he underestimated you, boss."

I nodded. "I'm not done yet," I said as I tossed the towel his direction.

Isaac tilted his head toward the ring. "You have a few takers if you're interested in stepping inside."

It had been over ten years since I allowed myself to fight, to feel the power of my knuckles connecting with a person's face. The sound of bones and cartilage crumbling was a drug, a high, and I'd been addicted, until it almost took me with it. I wasn't ready to start that addiction again. I had enough on my plate with the woman in my bed.

"I'm going to stick to the bag."

"I'll let them know."

By the time I unlaced the gloves, my clothes were drenched but my head was clear.

At least I thought it was… until I saw Charli again.

CHAPTER 28

Nineteen years ago

ADELAIDE

AS WEEKS PASSED, I became grateful to have someone beside me, someone who appreciated my father in a way Russell never had, yet at the same time, there was more happening around me that I didn't understand. Alton's relationship with my father was different than any I'd ever witnessed. Unlike Mother and I who simply agreed to each and every proposal, Alton's sentiments and opinions were valued, even sought.

When I asked Mother about it, she simply replied that it was the way it should be, a natural succession, a transference of power. It was what should have happened with Russell, but never did. On more than one occasion, I'd glean bits and pieces of conversations regarding Montague Corporation. They spoke about all aspects of the company, from diversifying investments to liquidating subsidiaries. For the first time in my life, I saw my father take pride in another individual.

I'd be lying if I didn't admit that my father's acceptance of Alton influenced my own feelings. The man I was about to marry was receiving the praise and appreciation I'd desired all of my life. I'd never have it, but the fact that Alton was entering the family through me allowed me a smidgen of pride. For once, I'd done something to meet my father's approval.

As Father had proclaimed, Alton and I became the talk of Savannah: the confirmed bachelor smitten with the young widowed heir. Invitations no longer came addressed to me, but to both of us. Our presence was requested at everything from charity benefits to political fundraisers. The society pages kept the world up to date on our latest social function.

It didn't take long to recognize that Alton craved what I'd taken for granted. The cameras documenting our every move, the mentions in the media, and the perks that came with the life of a Montague were his new drug. It didn't matter if I was tired or wanted to stay at the estate with Alexandria, declining an invitation was prohibited. We had a name to represent. Though he claimed that name was Montague, with each such occasion the name Fitzgerald gained prestige.

I quickly learned to read Alton's moods and his expressions. Of course, I'd been well trained with my father, but Alton was quicker to ignite. Even with Father present, Alton's passion for his beliefs was rarely tamed. When we were alone it was even more combustible.

Though I was a widowed adult, my parents forbade Alton to move into the manor until after our marriage. That didn't stop him from coming to my suite during his evening visits. My suite was the same one I'd shared with Russell and consisted of multiple rooms. The sitting room opened to the bedroom with a bathroom and dressing room attached.

Dinner was always precisely at seven o'clock, and Alton and Father often arrived home to the estate around six. Sometimes he'd join Father for a cocktail, and other times he'd excuse himself to visit me. The timidity of a new suitor was lost on Alton. His confidence and self-assured demeanor met little resistance even from my father.

With our elopement still weeks away, I received my first front-row seat to his determination. From the moment Alton entered my sitting room I sensed something was off. I swallowed the lump forming in my throat as I looked up into his eyes. Since the evening I learned about Bryce and Suzy, I continually searched for answers behind the slate gray. Once our conversation was done, it became a forbidden topic to everyone involved. It was as if the truth once freed was again captive to the shadows of Montague Manor.

Alton's gaze narrowed as he scanned my form, still wearing my dressing gown. Usually I was dressed, but I'd spent the afternoon with Alexandria, and time had gotten away from me. Though I used to balk at Russell's insistence of my interaction with our daughter, with him gone I found myself wanting to be with her. It might also be that she was getting older. No longer just a baby, even at nearly five, she was smart and funny. Merely the thought of one of her quick responses made me smile.

"Good evening, Laide." His voice echoed against the tall walls as the flames in the fireplace crackled and supplied warmth.

His presence stirred a mix of emotions inside of me. I found myself attracted, yet nervous, infatuated, yet apprehensive. I'd continued my sessions with Dr. Sams and consciously worked to boost the appropriate responses. Once our agreement was finalized, I asked for us to wait for sex until after we were married. Though he didn't argue, I sensed he wanted more.

Part of me feared that he wouldn't like sex with me. That he'd say the things Russell said, calling me names and making fun of me. I reasoned that if we were married, my inability wouldn't matter. It would be too late, and he couldn't back out. Then my father wouldn't blame me for another failed marriage. At the same time, there was the part of me that thought of Suzy. As if I didn't have enough issues, the idea of him comparing me to her, my best friend, added to my distress.

Standing before my fiancé, I wrapped my arms around myself. The satin of my robe suddenly seemed transparent under my own fingers. I knew it wasn't, but the look in his eyes told me it was.

"Alton, I wasn't expecting you this early."

He shook his head, closed the door to the hallway, and walked closer. Each step increased his breathing as he stared down at me. "It's after six." He ran his hands over my arms. "I've never seen you like this."

I took a step back. "I-I should be dressed. Let me just go…" I attempted to move toward the bedroom.

He held tight to my hand. "No." His chest rose and fell. "I've had a shitty day, but I believe it just got better."

I placed my hand on his chest and used my most appeasing tone. "Alton, let me get you a drink."

"I don't want a drink."

Desire filled the suite, thick like a cloud surrounding and suffocating. I tried to recall Dr. Sams' words. Senses. I inhaled, yet my lungs wouldn't fill. The flames in the fireplace no longer crackled. The usual scent of tobacco didn't register. Apprehension gave way to alarm as I tried to keep myself composed.

"A-Alton, we said… not until…"

His lips took mine: primal and needy. The tender, chaste connection we'd had in the past erupted into more. I tried to back away, to breathe, but I couldn't. His arms were around me, holding me close—too close. His body—shoulders, arms, and chest—eclipsed mine. I was gone, surrounded by him. His expensive suit coat was unbuttoned as my chest collided with his white shirt. He inclined my face as his fingers twisted in my recently styled hair.

That was the thought that crossed my mind. It was another example of how dysfunctional my thought process was. I'd just styled my hair and now I'd need to do it again. Instead of worrying about what he wanted, I concentrated on my hair. I couldn't go to dinner with my parents with my hair out of place.

"I've been patient." His words cut through the fog. They weren't soft or gentle nor were they meant to reassure me. They were simply his reasoning, his declaration. "In the two months since our agreement, I've been alone."

Two months? He bemoaned two months. I hadn't slept with anyone in nearly two years. Even Russell and I hadn't been intimate during the last few months of his life. The sting of my dead husband's last rejection twisted in the pit of my empty stomach.

"W-We're going to elope soon." I reminded him.

He pushed his erection against me. "Laide, I want you. You're mine." He forced my chin upward until I stared into his eyes. I sought the green and blue flecks that brought me comfort. The ones that glistened in the light of the fire, but they were gone. Cold determined steel stared down at me, leaving a chill as my breathing hitched. "Say it," he demanded.

"I'm yours. I-I'm just not…"

My robe was gone, lost to the floor. My only protection against the hard rod at my belly was the thin covering of his trousers and my bra and underwear. I considered screaming. After all, the manor was full of people: not only my parents, but staff too. They were everywhere. Yet my chest ached with the truth of my words: *I'm yours.* I was. I belonged to Alton Fitzgerald. Even if we hadn't said our vows, my father brokered the deal.

Questions of self-doubt surfaced. What if Alton didn't like me? What if he rejected me as Russell did? What if he preferred Suzy? He could decide to stop the wedding, and then it would be my fault.

I couldn't have sex with him. I would disappoint him. In an act of desperation, I dropped to my knees. It was something I'd only done a few times to my husband. Though it never appealed to me, I knew he enjoyed it. Would Alton?

At his feet, I reached for his belt and stared up at him through veiled eyes. "I can help you wait a little longer."

Indecision morphed his expression until a low rumble of laughter filled the room. His words came out thick. "Fuck yes." He lifted my chin. "If the world could see you now. Adelaide Montague on her fucking knees."

Acid churned and curled within me as he reached for his belt and covered my hand.

"You want to suck me?" he asked.

I nodded, hoping to sound convincing. "I want our wedding night to be special."

"You're fucking gorgeous on your knees."

I swallowed the bile.

"Say it," Alton demanded, his hand still covering mine.

I blinked as seductively as I could muster, my breasts heaving within their lace cups. "I'm yours."

"No. Tell me what you want to do."

I'd never said anything like this before. Nevertheless, to keep him from taking me, I formed the words. "I-I want to suck you."

In moments, he freed himself, his length jutting out toward me. A low growl resonated from his throat as he thrust himself into my mouth. "Keep your hands behind your back," he commanded as he moved me to his liking.

I did as he said, holding tight to my own fingers as his laced through my hair and held me in position. I wasn't sucking him as much as he was fucking my mouth. In and out. I concentrated on not gagging as his length pounded the back of my throat. Salty musk replaced the tobacco scent as he moved faster and faster.

My mind wandered. Did he lock the door? What if someone entered and saw us? What if Alexandria came in? What about my mother?

And then realization struck. I avoided sex. I'd won, but at what cost? He was about to come. I recognized the sounds, the labored breathing and grunts as he moved faster and faster. My fingers unlaced and I pushed against his thighs. I'd never allowed Russell to go this far.

It was degrading and wrong. I was a Montague, not a whore.

My manicured nails scratched at his skin as I shoved and pushed. It didn't matter; Alton was stronger. Tears filled my eyes and spilled onto my cheeks. My back arched. I tried to fall backward. It was to no avail. He was possessed.

Over and over he thrust. My scalp screamed at the pull of my hair. It was as if my fight fueled his actions. Sounds and obscenities came from his lips though I could barely hear them, the sound of him moving within me dominating my senses.

Even as he came, Alton didn't release my head. My mouth filled with his seed. My brain failed to comprehend the involuntary action. Spit or swallow? My cheeks distended as he continued to spew. No longer bile, vomit teased my throat as he filled my mouth.

"Swallow, Laide." His tone was soft as he spoke, petting my head and stroking my throat. All the while he kept himself inside my mouth, not allowing me to spit.

With tremendous will, I made myself swallow. It was like taking a pill that was too big. My eyes closed as I did it again and again until only dryness remained. Finally, I fell down to the floor, my knees collapsing with the awareness that it was over.

Alton took a step back, put himself back into his boxers and pants and buckled his belt. Then gallantly he offered his hand. As I stood, he pulled me close and kissed me, his tongue probing mine, no doubt tasting himself. "You are quite the surprise."

I tried to move away, but he held me tightly.

Brushing back my hair, he searched my face. "Go fix your hair and makeup. I'm going to go down and have that drink with your father."

New panic coiled though me. Was it not good for him? Did I do it wrong? Would he tell my father he didn't want to marry me? I was pathetic, and I knew it.

Alton wiped a tear that I didn't know I'd shed.

"You scratched the shit out of my thighs." He laughed. "Those will be fun to explain in the sauna at the club."

Shame reddened my cheeks. "I'm sorry. I've never…" My chin lowered.

"Look at me."

I did. The flecks were back in his eyes.

"You've never… blown someone?"

"I've never… he never came."

Alton cupped my cheek as a smile spread across his lips. "Then you're a quick learner. Next time I'll need to tie your hands. I don't like to be scratched."

There were too many things wrong with what had just happened. Too many things to even consider. Instead, I clung to the words *next time.* They meant he wasn't going to tell my father he didn't want to marry me. They meant I hadn't disappointed him or Charles. They meant I'd done something right.

Alton kissed my cheek and peered down my body, still only covered with a lacy bra and underwear. "I'm ready to be inside of you, but for the next month, I'll take this." He waited for my response, but I had none. "Clean up. Dinner is in twenty minutes."

With that, he left me alone.

CHAPTER 29

CHARLI

WHAT IF I'D ruined everything? What if he wanted me gone? Could he even do that?

I knew Deloris was outside the bedroom door when Nox and I argued. Despite the fact that she undoubtedly heard everything that happened, from the moment the two of us left the suite, she didn't mention it. She respected our privacy. That wasn't to say that the subject didn't loom omnipresent—it did. However, neither of us mentioned Nox, Jocelyn, or what I'd said.

Deloris possessed the answers to my questions, but I made the decision that I owed Nox the same courtesy he'd given me. I wouldn't learn my information from Deloris. I wanted it from Nox, when he was ready.

Entering my apartment that I had shared with Chelsea for three years was eerie. Just knowing that someone had been in there, touching Chelsea and our things, gave me the creeps. I walked from room to room. Nothing looked out of place, except tracks on the floor that I could only assume were made from the gurney

I was glad I came back. My time at Stanford and in California helped shape me into the woman I was now. Seeing it all again confirmed that it was time to move on.

I wanted to do that, at Columbia and with Nox.

Boxes of my things were neatly stacked against the wall. When I checked the kitchen cupboards, a lump formed in my throat. She'd packed everything that was mine, which was almost everything. Where our dishes had been were paper plates. Plastic cups replaced our glasses. I was leaving her with next to nothing when I wouldn't even be using the things she'd packed.

I began to pull the kitchen boxes out of the neat pile.

"What are you doing?" Deloris asked.

"If Chelsea decides not to move to New York, I want her to keep the things in these boxes."

"Doesn't it all belong to you?"

I nodded as I carried a box back to the kitchen. "Look in here." I opened the cupboard. "She'd be left with nothing. I won't even be using it. I can't do that to her."

There was something in Deloris's smile that told me she approved.

"I have the movers rescheduled. They're coming on Monday. Everything will be in New York by Thursday."

"That's fast, faster than the movers I had scheduled."

"Your friend needs to decide before Monday."

"I'll let her know when we see her."

"Is there anything you need from here?"

I shook my head. "No. She has everything packed. I don't want to…" And then I remembered something. "Wait." I found the many boxes labeled shoes. In the second box I found the shoebox I wanted.

"I bought you shoes."

"You did," I replied with a smirk. "These pumps have a history, and I'm hoping I can add to their escapades."

She lifted her hand. "I think that's all I need to know. But," she added curiously, "I'd love to know about that isolated rain shower the other night."

Pink rushed to my cheeks. "No, I don't think you would."

When we arrived at the hospital, Deloris was preoccupied with something on her tablet and suggested she stay in the car while I visit. Isaac waited outside the door as he'd done on each visit. I was glad to have some alone time with Chelsea.

The minute I entered, I sensed her readiness to leave.

"Are you here to break me out?"

I kissed her cheek, noticing how the bruise around her eye was beginning to change color and settle, moving down her cheek.

"I've decided I don't want to go back," she said.

I pulled a chair beside her bed. "Back…?"

"To our apartment. I remember…"

"Oh God, Chels. What do you remember?"

She closed her eyes. "Not enough to help but I remember him touching me."

"You didn't say…" I searched for the right words, but they weren't forming. "…he didn't…"

"No. I wasn't raped, but he touched me—not sexually. It was dark and he hit me with something from behind. I fell."

"You know it was a man?"

Her chest moved rapidly as her breathing became shallow. "I heard him talk. After he hit me…" Her eyes opened wide. "Oh shit. No. I just remembered. Never mind. I should tell the police."

"What?"

She looked toward the door. "Are you alone?"

I pressed my lips together. "No. Nox is paranoid. I have Isaac with me."

Chelsea reached for my hand. "Alex, he was angry. When he hit me from behind, I fell forward, face down. He rolled me over—when he did, he said I wasn't the right one."

Pulling my hand away, I jumped back as my heart began to race. "What the hell does that mean? Did you see him? Do you remember any details?" My questions ran over each other, not allowing her time to answer.

"I don't know what it meant, because even after he said that, he continued to hit me. Like he was sitting on me and punching me. I couldn't see him. Maybe he was wearing something over his face." She shook her head. "I can't remember anything but his form."

"Come to New York. If you get the job in D.C., fine. If not, at least you're close to me. You can decide to take more classes or look for a job there. I'm sure there's something. Please let Deloris take care of the movers. She's amazing. She'll get it all arranged."

"Deloris?" Chelsea asked.

"The lady who came to see you this morning. She said she was here, just before I got here."

"Let her take care of the movers?"

"Yes, she does, well, anything and everything. She works for Nox."

Chelsea nodded. "Do you trust her?"

"Yes." I laughed. "I know I said that really fast, and I'm not one to give out trust very easily, but Nox trusts her. So I do too."

"All right."

"All right? You'll come to New York?"

"Yes. I think I'll spend a little time with my mom. I don't really want to be on a plane with a shiner."

"You can always wear sunglasses."

That made her smile. "I seem to remember someone doing that and the flight attendant making a comment."

"Well, she was rude."

"No, girl, you were sulking. But look at you now. Your Prince Charming is back."

Prince Charming. Nox specifically said he wasn't, and I may concur. Then again, many a prince began as a toad. Maybe he was both.

I debated telling Deloris and Nox about Chelsea's memory. But as Isaac walked me to the car, I decided it could wait. I didn't want to set Nox off again. I wanted to offer him something else, something I took away.

For the first time since I left Nox in Del Mar, my perspective was different. I didn't think about being an employee or his being a client; I thought in terms of *us*. The idea that I may have upset him enough for this to end made me realize that I wanted there to be an us. I didn't care what Bryce said. I cared about Nox and the way I felt when I was around him—the way he was when he was around me.

The man who lay beside me and stared up at the ceiling as he spoke about his mother, the man who loved his wife enough to wear his wedding ring even though she was gone, and the man who made me feel adored and worthy of his attention—that was the man I concentrated on.

The suite was dark when we arrived. Since I'd had Isaac and Deloris with me, I couldn't help but wonder where Nox had gone. I prayed it wasn't back to New York. I didn't call him.

I believed he didn't and took his absence as a sign, a chance to show him my change of heart. I set a plan into motion, one I'd only toyed with in my head.

The first thing I did was order room service, complete with French wine. The man from room service must have thought I was crazy after trying repeatedly to convince me to order their premium California cabernet. Finally, I offered a finder's bonus for French Bordeaux. The rest of the order went much smoother.

Then I called my new accomplice and asked for Deloris's help. I was pretty sure she'd done this for Nox once before; nevertheless, my cheeks may have reddened a bit as I asked for long pieces of silk and candles. Thankfully, I was talking to her on the phone and she couldn't see.

That was, until she arrived. Handing me the shopping bag, I again saw her approving smile. She confirmed it when she whispered, "I know where he is. What time should I prompt him to return?"

Her clandestine support was exactly the strength I needed. A mischievous smile materialized. "Give me half an hour."

Deloris squeezed my hand. "Be patient with him. He's a good man."

I swallowed the lump forming in my throat and simply nodded.

As I continued to set my plan in motion, I thought about my conversation with Chelsea. I did trust Deloris. She'd said Nox was a good man. He'd said that people needed to earn his trust. I wanted to do that. I wanted it mutually. Bryce's accusations were only that. They hadn't been substantiated, and besides that, Bryce had a history of breaking my trust. Nox hadn't done that. Not yet.

The lavender bath I quickly took left its sweet aroma on my soft skin. My hair was up, secured in a messy bun with ringlets cascading down my back and around my face. My only attire was a rose-colored nightgown hanging seductively from thin spaghetti straps. Its style accentuated my breasts with a sheer lace bodice designed to hug all the right places and rich satin skirting that flowed to the floor.

I hadn't been this nervous since our first date in his presidential suite. The anticipation had my entire body on edge. My pulse beat erratically as my insides twisted.

While lighting the candles around the suite and pouring the wine, I decided to trust the man who was about to enter. It might not be the decision Alexandria was raised to make, but it was the one my heart told me was right. It was time to listen.

Precisely thirty minutes after Deloris left, the door to the suite opened and my breathing hitched. The sight of Nox Demetri took the very air from my lungs. I gripped the bedroom doorframe, my manicured nails holding tightly to the wood in an attempt to keep from falling.

Silently, he surveyed the suite as his presence emitted confidence and allure. He was the pure definition of sex appeal, and that aura surrounded him like cologne. I'd never seen him dressed so casually—apart from swimwear—standing in jeans and a light-colored button-down shirt, bunched at his elbows. Nox was the oxygen I required to breathe. Inhaling him gave my lungs what they needed, filling me with him.

I didn't say a word as he stood taking in his surroundings. As if each candle were a reminder and a light of empowerment, his shoulders broadened and stance straightened. By the time he'd turned completely around, the menacing gleam I adored shone from his pale blue eyes as they sought me out, finding me leaning against the bedroom doorjamb with a glass of wine in my hand.

Bravely, I moved forward. My bare feet padded against the floor. Each step brought friction from the lace of my nightgown as it rubbed my hardened nipples. With only his gaze he melted me, like the wax of the candles surrounding us. I was no longer solid, but pliable, wanting and needing more of his heat.

Coming to a stop before him, I lowered my eyes and handed him the glass. "Your wine, Mr. Demetri."

He took the glass and said, "I thought we should talk."

Since I was looking down, the strain in his jeans caught my attention. I longed to reach out and stroke it; instead, my tongue darted to my suddenly dry lips. "If you want to talk, I'll talk, but if that can wait, we can do something else."

I took a deep breath and sank to my knees, unsure what I was doing. I'd read books. I remembered Del Mar. With everything in me, I hoped this was what he'd meant by his unique tastes.

"Charli…"

"I won't mention it again, Mr. Demetri, except to tell you that I was wrong earlier today. I disobeyed you, and I believe I should be punished." I'd practiced that line multiple different ways, but saying it aloud was so different than each silent attempt. The spoken words heightened my arousal while simultaneously increasing a vulnerability I didn't know I'd feel. With barely a drink of the French wine I'd poured, I was deliriously intoxicated by my words, his proximity, and the uncertainty of his actions.

A deep sound, somewhere between a growl and a moan came from his throat. From my view, his shoes shifted. The hairs on my arms stood to attention as the room crackled, charged with energy. "Stand up, Charli."

My heart stuttered in its cadence as I looked up to his hand. Placing mine in the palm of his, I stood. His glass of wine was now on a nearby table. He lifted my chin, our eyes once again fixed on one another's.

"Tell me what you're doing."

It was a command, not a request. "I'm trusting you, completely."

His hands moved up and down my arms, their warmth comforting as I searched his expression. "You don't need to prove anything to me. I reacted—"

I pushed myself up to the tips of my toes and covered his lips with mine. "I'm not proving. I'm showing. I didn't even know your name in Del Mar, and I trusted you. Now that I know more about you, why would that diminish my trust?"

His arms surrounded me, pulling me tighter until we were one, fused together by the sheer heat of his embrace. The fervor of his kiss took what I offered and gave in return. Our tongues, no longer interested in talking, moved together, stoking the fire of desire. As the passion grew, his stance morphed. Subtle at first, his lips became more demanding, more apparent, as he fisted my tendrils of auburn, propelling my head back and making my neck vulnerable to his whims.

"Oh Nox," I gasped as the scruff of his chin abraded my sensitive skin, and his teeth grazed behind my ear.

"You're sure?" he asked, his voice now gruff and thick with desire.

Totally intoxicated by his presence, my answers wouldn't stand up in a court of law. I wasn't thinking straight. Mutual pleasure and fulfillment were all I could think about. Nothing else mattered. Accusations and fears were beyond my current comprehension.

"Y-Yes." I barely had the answer out when without a word he scooped me in his arms. I didn't know what awaited me in the future—near or far—yet as he held me close and our mouths joined in a bruising kiss, I didn't care. The concoction formed by the combination of his tenderness and force was addicting, and I wanted more.

Gently placing me upon the bed, Nox's eyes immediately went to the lengths of satin I'd laid across the mattress. His menacing gleam questioned with simply the furrowing of his brow as he lifted one length of the black satin and ran it over his palm.

Swallowing the saliva that moistened my throat, I simply said, "I trust you, Mr. Demetri."

"That punishment you mentioned," Nox said as he reached for the buckle of his belt.

My heart rate skyrocketed, but I refused to back down. Somehow I knew this was as vital to him as it was to me.

"Yes, sir."

CHAPTER 30

Eighteen years ago

ADELAIDE

THE BREEZE SKIRTED my sun-kissed cheeks as it rustled the skirt of my wedding gown. Not as elaborate as the first wedding dress I'd worn, this tea-length designer original was ivory satin with tulle and taffeta skirting. The sweetheart neckline dipped teasingly between my breasts, creating the perfect showcase for the diamond necklace shimmering in the setting sunlight.

"Do you take this man as your lawfully…"

The words flowed from the officiant's lips, words he'd undoubtedly repeated hundreds if not thousands of times. This was, after all, one of the top luxury wedding destinations. A former 11th-century palace on the cliffs beside the Amalfi Coast, Alton and I were saying our vows on a balcony above the Mediterranean Sea. Sparkling waves glistened in the vista of blue.

Though it was a private affair, the proceedings were extravagant, even by Montague standards. In many ways, the entire production was more elaborate than my first wedding. The ancient walls and fresco-covered ceilings gave the impression of being inside a work of art. From our suite to our nuptials, everything was planned to perfection. Unlike my first wedding, my mother wasn't the planner, and I had about as much say as I did the first time. This was all Alton.

"I do," I dutifully replied.

"Do you…"

I took a deep breath, the skirt shifting slightly as I settled my nerves and concentrated on the gray eyes drinking me in. Their contentment warmed my soul. This was it. I knew it with every fiber of my being. This was a wedding *and* the culmination of a business deal. There were no loopholes, no backing out. Even death wouldn't save me this time. Our only way to a future representative of the life I'd been born to live was through one another.

"I do," Alton said, squeezing my hand.

It made me smile to know that the gold band I slid over Alton's fourth finger was the first ring he'd ever worn. Of course, I wasn't his first love nor was he mine. This wasn't like it was with Russell, yet it was liberating. We held no pretense about feelings or the future. It was set, and we were but pawns in the grand scheme.

I'd sold myself for Montague and for my father. Alton sold himself for the Montague name, control of Montague Corporation, and assuring all of that for Bryce. The thought of my daughter's arranged future still turned my stomach, but Alexandria and Bryce's friendship gave me hope. They were only five and seven years old. At least they had a foundation.

It took me some time to come to terms with Suzy and the past she shared with my new husband. I wanted to hate her, as she said she wanted to hate me. But we were both sacrificing. Regardless, I found myself watching my fiancé and best friend for covert looks or clandestine touches. I searched for any sign that their relationship continued. If anything was present, I never saw it, or they did a good job of hiding it.

I was hopeful but not naive. Life had been too hard, even being to the manor born, to wear rose-colored glasses. Fairytales didn't exist.

Alton was my future, and as much as I detested that he and Suzy shared a child, she was still my best friend. I didn't want to, nor did I think I was strong enough to, continue without her in my life. More than that, we needed to stay close for our children and grandchildren. The Montagues and Carmichaels would come together. It would be easier for that to happen if we remained close.

"With this ring…" Alton's deep voice reverberated in my ears.

The diamond-studded band slipped over my knuckle, the stones glittering in the remaining Italian sunshine. The engagement ring I wore from Russell was a Montague stone, one passed down from my father's mother. For my new marriage, it was simply redesigned to a new, stunning setting, allowing the six-carat diamond to remain on my finger and in our family.

Even with our travel, I'd avoided sex, but the clock was ticking. After the ceremony and celebratory dinner, my time was up. I appreciated Alton's patience and knew I'd stretched it to its limit.

"I now pronounce you husband and wife," the officiant said, smiling at my husband. "Alton, you may kiss your bride."

Your bride. My husband. It was official.

I stared, mesmerized by my husband's lips. I couldn't tell Suzy, but I admitted to Dr. Sams how much I enjoyed his kiss. Strong and firm, his smile morphed to a pucker as my eyes closed, and our mouths joined. Sweet yet possessive, he claimed me as his.

"Mrs. Fitzgerald, you are beautiful."

It wasn't a declaration of feelings neither one of us was ready to proclaim. Still, his compliment and the use of my new name made me grin.

"Mrs. Fitzgerald." Gwendolyn, my matron of honor and Alton's sister, said. Hugging me, she placed my bouquet of fresh lilies into my hand. "Welcome to the family. I've always wanted a sister."

I smiled at her words. Our ceremony was supposed to be private. Though some might later question my choice, for obvious reasons I couldn't ask Suzy to stand with me. Therefore, Alton's sister seemed the natural choice. I'd known her for most of my life. We ran in similar circles; however, until news of Alton's and my engagement, we were never close.

The Fitzgeralds were content with their standing—until Alton. Gwen was an attractive woman and never seemed overly impressed with the Montague name. Though that wouldn't endear her to my father, it did to me.

Without understanding the truth behind my marriage to her brother or the urgency for us to wed, she welcomed me into her life. I especially liked how well Alexandria got along with her and Preston's son, Patrick. He was a year older than Bryce. When the three of them were at Montague Manor, I got the impression that Patrick favored Alexandria to Bryce. Briefly, I wondered if Gwen and Preston knew Bryce was their nephew. I didn't see any indication they did. Asking Alton wasn't an option. The subject was closed.

Only the eight of us, my parents, Alton and Gwen's parents, Gwen and Preston, and Alton and I were present at the wedding and the dinner celebration. As if relieved that the deal was complete, my father was uncharacteristically cordial, even jovial during the dinner. Toasts were made, and the alcohol flowed as everyone rejoiced at the blending of our families.

I would've liked to share the event with Alexandria. Even though she was young, this union affected her, but when I asked about bringing her, my suggestion was given as much credence as any other suggestions I'd made: quickly dismissed as if I'd never mentioned it.

Alton made plans following the wedding for a two-week honeymoon. He made no secret that he didn't intend to share me with Alexandria or anyone else during our trip. Our plans were to enjoy all the Mediterranean had to offer while our nuptials and romance were strategically leaked to the press. We were a couple in love, brought together after my tragic loss. I was the young widow who found love where there'd been friendship.

I'd read all the articles. Our pictures were shared on social pages beyond Georgia. Alton's place within Montague Corporation was the topic of speculation by many financial prognosticators. Concern for the company's future after Russell's death was lessening. Stock prices were on the rise.

The time finally came when we excused ourselves from the rest of the party. As we made our way to our suite, I thought about the flowing white negligee I'd found at an exclusive boutique in Savannah. Its sheer robe did nothing more than build anticipation of what was beneath, simply another layer to unwrap.

The champagne during our dinner did wonders to calm my nerves. Once we were alone, I excused myself to go to the honeymoon suite's bathroom.

"No, Laide."

I stopped. "No what?"

Alton stood in front of me, blocking my way. "I have no intentions of your leaving my sight, not tonight, not until I say."

I smiled, playing his words off as the jest I hoped they were. I kissed his cheek. "Don't worry, husband. I'll only be a few minutes. I have a surprise for you."

He didn't budge. "I've waited for this." He spun me around and busied himself with the back of my dress. In lieu of a zipper, there was a long row of pearl buttons. His large fingers patiently plied each button, slowly exposing my skin to his warm breath as the sound of his breathing hastened. "Don't you agree?" he asked between kisses to my neck. "I've been patient." His lips dipped lower, sending chills over my skin. "I've taken relief between your lips." He turned me back around, his gray eyes darkened with desire. "Now I want more."

His phrases were breathy and heated. They stirred a part of me deep inside, a part I hadn't felt in years. My head wobbled, falling backward as he pushed the material from my shoulders, allowing my wedding dress to pool around my pearl-accented heels. Only a silk slip, lace bra, and underwear protected me from his searing gaze.

"Alton…"

"Shhh, Laide, listen to me. Don't think. Don't speak. Give in to me."

I wanted to. I wanted to feel what I hadn't felt since before Alexandria. I wanted from him what I'd only experienced with my own touch.

"You're now mine. Tell me that you'll submit to me."

I already had. Admitting it wasn't difficult.

The next two weeks passed, days sightseeing and nights learning more about my husband. I was finally able to show him my negligee, and he was able to bring me to orgasm more often than not. It was more than I'd ever accomplished before. Even when I didn't, he did. I took comfort in that.

The part of marriage that concerned me was Alton's obsession with Montague. Even on our honeymoon, he was in constant contact with the office and my father. It was new to be together twenty-four hours a day. With so much time, I saw a side of him that I'd never fully recognized. The snippets I'd seen, I'd been able to rationalize. Now it was harder.

Whether it was business related, poor service in a restaurant, or a comment from me, Alton's speed to anger unnerved me.

It was different than my father, more than words. I was used to domination—a fact of my existence as my father's daughter—but being on the receiving end of a slap was new. The first time it happened was in our suite, less than a week into our marriage. He'd just finished a conversation with someone on the telephone. I knew he was upset, but we had reservations and a tour guide waiting. I don't recall exactly what I said, but I'll never forget the sting of his palm as it connected with my cheek.

With my eyes filled with tears, I stared, unsure what to do or say. I was fearful of more, but that didn't happen. Instead, he simply looked annoyed and asked, "What, Adelaide?"

"I-I can't believe—"

"Don't."

My lips pressed into a straight line.

"Don't push me," he warned. "Your job is to support me. Do you intend to quit that job—to fail another husband?"

I didn't respond.

"If you think you can tell Daddy what I did and our agreement will be null and void, you're mistaken. Moreover, I'm sure you don't want to disappoint him—again. You and I—we're in this for the long haul. I suggest you fix your makeup, plaster a smile on your face, and hurry. We have a tour to enjoy, Mrs. Fitzgerald."

Alton knew exactly what to say, which of my buttons to push. His venomous words stung, their poison exacting my obedience. Later I'd reflect and wonder how much Suzy told him about me and my insecurities, but at the time my mind couldn't process that far. My hands shook as I did as he said and reasoned that he was right about the agreement as well as my job or role, depending on who was describing it. My duty was to support him, not irritate him. By the time I stepped back into the bedroom of our suite, I had my smile securely in place.

It was a good thing. More than once our photo was captured as we toured the ancient ruins.

CHAPTER 31

CHARLI

WAKING EXHAUSTED YET content, I lay in the darkness of the hotel suite, listening to the beat of Nox's heart. My head rested against his chest while his arm surrounded my shoulder. His body warmed me and his hold reassured me. I'd never imagined the overwhelming joy that came with giving myself completely to another person.

Cathartic and liberating, the words seemed wrong for the actions of the night, yet from my soul I couldn't form others. The tension I'd caused was gone—cleansed away. Mindful of my tolerance, Nox ensured my punishment didn't last long, and the reward afterward made it worth every lash. With my behind on fire, he filled me, taking my attention away from the intensity of my outside to the sheer ecstasy happening within me. He was barely inside of me when I came with a release I'd never known. With no buildup or climb, a bomb exploded, the detonation shattering me. Starting from the tips of my curled toes, wave after wave crashed through me until forming words was beyond my capabilities. My nails bit crescent moons deep into my palms as my fists balled. The screaming of his name gave way to moans and whimpers. I was completely wrung out as my body convulsed around his, and the night had only begun.

At some point we drank wine and ate food. If I hadn't been the one to order it, I wouldn't have been able to say what it was we ate. Most of the meal came to my lips via Nox's fingers as my hands were useless, bound behind me in an elaborate weave of satin. The dependence made each bite of food or drink of wine more fulfilling, more intoxicating. It was as if the fine French wine's alcohol content far exceeded the legal limit. Each morsel or sip brought to my lips at his discretion was a hit from a drug, the lack of control stimulating my bloodstream like cocaine.

As we were about to fall asleep, I remembered things I wanted to say, information from Chelsea he'd want to know, yet settling into the cloud of musk, the lingering scent of sex, wax, and desire, I let them all slip away. I wasn't hiding any of it from him. I wanted to relish the aftermath of our reunion. Make-up sex was all my mind could comprehend.

Now, awakened by nothing in particular, those thoughts again weren't at the forefront of my mind. Another one was. Stirring, Nox turned toward me as my head slipped to his bicep, and I curled into him. Skin to skin, my fingers splayed upon his chest.

"Are you awake?" he whispered.

"Yes."

His gravelly voice rippled through the night. "Are you ready for round two?"

"Two?" I laughed. "I think you lost count. How about five or six?"

His lips brushed my forehead. "Then round seven?"

I shook my head. "Not really." I didn't want to admit how sore I was—in a good way. "I like this."

His arm tightened around me. "Me too, princess."

An unexpected tear leaked from my eye as the weight of our agreement settled over me. Quickly, I brushed it away, not wanting to ruin what we'd accomplished. Of course, I wasn't successful. *Mr. Intuitive* hovered over me, his handsome features shadowed by the darkness.

"What happened?" He stiffened, lifting his torso higher as if to see me clearer. "Did I go too far? I know what I said, but I was wrong. You may always express your limits. I never want to harm you."

I shook my head. "It's not… no." I reached up, caressing his cheek, loving the stubble below the tips of my fingers. "Nox, you absolutely overwhelm me. I feel things with you I never knew existed." I wasn't sure how to verbalize what I felt. "It's not just sex, though as you may have noticed, I'm not complaining.

"It's you, being with you, sleeping with you, talking with you… I just wish…"

I let my voice and words trail away, swallowing the emotion I didn't want to share.

"You wish what?"

When I didn't answer, he lifted my chin. "Charli? Don't make me ask again. You're the one who brought it up."

"I was stupid and impulsive."

"I know you're too smart to bring up a recent topic. What are you talking about?"

I pulled away from his grasp and threw back the covers. In the dark room, I found my robe lying on a nearby chair and wrapped it around myself, securing the tie. Before he could ask his question again, I said, "You know what I did. You just don't know why I did it."

Nox was out of bed, his nakedness coming closer. His height dwarfed me as we both stood barefooted, staring in the darkness.

"All right. Tell me. Tell me why you did it, and then I'll know what the fuck you're talking about."

Apprehension flooded my nervous system, fear that my honesty would sabotage our progress, yet equally fearful of leaving secrets unspoken. I noticed the clock near the bed. It was nearly three o'clock in the morning. We should be sleeping. Then again, that was six o'clock in New York, where we would spend the majority of our day.

"Nox, I'm sorry. We should be sleeping."

He quickly slipped into a pair of gym shorts, turned, and cupped my cheek. "If something is bothering you enough to interrupt your sleep, it should interrupt mine too. Give it to me, Charli. Let me help you."

I took a step back. "You can't help me." I shrugged, my arms slapping my sides. "Actually you did, but it's too late for more."

With my eyes now adjusted to the darkness, I watched as he ran his hand through his hair.

"You're infuriating."

"Me? Why?"

"Because," he explained, reaching for my hand and pulling me to a nearby sofa, "I hear you respond, but I have no fucking idea what you're saying or talking about."

"Infidelity." The word hung in the air, a reminder of my stupidity.

When Nox didn't respond, I went on, unsuccessful at keeping my words devoid of emotion. "I-I want to be here with you. After we left Del Mar, I cried… mourned… what we shared was more than I could've ever imagined. At first I wanted only one week. Chelsea told me I deserved it. She said men do it all the time. But, Nox, I couldn't. I couldn't separate sex with you from emotion."

I stood, needing to move. "Maybe it's because I'm female… but you got inside me…" My cheeks flushed. "…in more ways than one." *Okay, that wasn't what I meant.* "I hope you know what I'm trying to say."

He reached for my hand and pulled me closer. "I know exactly what you mean."

I collapsed on his lap, the warmth of his embrace surrounding me.

"I just wish that now…"

"Go on."

"I wish that it wasn't different. I don't want to be *owned.* I don't want to be obligated to a defined time period. I want real.

"I'm worried that the only reason you came back to the suite last night was because you had to—because of the agreement. I'm afraid that if you could've left me, gotten on the airplane and gone back to New York, you would have."

His words slowed, heavy with emotion. "You thought I'd leave you here?"

"No," I corrected. "I was afraid you *wanted to.* I didn't think you would."

"I didn't want to. I don't want to." His chest heaved as he smoothed my hair over my shoulder and tucked a piece behind my ear. "I was upset. I know there are things we need to share. It's difficult for me to explain. What made me… what made Del Mar special was that you didn't know me."

I looked up at his beautiful features—his chiseled jawline and the way his brow protruded—as he carefully chose his words. I considered telling him to stop. I didn't need to know any more if it brought him pain. But I couldn't.

"You didn't see me the way I've been portrayed. It was refreshing and invigorating. You even mentioned my boss or bosses. You weren't infatuated with money or standing. You were just you." He played with my hair again. "The most beautiful woman to catch my eye in years. I didn't enter our week wanting more, but I sure as hell left it wanting that.

"It took every ounce of self-control I possessed to let you leave me that morning."

"Why did you put your number in my phone?"

"Because I wanted you to break our rule."

"So you could punish me?" My behind still smarted as I asked the question.

"No, so I could see you again. I told you that I take what I want. I didn't want to take you. I wanted you to come back to me because you wanted me."

Another renegade tear descended my cheek.

Nox wiped it away with the pad of his thumb. "Don't cry, princess."

"I wanted to call you… "My phrases were separated by my stuttered breathing. "So many times I stared at your number, but my life is… was… hell, I don't know… it's crazy. I wanted to concentrate on school. And then it all imploded. I just wish I hadn't signed and you hadn't signed. I wish this was real and not a business agreement."

He kissed my forehead. "As far as I'm concerned it's real. I'm sorry you don't feel that way."

"But you made a point…"

His kiss moved to my lips. "I'm an ass. You'll learn that, if you haven't already."

I wasn't sure how to respond to that.

"I was livid when I learned of your agreement." He took another deep breath. "I wasn't planning on telling you this until I got my point across, but something tells me I've succeeded in doing so." He gently kissed me. "I didn't learn about your profile because I'm a client. I've never been a client."

My eyes narrowed. "W-What do you mean?"

He sighed. "Demetri Enterprises is heavily invested in Infidelity. I hate the company. I'm constantly concerned about its ability to stay covert. Deloris monitors it, making sure all their systems are hack-proof."

"So you didn't?" I shot up from his lap. "You didn't sign my agreement. You didn't buy it?"

Nox shook his head.

"B-But I received my first check."

"I said I'm an ass. I just kept thinking if you would've gone into the system, the people or person… I couldn't…" He stood and seized my shoulders. "Agreement or not, you're mine. You were mine from the first time I saw you in Del Mar. I just needed you to see that."

"So you lied to me? All this talk of honesty and trust and *you* lied?"

"Not really."

"What the hell do you mean *not really*?"

"I paid to buy out your contract."

My stomach twisted. "You did what?"

"Demetri Enterprises is an investor. Infidelity isn't my company. I couldn't just pull you from the system. Your signing the agreement meant that the company—all the investors—expected a certain level of return on their investment. On you. I gave them that. I bought out your year. Your name is gone from their records. I bought your freedom."

I staggered back to the sofa, sinking down. His words circled my mind: *Bought. Freedom. Investment.* "You were going to let me think that I was your *expensive whore*?"

"For a while," he admitted. "Like I said, I was mad. I wanted you to understand the ramifications of what you'd done." Nox fell to his knees with his hands on mine. "I didn't want you to experience it, not with someone else." He looked down, took a deep breath, and looked back up. "I'm a selfish bastard. I wanted you. I took the opportunity, and now you know the truth.

This is real. You're mine because I want you, not because I bought you.

"You could walk away anytime you want."

This changed everything. "What about living with you? I should stay in my own apartment."

Disappointment laced his response. "If that's what you want, but security is still non-negotiable."

My eyes widened. "I almost forgot… something Chelsea remembered."

Nox's grip of my knees tightened. "What?"

"Before I tell you, remember that we don't know what this means."

"Tell me. Now."

"She remembered the man attacking her. After he knocked her down, when he rolled her over and saw her face, he said she was the wrong one."

"Fuck!" Nox stood in one swift move. "No. You're not moving into your own apartment."

"You can't make me—"

Standing, he pulled me from the sofa into his arms. "I sure as fuck can. We don't need a written agreement. We don't need a fucking company. You, Alexandria Collins, are mine. You agreed to that, and I'm not letting you go, not without one hell of a fight. You've been seen with me. There are already social media posts. You're mine to keep safe, and I intend to do that. That also means away from your high school boyfriend."

Each phrase came forth with more determination than the one before.

"Do you have a problem with any of that?"

It was what I'd wanted, what I'd wished for. This was real, and hell yes, I wanted it too.

I lowered my lids, peering up at him through a veil of lashes. "No, Mr. Demetri, I don't have a problem at all."

I jumped as he swatted my tender behind. "Ouch, I'm a tad sore if you don't remember."

His gaze glistened as the rising sun seeped from the edge of the curtains, causing his light blue to sparkle. "Oh, I remember. I want more than your ass sore, and if it's not, I didn't do a very good job."

On the tips of my toes, I brushed my lips against his. "Real… this is real?"

"Yes, princess."

"I'm yours and you're mine?"

"Stop saying that like a question."

I had so many more questions, yet for the first time, I also had answers. The way he had berated my employment while being a client no longer seemed hypocritical. It now made sense. I wondered how much my freedom cost him and at the same time, was thankful to him and Deloris for saving me from my own impetuousness. None of my questions or concerns seemed as important as my new reality.

My smile broadened. "If I say '*Yes, Mr. Demetri*' will it result in another spanking?"

His grin quirked, lifting one cheek while pressing his full lips together. With the menacing gaze that twisted my insides, he asked, "Why don't you try it and find out?"

CHAPTER 32

CHARLI

AFTER WE STEPPED from the plane in New York, Deloris introduced Nox and I to a handsome, older gentleman. He wasn't actually old, but he was older than Isaac.

"Mr. Demetri, Miss Collins, may I introduce Jerrod, Miss Collins's new driver."

This man wasn't only my driver, but my bodyguard too, someone with whom I'd be spending plenty of time. I noticed Nox eying him up and down as they shook hands. Jerrod's dark hair mixed with white gave him a distinguished look, and his eyes were sharp and respectful of his employer. In his dark suit, my new companion appeared fit, not muscle-bound, but capable of protecting me.

"Hello, Jerrod," I said, extending my hand. "Please call me Alex."

"Ma'am," he said, taking my hand.

"Any questions," Nox said, "direct them to Mrs. Witt. If there's ever a problem or concern, contact me immediately."

"Yes, sir."

Before long, we were all in a dark limousine headed toward the city. Only Nox, Deloris, and I were in the back. Isaac sat in the front with Jerrod.

Through the closed dark glass I could only make out their silhouettes.

"He's been with Demetri for some time now. I consider him very trustworthy."

I wasn't sure if Deloris was reassuring Nox or me. For a moment, I considered pleading my case again for no bodyguard, but before the words formed, I knew my breath would be wasted. I thought of asking for Isaac—I'd gotten used to him—but I didn't. Nox and Isaac had more of a relationship than Isaac did with me. They had the same unspoken language that Nox and Deloris shared. I was the new person to the whole Demetri equation. It made sense that I'd have the new bodyguard.

In no time, the three of us were busy with emails and text messages. I didn't pay attention as Deloris and Nox discussed business. Their speaking of names I didn't recognize and exchanging looks became the background to my own thoughts.

I had a few text messages from Chelsea. The doctors were letting her out of the hospital in the morning. She planned to spend some time with her mother before moving to New York. I'd already informed Deloris of her plans. After Chelsea packed a suitcase for her visit with her mother, Deloris had movers ready to bring everything else to my apartment near the campus. Apparently, that was the destination of everything except my personal items. Those were going to Nox's apartment—our apartment.

Living with him without being required to do so made me happy. I wanted to wake up in his arms and fall asleep listening to him breathe. The idea of settling into a routine with the handsome man beside me excited me more now that I knew Infidelity wasn't party to it.

I didn't like that I was relying on him for my expenses, but he assured me it was what he wanted to do. That made it better than him having to do it because of an agreement. Of course, it also meant that either of us could walk away at any moment.

It made it real.

I texted Chelsea back to let her know we arrived. There were four new text messages from Bryce. I decided to delete them without opening any. I could read the first few words, but I chose not to. I'd made up my mind. I didn't care what he said.

I also had one text message from my mother. It was from her, but not from her phone. I wouldn't let myself think about that, about Alton and what she went through with that monster. I never understood why she put up with him or why she made me put up with him. Instead, I thought about seeing her without him.

Adelaide: "WILL ARRIVE BEFORE NOON. BRUNCH?"

I texted back to Jane's phone.

Me: "YES. LET ME KNOW WHERE."

Scrolling through my endless stream of emails, I found a few from my student counselor at Columbia. One gave a breakdown of my impending schedule. My fingers trembled with excitement. This was happening, my dream—and my fairytale. When I mentally added the last part of my thought, a silly grin graced my lips, and I caught a quick glance of the handsome man beside me.

I was busy pulling up the attachments and making notes when I looked up and realized we weren't in Manhattan. We were traveling too fast and too far.

I saw a sign for I-95 north just before the car slowed to exit the highway.

"Where are we? Where are we going?"

Nox looked up and reached for my hand. His furrowed brow and protruding neck muscles said more than his words. His comfortable demeanor from this morning and the plane were gone.

"I was trying to avoid this, but our trip made our relationship public quicker than I anticipated."

The scenery around us changed quickly, from the interstate to a nice neighborhood of manicured lawns and large homes. The houses grew larger as we continued. There were now driveways blocked by iron gates. Every now and then, when a break in the trees and houses gave way, the glistening of blue water would catch my eye.

"Where are we?" I asked again.

"Rye, New York."

"Rye? Westchester County? You were trying to avoid showing me your house?"

Nox took a deep breath and looked to Deloris, sitting across from us. "It is my house," he explained. "But it's also my family's house."

My heart beat faster. "Your family? I'm going to meet your family?"

I suddenly thought of Montague Manor and my attire. I'd only planned on traveling. I was wearing jeans and a comfortable flowing top. My hair was secured in a low side ponytail, and I wasn't wearing much in the way of makeup. "Nox, I-I'm not dressed to meet your family."

His serious expression shattered into a grin at my surge of panic. Tugging my hand to make me lean closer, he kissed me. "You're beautiful. My father doesn't deserve the grand treatment."

My hand fell to his thigh, feeling the denim below my fingers. At least this time we were both dressed casually. "Your father," I repeated. "Your mother?"

"Got tired of his shit a long time ago."

"They're divorced?" I thought she was gone, but then again, I didn't really know. I tried to learn as much as I could. *Shit!* We were stopped at a gate. Why hadn't he told me this sooner?

"They were," he confirmed. "Unfortunately, when she finally found happiness, she became ill."

The car stopped and I stared out at the front of the Demetri family home, a large modern stucco home with an ornate entry.

"She has passed," Deloris offered, completing Nox's brief explanation. "Lennox's father, Oren Demetri, usually resides in London. He's here, but will be leaving tomorrow."

"He wants to meet you," Nox added with an edge of apprehension.

Was this because I was seen with his son, or could he possible know what I'd done with Infidelity?

Isaac opened the door, and I hesitated. "Should I be nervous?"

Nox squeezed my hand. "No. I'm not letting you out of my sight. Just ignore most of what he says. He can be… brash."

We got out of the car and I fidgeted with my hair, waiting for Deloris, but she didn't move. Isaac closed the door with her inside.

"Deloris isn't coming?"

"No, Isaac will stay so he can drive us back to the city. Jerrod is taking her home." Nox tugged my hand away from my hair. "Stop worrying. You look beautiful."

"Back to the city? Tonight?"

Before he could answer my question, we both turned to the opening of the front door.

"Mr. Demetri," the woman with a welcoming smile said. "It's good to see you. Your father has been waiting."

"Thank you, Silvia. California is a long way away." He stopped before the woman. "Silvia, this is Alex Collins, my… girlfriend."

I felt like a teenager the way that title made me smile.

"Alex, this is Silvia, the longtime property manager and all-around boss of this house."

A bit of my nervousness waned at her welcoming manner.

"Miss Collins, it's nice to meet you. I haven't been here too long…" She winked. "…it's not like I have stories of a teenage Lennox or anything."

My brows went up. "Oh, Miss… Silvia, we do need to talk."

"No, you don't," Nox said with a grin as we entered the stunning foyer.

Unlike the shadows of Montague Manor, everything about the house was open and bright. The classic architecture boasted bleached wooden floors, light beige walls, and white woodwork. Fresh flowers adorned the large oval table in the entry. Beyond, farther into the house, the glistening waters of Long Island Sound were visible through tall windows.

"This is beautiful," I said, as much to Silvia as to Nox.

While he shrugged, Silvia smiled and replied, "Thank you. It's usually pretty lonely here. It's nice when people stay."

I had the feeling that comment was meant more for Nox.

"Your father's in his office. He's on a call, but I'll let you know as soon as he's available." She looked at me. "It's nice to have you here. I can't tell you how happy I am that Lennox brought someone here."

I heard the unspoken part, the *again.* That didn't mean I planned to recognize or vocalize it. Instead, I smiled and said, "Thank you. I apologize for not being more… presentable. We've been traveling."

"Oh nonsense. This is Lennox's home, not a formal occasion. You both are perfect. May I get you something, a drink after your travels?"

Nox pulled my hand toward the back of the house. "Some iced tea would be nice. First, I'm going to take Alex outside before the sun sets."

"Your father…"

"Can wait," Nox called over his shoulder.

I merely shrugged toward Silvia, my cheeks rising to expose my grin. Her smile was contagious. It seemed as if she genuinely adored Nox and might even approve of me. I couldn't help but compare her friendly reception with that of the staff at Montague. Theirs would be so much different and impersonal—well, except for Jane.

"I like her," I said as we stepped out through the glass door at the end of a long living room. My feet stopped at the magnificent view. "Wow."

More words didn't form as I took in his family's backyard. We were standing on a block patio that led to and surrounded a lovely crystal-blue pool. Beside the pool was what appeared to be a pool house, made mostly of windows. Beyond the pool was an expanse of green grass, freshly mown with perfect stripes, alternating dark and light green. The lawn led down to the beach where a narrow strip of brown separated the green from the blue. The water sparkled with shimmers of the late-day sun. In the distance on the other side of the sound was what I believed to be New York. I tipped my head.

"Long Island," Nox said, answering my unspoken question.

"This is so pretty. Why don't you come here more often?"

"Let me take you down to the water."

I held tightly to his hand as we crossed the lawn, my shoes sinking into the soft grass. "We're putting footprints in the grass."

His blue eyes narrowed. "We're what?"

I looked behind us, seeing the crushed blades indicating our path. "We're leaving footprints."

Nox pulled my hand closer, causing me to bump against him. "You're cute." He kissed my forehead.

Small round bushes partially hid a short wrought-iron fence. Going to the gate, he led me down a few steps until we were standing on the brown sand.

Clusters of large rocks dotted the beach.

"There, princess, no more damage to the grass."

I ignored his comment, let go of his hand, and reached for a small pebble. Throwing it into the water, I said, "Seriously, this place is beautiful. Do you not live here because of the commute?"

He walked out to one of the large rocks, climbed on top, and sat with his knees near his chest. Leaning back on his arms, he tipped his chin toward the water. It was his invitation for me to join him. The shoes I wore were flats, but their soles were hard. Worried that I might slip, I slid my feet out of them and with bare feet climbed next to him. Having spent the day absorbing the sun's rays, the dark rock was warm under my touch.

"It holds memories," he finally offered.

"Your mother?" I asked, placing my hand over his.

He nodded. "Yes. She loved this house. It was one of the few good things he ever did for her. He was hardly here, which made it better. When they divorced the house was hers. She left it to me. Now, whenever he returns, he insists on staying here." Nox shrugged. "I'm not sure if he stays here out of guilt or what. All I know is that it's better to have him here than in the city."

"Did she remarry?" I asked, trying to avoid the multiple emotional landmines he'd dropped.

"No. The happiness she found wasn't with someone; it was on her own. After living with him for so long, she'd forgotten how to be her own person." Nox turned his gaze from the water to me. "That's why I want you to go to Columbia."

My chest ached as my heart swelled. He'd thought about this. It wasn't just saving me from Infidelity. He'd actually thought about my goals and dreams. "I-I don't know what to say."

"Say you're going to kick ass at Columbia like you did at Stanford. Say that when you're done you won't settle for anything but the best damn law firm out there. Or…"

"Or?"

"Or you could work for Demetri?"

I lifted my brows as I widened my eyes. "Mr. Demetri, I believe interviewing for a job as a lawyer is a bit premature."

Our foreheads came together. "I think I'd like the idea of being your boss."

"I thought you were, Mr. Demetri."

His kiss was soft, more tender than usual. As our tongues found one another, Nox turned his hand and intertwined our fingers. It made me wonder if this house held other memories, ones of Jocelyn, ones he wasn't ready to share.

We sat silently for a few minutes, enjoying the soft lap of the waves against the rocks and shore. Occasionally, a bird would swoop down, diving into the water and back out. It was amazing how peaceful it was. I loved the West Coast and the Pacific Ocean, but it was wild and untamed compared to the serenity of where we sat.

"Come on…" He stood, offering me his hand. "…let's get this over with so we can go back to Manhattan."

"You don't want to spend the night?"

"Not with Oren here. Do you?"

I lifted my shoulders before jumping to the sand and picking up my shoes. "I wouldn't mind, but I have a brunch date tomorrow."

Nox stopped. "A date?"

"Not as in *date.* It's my mother, and now I feel bad for not telling you. I didn't know if I was ready for you to meet her or learn about my crazy family. But now that I'm here meeting your father, I'm embarrassed."

He shook his head. "Don't be. We wouldn't be here if I could've avoided it."

"Why would you have avoided it?"

"Because I told you I want to keep you safe and away from all things bad. Princess, I'm bad because I had the best teacher. My father is the devil incarnate. If he hadn't learned about you from the media, I would've avoided this for at least a few months, until he was back in the US or we had to be in London."

There were so many things in that statement, but the last one took my attention. "London. Nox, I can't run off to London while I'm in school."

"I just told you that my father is the devil, and you're worried about missing classes. No wonder you graduated with honors."

I kissed his cheek. "I know the devil. He isn't your father. At the worst your father is a minion. I've got you beside me and Isaac somewhere in the shadows. I'm not worried."

CHAPTER 33

NOX

CHARLI WASN'T WORRIED, but I sure as hell was. Oren's message was odd and unexpected. He'd seen a picture of us and called. I either had my phone off or was busy beating the shit out of a punching bag. Either way, I didn't catch it. I did hear his message.

It said that he was leaving Sunday for London, and we needed to talk. He was pissed that I left town with him in New York—until he saw the picture. From one photograph he'd ascertained that I was obviously thinking with my dick instead of my brain. We had things to discuss, and I better not have wasted my trip to California.

In other words, I better have made progress with Senator Carroll. And lastly, he wanted to meet Alex, or did he say Alexandria? I thought it was Alex. After all, that was the name they used with the picture of the two of us at the San Francisco airport.

I waited as Charli stopped halfway up the lawn to slip on her shoes. I wasn't sure if she went part way barefooted to avoid damaging the grass or if it was to remove the sand from her feet. Whatever the cause, while I paused for her, I looked up at the house and saw him standing on the second-story balcony of the master bedroom watching. Even from a distance, our eyes met.

My blue eyes came from him. Sometimes when we would stare at one another, it was eerie how similar they looked. I imagined he was my reflection in another thirty years.

"Your iced tea is in the living room," Silvia called as we entered the side door.

"Thank you," Charli replied.

She'd been talking about the house when we both stopped, silenced by his presence. Oren Demetri stood there, his smile too wide, too friendly. For a moment, I had visions of the Joker. That made sense. If I were Batman, my nemesis would be the Joker.

"Hello." His voice boomed through the air.

"Alex, this is my father, Oren."

She extended her hand to shake, but when Oren reached for it, he turned hers palm down and gallantly kissed her knuckles. "Alexandria, you are lovely."

Charli's eyes widened at the use of her full name. *What the hell?*

"Mr. Demetri, it's nice to meet you. Nox has told me many nice things about you."

"Then it seems as though you two aren't to the honest stage of your relationship. My son rarely has a nice thing to say about me." He turned toward me and back to Charli. "And please, call me Oren."

"Oren, please call me Alex."

"Let's have a seat, shall we?"

"Actually, Oren," I said, "we've been traveling. I know you wanted to meet Alex, but why don't we discuss the progress with the senator privately. I'm sure Silvia can keep Alex occupied. Then we need to get back to Manhattan."

"Don't be ridiculous. We have five bedrooms plus the guesthouse. You two will stay here. I'm sure you can each find a room or only one. It's really none of my business."

Asshole.

"We would, but Alex has a meeting tomorrow, and I have work."

"Tomorrow is Sunday. No one has meetings or work."

"I do," Charli volunteered. "I have a luncheon planned with my mother."

Oren's eyes widened as he stared at Charli. The silence lingered a little too long. What the hell was his problem?

"Silvia!"

Charli and I both flinched as he yelled for Silvia. God bless that woman. Anyone else would have told him to go to hell. I think it was living here alone all these years. Doing that, she could put up with his occasional visit.

"Yes, Mr. Demetri?"

"I think something stronger than iced tea is appropriate."

"Dad…" I said as Charli shook her head.

"What will it be? Mixed drinks? Wine? Beer?"

He wasn't taking no for an answer. Sure. What the hell? We had Isaac to drive.

"Wine," I finally answered. "We'll both have a glass of red."

Oren smiled. "You like wine, my dear?"

Charli's hand found its way into mine. "Yes, I do."

"White until six and red after?" He asked.

Charli's grip stiffened as Oren looked down at his watch.

"Yes, it is after six."

"Well," she said, "I find that an acceptable timetable."

When Silvia returned, she placed a tray with three glasses of wine on the coffee table. "Miss Collins, may I show you around a little more? Or would you rather stay here?"

I nodded toward Charli.

"Thank you, Silvia. If you'll both excuse me, I'm excited to see more of your lovely house."

"It hardly compares to yours, but it's home," Oren mumbled as Charli stood.

What the fuck is he talking about?

Her complexion suddenly paled. I worried she might be ill as the glass of wine teetered in her grip.

"Excuse me? What did you say?"

"I said it's home, dear."

Her golden eyes searched mine. All I could do was furrow my brow. I didn't have any fucking idea what was happening. Slowly, she turned and Silvia led her away. Once they were gone, I leaned closer, picked up my glass of wine, and asked, "What the hell is going on?"

Oren dismissively patted my knee. "Let's talk about Senator Carroll before we discuss your latest conquest."

"The fuck? *My latest conquest.* Alex isn't a conquest."

"I'm well aware of who Alexandria Collins is. I'm curious if you are."

I stood. "What the fuck are you talking about."

"Senator Carroll, Lennox. Does he think we have the votes?"

"How about Severus Davis? Maybe it's time you come clean with me."

Oren leaned back and crossed his ankle over his knee. After taking a prolonged sip of wine, he replied, "That girl may be better at her job than I've given her credit. What would you like to know?"

"Why did you meet with him?"

"Because he's damn good at what he does."

"He works for the other side."

"Oh son, if only life were that easy. There aren't two sides in this or any other dealing. There are so many more. Let's take the tobacco giants, for example. I mean, look who's in bed with them. Do you think they're all against the legalization of marijuana?"

Who's in bed with them? Severus Davis, the man you're courting is the one in bed with them. I didn't say that. Instead, I said, "Mostly. I thought we were discussing Senator Carroll and the votes needed for the bill to clear the Senate Finance Committee."

"We are. Severus is working to get the bill to clear with the current wording. It will benefit the tobacco and alcohol giants."

"And cost us millions. Carroll thinks we could guarantee a few more votes if we promise to move a few distribution centers to California."

"Which will cost us millions. Where are you planning to pull them? Don't you think we'll piss off the voters in those states?"

Sitting, I sighed. "I was thinking about opening new facilities."

"New? Why?"

"You just said it. Marijuana will be legal for recreational use in California before we know it. Let's get in on the ground floor. Napa Valley is a great—"

"You're jumping ahead, and you didn't answer my question about tobacco."

"I did. Most would be anti-legalization."

"What if they wanted to partner with corporations like Demetri Enterprises?"

"Why?"

"What if they learned we were getting in on the ground floor?"

"How would they know that, unless you told Davis?"

"I didn't tell Davis. I was feeling him out."

"Go back to London, Dad. You're seeing conspiracies where they don't exist. I'm going to go find Char… Alex. We need to go."

"She called you Nox."

"So?" I answered defensively.

Oren tilted his head to the side. "I haven't heard that name in many years."

"Stop. Don't go there."

I lifted my eyes from my glass in time to see Charli's golden stare. By the shadows running through it, I knew she now saw what I'd warned her about. Oren Demetri was the devil.

"Excuse me," she said. "Is it a bad time for me to return?"

I finished the glass of wine, placed it on the table and stood. "No. Your timing is perfect. We're going."

Oren stood. "I would so enjoy getting to know you better. It seems that Lennox has other plans."

"I'm sorry, Mr. Demetri. I'm exhausted from traveling and have the brunch date tomorrow."

He nodded. "I understand. Perhaps the next time I'm in the States we can visit. Please give Adelaide my love, and tell her that her daughter is as beautiful as she."

Adelaide?

Before I could question aloud, I reached for Charli. She looked as though she might fall as she stumbled backward.

"Y-You know my mother?"

"Of course. For many years. I had no idea her little girl had grown into such a beautiful woman. I'm sure she's proud."

"What the fuck is going on?"

Oren patted my shoulder. "Son, language. You're in front of a lady, a true blue-blooded American heiress. I'm sure you already knew that."

I didn't speak as I looked from Oren to Charli. What the hell was he saying? She wasn't an heiress. She was penniless. She'd signed her life away at Infidelity. He was wrong. This was just Oren Demetri being evil, doing what he did best.

"Silvia," he called. "Let Lennox's driver know they're ready to leave."

"Yes, sir."

I didn't tell my father goodbye or wish him a safe journey. I wasn't thinking about pleasantries as I snatched Charli's hand in mine and marched us both out the front door. I still didn't know what was happening, but by the way her hand trembled in my grasp, I knew it was something big.

When I looked down, her cheeks were damp and her eyes closed.

I didn't let her sorrow register. If I did, I'd go back in the house and confront my father. Instead, I concentrated on the peacefulness of the outside. With the sun almost set, the driveway was illuminated by the indirect lighting that shone toward the house and guesthouse. The sound of nature—waves and insects—filled the air as stars began to pepper the sky. I missed seeing stars. In the city, if they could be seen at all, they weren't as vibrant as they were out here.

Her soft body leaned into my arm, clenching my hand with all of her might.

I'd blown up at Charli yesterday. I wasn't going to jump to conclusions based on anything that Oren Demetri said. Besides, I had Deloris. She knew more about Charli than I did. She told me about the loss of her trust fund. Maybe she was related to someone, but an heiress didn't rent out her companionship for a year. It didn't make sense.

The almost-blue shine of bright white headlights came from the garages as Isaac pulled a black Mercedes up to the door and stopped. Silently, we both entered the backseat. Leaving the gates, I leaned closer and whispered, "Tell me what in the hell he was talking about."

More tears fell as she opened her eyes wide and nodded toward Isaac. "Please, can this wait?"

Wait?

I didn't fucking want to wait. Then again, she was upset. I was the one who exposed her to Oren. It was my fault he upset her. I hated that motherfucker more with each passing day. He could go back to London and stay there for all I cared.

I took a deep breath and wrapped my arm around her shoulder. She seemed smaller and more fragile, as I hugged her close. Kissing her head, I said, "Yes."

Charli nodded against my chest.

As I stared out the window I thought about Oren's words. I concentrated on the part about Severus Davis, about the House bill, and about marijuana. It was all connected, but I already knew that. What I didn't understand was what he meant about sides. Metaphorically I understood.

Did he intend to side with big tobacco and alcohol on the fight against legalization? Or did he think they were secretly in favor?

Fuck!

I needed to do more research, ask more questions.

The sweet scent of Charli's hair filled my senses as her head moved with even breaths. I lifted her chin, but her eyes remained closed. Long, damp lashes lay against her cheeks. She was out. She'd fallen asleep against my chest. I gently smoothed a few loose hairs away from her face. In the pale light from the front seat, I saw the pink in her cheeks and soft rosiness of her lips and smiled.

In the house she'd looked as if she were about to faint. None of it made sense.

What did she mean when she said she knew the devil?

Surely now she knew she was mistaken. She'd just met him, and in a matter of minutes he had her stumbling and in tears. That was Oren Demetri. The man knew how to make a first impression.

CHAPTER 34

Fourteen years ago

ADELAIDE

"MRS. FITZGERALD. MRS. FITZGERALD."

Jane's voice infiltrated my dreams, pulling me back to reality. Wherever I'd been mentally was better than here, better than the master suite of Montague Manor.

"Mrs. Fitzgerald, it's after noon. Alexandria's been asking about you."

I opened my eyes, only to quickly shut them again.

Why is the room so bright?

The floral wallpaper was an assault on my eyes. The matching draperies, bed covering, even the velvet sofas were color coordinated. It was all newly remodeled, seemingly seconds after my mother's funeral. Alton had the designers drawing up proposals to make the master suite ours.

"Jane," I moaned as much as spoke. "It's another migraine. Close the drapes. It's too bright."

The sound of rustling fabric let me know she was doing as I said. Each noise was magnified, making it much louder than it should have been. Every sense was exaggerated. I shifted, trying to sit up, but the intense pressure behind my eyes stilled my movement. I settled back into the soft pillow with a groan.

A warm hand skirted my arm, the one outside the blankets. The light touch caused me to flinch. My arm was sore, but the movement brought flashing lights behind my eyelids, colors like fireworks or static, and more symptoms of a migraine. "Ma'am, your migraine left a bruise on your arm. Do you need some ice?"

I barely shook my head. "No. I-It's not what you think. I fell. It was my heels. They were too high last night." I reached for the blanket and tucked my arm beneath it. "Go. Let me sleep."

"You need some food."

Food. Even the thought increased the nausea that my movement incited. Nothing sounded remotely good. I'd been the one to finalize the menu for last night's function, yet I'd barely eaten.

"Go. Take care of Alexandria."

"She's fine. She be outside with Bryce. Hannah, his nanny, and Miss Suzanna. She here too. She's askin' about you."

Outside… oh, keep them away from the lake. I didn't say that aloud. Jane had heard me say it a million times. My entire body ached. It was like the flu, but worse. If only I could go back to sleep. That was where I'd find relief.

"Tell her I'm indisposed. Then call Dr. Beck. Tell him about my migraine, my *real* migraine. Nothing else. Ask him to send over something for the pain. Tylenol isn't working."

"Yes, ma'am. I'll call. Last time he say he need to see you."

"If he says that again, tell him I can't come in. I'm too ill. Besides I was in a week ago for my regular exam."

"Your momma used to say—"

I pried my eyes open to the dimmer large suite. Having the curtains closed helped. Nevertheless, Jane's face was blurry, weaving back and forth. "Stop," I interrupted. "My mother isn't here anymore and neither is my father. I'm the lady of the house. Do as I say."

"Yes, ma'am. And Alexandria?"

"You take care of her." *She won't even know I'm missing.* Russell's words never left my mind. He might be dead and gone, but the pain he'd inflicted lingered. It was just another reason to burrow myself into this bed and sleep.

No one would miss me, not until…

As long as I was awake and dressed before six, before Alton got home, it would be all right.

I closed my eyes with a sigh. The click of the closing door gave me peace in knowing I was once again alone. I gave in, fading into the world of my dreams, a world that didn't exist.

I was almost there when the nausea hit again. It pulled at my insides, churning the emptiness until bile bubbled, clawing its way up from the pit of my stomach. I threw back the covers and staggered hurriedly toward the bathroom. Straight lines were waves as my equilibrium adjusted. The room around me bent and twisted as I found the doorway. My long hair fell forward and I tried to bunch it in my shaking hand as heave after dry heave wracked my body.

Exhausted, I collapsed onto the cool tile and curled around the base of the toilet, perspiration dripping from my body and making my nightgown damp. I think I fell asleep, but for how long, I had no idea.

"Mrs. Fitzgerald?" Jane's concerned call woke me as she rushed into the bathroom. "Ma'am, what happened?"

"It's this damn migraine!"

How many times do I need to tell her?

"This one is worse than usual," I added, ashamed I'd yelled at the one person who always seemed to be there for me.

Jane helped me sit. I closed my eyes and listened to her deep motherly voice.

"I brought you some crackers and water. The doctor say you needs to drink."

"Is he sending me some painkillers?"

"Let me help you back to bed."

I let her help me stand and I asked again, "Painkillers? Something stronger?"

"He say he need to see you. He say he'll come here."

She supported me as I rinsed my mouth, trying to get rid of the terrible taste.

"That's ridiculous," I replied as she helped me to the bed. "No one makes house calls anymore."

"Dr. Beck will, for you, Mrs. Montague Fitzgerald."

She said that as if I needed a reminder of whom I was. "When?"

"He be out soon."

I closed my eyes with a sigh. I couldn't let Dr. Beck see my arm. It was bad enough that Jane noticed it. Then again, she'd noticed other things in the past too. "Jane, can you get me a long-sleeved gown and my robe?"

"Yes, ma'am."

Wearing a clean nightgown, I leaned against the headboard with a long sigh. Vomiting must have helped. Maybe I ate something bad at the dinner last night. I couldn't remember what I'd eaten. I did have wine. Maybe that was it.

Last night's function had been in the planning for nearly six months. When the idea was first proposed, it was to Mother and me. It wasn't long after Father's passing. The plan was for a fundraising dinner to jumpstart the Charles Montague II scholarship for Emory University.

Originally, Mother and I'd thought it should go to Emory. That was, after all, where Father and I both attended. As the plans became more solidified, Alton decided the scholarship should stay local. He reasoned that it looked better for Montague to support local endeavors. With Mother's recent passing, I was the only one to disagree. The scholarship was going to Savannah State University.

The dinner was successful, raising over thirty thousand dollars. Much more money was expected from donations, but this did what it was supposed to do and began the intake of funds while bringing media attention to the scholarship. It was also good publicity for Montague Corporation.

Over the years, I'd learned it didn't matter what I did. If I socialized at a function, it was too much. If I sat quietly, I was rude. Though Alton doted over me the entire evening and we appeared the perfect couple, I knew. In his gaze and touch, I could tell he wasn't happy. And then when I asked to leave earlier than he wanted, I'd crossed the final line.

His displeasure started to become evident in the car with silent treatment. That was never a good thing. It meant he was holding back, calculating and waiting until we were home alone. Not that Brantley would dare stop Alton from belittling me the entire ride. Now that Father was gone, no one stopped him.

Once we were in our suite, he didn't strike me. The bruise on my arm was from him grabbing me. It was my reminder to pay attention and hear every degrading, derogatory thing he had to say. Apparently, it was much easier for Alton to yell when I was only inches away.

My only defense was that I had a headache coming on. That was why I wanted to leave the dinner. As I rubbed the sleeve of my robe, feeling the tender skin beneath, I knew the headache wasn't a viable defense.

The knock on my door forced my eyes to open. I wiped the tear from my cheek and called toward the sound, "Come in."

This was unnecessary and bothersome. If Dr. Beck had sent out the medication instead of wanting to see me, I could be sleeping soundly with a much better chance of being the perfect wife by six o'clock.

"Adelaide," Dr. Beck said as he came closer. "I'm sorry you're in pain."

I'd known Dr. Beck since I was a student at the academy. He'd been a new doctor to the area, taking over an established practice. Since Father's doctor had been the one to retire, Dr. Beck inherited the privilege of the Montague family. "I am," I concurred. "This one is worse than normal. If you could, please prescribe something stronger."

"Before I do, I'd like you to do something for me."

I sighed. "What?"

"I was looking at your lab work from a week ago. Have you noticed any other symptoms?"

I closed my eyes. "No. It's my head. I've had migraines before. You've prescribed pain medicine before."

"What about your breasts?"

My eyes opened. "My breasts? What about them?"

"Have they been sore or tender?"

I thought about his question. "Maybe. I haven't thought about it."

"Any nausea or vomiting?"

"Yes. I just did. I vomited. But that happens with these headaches."

"Last week you said your last period was three weeks prior to your appointment. Have you begun menstruating?"

"No. "I squinted my eyes. "Dr. Beck, you know I can't get pregnant. You're the one who told me that."

He reached for my hand. "I said that with the damage your uterus sustained during Alexandria's birth, conceiving another child was highly unlikely."

"We had difficulty conceiving her. You made it seem like it was impossible."

"Before I prescribe you a narcotic pain controller, I want to be certain you're not pregnant."

The nausea was back as my skin became coated in a new round of perspiration. I wrapped my arm around my midsection. "I-I can't be."

"You and Alton haven't had sexual intercourse in the last month?"

"We have. But I can't. He doesn't think it's possible." I closed my eyes as tears streamed down my cheeks. "Please, he… I can't."

Dr. Beck opened the bag he'd brought with him and pulled out a pregnancy test. It wasn't elaborate, much like the ones sold at the store. "I'm your doctor. I have been for most of your life. I won't tell Alton anything you don't want him to know."

I couldn't believe I was thinking this way. I couldn't believe the words were in my head, much less the possibility of my saying them. I also couldn't give Alton Fitzgerald a child of his own. It was bad enough that I subjected Alexandria to him. I refused to sentence another child to life with him.

I pulled back the covers and reached for the box he offered. "Doctor, if this is positive, what are my chances of carrying this baby to term?"

"We both know it would be a very difficult pregnancy."

"Difficult for the baby or for me?"

"Both."

It sounded selfish, but I also couldn't leave Alexandria. I may not be the world's best mother, but I was the only one she had. Her only family now that Russell and my parents were gone. I couldn't fathom who would raise her.

There was always the possibility of Gwen and Preston or Suzanna. Or Suzanna and Alton.

I clenched my teeth. What would happen to Alexandria if Alton didn't need her?

Very few of my life's decisions had been left to me. I was making this one.

"If this is positive, I can't do it."

Dr. Beck nodded. "We can take care of it, and no one will know."

"Thank you, Doctor."

CHAPTER 35

CHARLI

I WOKE AS the world came into focus. Soft lips warmed my head as a deep velvet voice rumbled from my dreams to reality. And then I remembered… everything.

My breakdown was completely out of character, but I'd felt blindsided—my two worlds once again colliding. How had Nox's father known my mother? Now I'd need to tell Nox everything, and I didn't think I was ready for that. My parents' betrayal was still too raw.

I sat straight, wiping my lips and my eyes.

I'd fallen asleep on Nox.

I turned, disoriented, as he reached for my hand. "Sleepyhead, we're here."

The building outside the car's window was unfamiliar, the glass doors similar to so many in the city. "Where? Where are we?"

"My—our apartment."

My chin dropped. "Nox, maybe Isaac should take me to my apartment. I need to think for awhile."

"No. You can think here. You have no furniture, food, or anything in your apartment. And most importantly, my apartment is safe." He lifted my chin and brushed his lips against mine. "If that isn't enough, I'm here and I have a fully stocked bar. After the way you looked with Oren, I think you could use one or both."

I could definitely use the bar.

"Both," I finally said with a weary grin.

I avoided looking up at Nox as we made our way through the lobby and into the elevator. I didn't even notice the surroundings. I was sure the building was nice. Of course it was. None of it registered as I contemplated my impending explanation.

I hadn't meant to fall asleep in the car. It was the emotion and probably the glass of wine. The last meal we'd had was on the plane. As the elevator rose higher and higher, I thought less and less about what I needed to say and more about food.

"Do you have food?" I whispered, though we were the only two in the elevator.

Nox grinned. "The correct question is 'do *we* have food?' And the answer is yes. We also have a cook, but she wasn't expecting us for one more day. So we have food, but I have no idea what."

I nodded. "I can cook."

His pale eyes widened. "You can?"

"Yes." For some reason, Patrick came to mind. "I'm not a gourmet chef, but I can make a mean spaghetti and meatballs."

"Meatballs? You do realize you're talking to an Italian here."

"Well…" I paused, scrunching my nose. "I've always bought my meatballs frozen."

His free hand flew to his heart. "The sacrilege!"

"How about toasted cheese?"

"Grilled-cheese sandwich?" he asked.

"Same thing."

"It sounds wonderful." The doors opened. "What wine do you suppose goes with grilled-cheese sandwiches?"

"A California one," we both said in unison.

Nox opened the door and flipped a switch. Lights turned on throughout the living room and dining area like soft-white liquid washing away the darkness. This building was older than Patrick's, but still modern by New York standards. The oak flooring contrasted with the light-colored walls. Like Patrick's apartment, the impressive feature was the windows. Two adjoining walls were filled with floor-to-ceiling windows. The view of the lit-up city was stunning in each direction.

He reached for my hand. "Let me show you around."

Silently, I agreed, following close behind as Nox took me from room to room. The first direction took us to a small hall with three doors. One led to a bathroom. The next led to a small bedroom with a queen-sized bed and other bedroom furniture. The last door opened to a larger bedroom, beautifully decorated in shades of brown and green. The four-poster bed was a California king that dominated the room. Directly across the room was a fireplace with a flat-screened television above. Near the windows showcasing more of the gorgeous city view sat a plush chair with a matching ottoman. Connected to the bedroom was a dressing room about the size of the first bedroom, except long and narrow with a padded bench in the middle. The walls were lined with cabinets and drawers. At the far end of the dressing room was a big, beautiful bathroom complete with a shower that had showerheads coming from all directions. The garden tub also had a view of the city below. The bathroom was accessible from the dressing room as well as the bedroom directly.

When we completed the circle, and came back to the bedroom, I said with a smirk, "I'll take this room."

"Yes, princess, you will."

"I hope you don't mind the smaller one."

His lips quirked into a grin. "I'd ask you the same question, but as you know, you get the large one."

I shook my head.

The other direction from the dining area was another hallway. It led to an office, a workout room, and another full bath.

"If you need your own office to study, we can have the second bedroom converted."

"But if you did that, then where would you sleep?"

He squeezed my hand. "All of your things from the Mandarin and from our trip are here. I meant what I said about shopping. Get whatever you need. The weather's different here than it is in Palo Alto. I'm sure you'll need things."

I didn't want to think about spending more of his money.

"Do those doors near the table lead to the outside?"

Nox led the way and opened the door. The balcony was the length of the dining area and the office. There was a small table for two as well as long chaise lounges. We were high above the city. "Nox, this is gorgeous. I love the view."

"Do you want to make those famous sandwiches or tell me what my father was talking about?"

"If that's an either/or, I'll make sandwiches."

"It's not," he said as we went back inside.

I rummaged through the refrigerator while Nox found bread and a frying pan.

"Does your cook live here?" I asked.

"If I want to live on grilled-cheese sandwiches she will."

"As I said… spaghetti."

"Not with frozen meatballs."

"They're not frozen once they're cooked."

"Her name is Lana," he said. "She lives in the building and works for multiple tenants. She also cleans and does laundry."

I nodded as I buttered the bread. "I don't know where to start. Remember when you said that my not knowing your past was refreshing?"

"Yes."

"The feeling was mutual. I wasn't hiding my family… I just don't like them. I spent four years in California pretending they didn't exist."

"Tell me how you're an heiress, whatever the fuck that means, and why you resorted to Infidelity."

The bread sizzled against the hot pan. "I had a trust fund and then I didn't. I was desperate. Someone told me about Infidelity. I went on the interview. It's just as I said. It was all true."

"How does my father know who you are?"

I shrugged as I flipped the sandwiches over. "From the photo in the media, I presume. It had my name."

"Alex Collins," Nox said. "I'm sorry. I'm pretty good at names. Hilton, Trump—I would've figured that out. Collins? I'm coming up blank."

"Collins was my father's name. And before you ask, yes, he's deceased. My mother's maiden name…" My head dropped forward as butterflies grew to bats in my stomach, making the sandwiches less appealing. "…is—"

Nox appeared behind me, his solid arms around my waist. "Wait. Before you tell me this—because I have the feeling it's important—let me pour our wine. Let's enjoy the summer's night on the balcony, eat our sandwiches, and bask in the fact that we met face to face with the devil and made it out alive."

I tilted my head against his hard chest. "What if we didn't?"

He spun me around and I looked up.

"We did, Charli," he said. "We're here."

"What if we can't escape, and what if there's more than one devil?"

"Then we'll survive, because there are two of us." He lifted my eyes to his and cupped my cheeks. "When I used to think about you, after Del Mar, when I didn't know if I'd ever see you again, I used to think about your beautiful eyes."

The pads of his thumbs caressed my cheeks.

"They're stunning and distinctive. Sometimes, when you didn't know I watched you, I saw shadows. I still do."

I tried unsuccessfully to look away, but his hold wouldn't budge. He was right. I hated how well Nox knew me without my telling him. I'd never considered myself to be transparent. Nevertheless, Nox saw inside of me, into my soul.

"I wondered about them," he went on. "How does someone as young and successful as you have shadows? I believe whatever you're about to tell me will answer at least part of that question."

I nodded. "You have them too. I saw them yesterday."

"I do." His chest inflated and deflated. "Charli, I won't rush you. Our agreement doesn't exist. Don't go anyplace to find the answers. I want you to wait until you're ready, until you're strong enough."

"I'm not going…"

He touched my temple. "In there. Don't go there." Then he touched my heart. His hand lingered, not sexually, but reverently. "Or in here. If you've buried things for a reason, don't uncover them until you can."

Suddenly, Nox let go of me as the stench of burning toast reminded us of our sandwiches.

"Shit!" I exclaimed as I turned back to the stove and moved the pan away from the hot burner.

Nox pulled two plates from the cupboard, and I scooped the sandwiches from the pan and plopped them on the plates, placing the golden brown side facing up.

I pursed my lips as I used the spatula to lift one corner of the sandwich and peek at the darker side. "That was your fault."

"Mine? You're the one claiming culinary genius."

"You distracted me."

He took the spatula from my hand and examined it closely. "Hmm. I just had an idea."

Snatching it away, I said, "I have one too. It involves wine. I'll take our sandwiches to the balcony."

Nox's sandwich was gone and mine was half-eaten when he refilled my glass of merlot.

"I guess it wasn't inedible?" I asked.

He grinned. "Well… I didn't want you to feel bad."

"Fine. Keep the cook. I have studying that I need to be doing anyway."

He reached for the remaining half of my sandwich and asked, "Are you going to eat this?"

"I was."

Tearing it in half, he handed me back the quarter. "I was hungrier than I realized and your cooking is divine. Now, onto whatever you were about to say in the kitchen before we were distracted by smoke."

I did my best glare, sending pretend daggers his way before nibbling another bite of my sandwich. As I washed it down with a hearty drink of wine,

I formulated my response. "My mother's maiden name is Montague." I stopped, waiting to see if it registered.

Does he know the name? Will it matter?

For what seemed like the longest time, he didn't move, not even a blink. Then he stood and walked to the clear banister with the silver railing and turned his back toward me.

"Montague?" he asked, looking out onto the city's lights. "I don't suppose Shakespeare wrote a play about your family?"

"Different Montagues, I believe."

He turned around, his arms crossed over his chest. The position pulled the seams of his shirt, straining them against his shoulders. "As in Montague Corporation—tobacco."

"Yes."

Nox's demeanor tensed. Just as quickly he seemed to see *me*. "You're the fucking heir to Montague Corporation and some asshole investors lost your trust fund? Why the hell didn't your family's legal team sue their ass? Why hasn't it been replaced? How the fuck did you end up at Infidelity?"

Each of his questions came louder than the one before.

I didn't respond at first. I didn't have the answers. I also didn't cry. I'd cried too many tears. Finally, I said, "It wasn't lost. It was reallocated. Deloris offered to look into it for me."

Nox ran his hand over the scruff of his face. "Reallocated? Deloris knows about this, but I didn't?"

"Deloris… well…" I shrugged. "…Deloris knows everything."

Nox nodded.

"I-I didn't want to talk about it," I continued. "It's still too raw."

The way his broad shoulders relaxed relayed his understanding. "I won't rush you, but you know, with Deloris and Demetri resources…"

"Please don't. I don't want to need them."

After a prolonged silence, Nox asked, "My father knows your mother?"

"I guess. It surprised me, too."

"Your mother will be here tomorrow?"

"Yes."

"Does she know what happened to your trust fund?"

"Yes." I finished the glass of wine and left it on the table as I walked toward him. His arms uncrossed in a silent invitation. The beat of his heart strengthened me. I craned my neck upward. "She knows because she sat there and watched as Satan himself took it from me."

Nox's embrace tensed, and then he rested his chin on the top of my head. "You don't need it, princess." He moved me to arm's length and looked at me curiously. "You *are* a princess, by American standards."

I shrugged. "I've never felt like one, not until I met you."

He brought me back to his chest. "You don't need the shadows or the devil… Satan, Lucifer, Alton Fitzgerald, or whatever name he goes by these days."

Every cell in my body went rigid. "You know him?"

"Not personally, but Montague Corporation has a reputation. Your stepfather is part of that."

I sighed. My temples throbbed, but my conscience was clear.

"Your schooling is secure," Nox reassured. "And you don't owe me anything except clear golden eyes for as long as you're willing to share them."

I looked up at the handsome man holding me in his arms. "If you keep saying sweet things like that, I may let you sleep in my room."

His chest rumbled with welcome laughter.

"You know," I went on, "if I'm a princess, I'm pretty sure that makes you Prince Charming."

"Not even close."

CHAPTER 36

One week ago

ADELAIDE

ALEXANDRIA'S PARTY WAS over except for a few remaining gentlemen with Alton in his study. They were talking and laughing. I didn't need to enter to know they were also drinking. I didn't care. Part of me hoped they'd continue until after I was asleep, and he was too drunk to notice.

On my way to our suite, I passed the kitchen and reminded the staff to clean each room as well as the patio. I had few responsibilities: the manor and the household staff were two of them. When we woke in the morning, if so much as a stray glass was found, I'd be the one to hear about it.

Other than the little blow-up in Alton's office, I wanted to think the night was a success. Alton was happy that Senator Higgins and Severus Davis were among the attendees. I didn't see Marisa Davis tonight. Perhaps she had her own party planned. Not everyone had as open a marriage as those two. I shook my head. The world was changing.

If only Alexandria would curb her remarks around Alton. The tension between the two of them was thick enough to cut with a knife. Perhaps it was my fault for not insisting that she understand her responsibility as I had. The way I saw it was that times were changing. I wanted—no needed—Alexandria to do her duty and marry Bryce. I didn't want her to feel trapped. I knew that feeling all too well. Unfortunately, Alton wasn't familiar with rebuttals and didn't receive them well.

As I made my way to the suite, I caught a glimpse of Alexandria and Bryce headed outside.

In our suite, I slipped out of my dress and heels, and wiggled my toes in the plush carpet of the dressing room. I'd seen the way Alton had looked at Suzanna when we were all in his office. Now with him downstairs drinking, there was a good chance I wouldn't be wearing my nightgown all night; nevertheless, I planned to enjoy it while I could. Pulling the pink satin over my head, I wrapped my robe around me and washed my face.

With a glass of Montague Private Collection cabernet in hand, I walked from our suite, down the long second-floor hallway and made my way to the library, more than a little curious about what was happening outside. The second-story windows in the library faced the back of the house.

Thick draperies hid me from the outside world as I stood at the tall leaded pane and took in the view of outdoors. The black sky sparkled with stars, little white dots shining with zest, competing with the large summer moon. The silvery rays of moonlight illuminated the estate, changing the color of the familiar red earth and green grass. The small lake my great-grandfather commissioned near the turn of the twentieth century shimmered like diamonds in the moonlight.

I twisted the large rock on my left hand. My mother's ring was equally as large. Charles Montague II couldn't allow his wife's ring to be less than his mother's. That diamond was secured away, waiting for the day Bryce would put it on Alexandria's finger. I'd been looking at some of the more modern settings. We could add to the large center stone. When the time came, I planned to ask Bryce what he wanted to do.

Bringing the glass to my lips, I sipped, watching the two shadowed figures make their way across the expanse of grass to the lake's edge. Warmth washed through me, the culmination of sacrifice and dedication. The children weren't standing on the edge of a lake, but on the edge of our future. I couldn't wait to have Alexandria back under the roof of Montague Manor, back in Savannah and with Bryce.

Nearly twenty years ago her fate was sealed. I sighed, leaning against the tall window casing. For almost two decades one goal had sustained me, for Montague to be hers. I've waited, not quite twenty years for the four of us to be a family. The future was close enough to touch. The anticipation brought hope to my soul and the jitteriness of pure exhilaration as I couldn't recall feeling.

My beautiful, intelligent daughter didn't know that she carried the weight of her family on her shoulders. I hadn't wanted her to know. I'd wanted her to experience life in a way I never did. When she left for Stanford, I knew it was a temporary reprieve, that eventually she'd be summoned home. I also knew the experience would be good for her. It would help her be stronger.

Just because her marriage was planned since she was a preschooler didn't mean she couldn't play a more vital role. I believed she would. Bryce wasn't Alton or Charles. He would be a good husband, a loving husband, the kind of man my daughter deserved. It would help that they were friends.

I was surprised to hear that she and Bryce were never intimate. While Suzy seemed displeased that Alexandria had never—what had she said?—*'helped him out,'* I was once again proud of my daughter's resolve. She did admit she wasn't a virgin. She's also almost twenty-four years old. Bryce wasn't a virgin either.

I shook my head. I don't know what that boy was thinking. This would all be much easier if we didn't have the incident with Melissa Summers hanging over our heads. Then again, it could work in our favor, his plea for her help being the final straw to bring her back.

In a way, it gave me hope. I could never imagine Alton asking for my help the way Bryce had today, in front of all of us. He was brave and had a good heart.

I took another glance toward the lake. The two children were standing facing one another. Their silhouettes stood out from the shimmering lake behind them. Bryce didn't even know the timetable, that by Christmas of next year they must be wed. That was why it was better to push for earlier, maybe *this* Christmas.

While the prospect of the impending marriage excited me, there was a twinge of guilt over the loss of Alexandria's law degree. After all, I was proud of her accomplishments. Being accepted at both Yale and Columbia was impressive. At the same time, Alton was right. It was a waste of money for a degree she'd never use, never need. I'd tried to reason that Montague Corporation had a legal team. She could work for herself. At the very least, it would give her more basis for understanding the workings of Montague, something I'd never been able to do.

He didn't agree. Bryce would provide.

I didn't correct him, but in actuality, Alexandria's name would be the provider.

Their marriage would seal the arrangement I agreed to years ago, but a baby…

I took another drink.

…A baby would cement it forever. It would join the Carmichaels and Montagues. Hell, it would join the Carmichaels, Fitzgeralds, and Montagues. Our grandchild would be the purest of blue-blood Southern royalty. Of course, people could only know about the Fitzgerald connection in name. The truth would cause too many problems.

Bryce was already fighting the accusation of rape and assault. He didn't need the world to know he was the bastard son of Alton Fitzgerald.

"Laide."

As if thinking his name had summoned the devil himself, my breath caught in my chest. "In the library," I called, not moving from my hiding place in the drapes.

Alton's footsteps reverberated through the large room as he came closer. "What are you doing?"

In my soft, flat slippers, Alton stood much taller and broader than I, even now with him in his mid-sixties.

"Shhh." I reached for his hand and pulled him closer. "Look."

He leaned toward the window. "Is that Bryce and Alexandria?"

"Yes." I couldn't contain the smile. "It's going to work. I can feel it."

"Don't try to change my mind about the trust fund. I let you convince me to allow her to go out west. How many times did she come home during the four years?"

I swallowed. "She's home now."

"And that mouth of hers. Really, Laide, you should be ashamed of the daughter you raised."

The small hairs on the back of my neck prickled. I'd done this dance so many times I could do it in my sleep. Agree with him, let him say his piece, and call it a night. I turned my gaze back to the lake. Pride in my daughter washed through me.

"I'm not," I replied.

"What?"

I turned back to Alton. "I'm not ashamed. I'm not fighting you about her trust fund. I want her home. That will do it. She'll learn to adjust, but I'm not ashamed of her."

Even in the darkness, I knew his neck and face were turning red. I didn't need to see the crimson. The color would be muted with only the light of the moon. I could feel it, feel the temperature rising.

"Of course you're not," he said, stepping close to me. The warmth of his growing fury became evident against my breasts. "Tell me why you didn't prepare her for tonight's meeting with Bryce and Suzy." He gripped my arm.

I didn't flinch. My eyes stayed locked on his. It was part of the dance.

"And why you thought it would be a good idea to allow her to embarrass all of us with her insolent responses. All you needed to do was to inform her today while you were out. That's what you said you were going to do."

I kept my tone even. "We were having a nice time. I mentioned that Bryce would be here, but she said she hadn't spoken to him. I was under the impression they did speak. You made it sound as if they did."

He took one last look out the window.

"Bryce has even made it seem as if they did. How does he know so much about what she's been doing?"

When Alton didn't answer, I added, "Have you told him?"

"Don't turn this around on me. You failed. You wonder why I don't trust you with more things. Jesus, Laide, you can't seem to handle much more than consuming your body's weight in wine."

I tried not to listen, not to let his words sink in. Instead, I thought about Alexandria, about how close it all was. All the years and it was coming together.

Once they were married, Montague would be hers and Bryce's. There were provisions for Alton and me, but my role would be over. It had been years since I'd read the agreement, and I wanted to check with Ralph Porter, but I was pretty sure that once Alexandria was married, I would no longer need to be.

Alton's monologue continued down the hallway and into our suite.

It wasn't a dialogue. It rarely was.

CHAPTER 37

CHARLI

"MORE WATER, MISS? Perhaps a drink while you wait?"

I looked down at my phone again. It wasn't like my mother to be late. I could easily compile an entire list of faults for Adelaide Montague Fitzgerald, but tardiness wasn't one of them.

I considered the offer of alcohol, but decided a clear head should prevail. "No, thank you. The other member of my party should be here any minute."

The Rainbow Room was one of the most ostentatious places in Manhattan to have Sunday brunch. I would've preferred one of the little restaurants in SoHo or even Tom's Restaurant, but this was more up my mother's alley. I wasn't the least bit surprised when she suggested it. Besides, I couldn't picture her sitting in a vinyl booth with Formica tabletops, even if it was iconic.

For a little more privacy as well as a spectacular view of the Empire State Building, I'd requested a table in the lounge. The restaurant was beautiful and newly renovated, but the clatter of diners as well as the gigantic buffet would make our uncomfortable reunion all that more difficult. And in the lounge, Jerrod could sit at the bar and inconspicuously keep his eye on me and everyone around me. Thus far we'd only said a few words to one another, but my new driver slash bodyguard seemed professional and competent. As I glanced his direction and our eyes instantly met, I knew he definitely had the omnipresent thing covered.

Nox's revelations as last night continued were borderline humorous. We were almost asleep when he sat up and said, "You have had drivers before, haven't you?"

I just laughed and waited for him to lie back down so I could cuddle close.

Though technically I was penniless, there was something about evening the playing field that was comforting for both of us. There was no doubt I appreciated Nox's financial support, but his realizing that money wasn't new to me did something for my self-esteem. Despite the entire Infidelity thing, I wasn't an expensive whore after his money.

The sight of my mother being ushered toward me brought me back to present. In the few seconds it took for her to reach my table, I did what I was sure she too was doing: assessing. She looked exactly the same as she did a week ago, the perfect Southern lady properly dressed with her chin held high. Adelaide had the look of complete superiority mastered. The only difference between today and a week ago was that today her eyes were clear, not red or puffy.

Did she expect mine to be? Was this meeting supposed to be where I begged her for my birthright?

As she approached, I stood, wondering what to say to my own mother. She stopped in front of me and nodded to the maître d', who quietly thanked her and backed away. The clatter of dishes and voices of other patrons disappeared as the tightness in my chest grew.

Before my very eyes, Adelaide Fitzgerald's mask of perfection shattered. Apprehension, concern, perhaps even love twisted her customary expression. The façade she'd worn for most of my life fell to the floor, shards of flawlessness broke into a million pieces as she wrapped her arms around me, squeezing my shoulders with more emotion than I could recall her ever showing.

I didn't move or reciprocate. I was paralyzed and dumbfounded.

I'd been mentally prepared to meet her ice with ice. I'd been ready to bask in my victory of remaining in school with the ability to live in New York, and all without her or Alton's help. But this was different. The woman clinging to me in the middle of a Manhattan lounge high above the city was *my momma.* Tears prickled my perfectly painted eyes as my arms found their way around her quaking shoulders as she cried silently.

Finally, she pulled away, her hands still on my arms and looked at me. It wasn't the scan for imperfections I was accustomed to. Her blue eyes glistened with tears. She was looking in my eyes, really looking.

"Alexandria, I love you."

I couldn't speak, could only nod as we both took ragged breaths and sat.

"May I start you ladies out with something from the bar?"

We both turned to the waiter who had either been watching our public breakdown or magically appeared out of thin air. "Yes," we said at the same time. Again our eyes met as our cheeks rose.

"May I suggest our Bloody Mary?"

"That sounds perfect," Mother said. "Alexandria?"

"Yes, thank you."

She reached out for my hand. "Darling, you're beautiful. I've been so worried about you, about how you'd live."

The indignation I'd harbored for the past week found its way back through the emotion. I kept my voice low. "You weren't worried enough to stop Alton from stealing my trust fund."

"Are you truly going to start with accusations? I came all this way to see you and your school and you're going immediately for the jugular?"

My school? Like this was second grade at the academy and I was going to show her the papier-mâché ornament I made.

I sat taller and smoothed the napkin over my lap. "I'm so sorry, Mother. Perhaps we should discuss the lovely view. Do you see the Empire State Building over there?"

Her lips pursed. "This is difficult for me."

"For you? Leaving me, the last Montague, penniless on the streets of New York is difficult—*for you*?"

"Dear, we never thought you'd leave. We never thought you'd walk away. That was your decision. You have a home. You don't need to be on the streets of New York." She leaned forward. "You aren't *on the streets*, are you, dear?"

The waiter placed our drinks. Undoubtedly sensing the tenor of our conversation, he wisely left without speaking.

"No, and you're right. It was my decision—my choice. I chose to have a life, one away from Savannah, one where I'm happy."

"You could be happy in Savannah," she replied.

"Like you?"

Her shoulders straightened. "I don't understand why you continue to say things like that, why you throw that in my face. Don't you realize that I did it all for you? You, Alexandria Charles Montague Collins. I did it for you."

I closed my eyes as I took a sip of my Bloody Mary. It was tart and strong, making my throat clench as the burn made its way to my stomach. Before its effects could numb the ache in my heart, I took another longer sip. "Then stop."

"Stop?"

She was stirring her drink with the large stalk of celery. Maybe that's what I should have done. I swear my sips were pure vodka.

"Yes, stop. If you're putting up with Alton and living under his thumb for me, stop."

After a prolonged drink, she spoke. Her tone was whimsical as if she were telling me a bedtime story. Not that I could ever remember her doing that. I was about to ask about Jane, but her words held my attention.

"Your father loved you very much. He didn't feel the same way about me."

I stared, silenced by her uncustomary honesty.

"He wanted to leave me, leave Montague, the company and manor. He detested everything to do with it, much like you."

There was something in that sad statement that gave me hope. Maybe I was more like my father than I ever knew.

"He didn't want to leave you. He told me that he'd take you with him.

You were all he cared about. He didn't want the money, name, or status. Only you."

I wiped a tear I didn't know I shed. "But he never got the chance?"

She shook her head. "No."

A new thought came to mind. He'd wanted to leave and then he died. My skin peppered with goose bumps. "Was he…? His accident…?" I couldn't make myself ask the question that churned the Bloody Mary in the pit of my stomach, a question I'd never before pondered.

"The police did a thorough investigation. There was no sign of tampering or foul play."

"So it was suspected? Why else would there be an investigation?"

"There are always investigations with accidents. Your father liked fast cars. He may have been driving that way because he was upset. We'd argued again over the telephone. He was on a business trip."

"Why haven't you ever told me this?"

Her slender shoulders moved up and down. "Alexandria, at what age is a daughter ready to learn the secrets of her past?"

"Did you love him? I've never heard you say you did."

She pressed her lips together before speaking. "Russell Collins was one of the few men I've loved. In college I believe we were both in love."

I exhaled. I wasn't sure why I wanted to know that, but it made me content to think that at some point in my mother's life, she was genuinely happy, that my parents were both happy.

"You may help yourself to the buffet at any time," the magically appearing waiter said as he refilled my water glass.

"Thank you."

As we stood, Mother reached for my hand and squeezed. "Dear, when I decided to visit you, I decided to share more than that story with you. Please give me time."

I squeezed her hand back and nodded.

The volume of the room increased as we made our way toward the buffet. Live entertainment crooned as chefs manned the many tables. Artesian breads, bagels, and rolls were just the beginning. There was a raw bar with tuna tartare and sushi, as well as an assortment of oysters, mussels, and crab. Traditional breakfast foods such as waffles, grits, potatoes, and eggs were also present. The dessert bar was too decadent to approach.

With plates overflowing we made it back to our table.

"Tell me about the man you're dating."

"I see you've spoken to Bryce," I said just before I took a bite of fruit.

"Yes. He's… well, heartbroken again. And Suzy…"

"He needs to move on." *And I don't give a rat's ass about Suzanna.* I didn't say the last part aloud.

"But, dear, you agreed just a week ago to stay in contact with him. He's been contacted by the Evanston police for a deposition."

My fork stopped somewhere between my mouth and plate. "I thought Alton had that all taken care of."

"He did. He had, but the girl's parents won't go away quietly. They're preaching something about clearing their daughter's name. They say she's a victim and since her name is public… well, it's all the fault of that campus newspaper."

"Stop, Mother. It's not the newspaper's fault. It's Bryce's."

Her blue eyes opened wide. "Alexandria, he didn't do it. She's just after money. That girl thought she found herself the goose that laid the golden egg. When Bryce rejected her, because you know his heart has always belonged to you, well, Melissa couldn't take it. She pursued him and convinced him to have sex. Then she had someone else batter her. With Bryce's DNA she had a case."

My head moved from side to side. "Talk about blaming the victim. Jesus, Mother, how in the world did you come up with that story?"

"I didn't. Suzy told me."

Melissa? Why does that name sound familiar?

"Oh, and I can see where she's impartial. Why would anyone do what you just described?"

"Things aren't always as they appear. The girl was living in a very nice apartment, yet her parents can barely pay their mortgage." Mother nodded as she took a bite of her brunch. "Yes, she was after money."

"You seriously think she had to convince Bryce to have sex? Do you think that was difficult? If he was done dating her, why did he do that?"

"You should ask him, dear. Talk to him. He's distraught over the deposition, especially now." Mother's blue eyes widened. "Just this week, she's gone missing. The evidence doesn't look good. He needs our support."

What the hell?

"The girl is missing?"

"Yes." She leaned closer and lowered her voice. "If you ask me, she knows that her lies will come out, and she's just trying to stay out of the limelight. It's a good thing Bryce was in California last week."

I shook my head.

"Why, Mother?"

Adelaide took a sip of her drink. "Because, dear, that was the last time she was seen."

"No. Why does Bryce need our support?"

"Because he's family. That's what family does."

I blinked my eyes, wondering if the scene would change. "No, Bryce isn't family. He's your best friend's son. I'm family and you sent me away with nothing."

"Alexandria, we did not send you away. I've done everything but get down on my knees and beg you to come home. You left. Never in a million years would we send you away. You're a Montague. You belong at Montague Manor. There you'll have all you need."

"I need more than money."

Her eyes opened wide. "What do you need?"

She is unreal.

"How about emotional support?"

"Where better than from your family? And dear, Bryce loves you. He'll support you."

"God, Mother, I feel like we talk in circles. What do you know about the man I'm dating?"

"Bryce said he's dangerous and involved in illegal activities."

"Wow. Need we forget that the man you want me to date has rape charges pending… oh and assault and apparently a possible kidnapping? Yet to listen to you, I'm dating a mobster or something."

Adelaide leaned forward. "Are you?"

"Of course not!"

"Well, I can see the attraction, the excitement, for a young lady such as yourself. You've been sheltered your entire life. A good looking man, wealthy—even if through dubious means—and mysterious." She took another drink. "It's every sheltered woman's fantasy. But, dear, it's not real life. Bryce, a man who's known you all of your life, who loves you despite this little infatuation, that's a real future."

Little infatuation? Is she talking about me and Nox or Bryce and Melissa?

I tilted my head to the side. "Was it yours?"

"My?"

"Your fantasy?"

"Oh, I learned a long time ago that fantasies don't come true."

"That's not what I asked. Do you know the name of my boyfriend?'

Adelaide's chest rose and fell as she studied the contents of her plate and moved the food from place to place. Finally, she looked up and straightened her shoulders. Her tone was different, determined. "Alexandria, you played right into his hand. You may not realize how much we are alike, but he did. The young man's name is Lennox Demetri and you must break it off with him immediately. Your future, our future, Montague's future is depending upon you.

"I didn't see it. I didn't understand it." She continued, reaching for my hand. "I was too stupid. But not you. You've been strong your entire life… and smart. Alton couldn't beat you, until now. Please, I will beg. Please come home."

CHAPTER 38

Present

ADELAIDE

"STOP ASKING ME to do that," Alexandria implored. "I don't understand a word of what you just said. What does Alton have to do with Lennox? And don't you care if I'm happy?"

I did. With all of my heart, I cared. My fingers trembled as I clenched the mostly empty glass of Bloody Mary. How could I possibly explain the web of lies and deceit when I'd played a vital role in all of it?

"Alexandria, I do want you to be happy. I believe Bryce can give you that."

"You haven't even met Lennox. How can you dismiss him?"

"I don't need to meet Lennox."

My beautiful daughter's eyes dropped to the table. "You don't even want to meet the man I think I love."

Love?

"Dear, you've only just met him."

"I didn't *just* meet him. We met—"

"In Del Mar," I interrupted.

"How? How did you know that? Oh, Bryce. That's right. I told him I met Lennox this summer on vacation."

"What made you choose to vacation in Del Mar?"

Alexandria shrugged. "Chelsea and I love the water, the coast. We wanted to go south."

"But why Del Mar? Why that week?"

I motioned to the waiter for two more Bloody Marys. I wouldn't be the only one needing it by the time I was done.

"Mother?" she questioned.

"Newport Beach, Laguna Beach, Half Moon Bay. There are so many possibilities, and you chose Del Mar, the particular week that Lennox Demetri was there."

"Fate?"

"That would be nice, but if you're old enough to learn the truth about your father, you're old enough to know that fairytales and fantasies don't exist and neither does fate."

"I don't understand what you're saying. If you're insinuating that Nox was there for me, it's not true."

Nox?

"I didn't say that. I'm saying you were there for him."

"This isn't making sense. I'd never heard of him. He'd never heard of me."

I took a deep breath and tried to explain, "Sometimes… it's a rare thing… but sometimes there's an attraction too strong to resist. An invisible pull that even though you shouldn't give into, you can't resist, no matter the consequences or repercussions. Call it chemistry. Call it love at first sight."

The waiter took our empty glasses and brought full ones.

"Was that you and my father?"

I smiled. "No. An attraction that strong never dies."

Alexandria sat back and stared. Her expression turned as if the words she were about to utter tasted sour. "You and Alton?"

I couldn't even justify that with words.

I tried to explain, "You were about ten. He was the only time I ever broke the rules. It almost cost me everything." I took a deep breath. "I'd do it again, and I wouldn't stop him. In hindsight, it would've made things better."

In the moments it took for me to collect my thoughts and decide what I could share, I remembered. I remembered how it all started.

It was another dinner party, another function. I knew my role. With my parents gone, it was even more vital. However, ever since the death of my father, Alton's power had grown. Both in and out of the boardroom, he was unstoppable.

Usually when he traveled, he preferred to be alone. I knew he wasn't really alone. I also knew that occasionally Suzy was unavailable while he was gone. I didn't know how stupid they thought I was, but the truth was, I didn't care. It was a break, a reprieve. It was time I could spend with Alexandria, time when I saw her smile.

This trip was different. Alton needed his wife by his side. We were in New York and it was almost Christmas. I would've much rather been in Savannah than freezing in the north. People say snow is pretty. It chills me to the bone.

Alton never told me about the business, about Montague Corporation. It was my name above the doors, yet I was too stupid to understand. At least that's what I'd been told. I wanted to know, to learn, but that wasn't my job. As we settled into the back of a limousine, with me trimmed out in jewelry and fur, decorated like a Christmas tree to appease the eye, I was reminded again not to speak, not to embarrass him. It was the same speech I heard before every affair.

It usually didn't matter. Once we crossed the threshold, he'd be off talking business and I'd be left with the wives to talk children, charities, and fashion. That was why I was always required to wear the finest and newest. It wasn't enough to know the designer: I needed to own them.

We always arrived in time for cocktails. According to Alton that was when deals were started. It was like fishing. Cocktail time was the time to bait the hook and cast the line. During dinner was the time to tighten the line, and after dinner, set the hook and reel them in.

The room was festive, elegant, and chic. Though I didn't know the amount, I was confident we'd spent a lot of money to attend this function. Busy with the other wives, some of whom I knew from other functions and many I didn't, I looked up and our eyes met.

I didn't know who he was or even his name. All I saw were his eyes, the palest blue I'd ever seen, and they were looking at me. Like a scene from a movie, the rest of the room faded into a fog. The music and chattering stopped, replaced by the sound of my beating heart.

"Hello." His deep voice echoed in my mind, sending ripples through my body.

I didn't know how we'd come to be standing before one another. One second we were on separate sides of the room, and the next, he was kissing my hand, his lips warm and full. His touch was gentle yet strong.

His black hair had just the right amount of whiteness. And from the way his tuxedo jacket hung from his broad shoulders, my imagination went wild with what was underneath.

It was completely out of character for me. I never noticed other men. I never daydreamed about sex. I'd gotten to the point that it was doable, acceptable, and while there were things Alton insisted upon that I didn't care for, I did it, and my body would react.

This was altogether different.

As the man before me spoke, my insides twisted and clenched with need. I imagined excusing ourselves and finding a coatroom, a bathroom, hell, I didn't care, a janitor's closet. All I knew was that for the first time in my life I was in lust.

My tongue darted to my lip as I spoke. His tone was kind as he offered his name, Oren, and asked for mine.

"Adelaide." I didn't add my last name or that I was with my husband. I didn't even consider it.

"A most beautiful name for an even more stunning woman."

Perhaps it was that I hadn't heard a compliment in years. I hadn't been told I was pretty or kind. Nothing I did warranted praise. All too familiar with criticism, my cheeks reddened at his flattery.

He noticed my wedding ring. How could he not? The ostentatious diamond was a neon sign glittering under the chandeliers. "Why do you act surprised? Surely the man who put that ring on your finger tells you so daily. He'd be a fool not to see the gem he has."

Words escaped me. There were the rehearsed answers I'd given for years: 'Yes, he's a wonderful husband.' 'I'm the fortunate one to have him.' *Or even,* 'It's as if we're newlyweds.' *But they were all out of my reach at the moment.*

The two of us talked for minutes or was it an hour? I didn't know. Never had I spoken so freely at an affair. Oren asked questions about me. He asked about my children, my child, her name, her age. He spoke about his son and his divorce, and I found myself enthralled with a life that didn't shun divorce but saw it as an opportunity for a new life.

He was a gentleman, acknowledging that I was a married woman. Other than the kiss to my hand, we didn't touch. It wasn't until another woman, one who with her husband often ran in the same circles as we, came up to me that I even remembered where we were.

"Adelaide, Alton has been looking for you."

The blood drained from my cheeks straight to my feet.

Oren reached for my hand. "Are you all right?"

Though chemistry set off sparks at our connection, my husband's name sent a cold chill of fear down my spine. I wasn't well, and apparently I hadn't hidden it well. Alton had been looking for me amongst the women and I wasn't there.

I squared my shoulders and remembered my place. Releasing Oren's hand, I turned toward the woman, Kate or Kit, I didn't remember her name nor did I care. "Thank you, I'll be right there."

Turning back to the handsome man who could be my downfall if I allowed it, I said, "It was a pleasure meeting you. Thank you for talking with me."

Oren bowed slightly. "Thank you, Adelaide. The pleasure was all mine."

"Fitzgerald," I corrected. "Mrs. Alton Fitzgerald. I must really get back to my husband."

As soon as I found Alton, I saw his disapproving glare and knew what my future held. Nevertheless, I stayed by his side throughout the rest of the night.

Thank God we flew in a private plane. If we hadn't surely TSA would have questioned us. Alton was usually skillful at delivering bruises in places easily hidden. That night he wasn't. It was the worst beating of my life. I didn't even learn Oren's last name until somewhere in the middle of Alton's tirade, when he said it.

I'd never forget the way it sounded: Oren Demetri. Alton accused him of underworld dealings, dangerous things.

Sometimes I wonder if I hadn't reminded Alton that night that upon my death, Alexandria inherited everything, if that would've been the last night of my life.

It wasn't the last.

It was only the beginning, the first time I met the love of my life.

I just became more skillful at my own form of hiding.

"What? Stop. Who?" Alexandria asked, her words slowing. "Does this have anything to do with Oren Demetri?"

I sat taller as my eyes narrowed. How did she know?

"I met him last night," she said.

My heartbeat quickened.

"He said to give you his love. You two know each other?"

His love.

"We met… a long time ago," I tried to speak with as little emotion as possible. "If Lennox is anything like his father, you need to get away before it's too late."

"What does that even mean?"

It means he'll hold your heart forever. That can't happen. I didn't say that. Instead, I said, "From what Bryce said, there's a history regarding his dead wife."

"Mother, Father died. How would you like it if people accused you of his demise? I trust Nox, just like I trust you."

My eyes fluttered as I debated. "There's so much you should know, but no way to tell you without making you hate me." I studied my daughter's expression. "More than you already do."

"I don't hate you. I don't like you very much. It doesn't seem as though you've ever backed me, supported me, especially in regard to Alton."

"I can't…" I swallowed. "Alton has been good for Montague Corporation. Bryce will be good for Montague Corporation. Montague is a renowned name for a reason. The business climate has been and is unsettled, yet Montague has survived."

"Good. Let it survive. I have no aspirations for CEO. Let Bryce have it. I don't care."

"It has always been a family-owned-and-operated company. The subsidiaries are publicly traded, but the infrastructure has a governing board of directors. It must stay in the family or it will be sold."

"What?"

"It may seem archaic, but it is the way it is."

Alexandria leaned back and crossed her arms over her chest. I hadn't paid attention to her attire until now. Her charcoal gray dress with a complementary jacket was very high quality and quite stunning. My daughter wasn't the little girl I'd raised. The woman across the table from me was just that—a woman.

"If you moved home, we could get to know each other, not as mother and daughter, but as friends."

"We could do that here. Appoint me."

My gaze narrowed. "What are you saying?"

"Appoint me as CEO. Throw Alton out on his ass."

"Alexandria, you know I can't…"

"Are you or are you not on the board of directors? Do you as a Montague have the lion's share of stock?"

"I am and I do, but in name only. Alton manages my votes and yours until you turn twenty-five, or you marry. Then yours will be managed by your husband."

"Then go to Hamilton and Porter and get our rights back. If the CEO must be a Montague, it's either you or me."

"It can be our spouse."

"I don't have a spouse. Make it me. I'll appoint people to run the show. I'll simply be a figurehead."

"And you'll move back to Savannah?"

Clouds passed behind her eyes. "I'm going to Columbia. I may even have a job lined up." Something about that prospect gave her a momentary grin. She turned her attention back to me. "I'll attend meetings but I won't move back."

The waiter took our plates and we stared for what seemed like hours. Finally, she spoke.

"May I take you to Columbia? Patrick said he'll meet us later."

I nodded. There were so many more things I needed to tell her and things I needed to sort out. "First, please answer my question about Del Mar. Who told you about that resort? Did you make the reservations or did that dreadf— or did Chelsea?"

Alexandria stood. "I did, Mother. I think I was looking at a few different places. It may have been Natalie from Hamilton and Porter who mentioned Del Mar."

"You were speaking to Natalie?"

"Yes, I was coordinating the withdrawal of funds from my trust fund.

After she mentioned it, I looked it up. It was lovely so I made the reservations."

"Why that week?"

Alexandria shrugged as she reached for her handbag. "As I recall, Natalie mentioned that the resort was normally booked far in advance, but she'd been recently looking and knew that they had some openings that week. It was too good of a deal to pass up."

It finally made sense. After all these years Alton wanted Alexandria to fail, wanted our agreement to fail. That's why he didn't fight me about her going away to Stanford. If she didn't marry Bryce, he'd get it all. He'd claim it was me that failed, but it was his plan all along. He'd gained the social status, and now the company and manor would be sold. The proceeds would go to Fitzgerald Investments. He'd walk away with everything, and Alexandria and I would be left with nothing.

My hands trembled at the revelation.

He'd used me to gain his status. In less than eighteen months, he could throw me away. Bryce wouldn't have the Montague name, but Alton would allow him every luxury resulting from his coup d'état.

"Mother," Alexandria asked, "are you not feeling well?"

I needed to think, to plan. I needed Alexandria and Bryce to marry. Alton couldn't win. He'd taken too much. I stood, looking down at the table, focusing.

"Dear, what about the check?"

She looped her elbow through mine and began walking toward the entrance. "The man you don't want to meet took care of it. We'll be going to Columbia in my car."

"Your car? I don't understand."

"I know you don't. Maybe someday you'll want to."

CHAPTER 39

CHARLI

IT WAS HARD to believe this was my normal. Over a month had passed since my mother was in the city. I spoke to her on and off, but her pleas for my return to Savannah were getting old and her reasoning becoming more farfetched. I'd completely blocked Bryce's calls. He told Mother that Nox made me do it. That wasn't the truth. I did it because I wanted to. Now, Adelaide was his messenger, relaying his accusations as well as his plight.

He'd been called to Evanston for his deposition. Mother said the Montague attorneys were happy with the results, but the girl was still missing. If she wasn't found, there was the possibility of additional charges. Mother emphasized Bryce's innocence, her concern that I was in a dangerous position, and how much I was needed in Savannah. She needed me, Montague needed me, and Bryce needed me.

I didn't need him, her, or Montague. As each day and night passed and Nox and I got to know one another better, her words lost their impact.

I was happy.

Such a simple statement that a month ago I feared I'd never be able to say.

Today was my first day of classes, and I was there. Not only was I there, I was there with support unlike any I'd ever known. It started during orientation. On the Saturday morning following that first week, I went running with Patrick in Central Park. Thankfully, Jerrod was a fitness guy and didn't mind running or keeping his distance. Having a security detail was becoming second nature. It was one of Nox's hard limits. Arguing it would be a fight I wouldn't win. Besides, ever since Chelsea's attack, I decided it wasn't a bad idea. Jerrod didn't talk as much as Isaac, but he was nice and non-intrusive.

That Saturday and every one since, my cousin was as animated as always. I didn't tell him that I was out of Infidelity. I suspected that to him it would feel like I cheated the system or something. He and Cy were good, and both were pleased that I was content. I did tell him that Nox and I had a past—a one-week past. I laughed at his response.

"One week to one year, little cousin, that's pretty cool."

He was right—it was. Except the one-year part was still under negotiation. Daily, weekly, monthly, the way real life and real relationships worked.

When I returned to the apartment early that afternoon, I found Nox waiting, looking amazing in his gym shorts and Boston t-shirt. He was smiling at me like the cat that had just eaten the canary.

"What did you do?" I asked.

"Me? Why do you presume it's me?"

I narrowed my gaze. "Because I do?" My answer came out more as a question.

"I know you said the dining room table would be fine for your studies, but you see, I'm slightly OCD."

I laughed. "I've noticed, but with you I think the *c* stands for control, and I also think you need to reevaluate the degree."

He shrugged and swatted my behind. "Guilty as charged."

"Ouch," I said playfully. The way his blue eyes shone with his characteristic menacing grin made my insides pinch. "Now tell me what you did."

"I'd rather show you."

"I like the sound of that," I said with a grin as he tugged my hand toward the bedroom. "But I just ran and I'm a little…"

My words trailed away as my feet stopped. Instead of entering the master bedroom, he took me to the smaller one. The bed that had been there that morning was gone, as was all of the bedroom furniture. In its place was a large glass desk, situated for optimal gazing at the city below. On the desk was a new computer, the screen as large as the one Nox had in his office. Along the wall, where the dresser used to be, were bookshelves—along the *entire* wall. I ran my hand along the woodwork beautifully crafted to match the rest of the apartment.

"How?"

The shelves were partially filled with the books that arrived from Palo Alto, as well as all the ones I'd already picked up from Columbia, with plenty of room for more. In the corner was a beautiful plush chaise lounge. The large modern light hanging above made it the perfect spot for reading.

"I-I don't know what to say."

Nox wrapped his arms around my waist and pulled me close. "Say you won't leave your school shit on the dining room table."

I laughed, stretching to my tiptoes and giving him a kiss. "Thank you. But how did you get all of this done in a morning?"

"I may have talked to your cousin and arranged for you to stay out longer than you planned."

"That's why he insisted on coffee at Tom's restaurant and seeing my apartment."

"Stop saying that," Nox reprimanded. "It's Chelsea's apartment."

"You're right. It is. And it's all ready for her, too."

"That's good, because you're staying put."

I stepped away from his embrace and turned completely around. "I still can't believe you did this."

"I did it for me," Nox insisted. "Remember, I'm the selfish bastard."

"Oh, really, Mr. Demetri? How is this for you?"

He reached for my hand and pulled me toward the hallway. "Because now I have to sleep in your bedroom."

"You do? There's always the couch."

That earned me another playful swat as well as a kiss.

That was over two weeks ago. Tonight, the Tuesday after Labor Day and after my first day of real classes, it was time to celebrate. While I'd been busy getting ready for school—there was a lot of reading expected even before the first day—Nox had been busy with his work. I didn't know in detail all that he did or how it was related to our lunch with Senator Carroll. I didn't ask.

After everything he'd done for me, I decided it was time I gave him what I owed him. It wasn't so much that I *owed* him; I wanted to thank him.

I sent him a text a little before five o'clock.

Me: "SURVIVED FIRST DAY OF CLASSES. LET'S CELEBRATE?"

Nox: *"SOUNDS GOOD."*

Me: *"MEET ME AT 7?"*

Nox: *"WHERE?"*

Me: *"NOT TELLING."*

Nox: *"THAT MAKES IT HARD TO MEET YOU."*

Me: *"IT'S COVERED. ISAAC KNOWS."*

Nox: *"WHAT THE HELL? MY EMPLOYEE. HE LISTENS TO ME. MY RULES."*

I grinned.

Me: *"NOT ANYMORE. THE RULES HAVE CHANGED."*

Nox: *"WATCH IT. YOU'RE DANGEROUSLY CLOSE TO CROSSING A LINE."*

Me: *"AND IF I DO?"*

Nox: *"PRINCESS, YOU DON'T WANT TO FIND OUT."*

Me: *"I THINK I DO. SEE YOU AT 7."*

Checking the time on my phone, I slipped it back in the handbag. Only a few more minutes and Nox would arrive. Isaac would be sure he made it to Mobar on time. This was the fantasy he'd told me about, the one in his note.

I intended to do everything in my power to make it come true. My mother was wrong. Some fantasies were real and so was fate.

Sitting at the bar, my hair flowed over my shoulders in silky waves of auburn, and my makeup was more than I wore during the day, but not over the top. I wasn't wearing excessive eyeliner or glittering eye shadow. If tonight ended in a shower, it wouldn't be because of my appearance.

As I glanced down at the beaded black dress I'd found what seemed like ages ago on the bed in the executive suite of the Mandarin hotel, I felt the pearl necklace around my neck. As appalled as I'd been at the idea of equating this choker to a collar, I no longer was. To me, it was like his note had read. To the world, a queen—a princess. Privately, whatever he wanted me to be. To the world, the necklace was chic and sexy. If privately it held other meaning, that was for us to know and enjoy. Though I'd crumpled his original note, if memory served me well, I'd followed Nox's previous directions, almost to a T. The only thing I didn't do was wear the shoes he'd bought; instead, I wore the Louboutin pumps from Del Mar. Their track record was too impressive not to include them in this night. Everything else he ordered was available. Besides my necklace and earrings, the dress and shoes were all I wore.

As he'd ordered, there were no other men around me. Jerrod's presence assured that. With only a look, he kept the bar stool on either side of me empty. A lemon drop martini sat on the bar in front of me. Slowly, I fingered the rim. With each slide around the edge, I imagined Nox. In my mind, it wasn't my finger on the glass, but his on me, teasing my nipples—the ones that were now as hard as pebbles beneath the dress. It was his taunting my swollen clit and plunging deep inside of me. Circle by circle, my breathing became shallower and my insides clenched in anticipation.

My handbag beside the martini glass vibrated, momentarily breaking my trance. I freed my phone and read the text.

Nox: "YOU TAKE MY BREATH AWAY."

Before I could move my head to find him, another message came through.

Nox: "DON'T TURN AROUND."

I shook my head, wondering again how he did that.

And another.

Nox: "ENTICING AND RADIANT. I KNOW IF IT WEREN'T FOR

JERROD, EVERY MAN IN THIS BAR WOULD BE HITTING ON YOU. THEY'RE LOOKING AT YOU. IT'S ONLY HIS PRESENCE KEEPING THEM AWAY. IT MAKES ME WANT TO PUNCH EVERY ONE OF THEM AND GIVE JERROD A RAISE, BUT MORE THAN THAT, I WANT TO SHOW EVERYONE THAT YOU'RE MINE."

I gasped.

Me: "I AM YOURS. YOU MARKED ME."

As I waited for the next response, a warm hand caressed my bare shoulder. I didn't turn. He hadn't given me permission. I didn't need to. His woodsy cologne combined with the possessiveness of his touch told me all I needed to know. My head to the side as his lips grazed my neck.

"I did," he said, his deep voice rumbling through me like thunder. "You're mine."

"Yes, Nox."

I stared at the sexiest man I knew as he eased onto the stool beside me. His gray suit coat accentuated his shoulders while the crisp white shirt glowed under the bar's lights against the blue of his tie. My mind imagined other uses for his tie as his voice reverberated through the soft music playing in the background.

"How's your martini?"

"I haven't tasted it."

With a knowing smirk, Nox picked up the glass and brought it to my lips. The cool liquid was both sweet and tart. It spread warmth over my tongue and down my throat. His other hand splayed across my knee.

"If I move my hand higher, what will I find?"

"Exactly what you ordered, Mr. Demetri."

His grip didn't move upward, but it tightened, the tips of his fingers blanching as they bit into the skin of my leg.

"I fucking wish we still had the suite here."

"Does that mean you're picking me up?"

"Oh, princess. I'm not picking you up. I'm keeping you."

The bartender appeared. "Sir, may I get you a drink?"

I looked down and ran my finger along the rim of my glass as he ordered.

When he was done, he asked, "Did you and Isaac make more plans, or is this it?"

"I didn't make any more plans with Isaac. I thought I'd leave the rest of the evening to you…" I licked my lips. "…Mr. Demetri."

He leaned closer. "Keep it up, princess. I'm getting fucking hard every time you call me that."

I looked down at my shoes and then lowered my lids. "I disobeyed you again."

He furrowed his brow. "Tell me."

"It's the shoes. They're not the ones you bought with this outfit."

His menacing grin twinkled in his pale blue eyes. "I recognize those shoes. I remember seeing them on the dashboard of a car. I think I'll let you keep them on while I punish you."

I closed my eyes, my breasts rubbing against the weight of the beaded dress as I exhaled.

"How was your first day of class?"

I kissed his cheek. "Do you have any idea how much it means to me that you even ask?"

"Why wouldn't I ask?"

I shrugged. In all my years growing up, I couldn't remember one time when Alton asked my mother about her day, unless there was something specific he was curious about. Did she call the florist or some other menial task he'd given her for the day.

"Lana has dinner for us," I volunteered. "Or we can eat here. As I said, the rest of the night is at your discretion."

Nox took a sip of his drink. "I'm sure they have wonderful food here, but I'd rather get you home to eat."

I swallowed. There was something in his tone. The warm trail started by the martini was now ablaze with flames brought on by his thundering pitch and devious undertones. Blood rushed to my cheeks as my breathing hitched. "Yes, Mr. Demetri."

He reached for some bills from his money clip and threw back the rest of his whiskey. With a menacing grin, he said, "You're going to pay for making me uncomfortable."

I picked up my purse. "I hope so."

Nox nodded to Jerrod. It was a routine that was becoming familiar. It meant that Jerrod would call Isaac. By the time we reached the door, with Jerrod watching over us, Isaac would be waiting with the car.

As we settled into the back of the sedan, I thought about the present I had back at the apartment for Nox. It was my vibrator. Whoever moved our things to the apartment from the Mandarin, put it with my bras and panties. With all that had happened, Nox hadn't mentioned it since the first morning when he told me not to use it. I hadn't. I couldn't imagine needing it with him in my bed. However, the morning he did mention it, he'd said he had some inventive ideas. I was ready to learn what those were.

As Isaac closed the door and Nox's fingers stealthily moved to my inner thigh, I laid my head against the seat and stifled a moan.

The anticipation was almost painful.

"Spread your legs for me, princess."

I did, thankful he'd whispered. This was a car, not a limousine. Nothing separated us from Isaac. Jerrod was driving the other car back to the apartment. My eyes darted to the rearview mirror. However as Nox lightly brushed the tips of his fingers against my folds, the world beyond us seemed inconsequential.

"Nox." I drew his name out to an untold number of syllables.

His lips hovered near my ear as he brushed my hair aside. His warm breath laced with whiskey intoxicated me, sending goose bumps over my skin. "If I wanted to make you come, right here in the car on our way to our apartment, I would."

I nodded with a whimper.

"If I wanted to make you scream my name, I could. Tell me, Miss Collins, would you object?"

From planning the evening, to sitting and running my finger over my glass, I was wound tighter than I ever remembered. His words were erotic but I needed more. I shifted toward his touch. It wouldn't take much, a pinch of my clit, a finger or two inside of me, and I'd be gone. "No, sir. No protest from me."

One hand stayed close, so close to where I needed it to be, while he continued his assault on my neck: from behind my ear to my collarbone and lower. Each kiss slow and warm as his teeth grazed my sensitive skin and the scruff of his cheeks abraded it. My tongue darted to my lips and eyes closed.

My head moved as he fisted my hair, exposing me to his desires. I winced at the tug against my scalp as I shifted toward his other hand. The pressure was too much. I no longer thought about Isaac in the front seat or that we were surrounded by other cars in one of the busiest cities in the world. Unabashed, I opened my legs wider, encouraging him to move higher.

"No, Charli."

My eyes opened.

"My fantasy. My rules. I'll touch you when I'm ready."

"Shit," the word came out breathily.

He grinned as his fingers possessed. More and more he teased and taunted. His grip of my thigh tightened blanching my skin as his kisses moved lower into the V of my dress.

"Please." I heard my own plea, but couldn't recall making it.

"What were you thinking about at the bar?" Nox's warm breath skirted my tender flesh. "Tell me what you were thinking about as you ran your finger over the rim of your glass."

"You." I could barely form the words. "I was thinking about you."

"What were you thinking about me doing?"

"This. More." It was hard to concentrate.

Why is it taking so long to get to the apartment?

His fingers skimmed over my clit, touching yet offering no relief.

I couldn't stifle the moan.

"More, Charli. I want more."

"Fuck, Nox. So do I!"

His chest rumbled with sadistic laughter at my plight.

My eyes opened again, and the brightly lit canopy of the apartment building came into focus.

"Thank God," I said.

Nox laughed again. As Isaac parked and got out of the car to open our door, Nox said, "Trust me, princess. I plan to help you out the second we cross that threshold. But it won't be a divine being you'll be thanking. It'll be me."

I practically panted with anticipation as we made our way through the lobby.

CHAPTER 40

CHARLI

PEOPLE. SO MANY PEOPLE.

The doorman, people in the lobby, and in the elevator. My feet staggered. I was drunk though I'd barely consumed more than a couple of sips of my martini. I was intoxicated on Nox and on life. His strong arm steadied me as he led me from the elevator and down the hallway to our apartment door. Each step reminded me of my arousal as my essence coated my thighs.

The key jiggled in the lock, the tumblers refusing to turn. Everything was happening in slow motion. I couldn't speed it up.

Before opening the door, Nox leaned down and kissed me. My body melted against his as he pulled me close. "I'm hurrying."

"Not fast enough."

The living room flooded with light as he opened and closed the door and flipped the switch. His lips captured mine, their heat the final degree to my combustion. Some scrumptious aroma emanated from the kitchen, awakening a different hunger I didn't realize I possessed.

My stomach growled—loudly.

The blush of embarrassment covered my cheeks as my arm crossed over my stomach.

A grin spread across Nox's lips. "Hungry?" he asked, his eyes widening.

"I want to say no, but I think you know the answer."

"I think I can satisfy both your needs. Go to the bedroom, take off the dress, but leave on the heels." He reached for my chin and his demands slowed. "Climb on the bed and spread those sexy legs. When I walk in there, I want you positioned so I can see how much your pussy wants me."

My mouth dried.

"I'll bring in a plate of food." He kissed me. "You may eat—after me. And princess, I'm not eating whatever Lana made."

My heart thumped against my chest.

"Yes, Mr. Demetri."

He rubbed his nose against mine. "Oh, just wait." His lips softly brushed mine.

I didn't want soft. I pushed myself toward him.

Nox shook his head. "So greedy. Remember, this is on my schedule. Now, go. I'll be in the bedroom in a minute, and you'd better be ready."

Excitement, curiosity, anxiousness… were only some of the many emotions flooding my bloodstream as I hurried toward our bedroom. Each step intensified the suspense. Being with Nox was like a high I never wanted to go away. If Nox were a pill, I'd sell my soul for a lifetime prescription.

I eased the dress from my shoulders and shimmied out. The urge to relieve my own tension fluttered across my mind. It would be so easy. I knew it wouldn't take long. Then again, on the bed was my vibrator, right where I'd left it. I had confidence that relief would be coming soon, and often.

"Charli." I turned toward the hallway, toward the sound of Nox's voice.

This was sooner than I expected. Nox appeared in the doorway. The passion and command of moments ago were gone. Even his tone was different. His eyes did a sweep of my body. "Get dressed. We need to get out of here."

"What? Why?"

"Now," he said as he scooped my dress from the floor and handed it back to me.

"What happened?"

He held out his phone. "It's the security system. Someone's been in here."

"Lana?"

"No. They didn't use her code. It was a bogus code, something only a professional could do. The system didn't catch it right away. It activated a delayed alarm. It only happened about twenty minutes ago. Deloris is on her way."

I pulled the dress over my head as my hands began to tremble. Sometimes Nox worked late. I could've been here alone. What if? "Are you sure they're gone?"

He looked down at the screen of his phone. "Yes. There are sensors throughout the apartment. No one's here now but us."

"You're sure someone was in here? Is anything…" I turned a circle and looked around the bedroom. The damn vibrator mocked me from the middle of our bed. An intruder saw that. "…missing?"

Nox's eyes followed mine. He quirked a brow. "I thought you didn't have plans?"

"I was hoping you could come up with something."

He reached for my hand and started to pull me out of the bedroom, but stopped. "We're getting out of here. Go put something on under that dress and throw some things in an overnight bag. Try not to touch anything other than what you need. Deloris needs to be able to do what she does."

I nodded. "You're sure… no one."

He kissed my forehead. "I wouldn't fucking let you out of my sight if I wasn't."

Hurriedly, I did as he said. Fear replaced my desire. Clothes for tomorrow, a nightgown, underwear: I made a mental list as I threw things in my small suitcase. I rushed to the bathroom and gathered my cosmetics and toothbrush.

"Do you want me to pack things for you?" I yelled toward the hallway.

I didn't hear his answer as I dashed across the hallway to my office and picked up the backpack I'd left there after class. It had all the books I'd need for tomorrow as well as my tablet.

As I turned to ask Nox again if he wanted me to pack for him, I saw the plain white envelope lying on the middle of my desk. Slowly, I moved forward, confident it hadn't been there earlier in the evening. My feet barely moved as I made my way around the desk. It was like a dream as I floated closer, as if the envelope were a snake and would sense my sudden movement and strike.

Alexandria was scrolled across the front.

My heart did triple time as I reached for it. Blood coursed through my veins and through my ears, muting the world around me. With shaking fingers, I lifted it and opened the flap.

The first page was a picture. I'd never seen the woman before, but she looked familiar. It was because she looked like me. Her hair wasn't auburn but beautiful rich shades of brown, long and flowing about the same length as mine. Her eyes were a soft brown, darker than mine, but with golden flecks. She was smiling at the camera and dressed in something red. It was only a headshot.

I sank to the chair. I didn't want to keep looking, but like gawking at a train wreck, I couldn't look away. My heart knew who she was, but it needed confirmation. I moved the picture to the back of the stack of pages and began to read.

Alexandria,
I'm sure you're mad or even freaked out that I had this put where you'd find it. I'm sorry. I won't say that I'm not trying to scare you. I am.

You won't return my calls. You won't return my text messages even when Adelaide explained how much I need you. Now I need you to listen. Please listen. Please keep reading.

You know who she is, don't you? The woman in the picture?

Her name was Jocelyn Marie Matthews Demetri.

My stomach sank. I needed to stop, to show this to Nox, but I couldn't.

Was, Alexandria, she was. She's dead.

Your boyfriend killed her.

The Demetris are dangerous. I won't go into all the illegal activities, including prostitution, but know that it's there. I just want you to know about the man you're sleeping with. The man she slept with. The man who killed her.

My empty stomach twisted violently.
Stop! Stop! Stop reading!
My heart screamed out, but my eyes continued to roam.

Lennox wouldn't allow her family to see her body. He had her cremated before any evidence could be found.

Evidence. Her parents have both sworn statements about his abuse. On more than one occasion they witnessed bruises on her wrists. They've both testified to that.

I looked to my wrists. There was a faint brown mark from where I'd pulled too hard against the satin. I continued to read.

He was a workaholic. They say she was sad and scared.

Their testimony is available. They have a civil suit pending against him. He bought off the judge for the petition of evidence in a criminal matter, but even the great Lennox Demetri can't stop all the wheels of justice.

Get out. Leave. Come home or at least move back to your apartment.

Alexandria, I'm scared to death.

I also think he's behind framing me with Melissa. He could be the reason she's missing. By getting rid of her, he can remove me from your life.

Lennox is dangerous.

I'm begging you. Your mother is begging you.

Ask him if he's responsible for Jocelyn's death… and get out!

Bryce

Why couldn't he let this go? Why would he think Nox was connected to Melissa? That didn't make sense.

The letter consisted of two pages. Each handwritten page surrounded the picture. I didn't want to move the last page of words. I didn't want to see her again.

I hadn't realized I was crying until a tear splashed against the paper.

When I looked up, my eyes met Nox's. His pallor matched his cold icy eyes, so different than only minutes earlier.

"You shouldn't have touched it."

I couldn't comprehend. "Touched what?"

"That letter, Charli. You're destroying evidence. Deloris can dust it for fingerprints."

My head moved slowly back and forth as I realized I was holding Jocelyn's picture.

How angry would Nox be?

Before I could think, I was up on my feet, my heels sliding across the wooden floor as I backed away from him. "Where's Deloris?"

"She's on her way up. What's the matter? What did that say?"

"I-I" I rolled my lips between my teeth. "I need to talk to her."

Nox took a step toward me. His expression morphed from concern to something more intense as I once again took a step back. "What the fuck, Charli? Are you afraid of me?"

"No," I answered too quickly and too loudly.

When he closed the distance, he snatched the papers from my hand. I didn't release them quickly enough. The momentary tug of war allowed them to fall. They fluttered to the floor, Jocelyn's smiling face looking up at us.

Color returned to his face as red covered his cheeks. The vein in his forehead bulged, and the muscles in his neck tensed. "What the fuck is this?"

I blinked, afraid to speak, yet unable to stay silent. I searched his eyes and worked to even my voice. "I think it's nothing. I think it's my family trying to scare me."

"You think?" He lifted her picture from the floor. "Your family broke into our apartment?"

I shook my head. "I doubt it. They probably paid someone."

Nox couldn't pull his eyes away from Jocelyn. The edge of the page crumpled as his grasp tightened.

"Please look at me," I begged.

The muscles in his temples flexed as he clenched and unclenched his jaw.

"Nox!"

Slowly, he looked away from her to me.

"Just tell me that you had nothing to do with her death. Tell me you weren't responsible, and we will go to the hotel, or stay here. There's no threat."

He didn't speak.

"Please, Nox," I begged, reaching for his hands, wanting to help him, to take away the pain this letter caused. "Please. I didn't gather this information. It was thrown at me. It doesn't even make sense. Just tell me you aren't responsible for her death, and I'll ignore everything the letter said."

The floor dropped out from under me as his answer echoed against the freshly painted walls.

"I can't."

The end of *Cunning*…

Learn what is next for Nox and Charli in DECEPTION

DECEPTION

CHARLI & NOX

Coming May 3, 2016, the continuing story of Charli and Nox, the Montagues and Demetris. As secrets are revealed and shadows are uncovered more than trust will be lost. Who will survive the depth of DECEPTION?

Book #3 of the Infidelity series, **DECEPTION**, by Aleatha Romig.

WHAT TO DO NOW...

LEND IT: Did you enjoy *Cunning*? Do you have a friend who'd enjoy *Cunning*? *Cunning* may be lent one time. Sharing is caring!

RECOMMEND IT: Do you have multiple friends who'd enjoy *Cunning*? Tell them about it! Call, text, post, tweet… your recommendation is the nicest gift you can give to an author!

REVIEW IT: Tell the world. Please go to the retailer where you purchased this book, as well as Goodreads, and write a review. Please share your thoughts about CUNNING on:

STAY CONNECTED WITH ALEATHA

Do you love Aleatha's writing? Do you want to know the latest about Infidelity? Consequences? Tales From the Dark Side? and Aleatha's new series coming in 2016 from Thomas and Mercer?

Do you like EXCLUSIVE content (never released scenes, never released excerpts, and more)? Would you like the monthly chance to win prizes (signed books and gift cards)? Then sign up today for Aleatha's monthly newsletter and stay informed on all things Aleatha Romig.

Sign up for Aleatha's NEWSLETTER: http://bit.ly/1PYLjZW
(recipients receive exclusive material and offers)

You can also find Aleatha@

Check out her website: http://aleatharomig.wix.com/aleatha
Facebook: https://www.facebook.com/AleathaRomig
Twitter: https://twitter.com/AleathaRomig
Goodreads: www.goodreads.com/author/show/5131072.Aleatha_Romig
Instagram: http://instagram.com/aleatharomig
Email Aleatha: aleatharomig@gmail.com

You may also listen Aleatha Romig books on Audible.

BOOKS BY NEW YORK TIMES BESTSELLING AUTHOR ALEATHA ROMIG

INFIDELITY SERIES:

BETRAYAL

Book #1

(October 2015)

CUNNING

Book #2

(January 2016)

DECEPTION

Book #3

(May 2016)

ENTRAPMENT

Book #4

(TBA)

FIDELITY

Book #5

(TBA)

THE CONSEQUENCES SERIES:

CONSEQUENCES

(Book #1)

Released August 2011

TRUTH

(Book #2)

Released October 2012

CONVICTED

(Book #3)

Released October 2013

REVEALED

(Book #4)

Previously titled: Behind His Eyes Convicted: The Missing Years

Re-released June 2014

BEYOND THE CONSEQUENCES

(Book #5)

Released January 2015

COMPANION READS:

BEHIND HIS EYES—CONSEQUENCES

(Book #1.5)

Released January 2014

BEHIND HIS EYES—TRUTH

(Book #2.5)

Released March 2014

TALES FROM THE DARK SIDE SERIES:

INSIDIOUS

(All books in this series are stand-alone erotic thrillers)

Released October 2014

DUPLICITY

(Completely unrelated to book #1)

Release TBA

THE LIGHT SERIES:

Published through Thomas and Mercer

INTO THE LIGHT

To be released June 14, 2016

AWAY FROM THE DARK

(Release TBA)

ALEATHA ROMIG

Aleatha Romig is a New York Times and USA Today bestselling author who lives in Indiana. She grew up in Mishawaka, graduated from Indiana University, and is currently living south of Indianapolis. Aleatha has raised three children with her high school sweetheart and husband of nearly thirty years. Before she became a full-time author, she worked days as a dental hygienist and spent her nights writing. Now, when she's not imagining mind-blowing twists and turns, she likes to spend her time with her family and friends. Her other pastimes include reading and creating heroes/anti-heroes who haunt your dreams!

Aleatha released her first novel, CONSEQUENCES, in August of 2011. CONSEQUENCES became a bestselling series with five novels and two companions released from 2011 through 2015. The compelling and epic story of Anthony and Claire Rawlings has graced more than half a million e-readers. Aleatha released the first of her series TALES FROM THE DARK SIDE, INSIDIOUS, in the fall of 2014. These stand-alone thrillers continue Aleatha's twisted style with an increase in heat. In the fall of 2015, Aleatha will move headfirst into the world of dark romance with the release of BETRAYAL, the first of her five-novel INFIDELITY series. Aleatha has entered the traditional world of publishing with Thomas and Mercer with her LIGHT series. The first of that series, INTO THE LIGHT, will be published in the summer of 2016.

Aleatha is a "Published Author's Network" member of the Romance Writers of America and represented by Danielle Egan-Miller of Browne & Miller Literary Associates.